The Wrong Game

Eden Chronicles – Book Five

S.M. Anderson

Other Books by S.M Anderson - and reading order:
All titles are available on Amazon and for Amazon's Kindle Unlimited Program. Audio versions for all books are available on Audible and have been released by Podium Audio.

The Eden Chronicles:
Book One: "A Bright Shore"
Book Two: "Come and Take it"
Book Three: "New Shores"
Book Four: "Bridgehead"
Book Five: "The Wrong Game"
Book Six: forthcoming 2024

The Seasons of Man:
Book One: "End of Summer"
Book Two: "Reap What You Sow":
Book Three: "Standing at the Gate"

Chapter 1

New Seattle

A new horizon indeed. Amona, a former Gemendi in the services of Lord Tima, felt the effects of the translation fade as he focused on the massive snowcapped mountain to the south—Mount Rainier. Twenty years of servitude on the Island of Landing his view of the horizon had never altered from the white rocks and endless sea. This morning, "going to work"—as his new boss called it—had encompassed a trip between worlds.

He'd gotten past the point where he felt like he needed to pinch himself each time he utilized the Edenite's portal. The Edenites and their Jema allies took new horizons, cities, and people for granted. For Amona, each journey—whether by aircar around Portsmouth, helicopter over the green hills of Caledonia, or portal to the other side of an entirely new world—still felt spiritual. Not all that overwhelming emotion tasted like discovery and sunshine. He could not forget what had been denied him by the Kaerin, and was still denied to the people of Chandra.

His group therapy sessions, which he'd attended three times a week for the first two months after his rescue, had been populated by rescued Chandrians from a half a dozen different clans. The sessions were part language training and part what he now recognized as emotional therapy. The Edenites and the Jema were slowly collecting refugees from around Chandra, and the reactions of the former Kaerin subjects varied between disbelief, terror, and hero worship for those who had rescued them. If there had been one thing that assured him the Edenites were, as they often joked, "on the side of the angels," it had been their insistence that they were in no way superior to the subject people of Chandra. The difference between them and the Kaerin in that simple statement had convinced him that his new friends were indeed worth serving in their attempt to free Chandra's people.

He'd needed those therapy sessions for an entirely different reason as well. Anger and hatred towards the Kaerin and what they had done to his world was natural, or so they were told. Especially for Chandrians like himself, who had worked so closely with the Kaerin. He hadn't needed the Edenite therapist to tell him that he needed to come to terms with the rage he felt. Early after his rescue, each new discovery—whether a piece of knowledge, a technical marvel, or especially the civil manner these different people interacted with each other—reinforced what had been stolen from Chandra. Help in understanding his anger and how to deal with it had come from an unlikely source - a Jema.

Audrin'ochal, or Audy as the Edenites called him, had become a friend. Audy worked closely with his boss, Derek Mills, in building out the city of Portsmouth and the other settlements across the island of Caledonia. Audy had pulled him aside one evening and told him that he needed to stop thinking of the Kaerin as demons—that they were a people as much a prisoner to the world they had built as the subject clans were. It was the Kaerin civilization and culture that was the enemy, not the people.

Thinking back on that conversation, Audy towering over him, Amona's eyes had gone to the Kaerin longsword strapped to the Jema's back. Everyone had heard how Audy had come by the sword. Audy had seen his glance and smiled.

"Yes, I needed to come to terms with my own demons. And I'll fight them every chance I have. But hate for them as a people can forge chains around your heart every bit as strong as the slavery they keep this world in. It gives them power over you. I won't allow them to have that ever again."

They were words he'd needed to hear. Words he was now trying to live by as he worked to rid Chandra of the Kaerin. He'd been cleared for work and assigned to Derek's team, now building out Portsmouth and Caledonia. The Jema weren't builders by nature, or civil administrators. They were warriors. The Edenites were simply too few to be everywhere at once. They needed someone to help corral and focus the people they'd rescued on building a new world.

Chandrian Gemendi like him fit the bill perfectly. As a result, his actual day-to-day work hadn't changed all that much. He was still focused on logistics, personnel manning, and schedules, though he was now armed with a compad, spreadsheets, and an application called Project that had become his personal savior and tormentor.

He started the walk from the open-air portal platform in New Seattle towards the program office headquarters, compad in hand. It reminded him of the mornings on Landing when he'd reported to Lord Tima, only now his superiors weren't likely to feed a dozen Junata to the crabs because they were behind schedule.

And they were behind. There simply weren't enough hands for all the work needed. Eden was still in the process of establishing itself and building its own infrastructure. As he understood it, those efforts had been impacted severely by the Kaerin attacks and the decision to take the fight to Chandra. Walking through the New Seattle city center, he could almost see where the skyline of Portsmouth was headed. As Derek often said, they were building a new civilization on Chandra. It started with concrete and ended with knowledge. The end of each workday included an hour of mandatory training and education for every refugee. Derek joked that they were trying to build an airplane as it rolled down a runway. It had taken him a while to grasp the metaphor, but it had quickly become his life.

Edenites and those few Jema who had found a passion in the civilian world worked alongside the Junata and the Creight in building the bones of that new civilization. If any of them needed more proof that the Edenites were not new conquerors come to supplant the Kaerin, it was the fact that all newly constructed housing on Caledonia was assigned and awarded via a lottery system. Amona had "won" a townhouse two weeks before his own boss had. Derek—his superior and an Edenite—had still been living in a prefabbed Quonset hut with his wife and young son.

Instead of jealousy and indignation, Derek and Denise had gifted him an Edenite microwave oven as a housewarming gift. Derek's only comment, delivered with a knowing smile, had been that he wouldn't have an excuse to miss meals anymore. It had been yet another pinch-worthy moment. His rescuers were not conquerors, not gods—they were colleagues, fellow citizens, and friends.

Derek had sent him to deliver their status report with an admonition to make certain that those "tight-fisted morons running logistics get him more nano-beds." While certain he wouldn't have to resort to name calling, the responsibility of delivering a report in front of Program heads like Colonel Hank Pretty or Dr. David Jensen was intimidating, especially where Dr. Jensen was concerned. The average Edenite, a beneficiary of a solid basic education, knew more about science than any supposed Gemendi from Chandra did. With Jensen and other Program scientists, that gulf was a chasm that would take a generation or more of education to remedy.

He spotted Dr. Jensen walking on the sidewalk ahead of him, no doubt headed to the same meeting as he was. He nervously slowed his pace out of instinct and then chided himself. David Jensen was a good man. His science-inclined colleagues, such as Breda and A'tor Bendera, were both so in awe of the man they had trouble speaking in his presence, which drove the Edenite scientist mad. For his part, Amona felt Jensen, or 'Doc' as he preferred being called, was one of the more approachable Edenites. Jensen may be a scientific genius—one of many he had met in the last six months—but the man's value to the Edenites was in his practicality.

A former soldier, Jensen cared little about how things looked, only how they worked. It was almost humorous to Amona, but at times, Dr. Jensen reminded him of an older, less homicidal version of Lord Tima. With the gift of hindsight, he felt Lord Tima could have become a man like the hard-edged Jensen had he not been raised as a Kaerin.

A week past, Jensen had interrupted a staff meeting in Derek's office in Portsmouth. The lead scientist of the Edenites had barged in without so much as the polite "good morning." The hammer he'd been carrying may not have been a Kaerin longsword, but Amona had recognized the anger in the man. Without a word, Jensen had nailed a poster to the wall before turning to glare at Derek's gathered staff of Program Managers. He'd huffed once—as if he didn't trust himself to speak—and then walked out, slamming the conference room door hard enough that everyone in the room had jumped in their seat.

Amona's use to Derek and the Program relied on his ability to read, and he'd picked up English quickly. The poster read, "Perfection is the enemy of Progress—Get your Shit DONE."

Derek had since added the same admonition to his own e-mail's signature bloc. Later, that same evening, Amona learned that Derek had known of Jensen's interruption in advance. His boss had laughed, saying that Jensen had asked for permission to "address" his staff. He'd been expecting Jensen to come in yelling. Amona had laughed at the rough-edged Jensen's tactics and made the comment that Lord Tima would have understood the display—though his message would have undoubtedly ended in one of the Program Managers being dragged out by High Blood warriors as an object lesson.

Amona timed his pace perfectly. Doctor Jensen had already disappeared into an elevator by the time he reached the lobby. Looking for the room number his compad was showing, he walked past the third-floor conference room he'd assumed was the venue. The room indicated was much smaller. Pushing through the opaque glass door, he was immediately struck by who wasn't there—the settlement chiefs. Their absence was odd because their cities and towns across Eden supplied Caledonia with everything it needed to stand on its own.

The first face he saw was Audy, head bowed in conversation with the Jema leader, Jomra Sendai. Jomra was not a person he'd never heard mentioned in the context of supply and logistics.

"Apologies," he stammered. He'd clearly walked into the wrong meeting.

Dr. Elisabeth Lassiter, the creator of the Chandran resettlement and training program who he'd met several times, smiled up at him. She was flanked by her husband Kyle, one of the men who had rescued him from the Isle of Landing, and Colonel Pretty himself.

"I think I make a mistake," he continued.

"No mistake, Amona." Elisabeth stood and motioned to one of the three empty chairs with a bright smile. "You are in the right place."

"Take a load off." Doctor Jensen turned around to face him and slapped at the chair next to him.

Amona held up his compad as he sat. "I was to give Mr. Mills' status report." He needed to relax—he was having a hard time finding the right words in English.

Jensen grinned. "Let me guess... your boss is tired of begging for another nano-bed, so he sent you."

Amona gave a slight nod, unsure of how to proceed. The Edenites' informality with one another was something all Chandrians struggled with. It wasn't only that they often discussed serious issues with humor. It was the complete lack of a rigid hierarchy. None of them seemed to have an issue with a subordinate disagreeing with them. Derek technically worked for Doctor Jensen, but Amona had heard them argue on several occasions.

"I believe a request for just such equipment is included."

Jensen laughed to himself. "You and I can discuss the report after this meeting. Derek's reports are usually the only ones that don't piss me off."

"Usually?" He did his best to smile. He was almost certain Jensen wasn't angry, but sometimes it was hard to tell.

Elisabeth had been listening to the byplay. "What did I tell you, Doc? He's a natural diplomat."

"He's also worth his weight in gold to Derek," Jensen fired back.

Amona was unsure which of them outranked the other. As was the Edenite's way, he doubted if either of them knew or cared.

"If we do this," Jensen waved a finger at the rest of the occupants, "one of you gets elected to tell Derek you're stealing his secret weapon."

The door burst open before a confused Amona could ask how in any way he was a secret weapon. Jake Bullock, another of his rescuers, stood in the doorway and pulled Breda in behind him.

"Sit down." Jake half pushed the Jehavian Gemendi at the empty chair next to his own before taking the last remaining seat.

"You all sure about this?" Jake's question was clearly directed at Elisabeth, but the Edenite soldier flashed a look of annoyance at Breda.

It would appear Breda's ability to anger colleagues wasn't limited to natives of Chandra. Amona had only seen Breda a couple of times in the last three months, even though they were both on Caledonia. The wiry, dark-haired Jehavian had been acting as a cultural translator, much like his own job. In Breda's case it was with the Junata and Creight who were actively being trained up to fight alongside the Jema and Edenites. It was a good fit for Breda as far as he was concerned, not that he'd ever say as much. His former colleague's temperament had always been a better fit for the military than as a Gemendi.

"Let's begin, shall we?" Colonel Pretty motioned to his deputy. "Kyle? This is your and Audy's idea…"

"Fine," Kyle responded in Chandrian. "First, I want to apologize to Amona and Breda. This is a sensitive matter and one we'll discuss using your own language. It's very important that there not be any misunderstanding on your part."

"We sure we want you giving the speech?" Jake joked.

It was evident to Amona that Kyle's Chandrian lacked a lot of natural flow, but he spoke very correctly.

"We are sure." Jomra flashed a look of annoyance down the table in Jake's direction.

Amona hid his own smile as Kyle looked at Jake and scratched his nose with his middle finger. "As I was saying, if anything we are asking isn't completely clear, please speak out and ask for clarification. Understood?"

Amona nodded formally. "I understand."

Breda looked like he was going to ask a question, but glanced at Jake, who was shaking his head slowly. "I understand."

"To be concise, you are both Hijala. I've debriefed you and A'tor extensively on that aspect of your former lives, and we are all very aware of the limitations that the Hijala network or system had or has. The fact that it has continued to exist at all, underneath the Kaerin layer of control, despite its limitations, is nonetheless impressive."

Kyle pointed at Breda. "From what we've been able to collect and piece together, in places like Kaerus—where Breda is from—and among the Jehavian clans, the Hijala network evolved to act almost as what we refer to as a 'black market' to facilitate low-level smuggling outside of Kaerin control. Would you agree, Breda?"

"It's not as simple as that…"

"Yes or no, slick," Jake growled.

"Yes." Breda squirmed in his chair, clearly wanting to say more.

"In Hatwa lands," Kyle continued, "according to A'tor, that particular evolution didn't happen since there were so few Hatwa Gemendi allowed by the Kaerin Lord there. In Junata lands—where we've made some intelligence-gathering inroads through our new Junata Gemendi—smuggling, although very limited, seems to have been the focus again. We are proposing a program to reach out and use the two of you, plus A'tor, to establish contact with subject clans across Chandra.

You would act as Hijala smugglers until you come across people you believe you can trust. We have a term in English called a 'fifth column.' It's an organization of people that would act in secret alliance with us against the Kaerin while they themselves remain under Kaerin control."

"Over time, the goal is to train them so that they are prepared to act when our forces are ready in their given area. Even before then, if the program is successful and robust enough, they can become active in sabotage. Or we can pull groups out by portal, secretly bring them here or to Caledonia for training before sending them back." Kyle stopped and looked at both of them for a moment as if he'd expected some sort of feedback by now.

"In short, we'd like to know what you think about the chances of turning the Hijala network into what its original founders meant it to be, an organization focused on resistance to the Kaerin. You would have our support each step of the way—secure transportation, as you know, is not an issue. You would work and travel in concert with small security teams that Jake and Audy have been training."

Amona was stunned. He had important work to do that he actually understood. Derek relied upon him. They'd given him a purpose, and now they wanted him to be a spy? He looked at Breda, who was shaking his head.

"You can't trust the Hijala," Breda almost shouted. "Most of them have forgotten what it was founded for, or have never even known. Your secret would die the first time one of them ran to the nearest High Blood."

"What secret would that be?" Audy spoke out. "That the Jema are on Chandra? That the Edenites are there with us? That we are at war with the Kaerin? The Kaerin know all this. This is what the Edenites call a win-win. Should your efforts be discovered, the Kaerin's control of whatever story they are peddling loses credibility. The Kaerin's reliance on and trust in subject host armies will weaken. Minor Kaerin Lords will learn they have been lied to by their superiors in Kaerus. What is the possible downside?"

"With respect, Audrin'ochal," Amona couldn't help himself. "The Jema should know what the downside is. They know what can happen when the Kaerin believe they can no longer trust a subject clan."

The silence in the room took on a weight that Amona could feel. He'd started the morning thinking he'd be talking about the progress on the sewer treatment plant and food stores in Portsmouth, and now he'd just offended the Jema as a whole, and his friend besides. Her he'd been worrying about Breda saying something stupid. He sighed. The look on Audy's face was unreadable, and Amona started in his seat as Jomra stood slowly.

"Well said," Jomra's deep voice was somber.

Amona had been so focused on his embarrassment at speaking that it took a moment for him to realize what Jomra had just said.

"I raised this same point myself." Jomra remained standing, glancing down the table at Audy and Kyle. "The Jema do not wish to see another clan… punished… as we were following our rebellion. I have been convinced that our allied forces could prevent such a culling." Jomra paused and looked directly at Colonel Pretty. "More importantly, I have been assured that we have the will to act in accordance with our full capability to prevent the same from happening again."

"Why wait?" Breda blurted out. "Why don't we use that same capability to destroy the Kaerin now?"

Jomra's face was a mask of stone. "We will do battle with the Kaerin where it is needed, whenever it is offered. We will not become them. We will not drop to their level and become murderers. Can you understand the distinction, Breda?"

"No! I do not. Given the opportunity, they would not hesitate to end all of you, all of us. They'd make such an example of you that no one would ever dare challenge them again."

A smile broke out on Jomra's face. "They've already tried that. Yet here we are." Jomra retook his seat slowly. "Your wish to just kill them all… this is not the first time I, nor anyone around this table, have heard that sentiment. It is shared by many Jema, and more Edenites than I would have wagered. As this struggle continues, I do not doubt there will be more voices calling for the same."

Jomra leaned forward until his elbows rested on the table. "Breda, I lead… *an entire people.* You are a Gemendi, or were. Perhaps the scope of that responsibility is not something you can imagine. My people's future within this world we are creating will not be built on mass slaughter. The Jema to come will be able to look back at their history with sorrow at that which was done to us, but with pride in our victory. We do not seek to supplant the Kaerin with our own rule—nor do I believe our allies would let us."

"No, by God we wouldn't." Jensen, speaking English, added quietly.

"Breda, we and our Jema allies know what we can and will do." Colonel Pretty cut in, dropping back into Chandrian. "The question before us today is the one Captain Lassiter has put before you and Amona. Would you be willing, with our support and under our protection, to reach out to other clans we have already been watching to try and gain us some more allies? As much as you think there is a quick solution we could take, I assure you there is not.

"As close as we can estimate, there are 300 million Kaerin controlling Chandra. Twice as many as we initially thought. That does not include over two and half billion subject peoples, who at this moment to one extent or another are being armed, trained, and made ready to fight us under the Kaerin's flag. That's almost three billion people, Breda. The need to spread the message of the opportunity we represent to Chandra is paramount. We will fight, as Jomra has said, but we need more people—more soldiers. We need to shatter the Kaerin's control over their subjects. Your Hijala network is our best opportunity to begin that process."

"The Hijala?!" Breda shook his head and looked back at him in what looked like disgust. For his part, Amona had already decided to agree to whatever his new friends wanted.

He knew Breda would need to vent. "Of the five Hijala members that found themselves together on the island of Landing," Breda began, "all of us were subject clan Gemendi, with the exception of Amona, whose people had always been there. One I had to kill before he ran to report our presence to the closest High Blood. He probably thought the Kaerin would reward him, though I knew they'd likely have killed him as quickly as the rest of us. The second, Barrisimo, was the greatest intellect on the island—but he was intent on kissing Kaerin ass and doing whatever was asked of him. That left myself, A'tor, and Amona. Each of us brought a different idea of what the Hijala was, what it was for."

"Yet we found common cause," Amona added quickly. He could see Breda winding up. "As I'm sure Breda is about to point out, A'tor and myself were not warriors, and perhaps we were even poorer spies, despite my friend's efforts. For myself, I would prefer to remain in Portsmouth to help our cause there. It is work for which I am trained... important work. But... if you around this table believe I would be more valuable as a... I'm sorry, I don't even know what it would be called."

"We'd call it an operative," Kyle explained with a smile. "Part diplomat, part spy. But a messenger of hope for all that. We can train you, but you already have the skills, Amona. You managed to communicate with the Hijala under the noses of the Kaerin for years."

Amona nodded to himself. "Fine, an operative. If you believe I would further our cause more in that role, rather than assisting Mr. Mills, I will do it."

"I sure as hell don't." Jensen whispered loud enough to be heard.

"The rest of us do." Kyle shook his head, smiling at Jensen, who swatted the air in defeat. Amona was left with the impression this was not the first time the two had argued over this.

"Your value to Derek and Dr. Jensen is well known," Kyle continued. "You will always have a role more suited to your training waiting for you. As Colonel Pretty has said, our greatest weakness is numbers. We need more people—it's as simple as that."

Kyle looked down at his wife in what seemed to be an apology before facing him again. "Your effort is not the only one we will be pursuing in this regard."

"Thank you, Amona." Jomra spoke from the far end of the table.

"Breda?" Kyle asked.

"Fine. Amona will need someone to keep him out of trouble."

Jake turned in his chair and slapped Breda on the leg, "Actually, Amona is going to be running point on this effort. We'll do it his way, at his pace. If and when he identifies some like-minded, local hot heads, your new role is going to be the leader of a partisan insurgency."

"A leader of… what?" Breda's confusion was complete. "What do those words even mean?"

"Means you would help them take the fight to the Kaerin and blow some shit up. Train them as I've been training you. You think I've had you shadowing me for the last few months because I enjoy it?"

Breda jerked his head back in momentary confusion. "I do not."

"Well, there you go!" Jake's hands came off the table in offering. "You've always been a sneaky, evil bastard. Now you'll actually be able to back it up. What do you say?"

Breda had not been an easy friend to make. Amona watched the grin slowly break out on the man's face. "This, I can do."

Chapter 2

"So… this other effort you mentioned?" Jake was the first to speak after Amona and Breda left the room. "We're going ahead with it?"

Elisabeth stood abruptly, collecting her things. "Sounds like you are," she said, flashing Kyle a look that made Jake cringe.

Kyle was in for an Abrahamic ass chewing, no doubt about it. He'd spent a good portion of his teenage years being yelled at by Elisabeth's mom. He knew his stepsister could bring the heat as well.

"Elisabeth, stay." Kyle tried.

"No," Elisabeth waved a hand over her head. "You're going to go. I can see that. I can even see the need for it, but don't ask me to approve." With that, she was around the table and out the door.

"Dude, I *did* warn you." Jake's shit-eating grin was almost too much to take at the moment.

"You're sure about this, Kyle?" Colonel Pretty's voice brought him back to the moment.

Kyle turned around and shook his head. "Tell me we have another option out there."

"We don't," Hank shook his head. "Doesn't have to be *you* is what I meant. Part of me wants to tell you it *can't* be you."

This was the part of the plan Elisabeth had an issue with. But he wasn't about to ask others to step through the portal and return to Earth when he wasn't willing to do it himself.

He looked his boss in the eyes. "You can't do that."

"Sure he can," Jake crowed. "He's our boss."

Hank grunted in what was almost laughter and shook his head. "I approved the plan… I'm not going to stop you. I don't think we have anyone else that can pull this off with the subtlety it needs."

"I can be subtle," Jake countered.

Kyle's anger was forgotten, and he struggled not to laugh. Doc Jensen barked in indignation, and Audy and Jomra were shaking their heads and smiling at the far end of the table.

"What did you tell Dere'dala?" Kyle asked. Jake's Creight wife was as tough as he was.

"I just said I had to go to New Mexico for a few days. To be fair, she might have assumed I meant on Eden. Earth wouldn't have meant anything different to her."

"You are a piece of work." Doc Jensen leveled a finger in accusation across the table.

Kyle wanted to call him out as well. Truth was, he was a little envious of his friend's situation. Elisabeth knew what Earth meant. Knew the risks it carried. She also knew New Mexico had been turned into massive open air holding pen for Americans that had been slow to appreciate what the government was doing for them. America had its own gulag archipelago and as far as they knew, it was full of people who might just jump at a chance for a new start. They had no idea what they'd be portalling into and no way to be certain until they could get their own eyes on the situation. His eyes, and Jake's.

He turned to Doc Jensen. "How long until the sensor package returns?"

"Forty-six hours," Jensen answered quickly.

Jensen and his team had put together a suite of sensors and added it to the *Phone Booth*, along with an automatic timer to initiate its return. The fact that the sensors hadn't tripped and initiated an immediate return, only meant nothing had approached their remote target landing site in northern New Mexico.

"Ok." Kyle nodded. "We'll be ready if the area looks safe."

"Two days?" Jake shook his head. "I thought we were ready to go. What if Elisabeth says something to Dere'dala in the meantime?"

Kyle offered a grin of his own. "Yeah… that would be tragic."

*

Indonesian Islands, Chandra - Danny

"What'd you do now?" Danny Carlisle waited a full two seconds before he punched upward into the bunk above him. The distended lumps of mattress held his brother on the other side. There was no response from Josh beyond a sleepy sounding groan.

Danny took another look at his compad. Yep, sure as shit, they were both supposed to report to New Seattle on Eden as soon as possible. He wasn't even sure it *was* possible at the moment. Their long-range patrol had been deposited in the middle of this jungle a week ago, part of a ten-person reconnaissance team that had been watching a local Kaerin-run plantation town. He still wasn't even sure why. There was maybe two squads' worth of Kaerin High Bloods running the rubber and coconut oil operation. Nothing that would have given their team a problem.

No such orders had come. They'd just watched, "collecting intel," which amounted to taking video and photos of the local serfs at work and their sword-wielding guards, who looked like they too would have preferred to be anywhere else. The musty-smelling shipping container was the solitary dry place in this hellhole, and it held two bunk beds. It would probably need to be disinfected with fire to be usable again. But, as bad as this mission had been at times, Danny loved it. He loved being in the EDF, which was why if his dumb-shit brother had screwed this up for him…

"Hey! Dumb-ass." He tried again, driving his foot into the mattress above him. He knew *he* hadn't done anything stupid in like a month.

"You kick me again, I'm gonna come down there and feed you your fucking leg."

"Hey, you're awake… check your compad. I think you screwed up or something."

One of the doors to the shipping container pulled open on rusty hinges. Everything was rusting here. The green-hued sunlight making its way through the thick canopy of foliage above them flooded the interior of the storage container. Danny looked between his feet to see the profile of First Sergeant Emory Tommens standing in the door. Tommens was backlit by bright green jungle and dark mud—the only two colors that made up their day unless they hiked to where they could see the ocean. Tommens was one of the Delta guys that had accompanied Colonel Pretty to Eden. As far as bosses went, Tommens was alright.

"What the fuck did you two do?"

"Just trying to figure that out, First Sergeant. We just saw the message." Josh responded from above him, suddenly awake and in full ass-kissing mode.

"Whatever it is, you pulled me into it. We are wrapping up here. The *Door Knocker* is due tonight. I've already radioed the on-site team to pack up and start back. You two, get your shit on and meet them on the trail. Give them a hand hauling the gear out."

It was six miles from their base camp to the two sites from where they'd been watching the large village. Six miles of snake-infested, boot-sucking mud. Danny's own groan was matched by one from above him. He wanted to say that they'd just returned from their own rotation the night before, but this was First Sergeant Tommens, and there would have been no sympathy and exactly zero fucks given.

"Yes, Sergeant," Josh replied with a lot more enthusiasm than Danny knew was real. His brother landed with a bang on the plywood floor of the container facing the doorway. "We're on it."

"Seriously? 'We're on it?'" Danny whispered as soon as Tommens' profile moved out of the doorway.

"Hey, I didn't do anything… I swear," Josh replied. "Just trying to get a start on the hole you dug for us."

"Me?" Danny dug around in his bag for a pair of dry socks that he knew he wasn't going to find. "Wasn't me."

"If we didn't do anything," Josh fired back, "why the hell are we getting hate mail and being pulled out of here?"

"How the hell would I know?" he yelled.

"Orders!" Tommens shouted back at them from somewhere outside. "You don't need to know why."

Twenty minutes later, Sergeant Tommens watched his two best troops—not that he'd ever tell them that—disappear down the trail. The jungle seemed to dissolve them slowly until they were gone. He glanced back at the message sent to him from Colonel Pretty. Whatever was going on, it was bigger than Josh and Danny. He was being asked to report as well.

*

Rotterdam, Chandra - Lupe

Lupe Flores had grown up hunting mule deer and antelope in the Owyhee high desert of eastern Oregon. In the fall, weekends had been for deer until everyone's tags were filled. They reserved weekends for going after bucks that his family had kept tabs on throughout the year. During the week, they'd rush to get after the pheasant, quail, and his favorite—chukar—before the sun went down. Hunting had been the single constant in his life. Even after he'd started drinking, hunting had been the one thing he'd sober up for.

A lot had changed in his life over the last three years, mainly because of the whole new planet thing—*planets*, he corrected himself. He hadn't touched so much as a beer since his first week on Eden. He was still a hunter though. These days his prey walked on two legs and carried four-foot-long razor-sharp swords on their backs. They had their own guns and wouldn't hesitate to chop him or his family up into chunks given half a chance.

He pulled the ventilated hood down further on his head, trying to protect his eyes and the back end of his rifle scope from the frigid mist that was so light it barely fell. It just seemed to hang in the air as if it couldn't decide to be rain or fog. The rain was a surprise, and they'd been promised it wasn't going to last. At the moment, he was trying to remember if he'd ever hunted in the rain in Eastern Oregon, and he came up with nothing. Snow? Sure, every year. Rain, not so much.

They'd also been promised some wind by the people who should know, but he'd already determined that weather people here were as clueless as they had been at home. The promised wind was why he was laying on his stomach atop the creaking roof of a storage shed at the end of a stone quay looking landward across a harbor at a Kaerin shipbuilding site. This location had been Rotterdam on Earth. Here on Chandra, it was a large city dedicated to shipbuilding, and the harbor, its shipways, the river estuary, and its docks smelled like a combination of high school wood shop, tar, and sewer gas. It was a powerful combination, and he didn't want to imagine what the stench was like in the summer.

A slight gust of breeze buffeted him, coming out from the land. Finally! This whole operation was going to be close to worthless if they didn't get their wind. Lupe spotted his two Jema warriors through his scope. They'd just appeared between two ships that he now knew were classified as frigates. Both of those farthest from him where the quay jutted out from the shore were of the new model the Kaerin were trying to turn out. Sheathed in steel armor and carrying a bunch of cannons, they still mostly looked like wood to him through the scope. They'd burn just fine.

The Jema appeared again, walking out from behind the ship. The bags of incendiaries they'd had with them as they'd gone ashore were gone, and they were almost to the landward end of his quay.

"Firebugs in sight. Three minutes out." He spoke into his open mic, reporting to Jeff Krouse, who had brought them into the harbor in the inflatable that was waiting in the water beneath his perch. Jeff clicked back once in response.

He liked working with Jeff, especially when he was hunting. He counted both Jeff and Jake as friends, but Jake never stopped talking, which could get a little annoying. On the other hand, one could almost forget Jeff was there—until or unless he was needed. In those situations, either one of the former SEALs was really good to have around.

His mentor, Carlos Delgado, a former Marine sniper and the man who had truly taught him how to shoot, felt both of the former SEALs were a bit bent. Tonight, Jeff was in charge. Their Jema, dressed in the common work overalls that seemed to be the uniform of most subject clans in this part of Chandra, made the turn onto the quay and started towards him, their pace picking up a little. He still thought it would have been better to have had the Jema dressed up as High Bloods, but the two Jema had insisted that no Kaerin would have been caught dead carrying around large bundles of anything.

"Slow down guys, you belong here." He switched to Chandrian, figuring that if it was him walking down there, with nothing on him besides a Glock, past ships loaded with High Bloods, he'd have been hot-footing it as well. They had to be tired. At this point, they'd been on the move for hours. They'd walked in with nearly a hundred pounds each of remote-detonated incendiaries. The packages were to be have been emplaced at each of the trough-like shipways.

The term "shipway" was new to him. Just one of a million new things he had learned or was still learning. But that one had struck him as just plain weird. The Kaerin were building ships at every harbor town and port across the planet. Thousands of ships were under construction, and the powers that be in Portsmouth wanted to keep the Kaerin convinced that the Jema and Edenites were concerned about being overwhelmed at sea. Lupe knew that wasn't close to being the case. Eden was turning out missiles, drones, and attack airplanes almost as fast. Not to mention the EDF's own growing navy.

It wasn't for him to point out how worthless this mission was. Tonight, was just one of many he'd already completed in trying to reduce the Kaerin shipbuilding effort. He'd been involved in sabotage attacks on Brest, Calais, Amsterdam, and Aalborg—all Earth names they'd assigned for places on Chandra. It was like trying to kill cockroaches. He knew whatever they managed to burn tonight would be back under construction within weeks if not days.

Movement on the deck of an old-style frigate directly ahead of the two returning Jema caught his attention. A High Blood, wearing a sword, had been given away by the directional lantern he carried. The Kaerin warrior must have been on someone's shit list. In Lupe's limited but growing experience, it was usually subject labor standing watch at this time of night. The Kaerin was situated atop the high platform at the stern of the frigate, leaning over the railing and watching the two Jema below come closer.

"I have a shot." He spoke slowly. The Jema wouldn't have missed the dude with the lantern suddenly appearing above them. They stopped and were shouting something up at the Kaerin. He was too far away to hear what was being said, but Lupe couldn't imagine any conversation in the middle of the night with a Kaerin guard going well for anyone. He was already on target and didn't have to move anything other than his right hand. The laser range finder integrated into his scope put the Kaerin at 337 yards, and he'd been clicking off the elevation at regular intervals as the Jema approached.

The actual trigger pull was a whisper of movement. He'd been practicing… a lot. He knew it had been a good shot before regaining his sight picture post recoil. The Kaerin was a lifeless pile on the deck. His lantern though had dropped overboard and fallen onto the quay, where a small patch of lamp oil burned. The two Jema were already moving, looking behind them as additional lanterns suddenly appeared atop the deck of the ship on the opposite side of the quay. Lupe's Lapua .338 was suppressed, but its bullet wasn't, not by a long shot. The supersonic crack had been very loud across the harbor.

"They're alerted." He spoke into his collar.

"No shit. Delivery boys clear?" Jeff's voice was calm, which was always welcome.

"They are clear, no packages on them." The last thing he and Jeff wanted was to turn the Jema into human torches.

"Fire in the hole," Jeff announced.

Lupe pulled his face off his scope and looked across the waterfront to the line of distant lanterns marking the covered construction ways, piles of lumber, barrels of tar, and reels of cordage. There weren't any fiery explosions—not with the incendiaries that the Jema had tried to hide among the clutter—but half a dozen small fires appeared a moment later.

The Jema were running full tilt at this point.

"Friendlies' inbound—thirty seconds," Lupe reported, ducking back to his scope.

Ships were coming to life all along the quay, High Bloods and subject sailors coming up on deck. Some were coming down the ladders to the quay itself, but their attention was focused landward. A few broken shouts reached him, but it all seemed to be happening behind the Jema.

He broke down his roost by slinging the heavy sniper rifle on his back and retrieving the soft bag that he'd been perched across. He looked back once to the waterfront and was amazed at how fast the fire was spreading. Flames flared on the deck of a ship close to shore, the fire climbing its masts and spars as if they'd been doused in diesel. The light from the burning lumberyards was growing by the second, and the ways themselves were a line of fire outlining that portion of the harbor's edge.

It wouldn't matter, he thought. He was just a small piece of the EDF, but even he knew this wasn't going to be enough. What they'd done here tonight wouldn't mean dick in the long run. All they'd done was step on a few ants at the edge of the anthill. They were up against a whole planet of these bastards, and all the EDF, the Jema, and their Junata allies had was the British Isles—that was it. After a moment's reflection, maybe taking out their ships like they'd been doing all fall and into the winter suddenly made a little more sense.

Two hours later, back on board the E.N. *Independence*, Captain Jack Harper stepped into the small ready room behind his high-tech bridge.

"You're Lupe Flores, correct?"

Lupe flashed a look of concern at Jeff, who just shrugged back at him and moved the dip of tobacco in his lip from one side of his mouth to the other.

"Yeah, that's me."

The captain, who reminded him of his elementary school bus driver, rather than the Hollywood image of a ship's captain he had in his head, held out a piece of paper to him. "This came in about an hour after you guys cast off. I'm supposed to get you boys back to Portsmouth ASAP, and you," Harper nodded at him, "are supposed to get yourself to the portal for immediate return to New Seattle."

"What for?" Lupe asked.

The captain offered a shrug of his own. "The orders didn't say. You boys might want to catch some sleep while you can. I'm going to run this thing out, and the sea's a lot rougher than it was during our trip in. It's liable to get a bit bouncy. We're looking at about a seven- or eight-hour run-though—depends on the wind. I'll make sure Chief Savvo gets you something warm to eat."

"Thank you, Captain," Jeff answered and pointed at their two Jema delivery boys. Both were stretched out on the floor, asleep. "They'll likely be hungry."

Lupe waited until Harper had slid the heavy door to the bridge shut. "You know anything about this?" He waved the paper in front of him.

"I might." Jeff looked at him and shook his head. "Not for me to say."

"I screw up or something?"

"I don't know. Did you screw up?"

"I don't think so."

"Don't worry about it then. In my experience, people know when they've fucked up."

"It's all good, right?"

Jeff grinned as he closed his eyes. "Yeah, what could go wrong?"

*

Portsmouth, Caledonia—Chandra - Dean

Dean Freeburn would have had to have been blind and deaf to miss the change in the tempo of work going on around him. His two Edenite foremen, educated on Earth and who actually knew what they were doing, were still shouting instructions, but his workforce of mainly liberated Junata and several dozen Creight tribesmen suddenly stopped their bickering and went quiet. For just a moment, the sound of hundreds of shovels slicing into gravel was all he heard. He looked up in expectation, and sure as shit, Derek Mills' aircar was circling the railhead that was less than ten miles from Portsmouth.

His railway, at least until it was complete. The first Chandrian railway, the Caledonian Freight Line, linking Kirkton Base with nearby Dumfries, ran east across the neck of Northern England to link up with the base and growing settlement at New Castle. From there it ran south, and they were now, after six months of 24-hour-a-day work, within ten short miles of linking up with Portsmouth. Derek had just been out to check on their progress two days ago. His boss wasn't ever satisfied with the pace of the work, but he hadn't been upset either. Dean couldn't imagine what had brought him back so soon.

Granted, the CFL railway wasn't anything that the Union Pacific would have recognized, but it was, in Derek's words, "Chandra-good." At the moment, their locomotives were farm tractors. Produced on Eden, they had the torque, transmission, and horsepower to pull four or five railcars at a time, their massive back tires straddling the tracks and running on the striated concrete road bed on either side of the rail ties. Eden, his actual home, still hadn't developed a rail system of its own yet, and he had to wonder if it ever would.

Eden's settlements were scattered across an empty world. Moving shit from place to place across a continent or a region on Eden was generally easier if you could just get it to a portal site, send it to Kirkton or Dumfries on Chandra, and then send it back to Eden and its terminal destination.

Their bridgehead on Caledonia was different. A lot of people traveled from the north to Portsmouth via the portal, with the quantum bridge mechanics requiring the waypoint stop on Eden. But the scope of traffic on Caledonia, heavy as it was, was local on a planetary scale, and another mode of heavy transportation was needed that didn't tie up the portals. Roads were still being improved, though somebody, in his opinion, needed to put some real thought and effort behind getting the Junata—and especially the Creight—some more driver's education. Creight behind the wheel of anything was just asking for trouble. The Junata were only slightly better.

Junata road rage and the Creight's lack of basic depth perception while moving at any speed faster than one could walk, were just symptoms of a larger problem. There might be a couple billion potential allies on Chandra, but at the moment, running a shovel was pushing their limits of dealing with technology that most of his workforce still considered magic.

Tam'gus, a local Junata liberated from a Kaerin plantation north of Portsmouth six months ago, was his quickest learner. The former blacksmith had a lot of potential and was standing next to him, pointing at the circling aircar with his chin.

"The boss come again?" *Gus'* English was at about the same level as his Chandrian, which wasn't anywhere close to where it needed to be.

"It's alright, Gus. Your team is doing well."

The Junata were still overly sensitive as to what their superiors thought of them. It would probably take a generation to fix. It wasn't like anyone could fault them for being a little hyper sensitive—not when the Kaerin had been willing to kill as their idea of workplace motivation. Keeping the Junata convinced they were free and being paid for their labor was a constant struggle.

On the other hand, the Creight didn't feel like they needed to answer to anyone, ever. They might show up for work, or they might go fishing. He'd lost half a work crew of Creight a couple of days earlier when they'd spotted a herd of deer in the distance. In the middle of the day, they'd just dropped their shovels and picks in place and gone hunting. He wasn't certain any of them had come back yet.

"More Creight left last night," Gus reported in Chandrian as if he could read Dean's mind.

"I know." He nodded, watching the aircar drop down behind the tree line as it landed. "They aren't prisoners, Tam'gus."

What he really needed was another dozen or so Edenites. Edenite founder stock or Earth-educated, it didn't matter. He'd settle for anybody that understood that quality concrete had to be mixed correctly—or, in his waking dreams, half a dozen people who could operate a front-end loader or a backhoe without killing those around them.

"Gus, I want you to hammer check those concrete rail ties." He pointed at the recently delivered load of concrete ties that had come down the rail line from the plant in New Castle. Nearly twenty percent of the last load had been unusable for anything beyond fill material. "Mark the bad ones."

Gus nodded in understanding and then lifted his chin at something behind him. "Not the boss. Is soldier—Kareel."

Dean knew enough Chandrian to know Kareel was just a step below God, if the Kaerin had such a concept. He turned to see Kyle wading through the suddenly industrious workforce, coming closer and waving.

He waved back. "He's a friend, Gus. Make certain only the good ties get laid down."

"Right." Gus nodded and moved away as quickly as he could without breaking into a run. The Junata wanted no interaction with the big soldier boss man.

"Dean, this is amazing!" Kyle shook his hand. "Seriously, you've got as many Junata working for you as anybody does."

Dean pointed back at him. "Thanks to big soldier boss man arriving in his magic flying machine, they are going to work really hard until you leave. Half of it will need to be un-fucked later, but thanks all the same. My standing probably just went up a notch."

Kyle nodded knowingly. "It's even worse in the army. Half of them still think we are going to use the poor performers as targets."

Dean laughed and shook his head. "Just between us, there are days—moments—when I think the Kaerin might have been on to something. They'll come around."

Kyle pointed back down the railway toward New Castle, just less than 300 miles distant. "Still, what you guys have done is nothing short of a miracle."

Dean had known Kyle since they were kids. He'd been two years behind Kyle in school, but old enough to play on the same football and baseball teams once they were both in high school. After Kyle had left town for West Point, they'd probably seen each other half a dozen times before Kyle had shown up three years ago with a wild ass story about a new world. Kyle's timing had been fortuitous. Dean had already skipped town to avoid his New Civilian Works Administration, or NCWA, subpoena. The government had thought his skills would be more valuable somewhere other than where he wanted to live.

He pointed up at the railway. "Lots of hands, most of it was Army in the beginning. I'm just the walking boss."

That wasn't exactly true. He, his youngest son Patrick, and his dad Mike had founded Freeburn Engineering Inc. and they, and Edenites like them, were now worth their weight in gold on two different worlds. Dean's oldest son, Jacob, had discovered he liked the Army and was still serving for the time being down in Portsmouth. If everything came together, Freeburn Engineering would come out of the CFL railway project owning a full percentage point of it.

"You're far more than that, and I know it. I pissed off Derek when I gave him a heads up on what I wanted to talk to you about."

Dean felt himself smile. "Yeah… I already heard. You're stealing Amona from Derek. You're right, he's pissed. So am I. That little guy has been critical in getting us Junata that will actually stay on the project long enough to learn enough to be halfway useful. Amona is a rock star. Save your breath, Kyle—there's nothing I could do to help Amona recruit local tribes."

"I can't argue with any of that."

Dean pulled his head back and looked at the grin on Kyle's face. "You know I'm always glad to see you. I'll never forget the opportunity you gave me and my family—or the fact that you used to buy me beer in high school. But I know you are helping run a war and are too freaking busy to swing by for a chat. What's going on? Everything okay with my Jake?"

"Far as I know. I understand he made it through the first round of selection for Captain Souza's *Door Knocker* Assault Team. That's not easy. He's doing well."

"He likes the army." Dean shrugged. "And he's a lot better at it than I ever was. Freeburn Engineering is keeping his seat warm in the meantime. Come on. Kyle, just give it to me."

"Jake Bullock and I just got back from a quick trip to New Mexico. I'm headed back very shortly, and I could really use your help there. For a couple of weeks, probably."

"I wasn't aware the Program had much development planned for New Mexico at the moment. Is this strictly an EDF project?"

"Dean…"

"Dad still handles most of the contractual stuff for the company, but he's just going to ask me what I think in the end. What are you thinking? A new training base?"

"The other New Mexico, Dean… Earth."

It took him a moment to process what he'd just heard. "Oh… no. Hell no, and fuck you while I'm at it. Are you nuts? It's a freaking prison. The whole country was coming apart the last time you guys were there. No way I'm going to risk getting stuck there."

"We have a good plan." Kyle ignored him. "No issues portalling in or back out. I was just there for a quick twelve-hour trip. Think of all the people there that would give their left nut for a chance to get to

Eden. The same chance we had. We need more people, Dean. It's as simple as that."

"I couldn't agree more. You go get them. I'll give them jobs when they get here."

Kyle grinned back at him. "You could consider it one of those company recruiting trips."

Dean scratched his nose. "Look, I know what we're doing here is not saving the planet or anything, but for the first time in a very long time, my old man is happy. We are building something together. Something that's going to outlast us and that his grandkids will have. You're asking me to risk all that. I won't do it."

"Dean, you're not seeing the big picture. What you are doing *is* going to save the people of Chandra. We have to get big enough and produce enough fast enough to take them on—and we don't have the numbers to do it. Period. Not without years of bombing civilians into submission. We've practically gutted Eden's building plans to get this place up and running. I know how many projects you have waiting for you after the railway is finished—Derek made sure I knew. Enough work for decades, in his words. Dean, we don't have decades. We've beaten as many plowshares into swords as Eden's population can handle. How many construction outfits from Eden like yours are there? Three? Four? Can you train Junata up in time? Or the Creight?"

"But we'll take another city, get another subject clan on our side."

"You're right, we will," Kyle agreed quickly. "You think they'll be happy to leave? Be uprooted from their homes to come to Portsmouth to finish building out the Junata's and Jema's new home? Or do you think they might want to stay where they have roots and build up from there? Militarily, we'll have to keep them in place and build up a local defensive capability wherever they are. If we don't, it will just get taken back, especially when we start going after places that aren't surrounded by an ocean. Yeah, we'll get more locals, but your workload, the logistical load is only going to get heavier."

Dean hadn't thought about it those terms and admitted as much.

He could see the headache that guys like Kyle, and worse, Derek, were facing down the road.

"I can't imagine why you'd need me. You going to build a house while you're there?"

"I need people who can talk to them. People that aren't soldiers, people that would probably be living next to them under the New Mexico sun if they hadn't made it to Eden. Back in Oregon, how many weeks away do you think you were before they would have arrested you?"

"I wasn't going to let myself get arrested." He had taken Sonja and the boys up into the hills above Baker, to his dad's cabin, to escape.

"I'm not doubting you, Dean. I know how stubborn you are. I'm betting a good number of the current prisoners of New Mexico probably said or thought the same thing before remembering they had children and families. You've been where they were. There are precious few people in the Program that truly understand what it was like to live under that threat. Most of the people associated with the Program operated under the mindset of having an out. You lived the reality of having it all taken from you. I can sell the fight, and I can be honest with them all day long about the opportunity Eden represents, as well as the risks. But at the end of the day, I'm some lucky bastard that always had an out."

"I can't be the only—"

"You're not," Kyle interrupted him. "Grant Ballard is coming as well... so's his mother. But Grant is a now a soldier, and his mom's a nurse for the EDF. I'd like somebody who could convince them that there's more to our offer than an ongoing war."

Dean glanced around at the hundreds of people working for him. He knew there were Junata watching him right now, who probably thought he was insane for arguing with a "Kareel" or a "War Leader" or whatever the hell it was they thought Kyle was. What else were they going to think?

It *would* be a relief to have somebody close by, who just *knew* that a foot, as in twelve inches, wasn't *his* literal foot at the end of his leg. Or that a backhoe wasn't some sort of device for executing problem workers. How many times had he told *that* story over a beer? An entire contingent of Creight had taken for the tree line when he'd opened up the claw-toothed bucket. The only reason he hadn't lost a few Junata that day was because they had all assumed it was a Creight that was going to be clawed in half.

"Can I think about it? I'd have to tell Sonja about it—and my dad. He'd blow a nut over losing this project."

"Absolutely." Kyle clapped him on the shoulder. "And you're not going to lose a thing—I have Derek's word on that. Get to Seattle tomorrow morning at 1130 hours, Seattle time. Jake and I will brief everyone on what we learned. Then you can decide. As for all this, Derek may bitch—and believe me, he has. None of this will affect Freeburn's completion bonus."

"I'll think about it."

Kyle grinned at him. "You know, if we do manage to convince a bunch of folks to come back with us, you might tell your dad that you'd have the first shot of recruiting them. It's a hot job market out there, and it's only going to get hotter."

Dean shrugged, not certain that would make up for the risk of getting stuck on Earth. Then again, Pops *was* a businessman. "I can make your meeting, then decide?"

"Sure, if we stay on schedule, you'll have a day or two."

"Is Elisabeth okay with this?"

"She's better now that we've done our recon and know a little more."

Dean smiled and shook his head. "So, not okay?"

"Not so much," Kyle admitted. "She does understand we don't have a choice."

*

Chapter 3

Kaerus (Kaerin Capital), Chandra

"How are your injuries today?"

Lord Tima Bre'jana looked forward to his daily discussion with the Edenite prisoner. It was an interesting distraction from the administrative work of helping Lord Noka manage a war involving every Kaerin on the planet. The title "prisoner" wasn't quite right—the man had come to them of his own volition as a traitor to his people. While it was true that Daryl Ocheltree would never leave this suite of rooms alive, he was treated well.

Lord Noka had personally put the traitor to the knives before Tima had ever been told of his presence. The process had broken something in the prisoner beyond the flayed skin. Tima had worked daily to try and fix some of that damage. The more he learned at the prisoner's side, the more convinced he was of the man's value.

Tima suspected Ocheltree felt somehow betrayed by his captors, as if the Kaerin should or could have welcomed a traitor. The Edenite's stubborn naivete had worn off to be replaced by an acceptance of his fate and a corresponding crisis of spirit that had threatened to destroy what was left of him. For months, Tima had worked to undo the damage Lord Noka's questioning had wrought in the man's mind even as his broken body healed. The key had been convincing him that his role was critical, that his original purpose in coming to them—to end the fighting between the Kaerin and the Edenites—could still bear fruit.

"Injuries suggest an accident." The prisoner's accent was grating, but it was improving. "Not the fact that I was tortured." The Edenite wagged a finger at him in admonishment.

This concept of what the prisoner had termed "morality and human decency" was foundational to how the prisoner thought. It was as if those concepts somehow existed on a higher plane of reality that should somehow supersede the very simple fact that his people were at war with the Kaerin.

"Daryl." He'd long used the prisoner's informal name. It was clearly important to him that he be liked, and Tima had done nothing but reinforce the idea that he was here as a friend. "We've spoken of this— you were questioned under the knives, as is our way. It was not torture. You responded well, and truthfully. Your injuries are but a reminder of what could and would recommence should your cooperation falter for some reason."

Ocheltree's face dropped at the mention of the knives. "I'll continue to assist you in every way I can."

"I believe you, and I appreciate your cooperation. The misunderstanding surrounding your capture was unfortunate. The idea of someone volunteering themselves for the... *diplomacy*? Did I say the word correctly?"

"You did." Daryl smiled, as if taking pride in a student.

"Diplomacy... a strange word. Relations between two states, yes?"

"Basically, yes."

Tima could hardly imagine the world of the prisoner's origin—not Eden, but the other—Earth. Hundreds of polities and massive clans called countries, each with relations with one another—and they named it diplomacy. Chaos was the word that came to his mind. More sobering was the fact that these Edenites were the descendants of a people that had been fighting one another for thousands of years. That had been an eye-opening discovery, the implications of which he was still trying to gain a better grasp.

"There has been only the Kaerin, and our subjects. The two are not equal. We could not have known anything of your intentions. The concept of diplomacy itself is… what is that word you have used before?"

"Alien?"

"Yes… that's it. *Alien* to us."

"I understand that now." Ocheltree nodded somberly.

"We are, however, willing to learn." Tima patted his own leg. "So is Lord Noka. We wish you to write a letter to your people."

"A letter? Saying what?" The prisoner's face lit up.

"We'll have time to come up with something together. We'll combine the effort with my language lessons. After all, if the two of us are to be representatives of our people and trying to end this conflict, I'll need to learn to speak your tongue much better than I do presently."

The Edenite seemed to grow before him. He sat up straight—or as straight as his forearm allowed. It had been stitched to his stomach and forced to heal into a manacle of scar tissue binding his arm to his body. Daryl rubbed at his tear-filled eyes with the one arm that still functioned.

"Together? Your Prelate would be willing to talk? This is all I wanted. It is why I came here."

"Lord Noka will listen to my suggestion. But the decision, of course, would be his in the end." Tima would sooner stitch his own arm to his side before taking such a proposal to Lord Noka, but he'd surmised early on that blind hope was all this creature had left.

The Edenite regarded him closely for a moment before looking up at the small basement window that let in a shaft of light from the courtyard above. When he turned back, he was shaking his head.

"We have a saying—we call it 'burning a bridge.' You choose a path as you make a decision, your path is chosen, and the 'bridge' behind you is burned. There is no going back for me, Lord Tima. I'm not certain anything I say would be believed by my own people. Anything I compose on your behalf would likewise be deemed suspect."

Tima nodded in agreement, hiding his surprise. The prisoner's mind wasn't entirely gone, just deluded by its righteousness to the point of being nearly useless. Just now had been the closest the prisoner had come to taking some responsibility for why his own people might despise him. It was an improvement that spoke to Tima's own challenge with respect to the strange man living in the bowels of Lord Noka's citadel.

He had to find a way to get the truth from Ocheltree. The actual truth, and not the opinionated delusions of a broken man who still felt justified in betraying his own people. Tima wondered at the odd type of strength it must take to delude oneself to that degree. Hope was the key. He had to keep the prisoner hopeful that he'd made a sacrifice for his own people, rather than having committed a tragic error based on delusion. Daryl Ocheltree so wanted to be right.

"I admit," Tima began, "my concerns align with your own on this point. Yet, how else can diplomacy begin? As you have said many times, Daryl—at some point, the two sides must talk, yes?"

"Yes, of course." Daryl's excitement seemed to fade with the answer.

Tima recognized the faraway look on the prisoner's face. These swings in emotion were the hardest part of their discussions. If he lost the prisoner to despair, it could be days before another fruitful interaction.

"Think on what I should say in the letter." Tima spoke as he stood and took a step towards the door. He stopped mid-stride and turned back, pulling a small cloth bag from his tunic. "I nearly forgot—the carpenter I asked to make your game pieces has finished these. If they meet with your approval, he is ready to make the rest." Tima dumped the alien wooden shapes out onto the tabletop. There were six different forms of caricatures representing different roles in some ancient Edenite game of strategy.

He watched closely as the prisoner's face lit up. "These are great! Please pass on my admiration to the craftsman."

The 'craftsman' was a Jehavian clansman in the employ of Lord Noka, who would never hear of who he had produced the game pieces for, or why.

"I will be sure to do that."

"We'll need two identical pairs of these five larger pieces, one pair black, one white. And then sixteen of these smaller pieces—the pawns. Half white, half black."

"And then you'll be able to teach me this famous game of strategy you have spoken of?"

"Chess." The prisoner beamed. "Yes, though we'll need the game board the pieces set on as well. Did the craftsman get that drawing?"

"He did. I was told it was still curing. I would have brought it otherwise. You'll need to be patient with me, Daryl. I understand games of strategy very well, but learning a new one takes time."

When the prisoner had first mentioned the game—one that the Edenites had been playing for millennia and referred to as the game of Kings—he'd seen it as an opportunity to learn *how* his enemy thought. How they planned and strategized.

"I'm very much looking forward to it, sir."

"As am I." Tima realized he was telling the truth. He enjoyed his time spent with the prisoner, learning of technologies that he could barely imagine. The Edenite was a goldmine of knowledge and had shown a willingness to talk freely when his mind was otherwise occupied. Much of what he had learned was already being applied—especially with the shipbuilding effort.

"We'll play in English as well—I must learn your tongue if I'm to become a di…" He stumbled over the word.

"A diplomat," Daryl finished for him. "You are a very fast learner."

"As you say, a diplomat. You'll teach me more of your tongue, and I'll see if I can get approval to have your arm's use returned to you."

"You can do that?" The man's surprise seemed genuine.

"I do have some authority in these matters."

"Of course, of course," Daryl sputtered. "I didn't mean to suggest otherwise—I meant technically. You have people who can do that?"

Tima forced himself to smile. The prisoner's appreciation for the technical ability of the Kaerin, or lack thereof, spoke volumes. It wasn't a comfortable thought.

"Our abilities in these matters are quite advanced. The skin of your forearm was removed during your questioning, as was the patch on your torso to which it is attached. When they were stitched together, the healing and the resultant scars bind the subject quite well, as you can attest. The practice also serves as a visual example to others, should a subject ever be released."

"I can imagine."

"Often the leg bones are broken and those limbs are bound by the same technique in some unnatural manner as well, but I don't see a need to progress to that level. Excuse me." He smiled again, having enjoyed seeing the blood draining from the man's face.

"I didn't mean to suggest," Tima waved his hand. "I meant to say— the process can be reversed if accomplished before the limb becomes useless. And your powers of healing are nothing short of miraculous."

"That would be… wonderful."

"As you can imagine, there would be some pain involved in the process."

The prisoner waved away the concern with his free arm. "If it would return the use of my arm, I would welcome it."

Tima, still standing, nodded once. "It would seem I have my duties laid out then. Until tomorrow, think on what I should say in my letter of introduction to… I'm not even certain who it should go to."

"Colonel Hank Pretty," Ocheltree responded without a pause. "Or someone in his military junta—that means his council. It's a group that shouldn't have the authority it does, but they claimed it, and there has been little pushback from the Program council, which represents the will of our people. I suppose it is the fact that we are at war."

"Ah, yes, the civilian-military divide. You have spoken of it before."

"Exactly. Before the Jema came, before your invasion of Eden—we were ruled by a committee of civilians. War shouldn't have changed that, and technically—or officially rather—I suppose it hasn't. But Colonel Pretty and his people have all the influence now."

Tima was well familiar with the prisoner's dislike and distrust of his own military, an organization to which the man had sworn service. The Edenites were alien to him, to use the new word he'd learned. More and more, he was convinced that his prisoner's mindset was probably just as alien to the people he had served.

"I would wish to avoid offending others on this Program council by addressing the letter to a single one of its members. It's one more thing we can discuss as we create the letter." He turned to go before remembering the English phrase Daryl had taught him. "Have a good day, Daryl."

Tima shut the door to the suite of rooms behind him, shaking his head. 'Alien,' as he understood the term, was a very good word. Beyond the tools and technology of his enemy, of which he had already learned a great deal—it was how they thought which concerned him. His biggest fear being that the single Edenite in his possession was by no means the norm.

"Sir?" One of the two guards standing on either side of the door—part of Lord Noka's personal security—spoke up.

"No tears today," he answered.

The guard who had spoken nodded in approval. The other grunted in disgust and handed a single coin over to his watch-mate.

Guarding a prisoner was far beneath a warrior's time, but Lord Noka had made it clear to his guards that this particular prisoner's existence was to remain a secret. He couldn't fault the guards for finding some entertainment in their task.

"I've ordered Gemendi here this evening. They are going to administer something to the prisoner in his evening meal to knock him out. Make certain he eats his entire dinner. They'll be working on him through the night to restore the use of his arm." He glanced at the guard who had lost this day's wager. "I personally guarantee there will be tears tomorrow."

"We are going to heal him?" The first guard sounded more curious than shocked.

"I'm after what's in his head. He's very cooperative, and I'll continue this pretense of respect as long as he remains so. Do not mistreat him."

Both of the guards saluted him, the second speaking. "Lord, you asked to be notified when another shipment arrived from Landing. The crates have been moved to your work-shop."

"How many?" He dared to hope. To date, the effort to comb the site of destruction on the island of Landing, his abandoned fief, had so far proven fruitless. Dozens of crates had been delivered to him here. Hundreds of burned, crushed, and broken artifacts from a useless Kaerin past littered his workshop in the hope that he could find an answer to the Edenite's technological advantage.

Lord Noka had provided everything he'd asked for. His workshop, formerly a half-used wine cellar and auxiliary barracks room, had been transformed since Tima had taken up permanent residence in Kaerus. At the moment, he stood staring at six large packing crates stacked between his work benches.

Lord Noka had also seen to it that he had his own security detail, which had been one of the first public—if still unofficial—signals to the Prelate's Council that a successor had been chosen. It was a fluid situation, and no one in or out of Lord Noka's pool of supporters believed that a handover of the Prelate's office to a non-hereditary successor would go unchallenged. Tima was often driven to the memory of Lord Noka telling him that he would not wish the role of Prelate on someone he thought of as family.

At the moment, the presence of his security detail meant he didn't have to deal with the crates himself. He had two fingers of warriors under his personal control—ten warriors who had sworn in Lord Noka's presence to defend his life. Four of them guarded this workshop at all times.

"Let's begin with the crates that just arrived." He only had to point.

They stood ready with pry bars, and by now they knew the drill. They would unload each item, and if it was a piece of ancient material, it went into the growing pile at the end of the room. If it was a whole undamaged piece of anything, it would be inspected by him before being catalogued and passed onward to one of the many teams of Gemendi reporting to him.

Lucky for all of them, he thought as the warriors fell to tearing down the crates, much of the production of the newly designed weapons had already been shipped offshore before the Edenite raiding party had turned the Kaerin pavilion on Landing into an unstable crater half a kamark across.

Those same weapons—based on recovered Edenite weapons— were a vast improvement over what had been used for centuries. They were still a weak answer to the *technology*—another word that Ocheltree had taught him—of the Edenites. It was technology he'd dismissed as rumor, along with most of the Kaerin leadership. It was now an accepted fact.

The seizure of Irinas in a single day of fighting—as well as his conversations with Ocheltree—had proven the Edenites had yet to show the true extent of their abilities. If the prisoner was to be believed, the Edenites had airboats that could exceed the speed of sound, and explosives of such unimaginable power that Ocheltree's home world of Earth had lived in fear of global annihilation. He had to find an answer to the Edenites, or he truly would be the last Kaerin Prelate.

"Lord Tima?"

He looked up to see one of his detail holding up the barrel of an ancient Kaerin rifle. He'd seen its like a hundred times, and he knew it wasn't a rifle any more than the sword he carried. The model numbers etched into its strange alloy frame mocked him: *tar* 14.2. A Kaerin letter, near the end of the list, then 14.2? As if hundreds of earlier models had existed before and been approved upon. Yet he had no idea how the weapon had been powered or even what it fired down its magnet-lined barrel.

"The magnets within are useful. Put it in the disassembly pile."

More of the same. Perhaps he was wasting time with this recovery effort. The site of the devastation on Landing was riddled with collapsed tunnels and unstable chambers. His recovery efforts had been costly for the Subject residents of Landing, but with the Pavilion gone, it wasn't as if he had another purpose for them. They and their ancestors had served the Gemendi on Landing for generations. They knew far too much to be re-located, and there were too many mouths to feed. Better their deaths come sooner and possibly amount to some gain as they dug.

"Lord? This is new, at least to my eyes."

His guard was holding up what he took at first to be a thick short hose, stiff enough that its ends bent towards the floor under its weight rather than drooping. He nearly pointed toward the materials pile without a thought, but something about the flexible, clamshell pattern of its metal sheathing pricked at his memory. He'd seen cabling like that before. He waved the guard over to him.

The weight of the short cable surprised him. He laid it out on the tabletop, and it took both of them to bend the ends towards each other. He let out a satisfied grunt when the male and female terminals mated perfectly.

"Is it of value, Lord?"

He pulled the terminals apart and stared at the female end. He'd seen a receptacle like that before. "Perhaps, if we had the correct object to plug it into."

The guard waited a moment before dipping his head and moving back to his crate. Tima ran his hand over the flexible sheath that had jogged his memory… where had he seen this before?

The boat! The ancient Kaerin boat the old Subject Gemendi had gotten to work in the sun. It had had cables such as these buried throughout its hull. Had the cables merely plugged into a portion of the hull—the part that was exposed to the sun? Had they even bothered to look? Power was power. Impetus powered lights and manufactories across Chandra, and they used heavy copper for the purpose—was this merely a more advanced cable? Could the boat power its own battery pile by the sun using such cables? Why couldn't it be made to power something else? He glanced at the female end of the cable again. His legs almost gave out when he remembered where he'd last seen that pattern. It hadn't been on Landing. It was on the ancient beacon device under guard in Lord Noka's office.

He went directly to his own private office with the cable over his shoulder. He shut the door, wondering what he could or should tell Lord Noka.

Back in the workroom, his guards looked at each other in surprise before their Teark shrugged and motioned the rest of them back to the crates. "Must have been something important."

One of Lord Tima's new guards silently agreed. The Kaerin Lord he actually served would perhaps find it interesting as well.

*

Chapter 4

New Seattle, Eden

"I'm in agreement." Paul Stephens came around his desk in his wheelchair. He waved a book in front of him with the hand not controlling the joystick. "I think with some obvious modifications, the foundation of our overall strategy is in here. I'm just surprised that an Army guy came up with it."

Kyle smiled at the joke. Hank Pretty and Paul Stephens had been friends for a long time. Hank grunted as he took the book and handed it over to Kyle with a sadistic smile.

"Read this in your free time."

Kyle rolled his eyes. Luckily for him, he'd read the book while at West Point. Hank knew that and that Kyle was already familiar with his long-term strategy. Alfred Thayer Mahan's *The Influence of Sea Power upon World History: 1660-1783* had been required reading for almost every officer of every military service worth the name since its publication in the late 1800s. The principals and theories espoused in it had helped Hank, Jomra, and him formulate a long-term strategy for Chandra.

"We aren't going to be building any battleships or ships of the line anytime soon." Stephens shook his head. "But with our control of the sea, I think this idea of cutting the land masses of Chandra off from one another, gaining footholds on every island we need and are able to, liberating the Chandrians on those islands, and hopefully convincing them to join us is our best option. If we are given the time to do it."

If... there we a lot of ifs in their plan. Then again, what plan didn't have them?

"Caledonia is a template of sorts," Hank started. "We are going to duplicate those efforts on the Japanese island chain, Madagascar, and the entire Indo-Pacific. Australia and New Zealand are nearly devoid of Kaerin presence, and the indigenous people there are less like the Creight than they are remnants of whatever folks weren't rounded up by the Kaerin a thousand years ago. They aren't escaped slaves. They've always been free as near as our recon efforts have been able to discern."

"I've read those reports." Stephens said. "We'll do what we can for them, but we'll leave them alone if they wish. Frankly, there aren't enough of them to be useful to us, and they don't need to be liberated."

Hank nodded in agreement. "To continue, the Indonesian archipelago is controlled by the Kaerin and runs like the plantations we found on the British Isles. They are on the list. Eventually I want to be able to take Cyprus, Crete, and Sardinia and drop bases right in the middle of their gut. The minor islands are uninhabited for the most part, and we could take them now... but unless they offer some strategic depth—as in lots of water between them and the mainland—we aren't ready for it. I don't want an island outpost we can't defend any more than I imagine you do. If they manage to put their numbers ashore on any island we manage to take, we'll be hard pressed to hang on to it."

"What about North and South America?" Stephens asked. "Lots of Kaerin there too, though not as many as in Eurasia."

"Cuba," Kyle answered. "For starters." He and Jake had personally undertaken that recon mission. "It's set up a lot like the British Isles were, except that it has two large Kaerin settlements: one in the location of Havana, and the other at the opposite end of the island. We designated it Guantanamo, but it's a different natural bay. When we have the numbers, we'll take control of the Panamanian isthmus and wall off North and South America from each other. We'll be able to deal with their land-based centers of power piecemeal, or hopefully the local Chandrians will—with our help, of course. Choke them off, prevent any reinforcements from one continent to another that won't have to march to get to a fight. In the meantime, we just keep recruiting and training Chandrians."

"This could take years." Stephens sighed.

"Decades, perhaps," Hank agreed. "Until or unless the Kaerin can be convinced they have a future that lies in change and compromise. We needed a strategy that informs our tactics and next steps. This fulfills that need, but it's a long-term strategy, Paul. It's not a plan. We'll stay flexible, take opportunities when and where they come. It does provide you with an overall framework that should be sellable as a policy to the Council. They need to understand that this is a long-term process, but it's the only reasonable one we've come up with that doesn't involve the wholesale slaughter of the Kaerin and untold numbers of Chandrians."

Kyle wasn't too worried on that score. A lot of Edenites who had initially thought Chandra should be left to its own fate—or who had wrongly felt that the war was the fault of the Jema—had changed their minds after the Kaerin attack on New St. Louis. The attack had been dealt with quickly, but the path of death and destruction between the Kaerin force and the outskirts of the city had been all the proof needed to convince most Edenites that the Kaerin issue wouldn't resolve itself.

There were always exceptions. One of those had taken his concerns directly to the Kaerin in person. Kyle didn't like thinking about the potential damage Ocheltree could do to them. On the flip side, Audy and Jomra had painted a horrific picture of what the Kaerin would likely do to him. To be sure, whatever Ocheltree knew, the Kaerin would know as well.

"That's not the problem it was," Stephens spoke as he motored his wheelchair back behind his desk. "I was never deluded into thinking we'd avoid politics on Eden, and we haven't." Stephens' wheelchair pirouetted and came to a stop, facing them. He offered up a sad smile.

"And we won't even try. The Program was meant to go away as quickly as possible, and, good for us, our body politic doesn't seem to be evolving along the lines of a zero-sum, two-party system that can only exist to feed itself.

"The bad news..." Stephens grinned and pointed at a stack of papers on his desk. "I've got eleven party formation applications here, and they've all got the numbers to be approved. Each one has a foundational issue, or several in a couple of cases. At the moment, with one exception, they all support what we are doing on Chandra. Nine of the eleven favor continuing to support the Jema by any means possible."

Kyle did the quick math in his head. "You mean to say that we have a political party that supports what we are doing on Chandra, but thinks we shouldn't support the Jema?"

Stephens laughed. "You caught that, huh? You think I could make something like that up? It's democracy at work. Frankly, the party that thinks we should glass the Kaerin and put the Jema in charge of the planet is more worrisome, but they're just very energetic, small minorities. More to the point—they're my problem. Overall, the Council will support you. The liberation of the Junata on the British Isles played well. Very well, indeed. If we keep that kind of feel-good end in mind, we'll have the long-term support you need."

"Here I was thinking we'd left all this bullshit behind." Hank tried to smile and failed.

"Hank, you're too damned smart for me to believe you actually thought that. People are people. Always have been, always will be. How's that for a deep thought?"

"You've done better."

Stephens laughed in agreement and then turned his attention to Kyle.

"Okay, that brings us to our biggest problem: numbers. We need more people—period—on Chandra *and* Eden. I'm just not certain returning to Earth for them is worth the risk, and I don't need fringe political elements to help me come up with reasons why the idea may be batshit crazy."

"Paul, it always comes back to the numbers." Hank beat him to the punch. "The industry we need to support our strategy—let alone defend ourselves while taking the fight to them—requires numbers we don't and won't have for a generation."

Stephens stopped him with an upraised hand. "I'm going to play devil's advocate here, because I know the first question I'm going to get asked is, 'we were told the Chandrians would fight their own war—we would just support them'"

Hank looked at him. "Kyle can answer that better than I can."

"The Junata are our best sample to date of who we can expect to liberate as we move forward. It's a mixed bag. They are trainable—and most are even motivated—but it takes time, resources, and most critically, our own people to train them. As we liberate another area, our logistical load—and most of all the managerial tasks of training whatever Chandrian clan it happens to be—gets heavier, not lighter.

"At some point, it will become an advantage for us as we further train them and they become better integrated. We've all met Chandrians that we can see taking on that role in the future—but so far, it's a small number drawn from primarily Kaerin Subject Gemendi. They were already a step ahead of most of their fellow clansmen—a breed apart, really. We are a ways off before we'll have a corps of Junata able to do the same."

"Okay," Stephens relented. "You've convinced me of the need and the potential benefit. Explain to me how to balance the risk of the authorities on Earth discovering that Eden is real balanced against that need for numbers."

"Sir Geoff didn't try to hide who we were and where we were going." Hank immediately jumped to the point Kyle had been ready to deliver. "They didn't believe him."

"I know, I know." Stephens patted his paralyzed legs. "I've made a study of the debriefs provided by Captain Souza and the rest of her

Task Force Chrome. There *were* elements in the government who were likely acting as if Sir Geoff was telling a true story."

"That's a leap, sir," Kyle interjected. "Yes, they were pursuing Sir Geoff and Souza's team, but she'd just absconded with their prisoner. General Gannon had just been arrested, and he was killed very soon after. Brittany Souza had no idea what Gannon said about Sir Geoff, if anything. I've gone over those reports in detail myself and while I can't prove a negative, we have zero evidence that any Earth government is focused, either theoretically or practically, on the existence of Eden. The team pursuing them was killed. For all we know, they think Sir Geoff is still on Earth and still on their most wanted list."

Stephens' lips were pursed as he turned to Hank. "You agree with that assessment?"

Hank opened his hands in front of him. "There's not enough evidence to call Kyle's reasoning an assessment. I do agree that we have no evidence indicating any official governmental belief in the existence of Eden, or the Multiverse, or whatever we are calling our neighborhood these days."

"Let me change the question." Stephens' sharp eyebrows danced for a moment on his forehead. "Wouldn't the disappearance of several people imprisoned there lead the government to realize what could be happening, or come to believe the story Sir Geoff told them all in his broadcast? Keep in mind Dave Jensen believes the US government could effort a transition-capable program to Eden within a year, *if*, in his words, they were to get "Manhattan Project serious" about it. And Jensen has an even lower opinion of government-led research programs than I do."

"Sir, if anything, that's a fact on our side." Kyle had spent a lot of time with Doc Jensen talking about this. "We are almost on our fourth year since the great escape. To date, we haven't seen any evidence of a transition coming from Earth, and we've been watching."

"People don't just disappear without a reason…"

Kyle shook his head. "Sir, people have been and are still being sent to New Mexico for the express purpose of disappearing. Have you had a chance to read to our report from our recon mission?"

"Just the summary." Stephens indicated his desktop, which was just a series of piles of paper.

"We only had time to get close enough to one decent-sized town. We chose it because it was a border town on a freeway. It's a hellhole, sir. The government just dumps people, brings them in on buses, and offloads them. Some transports would just drive through—we assume taking prisoners elsewhere in the state. As near as we could tell, there is just border security at the state line. Guards, fence lines, and cameras and probably a minefield."

"I can't imagine…" Stephens trailed off.

"We could hardly believe what we saw at a distance," Kyle agreed. The prisoners in New Mexico might prove to be valuable immigrants to Eden at some point, but with the absence of any law and order, many had devolved into a slice of humanity that wasn't going to get an invitation.

"The point I'm trying to make, sir, is Jake and I could have walked into that town and the only security concern we would have faced was getting mugged for our boots. There was no official presence that we could see."

"Is that an element we risk bringing here?" Stephens asked.

"No," Hank answered for him. "It's an element that will need to be dealt with. As best as we can tell, the observed town is run by a warlord. Every community is probably different. It's nothing we haven't seen before in a dozen other countries. You remove consequences, deny the average person the means to protect themselves, and at some point, you get a failed state run by those most comfortable with violence."

"But this is America." Paul shook his head and held up a hand, forestalling the answer he knew was coming. "Was… I know."

Paul Stephens was probably the smartest person Kyle had ever met. For a former CEO of a company that had made nano-manufacturing a reality and one of the richest people Earth had ever produced,

Stephens was remarkably normal and a 'good guy' as far as geniuses went. But the man had also led a somewhat protected life and had a hard time believing the depths some people could sink to.

"You said it yourself, sir," Kyle added. "People are people."

Stephens nodded to himself before looking up at both of them. "First sign of any official awareness of any type, of your presence, you return immediately. In a manner that doesn't raise questions."

"Understood, sir," Kyle replied.

*

"Damn…" Josh Carlisle paused at the top of the classroom-sized auditorium. "Bunch of folks must have screwed up."

There were close to fifty people spread out below them in small groups. Others were pushing in behind them through the double doors. Most were EDF, but enough weren't that Danny picked up on the fact that they probably weren't in trouble. Grant was in the second row from the front, waving them down to him, and he knew Grant had never been in trouble in his life—at least on his own.

"I think we're safe, brother. Grant's here too."

"You two idiots are blocking the door," Sergeant Tommens complained as he squeezed past them. "I'll catch up to you later."

Grant was grinning from ear to ear by the time they made their way down to him. "I'm glad you guys are going… be like old times, eh?"

Danny exchanged a look with his brother before turning back, confused. "Going where? We thought Josh had stepped on somebody's dick."

"I didn't do anything!" Josh fired back.

Grant laughed. "They didn't tell you?"

Danny was looking for some indication that they were being played as Grant's face went white and his jaw dropped open in shock.

"Mom?! What are you doing here?" Grant was looking past them out into the aisle.

"Same thing as you, I suspect." Mrs. Ballard quipped before

squeezing past them. "Watch your feet, boys."

"Mrs. Ballard." Both Carlisle brothers dipped their heads in greeting and stood to let her by. They'd learned a long time ago that Grant's mom was psychic. She'd known what they were thinking since they'd been kids. Josh elbowed Danny as soon as they were back in their seats. "You think she's in trouble too, dumbass?"

Danny elbowed Grant. "Going where?"

Grant was still gob smacked at his mother's presence. Captain Lassiter walked across the bottom of the auditorium and hopped up to take a seat on the table. He was center stage facing all of them. The murmured conversation dropped to almost nothing in an instant.

Danny elbowed Grant again. "Dude?"

"Earth," Grant whispered.

"Earth?!" Danny belted out, further silencing the room. He realized immediately that he might have just stepped in it and looked up at Kyle Lassiter, who was staring back at him with that look he had—the same one that had threatened to fill his ass with birdshot the last time they'd been on Earth.

"Sorry, sir."

Kyle felt himself grin. Part of him felt the same way.

"I think that's my cue," he started. "First off, I want to thank everyone for coming. If it hasn't already been explained to you, this trip is completely voluntary. Hear me out and then make your decision. No one's going to think any less of anyone who opts out."

"I've heard enough," Josh whispered, almost to himself. "Not this cowboy, not today, not ever."

Kyle gave the presentation he'd intended, answering questions as he went. They were all in keeping with what he'd answered previously to half a dozen different audiences as he'd fought to get the mission approved.

"Sergeant Tommens?" He pointed at the upraised hand.

"How do we explain to these people we are at war? Who the enemy is? Where they're from? You see my point, sir? I still can't hardly believe it, and I just spent the last two weeks outside a subject plantation on Chandra."

"I do." He answered, part of him still worried that he could be making a huge mistake here, that the juice wasn't going to be worth the squeeze. Yes, they needed people. They also needed to know what was happening on Earth.

"We've developed a strict contact protocol that we will all follow. In a nutshell, we're going to make contact with small groups and take it slow in terms of what we tell them. We'll be flexible and deal with issues as they present themselves. First step is to find people we can trust. A lot of the folks who have been sent to New Mexico are there for the same reasons a lot of you came to Eden. Others were probably just caught up in the sweeps, or had the bad luck to be living in a town that pushed back. My point is, it's a mixed bag in terms of people. We don't even know if the citizens of New Mexico were moved out or just became prisoners based on where they happened to live.

"But rest assured, we aren't interested in any bait and switch approach. Before any of them make the trip, they'll know the full story. And none of them will know the full story until we are sure we can trust them. Remember, we need numbers to backfill the people that have taken work on Chandra. It doesn't matter if they want to farm on Eden, help build a railway on Chandra, join the EDF, or serve beer at the pub—we can use them. We need more people—period. The one thing we know about New Mexico right now is that there are a lot of people there that don't want to be."

The younger Carlisle brother, Josh, raised his hand. Kyle immediately scanned the audience for another question, for anyone else. *Shit...* he'd probably regret this.

"Yes, Josh?"

"My fiancé and her family were sent there. Any chance we can find them? I mean like specific people?"

He remembered the story. As Danny Carlisle had told it, Josh's fiancé had dumped him long before the brothers had been caught up trying to save her and her family in Nebraska. As for the question itself, it wasn't as bad as he'd feared.

"I can't speak to the probability of locating anyone specific right now. If this does work, it won't happen overnight. We'll just have to see what we see. I hope to have a better answer for you in time. You aren't the first person to ask that particular question."

"I'm in, sir. When do we leave?"

Kyle doubted if Josh had even been listening.

*

Chapter 5

Raton, New Mexico (Earth)

Patrick Loukanis had listened to his friends tell him for over a year that now was not the time to get serious about someone. Hell, he'd tried to tell himself the same thing just as often. He'd never been much of a listener. Whether the trait flowed from his mom's Irish side or his old man's Greek blood, he'd never been told anything in his life by anyone where his first reaction hadn't been, "Oh, yeah?"

He looked across the fresh mound of dirt that was Benny's grave, at the rest of the Orosco family standing beyond it. Sandra, Benny's sister, was the reason he was here. She was the only thing in his life that hadn't gone to shit. Sandra was doing her best to comfort her mom, Emilia. Everyone in the family had assumed the old lady would be the next to be buried here—she wasn't doing well, and today wasn't going to help in that regard. Benny was the second brother Sandra's family had buried in the dry, crumbling dirt of New Mexico.

Patrick had never met the eldest Orosco sibling, John. John Orosco had been wounded in the same fighting around Lubbock that had seen Sandra's family, some five thousand other refugees, and most of his own Missouri National Guard unit arrested, transported, and dumped into the open-air prison that had been New Mexico.

Sandra had one brother left; Noah was staring across the empty highway in the direction of town—towards the revenge that he probably felt entitled to. If Patrick didn't do something about the kid, he'd be back here at this same barren hill burying another Orosco too soon. Ellsworth and his goons ran Raton. There wasn't anyone to tell them they couldn't, and they all pretty much had it in for Noah at this point.

Benny had taken issue with Ellsworth's tax collection efforts while he was taking a load of squash the family had grown to the local market. Benny hadn't wanted to pay Ellsworth's tax, or at least not all of it. Noah's mouth had started a fight that his older brother hadn't come out of.

Sandra's dad, Juan, was defeated. He stood like a scarecrow with one hand on Sandra's shoulder, staring at the dirt that awaited all of them. Patrick couldn't speak to the rest of the Federal holding pen that had been New Mexico, but he knew a lot of folks like Juan and Emilia who had just given up. Their lives had been reduced to a slow, painful timer counting down.

There were times when Patrick almost wished he and others of his Missouri National Guard unit hadn't refused orders to fire on the civilians of Lubbock, Texas. There were a lot of units like his in New Mexico. Soldiers who had refused orders only to be crushed by the big Army, or worse, an ISS security team. There'd likely be even more, but at some point, the feds had wised up and figured out that state-run National Guard units were somehow reluctant to fire on their neighbors. It's why his Missouri unit had been sent to Lubbock. It was why Texas guard units were sent to California, and so on. Except that people being people, the plan didn't always work.

Lieutenant Vroom had challenged his orders to fire into a mob of by then starving and desperate citizens of Lubbock. Patrick couldn't have known it at the time, but Sandra and her family had been part of that crowd. The entire unit had breathed a huge sigh of relief when Vroom had delivered his "no fucking way" response over the radio. The relief had been short-lived. Two companies of infantry from the 10th Mountain Division had moved up from somewhere behind them and carried out the orders. It was impossible to know, but he figured that might have been when John Orosco had caught a bullet. An ISS security team had been close behind the 10th Mountain. They'd arrested and executed Lieutenant Vroom on the spot.

His own Guard Company hadn't been cowed and returned the favor. Patrick had personally pulled the trigger on the ISS asshole that had given the order to kill Vroom. Within an hour, they'd been surrounded, disarmed, and folded into the refugees from Lubbock and sent on their way to New Mexico. It had been a year and a half since his unit had surrendered, and he'd been doing it every day since. Sandra was the only thing he had worth hanging on to, but it was no longer just Sandra, not that it ever really had been.

Benny's seven-year-old daughter Erin was holding her grandfather's hand. Her face looked slack, cried out. Behind her stood her older cousin George, fatherless since burying his own dad on this same shitty hill a week after they'd arrived. Juan and Emilia Orosco had raised their children only to lose their two eldest sons to a revolt against their own government or to the prison the rest of them had been sent to.

It would fall to Sandra and Noah to raise their siblings' children, which meant it would be Sandra and his own dumb ass doing it. Noah was a hot-headed idiot, one temper tantrum away from his own grave. Patrick knew firsthand just how close Noah had come to being killed. He was neck-deep in Ellsworth's prison mafia. It had taken every bit of persuasion Patrick could muster to buy Noah some forgiveness, except it was more of a pay-as-you-go rental arrangement. Ellsworth had used Benny's "accident" to sink his claws further into Patrick's own little business, and he was done surrendering.

The words of the Catholic priest, his dark cassock unwashed and graying with dirt, were lost as a wind devil kicked up a wall of dust that seemed to form atop Benny's grave. It seemed a fitting end to the ceremony. Patrick had long since given up practicing his mother's Catholic faith, but he prayed now with his eyes slammed shut against the dust. *Just a little help, Lord. That's all I'm asking.*

Sandra's father was looking at him when he opened his eyes. There was an unspoken ask in the old man's gaze that he couldn't have avoided and still faced himself in the mirror. Patrick could feel the weight of the request from a father who, a year ago, had looked at him like a piece of shit for showing interest in his only daughter. In that short distance across the grave, the old man was passing something more than his daughter to him.

Sandra hung back as the rest of her family started the long walk back to the shitty two-bedroom house they shared with another family.

"My father needs to talk to you."

I think he just did... "What about?"

"He wants us to try for Silver City."

Patrick glanced over Sandra's shoulder at her family moving slowly away. They were moving at Emilia's pace as she leaned on Noah for support. He'd been surprised the old lady had managed the trek to Benny's grave.

"It's a month on the road—they wouldn't make it."

"No," Sandra agreed. He'd been expecting her to explode.

"Me, Noah, and the kids." Sandra shook her head. "With you. My parents will stay."

How many times had he tried to convince Sandra to make the trip? Suddenly it was him having doubts.

"Package deal." Sandra looked sad saying it. "I'm not ready to be someone's parent, but I don't have a choice."

Neither did he, and he knew it. He loved her. Sandra was a beautiful woman and wouldn't last past the first road gang she and Noah encountered, and that was assuming Noah didn't get them all killed before that.

"Can you sit on Noah for a few days? I mean, keep him from leaving the house. I managed to buy him a little forgiveness, but his mouth will kill that deal in a heartbeat."

"Will Ellsworth come after us?" Sandra asked. "By us, I mean you."

Like a starving dog let off his leash. "Let me worry about Ellsworth.

He's why I need a few days to pull something together."

"Will they come with you?"

He knew Sandra meant Allen and Mitch. The three of them were a team, and—to varying degrees—they all worked for Ellsworth.

*

"How was it?" Allen Okamura looked up from the book he was reading as Patrick entered the three-bedroom house that they shared with a total of twelve other guys from their guard unit. He'd long since stopped wondering what had happened to the family who had lived here. There were still photos of them lying around the house. Had they been killed when this part of New Mexico revolted? Or had they been evacuated, like so many others, to make room for the influx of political prisoners?

"We buried him. How you think it went?"

Allen snapped the college chemistry textbook shut and reached for a mason jar of clear liquid on the coffee table. He took a sip of the moonshine that kept them all fed and alive.

"Here, looks like you need a pull."

A small part of him wanted to ask why they were drinking their inventory. Allen was usually the stickler for not cutting into their profits. He nodded his thanks and took more than a sip. Every batch was different, made with whatever they could scrounge, but Allen had been a chemistry teacher at Ozarks Technical Community College in Springfield and knew what he was doing. It burned a trail of fire down his throat.

"I'm done, Allen."

"With Sandra?" Allen looked at him like he was crazy. "Don't be an idiot. It wasn't your fault. She knows that."

"I mean, it's time… I'm going."

"Silver City?"

He nodded before taking another pull. "I'll take Sandra, Noah, Benny's little girl, and I guess the other kid too."

"Dude, it's a probably pipe dream." Allen was shaking his head. "The only thing Silver City has that Raton doesn't is a better PR program. Everybody that shows up on their doorstop will get put through a meat grinder, same as here. Why would it be any different?" Allen reached for the jar. "Besides, what about your long-term plan? Another two, maybe three years of playing the good little socialist, you might get released."

"Fuck you."

Allen smiled back at him. "You got options, is all I'm saying."

"Come with us."

Allen struggled not to cough and waste a pull of the best moonshine in Raton. He wiped his mouth with the back of his hand, grinned, and shook his head. "My turn—fuck you. I've got a good gig here."

"That's not an option," Patrick explained as he took the jar back. "With me and Noah gone, and Mitch too, who are you going to be able to trust to watch your back? Inside a week, you'll be chained to your still in Ellsworth's basement."

"Mitch is going with you?" Allen's whole face jerked back in surprise.

"He owes me." Patrick nodded. "He'll come with."

Allen's eyebrows scrunched up in what looked like suspicion as he leaned over the back of the couch.

"Mitch! You awake? You hear that?"

"Ugh yeah, I heard him."

Patrick looked over the back of the couch himself. Mitchell Bennett, six foot five without the military issue boots, was laid out on his back, his face covered in the crook of his elbow.

Patrick looked at the Mason jar again. It was down to a third. For all his artistry, Allen wasn't a big drinker. "I should have known. He filched it?"

"Yeah." Allen rolled his eyes. "He couldn't string more than a few words together, but he swore he'd found it lying around."

"Quality control." Mitch groaned from the floor behind them.

"You hear him?" Allen yelled a lot louder than he needed to. "You going to go too?"

Patrick was certain Mitch would either laugh it off or tell him to fuck off. His former corporal could be a real asshole when he was sober, and he was a mean drunk to boot. Nobody in their right mind fucked with Mitch.

"He's right… I owe him."

Allen swore under his breath before looking back at him. "How the hell am I supposed to take the still with us?"

Patrick looked back at Allen, feeling a little bit sorry for his friend. Maybe they could carry the copper tubing with them—that had been the hardest part to find.

Allen seemed to deflate in front of him. "Shit."

"Going to need wheelsh." Mitch spoke up from the floor, slurring his words. "Unleth ya think you can out-walk whatever Ellshworth sends after us. Not sure what he wantsh more, the profethor's brain or your girlfriend's ass."

"Drunk or not, he's got a point," Allen said, handing the shine back to him.

Patrick accepted both the jar and Mitch's wisdom. "What if we deal with Ellsworth first?"

"We do that…" Allen perked up. "Why would we need to leave at all?"

He and Mitch had kicked around the idea of replacing Ellsworth for almost a year. It came down to the fact that they didn't have nearly enough men they could count on to hold Raton. Ellsworth had too many rabid dogs underneath him that would fight each other for control. They just needed to start that fight and get good and gone before the dust settled.

"'Cuth we'd get our ath'es kicked." Mitch grunted.

"I think I can get us wheels." Patrick took a swig of the clear spirit. "Going to take some serious groveling, but I think I can do it."

"We doing this now?" Mitch asked from the floor.

"No way," he replied. "I need a couple of days and you sober."

"'Kay," Mitch responded. He was snoring a few seconds later.

Patrick smiled at Allen and held up the jar in a toast. "So… Mitch is in."

Allen just shook his head and reached for the jar. "You do know he's not going to remember a thing from this conversation."

Patrick thought about that for a moment. "Probably better that way."

*

Kaerus, Chandra

"You are certain?" Lord Noka asked.

To Tima, the Prelate looked tired in a manner that would not be remedied by a good night's sleep. Most of the other Lords who would be arriving over the next couple of days had not witnessed the gradual change in the Kaerin leader over the last six months. To them, it would come as a shock as they realized their Prelate had grown old. In a time of peace, it would not have mattered. The S'kaeda Prelate would have been replaced by his son, as had happened for the past two centuries.

Tima knew the next ten days would be critical for both of them. They were at war, and Noka S'kaeda had no son. By now, everyone knew Lord Noka had informally picked Tima as his successor, and the Kaerin Lords had been given time to make their acceptance or displeasure known. There were more than enough grounds for displeasure—they were at war and had yet to win a battle against an enemy that took pains to avoid one.

And now Tima needed to tell Lord Noka that he'd made a mistake.

"I'm certain. The impetus cable mates perfectly into the beacon's receptacle. Further, I'm sure the cable is the same as those in the ancient watercraft we found in Landing. If memory serves, several such cables form the link between the craft's power plant and whatever is in its hull that allows for the conversion of sunlight into energy."

Noka blinked slowly. "The same water craft you had me gift to Lord Oont'tal?"

"Yes. At the time I suggested it, the boat showed little potential. Its range was limited, and—"

Noka waved at him to stop. "I'm not blaming you, Tima." Noka stood up from behind his desk and went to the bank of windows overlooking the interior courtyard of the Prelate's pavilion. "Oont'tal and his navy had much more of a natural call on the artifact than I do— he still does. It also helped assuage some of his suspicions, which neither the Kaerin, nor the two of us, can afford at the moment. How does the discovery of this power cable alter any of that?"

"Lord, if I'm correct, the boat itself may represent the only means we have of powering the depleted energy cells that activate the ancient weaponry or the beacon. More than that, I'm concerned about anyone else having the ability to charge the beacon I found on Landing. You said yourself the other beacon is unaccounted for."

"Perhaps you should just destroy the cable."

"My Lord, the ancient water craft has several such. I made the connection, and Lord Oont'tal has several talented Gemendi in his house that I respect. They could possibly reach the same conclusion I did—and there is another beacon out there. My studies of your library revealed that it was likely in the keeping of High Kareel Lomas'tal at the time of our people's arrival here. He was the second-highest ranking officer at the time."

Lord Noka was shaking his head as he turned away from the window and faced him. "That line died out six or seven centuries ago. There hasn't been a Lord Lomas'tal since, not even among the minor houses."

"True, Lord—but at the time of his death, the Lomas'tal line had long held Pagasta as their seat of power. Authority there passed to a Lord Cras'tal who is an ancestor of the current—"

"Lord Oont'tal." Lord Noka interrupted him as he pinched the bridge of his nose. "You're thinking he may have the other beacon?"

"It's impossible to know," Tima acknowledged. "But on the chance that he does, I have devised a proposal to get access to the boat. I should at least be able to discern if his own Gemendi are on the right path." He stopped himself. "Or the wrong one, as the case may be."

Lord Noka grimaced. "Oont'tal is suspicious by nature, and he has made no secret of his desire to supplant me. If I were in his place, I would stand on my rights. The watercraft was gifted to him—it's his. We'd only be alerting him—and possibly his Gemendi—to its potential. No."

"The craft has other potential, my Lord… beyond anything related to the beacon."

"Then why did I give it to him?"

"The Shareki prisoner calls it a propellor. It is very similar to a child's wind toy. Larger versions are what they use to propel their own watercraft. As he was describing it to me, I sent for my drawings of the study we had made of the ancient water boat at Landing. They are remarkably similar in design and stand free in the water at the rear of the ship, or they can be enclosed in a tube of sort to drive the water away from the boat. The shape and the angles of the blades are critical. It's quite remarkable—and frightening—when you think that our ancestors and the Shareki observed and made use of the same physical principals."

"Tima…"

He looked up to see Lord Noka's jaw set in frustration. This is where he and the Prelate differed. Lord Noka could recognize the importance of something, but he would never share his enthusiasm. Or—if he was being wholly honest—even a concern for the why.

"My apologies, Lord. Discussions on the subject with the prisoner occurred after we had given the boat away. I meant to say—or ask you rather—what is the quickest way to disable one of our warships?"

"Destroy its drive paddles." Lord Tima shook his head in frustration.

Tima nodded in agreement. "Bear with me for a moment. The

propeller of the ancient boat is located at the stern of the craft. It is submerged completely, hidden from view, and protected by the water around it. Shareki boats use the same principle, and, not long ago, they were powered by steam just as ours are. I'm suggesting we be open with Lord Oont'tal about this breakthrough, if not the source of the information.

He is focused on his naval forces and has more boatbuilding capacity than any other three Lords combined. I'm suggesting we share the knowledge of the propellor with him—with all the Lords—for all our ships. He would have the most to gain, but as you have said, we need to do all we can to tie his efforts to our own."

Lord Noka's head slowly lifted in understanding. "And the required work would necessitate your access to the ancient boat."

"Just so, Lord."

"Fine." Lord Noka nodded. "Detail the request in a manner I and Lord Oont'tal will understand. It will give me some salve to apply to his pride when I call him out for his machinations with Lord Atan'tal."

"Within the Council?"

"Of course not. If I accuse him publicly, it would mean war between us. His pride—and my own writ—would box us both in, leaving little room for maneuver. His secret communications with Lord Atan'tal were meant to be discovered. He's testing me, Tima. I will remind him that his fate is tied to mine, and none of us can afford a war of succession at the moment. But I will leave no doubt that I'm ready to fight one if necessary. I think even he will understand that."

Tima hoped Lord Noka was right. The more technical subjects he covered with the prisoner, the more he came to realize how stunted Kaerin knowledge was in comparison. Darryl Ocheltree was no Gemendi, or scientist, as the Shareki named the calling. He was a soldier—an educated officer to be sure—but one whose technical knowledge was limited to what Ocheltree had referred to as "a couple of courses in the general sciences at college." Tima's current understanding of what a college was left him with feelings of longing, and perhaps, if he chose to admit it, jealousy. He had no doubts that his ancestors on their home world had possessed such institutions.

"How many more such gifts does your prisoner have in his head, Tima?" Sometimes it was as if Lord Noka could read minds.

"He doesn't know the value of his knowledge. For their people, his level of knowledge is commonplace. I learn a great deal every time we speak, but each subject is like opening a door to a massive undiscovered library that is only partially lit. Many corridors within are dark to him, but he at least knows they are there."

"And the game playing?" Noka's hand waved towards the untouched chess set Tima had made for the Prelate.

"It's a strange game, but easy to learn. The advantage goes to the player who can think ahead and imagine the pieces on the board down disparate paths. We play every day. The prisoner seems to be more forthcoming on a number of subjects when his mind is occupied. As for the game itself, I'm beginning to hold my own. I've beaten him a few times."

"Truly?"

"Like much of his knowledge, I believe his interest in the game itself is at the surface level. He does not pretend otherwise. He described himself as a good player, but not great."

Lord Noka walked back around his desk. "Edenites -what an enemy. Nothing more valuable than a good stone to sharpen our edges against, yes?"

Or blunt them. Tima winced internally. For all they'd learned, Lord Noka still thought of the enemy as individuals out for blood or conquest. As if he could challenge their leader under a black flag. It wasn't that kind of war. Tima was now certain that the Terrans didn't even think in those terms. From Ocheltree, he'd learned it was the enemy's culture, their combined knowledge, and most of all, their commitment to this concept of liberty for all individuals that was the real threat.

"Our swords have never been sharper, my Lord."

"Tima!" Lord Noka barked out a laugh. "Do I need to remind you that I have no need for another ass-kissing noble? You needn't fear being impressed by the enemy. For all that I don't understand any of the why behind their actions, I can appreciate their attributes and skill in battle. In fact, for all their apparent weakness of will—even with their limited numbers—they no doubt have warriors with whom we could find much to admire."

*

Chapter 6

"My nuts itch," Jake announced as if were sharing that he had a headache.

Kyle glanced at Colonel Pretty as he tried to keep his grin under control. The colonel had just arrived and wasn't going to be goaded by Jake.

"Just a one nut itch?" Pretty asked, full of concern. "Or is it more of a full-scrotal issue that's going to require medication and an EDF-wide public service announcement?"

Jake smiled and shook his head. "Just an itch, sir."

"Glad to hear it." Pretty deadpanned. "Look, I know you both think I'm here to play nursemaid. I just wanted to see your team off personally."

"Not a problem, sir," Kyle answered. For all that he understood the need, Hank wasn't a fan of the mission. "We've got a very tight ROE," Kyle added. "We're going to sit on them."

Rules of engagement were all fine and good, but the best way to keep people safe would be to minimize their exposure or interaction with anybody on Earth, at least for now. The numbers they were taking were more of an insurance policy. If the worst happened, they'd need enough firepower and ammunition to last the 72 hours until the *Door Knocker* came back for them.

"Fine, fine," Pretty agreed. "Just to reiterate—you're there to collect enough ground truth that we can plan for a next step. That's it."

"Understood," Kyle replied. Pretty was a clearly having second thoughts.

"As for you…" Hank stuck a finger in Jake's chest. "That means no kidnapping of mentally challenged goat herders, no bar fights that lead to your arrest, and no chasing tail with a herd of cattle."

"In my defense, sir, I married that piece of tail and forged an alliance. And you," Jake's face broke out into a grin as he waffled a hand back and forth, "are dangerously close to sliding into nursemaid territory."

Pretty nodded knowingly and looked at both of them. "Never thought I'd be *that* guy." He shook his head. "Just please, both of you get your asses back here in one piece without anyone ever knowing you were there—and maybe not even in that order. Lowest profile possible."

"Understood, sir," Kyle answered as the two-minute warning beep sounded from the *Door Knocker's* deck above them.

"We got this, sir." Jake sounded serious.

They both watched Pretty amble off beyond the safety line of the orange concrete bollards that marked the safety zone for the *Door Knockers'* travels. Another empty ring of bollards was just visible in the distance. It was the landing pad for the *Party Favor*, the second ship of the 'Land Yacht' production model that Doc Jensen referred to as Independent Quantum Field Generating Platforms. The *Party Favor* had departed hours earlier with Amona's team of Chandrian Gemendi agent provocateurs and a security force headed up by Tom Souza. They'd gone a different direction down the Quantum tunnel to the Indonesian island of Sumatra on Chandra.

"Sounded pretty nurse-maidy to me," Jake offered as they started up the metal staircase to the ship's deck.

"Ish," Kyle agreed. "Not like I can blame him."

"No shit," Jake agreed. "Can you imagine having to deal with Audy and Jomra without us? Pretty would pull his hair out—I mean if he had any. He rocks that Mr. Clean look."

"Yeah, I'm sure that's what he's worried about."

They were both still laughing when they joined the rest of their team beneath the *Door Knocker's* pilothouse.

"Red River Peak Campground doesn't sound so bad."

Kyle wasn't sure which of the Carlisle brothers had spoken. He looked in question at Jake.

"I did tell everyone it was a dirt parking lot in the middle of a barren high desert."

Jake twitched his head to the side in disgust. "You did."

"They said unimproved campground, dumbass." Grant Ballard delivered the ground truth. He looked tall and lean between his two troll-like brothers-in-law on either side of him. "Probably just a shitter in the middle of nowhere, feeding flies."

Everyone tensed as the electronic beeps got closer and closer together. In the final ten seconds, the alarm went silent, and all eyes were on the LED timer counting down on the side of the pilothouse. Everything stopped until suddenly they were in northern New Mexico, on Earth. The cacophonous rolling boom of their arrival brought them all back to a new here and now. Kyle imagined that if the human brain could skip like an old-time record player, that's what his brain had just done.

His finger shocker was delivering an unpleasant tingle to one index finger, but it ended quickly and prevented the low-grade headache that he'd always come away with after a translation. They were all equipped with the same device, and some of them, like Danny Carlisle, were spared a bout with psychosomatic "space spiders." One of the EDF soldiers bolted for the ship's railing. He almost made it before he sprayed the deck with whatever he'd had in his stomach.

Jake was chuckling to himself. "How hard is it to check a fucking battery?"

Kyle glanced at the top of the pilothouse, where powerful search optics were scanning the skies for threats. A suit of antennas passively listened for signals, and more than a dozen *Door Knocker* crewmen were scattered around the pilothouse's outer catwalk with binoculars. The location was the same that he and Jake had inserted into a week earlier, and he didn't expect the *Door Knocker's* crew to find anything. That said, he couldn't hide his relief when the ship's Captain, August Reverte, stepped out onto the boardwalk and flashed him an upturned thumb.

They were going to operate under a strict zero-EMCON protocol: zero emissions, electronic or otherwise, until they could confirm the noise floor was in the immediate area hadn't changed since the last visit. Even then, they were going to be damn careful.

"Alright!" he yelled. "Just like we planned. Everybody knows their job. Let's get unloaded and set up behind that ridge."

The *Door Knocker* sat astride a dirt road that was quickly being reclaimed by desert grass. That said, the area was characterized by arroyos, gullies, and large hills. If anyone did come out here, they'd have no choice but to use the road. He wanted their camp hidden from anybody using the road.

"Not even a shitter." Danny Carlisle grabbed up his heavy pack and squeezed past them, mumbling to himself.

Desolate was the only word that described this place. Even the wind felt lonely. He imagined that at some point in the past, the parking lot had been used by people transporting their motorcycles or ATVs out into the desert for a day of trail riding, or—judging from the carpet of desiccated cow pies—a place where ranchers had parked their stock trailers. But the location fit their purpose. Interstate 25 was just less than ten miles due east of them. The border town of Raton sat another six miles north of that. It was the single town that he and Jake had observed from afar during their scouting trip. The town looked more populous now than it had before the government started interning rebellious malcontents there.

"Let's go, move it!" Jake yelled over the sound of the front bow ramp cranking down.

It could be dropped quickly if needed, but shaking the *Door Knocker's* field emitters was never a good idea and always avoided when possible. They'd brought four, four-man electric ATVs, as well as three old beat-up pickup trucks that had made their way to Eden over the years before the mass exit. Under the hood, they'd all gotten a once over in the last few weeks, but to look at them, they'd fit right in with the few jalopies he and Jake had seen moving around Raton before. All but one of the ATVs were pre-loaded with supplies.

Lupe Flores sat behind the wheel of the unburdened ATV. "Who you sending with me?"

Kyle stopped Grant as he was moving toward the trucks. "Pick somebody to partner up with Lupe. They'll keep an eye on the freeway, and we'll swap them out tomorrow."

"Yes, sir."

"Make sure they can shoot!" Lupe added loudly from his seat before following the vehicles in front of him towards the ramp.

"That'd be me." Josh Carlisle elbowed his brother-in-law.

"Fine, go." Grant pointed towards the ATV.

"Grant." Danny stopped moving and spun back around. "You know I can outshoot him—don't forget old man Macpherson's dog."

Grant just shook his head and forcibly turned Danny around by the shoulders before giving him a push. "Next time. Go."

Jake glanced at Kyle and gave an approving nod in Grant's direction. "I almost want to ask."

"Please don't." Kyle gave a laugh.

Josh flopped into the passenger seat next to Lupe. "Don't listen to Danny. It was dark, I was only ten years old, and he told me it was a coyote. I missed anyways... well, mostly. The dog did kinda run funny after that, but it was just a .22. It looked like a horse at a gallop."

"What the fuck are you talking about?" Lupe asked as he swung his helmet mounted NODs down in front of his eyes.

Josh flashed him a confused look. "You know what? Not important. Never mind."

"Get your night vision on."

*

Raton Internment Site, New Mexico—Earth

"This feels wrong, man." Mitch almost came to a stop by the steps leading up to the palatial doors of the former Raton Community Library.

The sandstone and granite edifice was one of those late nineteenth-century buildings built when robber baron capitalists tried to do something useful for the civic good with their fortunes instead of donating to a worthless political action committee or investing in pie-in-the-sky longevity drugs.

Currently the library was the headquarters of the Raton NCWA District. The presence of the *"Nick-Wha"* in Raton had the stated purpose of rehabilitating internees or to "clear" anyone who could prove they'd been unfairly or unjustly interred. Patrick knew firsthand that "rehabilitate" was a more palatable word than re-education or re-programming, which was what truly went on within the walls. He'd yet to hear even a rumor of someone being cleared. A year ago, the new sign at the edge of the library's lawn had read Raton District Clearance and Rehabilitation Center. It had lasted in that form for a day until it had been tagged with competing graffiti. For the last month or so, a giant penis and the words "bite me" seemed to have won out.

Patrick walked back to where Mitch had come to a stop.

"Dude, we have to play their game. They're as evil as fuck, but they aren't stupid. They've got informants everywhere, and they know all about you, us, Ellsworth."

It had amazed Patrick how fast the internees would report on their fellow prisoners for an extra food chit, better housing, a set of clean sheets, or even a roll of TP.

"They going to know what we do for Ellsworth?" Mitch's eyes were wide open in panic. This was a point where people usually got hurt. It was hard enough to keep Mitch focused when he wasn't wound up.

"They already know." He'd explained this all before, but Mitch had been drinking at the time.

"You sound pretty fucking sure about that."

Patrick clapped Mitch on the arm and grinned. "I should be. I'm the one that told them."

Mitch blinked at him in confusion. "They're okay with that?"

"They don't give a shit what Ellsworth or anybody else does here. Gabriel just wants his cut and for his goons to have regular access to Ellsworth's girls. As far as Gabriel is concerned, he thinks he's been working me for inside information on Ellsworth. I've been playing both of them."

"Yeah, I know that." Mitch frowned. "It's a miracle you're not already dead. I don't think I'm smart enough to play games with these assholes."

Mitch was a lot smarter than he showed. He was generally happy to play the rube and then surprise the hell out of people. Mitch had told him, long before they'd been made enemies of the state, that if people made the mistake of thinking he was stupid because of the way he talked or the fact he wore steel-toed boots to work—it just let him know who he was dealing with.

"We're all dead if we don't get out of here," Patrick answered. "Tomorrow, or a month from now—it'll happen."

Patrick felt his own words in his bones. Ellsworth was just looking for an excuse to off Noah. That would probably equate to killing him and Mitch as well in the process. With them gone, Ellsworth would have Allen's moonshine operation free and clear, as well as leave Sandra in his clutches. When he thought about the win-win-win that his death would mean for Ellsworth, he was half-surprised it hadn't already happened.

This close to the entrance, there was probably somebody inside watching them right now.

Patrick stepped a little closer to his friend. "Remember, you've seen the errors of your ways, and you want to join me in doing whatever it takes to get rehabilitated and sent back home. Play it like you're having second thoughts all you want—but remember why we're here."

"Back home?" Mitch snorted in derision. "Like that's in the cards. NCWA ever takes me in, I'll probably be slinging power lines in Alaska or some shit."

Patrick couldn't argue with that. At least Mitch had a tangible skill as a lineman for the power company. He'd been an assistant dean of admissions at a community college, and there was no way the NCWA would ever let him work in another school, ever. Any job in higher education was wholly staffed by approved party members.

"You sure this will work?" Mitch was getting his game face on. Patrick didn't need that Mitch either. That was the break-glass-and-duck Mitch.

"No." Patrick answered. "But it should. Gabriel trusts me. If it doesn't, we'll have to go the hard route."

"Can't we just start with that?"

Patrick smiled, knowing Mitch was just fucking with him now. "You want Ellsworth *and* the NCWA on our asses before we can even get out of town?"

"Fine... I'll be polite."

"Good evening, Patrick." Cory Gabriel was a young, rich kid from the Northeast. He'd probably never even seen the inside of a public school. Everything from the way he held himself to his precise, clipped speech screamed big-money privilege. Gabriel had come to his feet behind a massive hardwood desk when they were ushered into his office—after being patted down by the ISS goons sitting behind the library's checkout kiosk.

"Good evening, Secretary Gabriel." Patrick felt like an idiot. He could feel Mitch's surprise and derision coming off him in waves.

"You must be Mitch." Gabriel leaned across his desk and held out his hand, perfectly aware that no one would be dumb enough to try and hurt him here. It wasn't just the ISS guard in the hallway, or the two on duty at the front desk, or the CCTV camera mounted in the back corner of Gabriel's office. If anyone started trouble here, there was nowhere to go, even if they made it out of the library. Patrick just prayed that Mitch played nice and didn't pop any bones in the bureaucrat's hand when he shook it.

"Yes, sir. That's me," Mitch offered up after a brief second when he wore the look of a wild animal considering running for the door.

No one would have stopped him. They were already in prison—the NCWA office was a stand-in for the warden's office, and the single path for potential trustee status that might—at some indeterminable point in the future—lead to a release. The fact that someone of Gabriel's background had chosen to work here just painted him as a true believer. His tour in Raton would no doubt help him with whatever future political ambitions he had.

"Relax, Mr. Bennett." Gabriel's easygoing smile was genuine. "Patrick tells me you're interested in working your way out of your present situation."

"Well… yeah." Mitch nodded. "I guess I am. Never been afraid of hard work."

"Nor has Patrick." Gabriel turned and acknowledged him with a salesman's smile. "Please sit, both of you. I've explained to Patrick that your personal situations necessarily lead to a longer road of rehabilitation than it might for the average internee."

"I don't understand." Mitch remained standing, as if he hadn't yet decided whether he was going to stay. "There's nothing special about us."

Gabriel stayed quiet, nodded at the chair, and waited until Mitch sat himself. "Maybe I should have said a longer journey than the average *civilian* detainee. I understood from Patrick that you were in the same military unit."

"Yeah, but we were following orders. Pat here was my Sergeant. I did what I was ordered to—so did he. Lieutenant Vroom gave the orders. We followed them."

"That's accurate, yes." Gabriel nodded knowingly. "But your Lieutenant Vroom ordered you and the rest of your company to ignore a legitimate order from his superiors."

"Lieutenant Vroom paid for that," Mitch explained. "We did what we were told to do—or not to do—as the case may be. We weren't party to the lieutenant's comms."

Patrick could sense Mitch getting spun up. They'd both been standing right next to Vroom when the butter-bar lieutenant had told the disembodied voice of the major on the other end of the line "no fucking way" in response to the order to fire on a group of unarmed, half-starved civilians trying to walk through the cordon set up around Lubbock.

"I'm not disputing what you say happened." Gabriel moved his hands apart in apology. "I just want to be honest with you. The government is committed to returning citizenship status to as many detainees as possible, but it is the NCWA that has been tasked with 'filtering,' if you will, applicants such as yourself. The mandatory retraining and rehabilitation courses are federally mandated.

"And for former military personnel like yourselves," Gabriel shook his head. "I'm not saying there isn't a path for you, I'm just being honest. Your personnel files will always carry the fact you were part of a military unit that was disbanded due to its political unreliability."

Disbanded was a funny word to use when the fact was they'd been chewed to pieces by the Bradleys of the 10th Mountain Division and any survivors of that thrown into prison.

It was difficult for Patrick to sit there and listen to this same speech again. He'd warned Mitch what he was in for. Patrick knew Gabriel well enough at this point to know the man meant what he said. He could sit there behind his desk in a clean shirt and actually believe he was on the side of the angels, enforcing laws written by socialist functionaries back in Washington. Lawmakers who didn't even recognize the term citizen, at least not in its original American context. They were all just raw material for the giant, centrally managed construct that America had become.

"We know we have a long road in front of us," Patrick broke in. "And we are," he paused and nodded in Mitch's direction, "both of us—committed to getting to the point we can contribute again. But Ellsworth isn't going to let that happen. Mitch here has been roped into working for Ellsworth, just like I have. We're both dead men if we can't figure a way out from under his thumb."

"Mr. Ellsworth's influence in the Raton district is well established." Gabriel nodded gravely. "I think all detainees understand that the Free District of New Mexico was established for them. If they don't wish to live within the guidelines of the United States, this is what is left to them. By design, we maintain a hands-off approach as to how those interned organize themselves—to include opportunists like Phillip Ellsworth."

"Opportunist?" Mitch blurted out. "That's giving the asshole a lot of credit."

Gabriel ignored the outburst and offered a weak smile. "I'd be lying if I said I wasn't aware that both of you gentlemen, from time to time, act as his muscle. If something has occurred to create friction between you and him, I'm not sure what role I or the NCWA have to play."

"I explained to you—" Patrick jumped in before Mitch could. "We didn't have a choice about that. But we do have a possible way out—one that would benefit your efforts here."

Gabriel nodded once. "I assume Ellsworth would be the loser in your solution?"

"Oh yeah," Mitch agreed.

"Yes," Patrick added, and then flashed a look at Mitch that he hoped conveyed 'shut the hell up'. "But it's not about that. It's a win for your status here—and admittedly, it might keep us alive."

"My status?" Gabriel twisted his head to the side in question.

"How many people have you averaged each day that show up and pretend to listen to your pep talks and your testimonial speakers?"

"The education system is brand new," Gabriel offered in defense. "It's less about numbers right now."

"How many, Mr. Gabriel?" Patrick pressed him.

"Fuck all," Mitch answered. "Except when we get a cold snap.

People will line up for a few hours of central heat."

Patrick held a hand out to stop Mitch. "Right now, Ellsworth controls the distribution of everything the Feds provide here. The limited meds, the water when it flows, and the food chits—not to mention everything that gets produced by all the cottage industries under his control."

Gabriel just looked back at him and nodded knowingly. "To include the largest and some say best distilled spirits in the district."

"To include our distillery," Patrick admitted. "A distillery he wants for himself—a distillery that could provide the NCWA clinic with antiseptic and your daily information sessions something a lot more enticing than lukewarm coffee and an hour of AC or heat."

"You're here to get a better deal from me than you get from Ellsworth?"

Patrick wanted to just say yes. "We're thinking everyone in this hellhole could benefit if they saw the NCWA as having something to offer. Right now, Ellsworth controls everything they need to live."

Gabriel was clearly thinking about it. Patrick wasn't sure which aspect would give Gabriel the most heartburn: the helping-everyone-out part or how pissed off Ellsworth would be.

"I'm not blind to the depravations that exist here, gentlemen." Gabriel started with his standard I'm-sorry-you've-brought-it-on-yourselves spiel that Patrick had heard a hundred times. "People have been sent here for a reason. My position exists to identify those willing to work for a second chance—not to make their lives better. Many of my superiors, perhaps most of them, would see that humanitarian goal as antithetical to the very purpose of the Free District."

"Meaning they don't give a shit," Mitch surmised.

Gabriel's hands went out to the side in apology. "I would never put it that way."

"That's just great." Mitch shook his head. "Why even try to do the right thing?"

Gabriel flashed Patrick a look that seemed to ask whether he was going to control his attack dog. Patrick wondered what Gabriel would be thinking if he knew plan B was to turn Mitch loose.

Gabriel sat forward until his elbows landed on his desk. "None of that is to say that a case couldn't be made that Mr. Ellsworth's degree of control over the Raton District is preventing internees from seeking out the second chance that we are offering. I can't think of a reason why your distillery couldn't work to augment our efforts here and supply the free clinic, as you suggested."

Patrick worked hard to keep the smile off his face. They had him. Gabriel was probably already thinking of a moonshine reward system for the re-education classes they offered.

"Ellsworth is set to make a grab for us and the distillery tonight." Patrick struck while the iron was hot.

"Forgive me for assuming you've already thought of a way to pull this off." Gabriel's knowing smile was almost a frown.

"We need a truck," he stated. "Or maybe just one of the NCWA's buses to move it tonight. We could set it up in one of the vehicle bays in your team's garage. It wouldn't take us more than three or four hours to get it moved."

The suspicion in Gabriel's eyes was impossible to miss.

"And one or two of your guards riding shotgun," Mitch added immediately. "Ellsworth wouldn't dare stop us if we had some ISS cover."

Patrick wanted to jump up and hug Mitch. It was what Gabriel had needed to hear. A vehicle was a way out of Raton, and he had clearly been thinking it was all a ruse to get access to some wheels.

"No... I don't suppose he would." Gabriel pointed out the door in the direction of the ISS guard in the hallway. "I'll provide a guard to accompany you. I take it from the hour of this visit that you're looking to do this now?"

"We appreciate your understanding, sir." Patrick sat forward. "Could I recommend that you don't allow any of your people out into the town this evening until we get back? Should take us four hours, tops."

Gabriel did a good job acting as if he couldn't understand the request. The fact was the NCWA limited its presence in the Free District to just a few large cities and border induction centers like Raton. In similar fashion, ISS deployments were limited as well. The Free District of New Mexico wasn't exactly a sought-after posting for federal law enforcement, and Patrick had heard Gabriel complain about how hard it was to get "good people" posted here. ISS goons that did get sent were of the type that either wanted to be prison guards or had somehow screwed up elsewhere. The vice didn't matter—Ellsworth made certain the guards stayed entertained and friendly with him. Raton's warlord owned most of them.

Gabriel wasn't going to admit that. "I'm not in the habit of locking up my staff as if we have anything to fear from Mr. Ellsworth."

"Then we'd best get started," Patrick rose to his feet.

"Sergeant Acker!" Gabriel raised his voice. "I assume you've been listening. I'd like you to check out one of the trucks to Mr. Loukanis and his colleague. They are going to be moving their distillery this evening, and I'd like to make certain there's no issues. Please accompany them."

"Sir? Say again?"

Acker was deeper into Ellsworth's pockets than most. His taste in girls ran young, and Patrick glanced over at Mitch, who was nodding to himself, probably thinking the same thing. The world wasn't going to miss Sergeant Acker.

"You are the two dumbest motherfuckers in this shithole, and that's saying something." Acker waited until he closed the rear door of the F-350 crew cab, taking up a position in the back seat.

Patrick was behind the wheel and ignored the comment. He was struggling not to do a fist pump as the fuel gauge swung up to the three-fourths mark. There was another tank as well, but he'd wait to check that one. Acker was already suspicious.

"Relax, sergeant," Mitch responded. "We'll have you back on guard duty in a couple of hours."

"You assholes *do* realize that Gabriel isn't going to let you live on this compound, right? You're going to have to go home at some point. Ellsworth won't let this slide."

"Yeah? Well, Mr. Gabriel believes otherwise," Patrick answered before starting up the truck and pulling slowly through the NCWA's motor pool.

The rolling gate was slid open by two more guards. They were shaking their heads in surprise when Acker stuck his head out his window and gave them the all clear.

Acker laughed to himself as they pulled out onto the road. "It won't be Gabriel's nuts in a jar on Ellsworth's desk. One thing's for sure— he tries any shit tonight, I ain't going to raise a finger to help you limp-dicked morons."

"Good to know, sergeant." Mitch sounded almost pleased. Patrick glanced over at his seatmate and took some comfort from the grin on his face.

Acker mercifully shut up for the rest of the five-minute drive past the massive trailer park where the majority of the internees were housed. By the time they pulled into their neighborhood, Acker was leaning forward between them, his head hanging over the back of the front seat.

"Maybe you all could slide me a bottle of your good stuff for helping you out."

Patrick slowed as their driveway approached. "What happened to not lifting a finger to help us?"

Acker was winding up again as Patrick turned into the driveway. The headlights framed the group of people waiting outside the carport entrance: Sandra, Noah, Allen, and the kids. The distilling master stood there with close to forty feet of coiled copper tubing looped over a shoulder in front of Sandra's niece and nephew. Clive Denny, another one of their Missouri National Guard guys, was sitting on the back steps.

"Who the fuck are all these people?!"

Mitch reached over and grabbed a handful of Acker's hair as his other hand came up with a knife held to the ISS guard's throat.

Mitch twisted the man's head. "Not important, sergeant, but I'm pretty sure you're in their seat. Move your hands, and I'll give you another smile."

"You assholes are dumber than I thought." Acker grunted.

Patrick killed the engine and leaned over the seat to pull the handgun from Acker's chest holster. The ISS guard was probably right, but it wasn't like they had an option at this point. He got out, popped the back door, and relieved Acker of his assault rifle and two extra magazines.

"Clive!" he yelled. "Get him out and frisk him." He kept the Glock trained on Acker's head while the guard did his best to look at him, but Mitch still had a handful of his hair.

"You're dead. All of you." Acker winced as Mitch tightened his grip.

Mitch reached further into the truck until the muzzle of the gun was against the ISS man's head. "It's why we're leaving, sergeant. You just need to ask yourself whether this shitty truck is worth your life."

He gave a nod to Denny. Acker was dumped onto the driveway on the far side of the truck. Clive and Noah fell on the ISS guard. Patrick ignored the grunts, cries of pain, and the silence that followed. It had been a long time since Patrick had given a shit about doing the right thing. Besides, Acker deserved whatever he got this evening and more.

"Get him inside!" he yelled through the cab of the truck.

Their neighbors wouldn't care about a fight—they saw worse every day. But the presence of a NCWA truck sitting in their driveway would get some attention, and there were always people willing to inform for some extra water or medicine. Lucky for them, none of their neighbors had a working phone, and it was a long walk back to the center of town.

"We got gas?" Allen asked from behind him.

"More than we have cans for." Patrick grinned. "Start siphoning off both tanks. We'll go as soon as you're finished."

He watched as Allen and Mitch started snaking rubber hoses down the two fill caps.

"What are you going to do with him?" Sandra came at him from around the front of the truck. She was pointing back at the house where her brother and Clive had just dragged the unconscious Acker.

"I haven't decided."

"You know what he is." There was no question in Sandra's eyes. Every parent or guardian of a child in Raton knew about Acker.

"I know," he responded. "Get the kids loaded up. We'll be leaving in about twenty minutes."

Chapter 7

By the time they'd transferred most of the gasoline into cans, Acker was conscious, gagged, and hogtied in the back of the truck with Mitch for company. Patrick had to yell at everyone to shut the hell up as he'd started backing out the driveway. Sandra's niece, Emma, hadn't stopped crying since. He didn't know what was worse, the sounds of the little girl's sobs, or the look that Sandra had thrown his way across the cab.

It was hard to drive slowly. Patrick was anxious to be gone, but the NCWA would be hot on their tails unless Gabriel could be convinced that Ellsworth had taken them out. There was no shortage of reasons why Ellsworth himself would come after them. The asshole wanted Sandra for himself, he wanted Allen for his distillery, he wanted Noah dead on principle—and where he was concerned, Patrick figured Ellsworth would just kill him for fun because he'd know whose idea this had been. The math was easy... they had to take Ellsworth out before they left.

Patrick drove an extra two blocks south of Ellsworth's headquarters: the old Boardman Hotel in the middle of what had been Raton's historic city center. He rolled to a stop to let Sandra and the kids out.

"If we don't come back, just keep running. We'll be in Ellsworth's Suburban. I'll flash the headlights three times."

"Be careful," Sandra said as she slid out and gave Noah a kiss on the cheek. Sandra stood at the open door for a moment, looking back at him. "Please, come back."

That's the plan, he thought, as he made sure she and the kids all had their backpacks with them. They carried enough water to keep them alive until somebody caught them.

"We will." The words came out with a lot more confidence than he felt.

It was a quick drive back to the hotel. From a block away, he scanned the small park at one corner of the intersection. Small groups of people were coming and going, most of them in the process of buying or selling something from Ellsworth or scoping out the weak among said buyers and sellers. Others just stood around because there wasn't anything else to do, sunup or sundown.

"Remember, nobody shoots anyone until I take Ellsworth out. Until then, knives only—and when we do shoot, make every shot count."

"Should be easy," Allen called out from the back seat. "You gave me three rounds."

"Why don't I get a gun?" Noah barked.

"I don't have one to give you," Patrick answered. It was the truth, and it sounded a lot better than saying he didn't trust Noah not to fuck this up. "You got one job, Noah. Start transferring the gas to Ellsworth's Suburban as soon as we get inside, or we won't make it out of town. Any extra, make sure the cans get stored in the back."

Noah wasn't one to hide the fact that he was unhappy. The teenager glared back at him until Allen leaned forward and slapped the kid in the back of the head.

"Hey! We wouldn't have to be doing this at all if it wasn't for your fucking mouth. Least you can do, is what he's asking."

Noah looked at Patrick for a moment as if he expected to be defended. The kid had been babied by his mom and his older siblings his entire life. When it came down to it, he couldn't blame Noah for Benny's death. That was on the "Free" District of New Mexico, Raton, and Ellsworth, but Noah's mouth sure as shit hadn't helped.

"Can we count on you?"

"Yeah, I got the gas."

"Good."

He looked at the backseat in the rearview mirror. "Allen, you follow with the cocktails sixty seconds behind Clive and me. I don't want to risk you getting into a scuffle."

"I packed it real well. I'll be fine."

It was the part of the plan he liked the least. Then again, what good was having a college chemistry professor if he wasn't willing to mix up a batch of nitroglycerin?

He was about to answer when Noah reached across the seat and slapped him on the arm. "Look out!"

Patrick almost came out of his seat, standing on the brakes as the tires locked up and they squealed to a stop. He looked up and watched a trio of bodies scramble out of the way to either side of the truck. One of the men he'd almost run over jumped up from the ground, pounded a fist on the hood, and wordlessly leveled a finger at him through the windshield. He didn't recognize them, but they looked new. Really new: well fed, healthy, and way too clean. *ISS!* a voice in the back of his head was screaming.

"Watch where you're fucking going!" Noah had his head stuck out his window. "Fucking newbies!"

Patrick reached across the cab, grabbed a handful of Noah's jacket, and yanked hard, pulling him back into his seat. He lifted both hands off the wheel and waved a two-handed apology at the lanky looking shadow standing in front of his truck as the man moved to the side to let him roll past.

"Lighten up, fuzz-nuts," one of the almost-victims called out to Noah as they rolled past them. Patrick gave his own collar a pull—he was drenched in sweat and wondering how close he'd come to just killing all of them.

"As I was saying..." Allen drawled. "I packed it real well."

"Mitch? You okay?" he shouted over his shoulder through the open back window.

"Don't do that again," Mitch called back. "Sergeant Snuffy here seems to have bumped his head again."

He actively didn't care if he'd just broken the ISS guard's neck. He'd already made the decision that, no matter what, Acker wasn't going to live much longer. The Universe would thank him. He continued past the Boardman on the main drag and turned into the alley leading to its back door. It was where they'd always made their deliveries, though it had been by foot or bicycle in the past—one crate at a time. Rolling up in a NCWA truck was a first and would raise a few eyebrows on its own.

"That is a fucking stop sign, right?" Jake yelled at Danny as he pointed back at the intersection where they'd almost been hit. All he could think of was having to explain to Colonel Pretty that they'd been discovered because he'd mistakenly assumed people still stopped at freaking stop signs.

Danny took the question at face value and stopped to look back at the intersection.

"Yes, sir."

"It was a rhetorical question. And drop the 'sir' shit."

"Yes, s… right."

"Guys?" Grant had been watching the truck and had seen it turn into an alleyway behind the hotel bar that seemed to be the center of whatever nightlife this place offered.

"I mean shit, it might be a prison, but a stop sign should still be a stop sign, right?" Jake was more embarrassed than frazzled. He'd been leading the way and had been the one closest to being hit.

"Guys!" Grant yelled again. "Did you see the back of that truck?"

"No, but I got a real good look at the front grill." Jake countered. "What about it?"

"The guy in the back was kneeling on a body."

"What?" Jake had been eyeballing the driver as the truck had slid past them. "You sure?"

"I'm sure," Grant nodded. "And it was a NCWA truck."

"Those weren't NCWA guys," Danny blurted out. "No way. That mouthy little shit on the passenger side couldn't have been eighteen."

"The body in the bed of the truck was wearing BDUs, I'm sure of it. Maybe *he* was NCWA?"

Jake was quickly forgetting about the near-death experience. "Grant, you're sure about the truck?"

This was their last night for this recon mission. So far, they hadn't learned shit—other than everyone lived at the whim of a guy named Ellsworth who ran the city out of the old hotel across the street from them. He'd managed, barely, to talk Kyle into a little walking recon through town.

Danny turned away from the hotel and faced him with a big grin. "Why don't we go in? Get a drink?"

"We don't have any of their chits, and we look like we're dressed in our Sunday best compared to these people," Grant answered for him.

Jake was nodding to himself. They'd already noted that for the next trip, a serious downgrade in clothing was needed to blend in. He pointed ahead at a bench outside an old barbershop with broken windows and a missing door.

"Let's just camp for a bit and report in, shall we?"

"We going to tell them about the accident?" Danny asked

Jake gave Danny a confused look, shaking his head in disappointment. "What accident? Seriously? You've still got a lot to learn about reporting to higher." Jake pulled the wire for the microphone and ear shroud from inside his jacket.

"Hobo One for P.T. Barnum."

"Go Hobo One."

Kyle's voice came back quickly. They'd found enough walkie talkie and CB radio traffic in the area that they'd relaxed their prohibition on radio use. Some enterprising prisoners had even kept an AM radio station broadcasting between the hours of 6pm and midnight. Between the country music songs were blatant public service announcements that left no doubt the Feds were underwriting the operation.

"Can you put the bird on a white F-350… should be behind the Boardman Hotel?" Jake was wracking his memory. How the hell had he missed the NCWA markings on the truck?

"The one that almost turned you into roadkill? That one? We've been watching it since it almost pasted you guys."

Shit. "Oh… you saw that?" In retrospect, it had probably been too much to hope that Kyle wouldn't have been tracking them with the drone.

"Yeah, we saw that."

Jake could tell Kyle wasn't laughing, and the incident would become one more item added to the long list of shit that he'd never hear the end of.

"Anything strange about it? Did you see the cargo?" Jake asked, looking down the bench at his two companions and nodding in appreciation. At least Grant had been paying attention.

"Yeah, and it's gotten even stranger, Hobo One. We are pretty sure they just dropped a couple of the guards at the back entrance of the Hotel. Start back to your ride, *immediately*. Something is going down, and I don't want you all caught up in it."

"Say again, Barnum?"

"I know you heard me. Now, Hobo One."

Shit. "Copy last."

Jake pulled the earbud out and tucked the mic wire inside his jacket. "Time to go."

"Where to next?" Danny asked.

"Back to the ATV," Jake answered.

"Already?" Danny complained loud enough that it caught the attention of two sketchy-looking young men who had just walked by.

Jake came to his feet as he gave the pair of hungry looking young men a hard look of his own. They wasted no time in looking away and moving on to easier pickings. They'd probably been more interested in the nice boots they were all wearing than anything they'd overheard.

He waved Grant and Danny to their feet. "Come on. Orders."

*

Lou Ellsworth came to his feet behind his desk, flanked by a pair of prison system parolees that staffed a good portion of his goon force. The steady murmur of the jukebox and the bar crowd on the other side of the back wall provided a muted, steady low frequency drumbeat.

"It true you just drove up in a commie wagon?"

"It's true." Patrick gave the crate of moonshine he was carrying a slight shake and jerked his chin around at Clive, who had followed him in with yet another crate. "Figured I'd use it for a delivery while I had it."

"This I gotta fucking hear." Patrick had never seen Ellsworth smile, not ever. The guy had a half a dozen different versions of cynical smirks that had taken some time to get a handle on and label. Right now, he thought he recognized Ellsworth's "you're full of shit" grin. It was a much better starting point than the "I've decided you are of no further use to me" grin. That one usually preceded somebody dying.

Ellsworth stuck his thumbs in his belt. "You decide to quit pretending and go full commie on me?" It sounded like a challenge.

"Not hardly." Patrick gave a laugh as he set down the milk crate holding half a dozen mason jars of Allen's best stuff.

He went to one knee and grabbed the Glock he'd liberated from Acker, thinking that Mitch was a much better shot than he was. But Mitch was guarding the back door, covered in blood after killing two guards with a knife. Mitch was just plain better at this kind of thing than he was, period. He didn't stand, raising the Glock and taking careful aim at Ellsworth from one knee.

He pulled the trigger, the once familiar recoil feeling almost alien in his hands. Hit in the chest, Ellsworth sagged back into the bookshelf behind his desk as Patrick spun counterclockwise and fired twice in quick succession at the guard closest to him. A shotgun blast went off from the other side of the room and a flash of pain exploded across his back.

Patrick was driven forward across the milk crate, his vision swimming, as he heard Clive open up behind him. Lying on the floor, it was strangely quiet for a moment. He could still hear the deep bass pounding of the music through the walls. He saw Ellsworth's desk chair move behind the desk, and then Clive was behind him, pulling him up by the shoulders. Patrick screamed in pain and managed to shake the help off, holding himself up above the crate with one arm.

"Kill him!" He held his gun out and pointed at the desk.

Clive took the gun and ran to the desk just as Ellsworth came up holding his .357 wheel gun. Lucky for both of them, Ellsworth had climbed up over the edge of his desk, pointing the gun in his direction. Clive took one step around the side of the desk and put a round into Ellsworth's skull. Patrick almost passed out in relief, but instead nodded in appreciation as Clive retrieved the .357 and went to the first guard to grab his rifle. By the time Clive made it back to him and started dragging him to his feet, he could feel himself slipping away. The last thing he saw was Mitch coming into the room, firing a rifle back the way he'd come. *That's not good...*

Jake and his recon team had made it about four blocks when it became clear all hell had broken out back at the hotel. There were a few distinct gunshots outside the building, but it was the boom of a large explosion that brought them to a stop. By the time he turned around, a fireball centered over downtown was rising over the trees of the residential street they were on.

Okay, good call. He silently thanked Kyle for ordering them out of the area and struggled to keep up the fast walk as he reinserted his earpiece.

"P.T. Barnum, Hobo One—what's happening back there?"

"Your hit and run crew started it. They just blew the shit out of the back of the hotel and their own truck. They're now in a black or navy

Suburban and have left the area with at least one wounded. I'm guessing here, but it looks to me like they just decapitated the snake and the next in lines are now holding a warlord election."

"Barnum, did you say they blew up their own truck?"

"Affirmative."

Jake turned to Grant and Danny. "The guys that almost ran us over just blew up their own truck?"

"Pretty decent truck for this shithole." Danny observed.

"P.T. Barnum, Hobo One—Hobo Two is certain that it was a NCWA truck and the guys inside weren't NCWA or ISS. You think they might have stolen the truck?"

"Makes as much sense as anything else. Oh yeah, the guy in the back wasn't a stiff," Kyle came back. "He is now, though. They executed him in the parking lot just before they torched their truck. Stay up on comms and make best speed to your ride. Let me know when you are mobile. We're tracking them."

"Copy all, Hobo out."

Jake filled Grant and Danny in on what the drone had seen.

"Sounds like maybe these are people we should talk to," Danny remarked.

They were half-jogging through the neighborhood at this point. They'd left the electric ATV in a washed-out arroyo east of town, and they had at least another mile to go.

"They just executed some dude," Grant argued.

"Yeah, but if he was a soldier or ISS?" Danny countered. "Are we supposed to give a shit?"

Jake realized both of his charges were looking at him for an answer. "I can think of reasons why we wouldn't, and some why we would. We have no idea what happened back there."

Danny shook his head as they all broke out into a steady jog. "I'll bet they stole the NCWA truck, then blew it up to make it look like the asshole that runs the town did it. Now they have a clean ride out of town."

"Or maybe… it was just… one gang trying… to take out another." Grant spoke between breaths.

Jake stayed quiet. Audy's mantra, "it would be one thing in the end" was on the tip of his tongue, but he was too damned old to be trying to have a conversation while running.

Allen clapped him on the shoulder and screamed in his ear, "Somebody's following us!"

Mitch had already figured that out. He'd been watching the rearview mirrors closely. The narrow space between the headlights screamed jeep in his head, and that probably meant it was one of Ellsworth's goons.

Allen had to scream to be heard. The interior of the Suburban was pandemonium. He was pretty certain everyone was crying, screaming in pain, or—in Clive's case—mumbling to himself incoherently.

The one exception was the young boy next to him, his ass planted on the front seat divider. Sandra's nephew hadn't made a sound, and it was starting to freak him out a little bit. Patrick was kneeling in the middle of the backseat, facing the wrong way with a back full of buckshot. Noah had been shot twice and would be dead in a few hours or sooner. Sandra had probably figured that out and was frantically trying to stop the bleeding while alternatively shouting at her niece to stop crying or at Mitch to stop the Suburban and help them.

What the hell could he do? If he stopped and let their pursuers catch up, they were dead. If they couldn't stop soon and clean out Patrick's back, he would die from infection. Noah needed a hospital trauma center, so it was just a matter of time for him either way. Patrick was probably on borrowed time even if they could clean out his back—it wasn't like there were any antibiotics in his immediate future.

They'd just shot down the on-ramp joining the freeway's southbound lane. Between the peaks in the cacophony of the screaming, Mitch was pretty certain he could hear—or was it feel—the sound of the Suburban's lifters trying to pull three-year-old oil up out of the pan. This thing might have been Ellsworth's prized ride, but it was still a POS. Glancing at the speedometer, he was holding steady at seventy mph and was afraid to push it any harder. He knew whoever was following him wouldn't be in any better shape. There were very few vehicles running at all.

"Allen! Get in the far back with that AR."

"It's only got half a mag."

"Well, don't miss then!" He realized he was screaming and probably not helping matters. Shit, he needed Patrick. They all did. He was so much better at this shit than the rest of them. "Allen, don't shoot until I can bring them closer." He looked down at the young boy. *George.* He remembered Sandra yelling the name when they'd all crawled in.

"George, you and your sister get down on the floor back there. Way down, okay? Can you do that?" The boy just nodded silently, but he crawled back into the already crowded rear seat. The third row of seats was down, and the back of the vehicle held all their shit, the gas cans, and now, Allen.

"Sandra!" He hated yelling. Hell, he didn't even like talking all that much, but Patrick's lady had pretty much lost her shit when she discovered both Patrick and her brother had been shot up. "Lay Patrick down on the seat. You get on the floor with the kids and Noah."

Noise from the engine forced his attention to the dashboard. While he'd been yelling, he'd pushed the Suburban up to almost eighty, and it was complaining. He let up on the gas and waited until they were back down to a still-too-fast sixty-five.

"Sandra?"

"Noah is unconscious! Oh my God! What do I do?"

"Sandra! Get him on the floor with you and the kids. Keep pressure on his wounds!"

He looked across at Clive in the passenger seat. He'd stopped talking to himself for the moment and was leaning forward, staring into his side-view mirror.

Mitch reached across and punched him lightly in the arm. "You have anything left in that Glock?"

"Uh…"

"The Glock!"

"It's empty." Clive seemed to snap out of it a little.

He liked the guy—they all did. They'd always given the former car salesman a hard time because he'd joined the Guard to help pay for his divorce. Worst excuse ever. Then again, he'd used his Guard pay to help pay for a new bass boat and that hadn't worked out any better.

Clive lifted the stock of the shotgun, the barrel resting on the floorboard. "One shell left in the shotgun."

Shit. "All right, pass it over real careful." Driving or not, he wanted to be armed.

"I checked," Clive added. "It's just a low-brass bird shot. Ain't going to do shit."

It was the same gun that had shot Patrick. It was more than enough to kill his friend over the next few days if they couldn't get somewhere soon and clean out his back.

"What are they waiting for?" Clive asked.

Mitch had been wondering the same thing. "If I was them, I'd wait until we were further out of town. No chance of people seeing anything. They probably still don't even know who we are. They just want the ride and the gas."

"How far out of town?" Clive asked.

"Let's find out." He let up on the gas further, disgusted at how fast the Suburban slowed. A moment later, the glow of the jeep's brake lights was clear to see across the expanse of the empty freeway behind them. *Farther than this…*

"Hobo One? This is Barnum, you mobile yet?"

Jake could see the mound of brush covering the electric dune buggy thirty yards away. "One minute."

"Just when I thought this couldn't get any stranger, the attackers stopped on their way out of town and took on a woman and two kids. They are almost to the freeway."

"Hostages?"

"Negative," Kyle answered. "They pulled over, and passengers came running and hopped in. Something else is going on. They are also being pursued by another vehicle: open-air jeep with three pax, all armed."

Jake pulled up as they reached the ATV and signaled for Danny and Grant to start uncovering it. "Hobo Three had a theory - they stole the truck and torched it to make a clean break out of town. If they'd taken the NCWA truck, shit is probably beaconed, right?"

"Sounds as plausible as anything I can come up with."

Jake glanced upward. The moon was up but hidden behind thick clouds. "You want us to intercept their tail?"

"If you think you can—and the Suburban makes it far enough away from town that no one is going to see you do it. This needs to be private. Do you copy?"

"Copy all," Jake replied as he swung behind the wheel and grabbed the NODs Grant was holding out to him. "They driving with headlights?"

"Affirmative, both of them."

Idiots. Jake shook his head. "Let me know when your drone picks us up in the sight picture."

"Will do. Barnum out."

*

The electric ATV flew over the loose dirt at the edge of the interstate, fishtailed up the embankment, and hit the pavement like it had been shot out of a cannon. Jake was driving without lights, using his night vision. The steady whirr of the heavy off-road tires almost felt like he was driving over rumble strips. Without the tire noise and vibration, they could have been flying.

They were still far enough behind that they hadn't spotted their quarry, but the light-gathering and magnifying qualities of the NODs gave the canyon up ahead of them an unnatural glow that he knew was from headlights. Jake couldn't risk taking his eyes off the road—twice there'd been abandoned wrecks in the middle of the freeway that some asshole had been too lazy to move off to the side. Grant was hanging onto the dash's grab bar as if it would somehow save him, and Jake imagined that Danny was behind him with his head stuck out into the slipstream eating bugs.

Five minutes later, the rear lights of a jeep swam into view ahead of them as they hit a straightaway. He was thankful the fast rate of closure allowed him to let up on the accelerator. The ATV slowed for a good bit before the speedometer that had pegged at fifty mph caught up. He'd closed to within a half mile of the rear vehicle.

"Hobo One—Barnum here. Drone has you. I'm on my way to our OP with support."

"Why they driving so freakin' slow?" Jake asked. "We sure these guys aren't working together?"

"Unknown," Kyle answered. "I've ordered Lupe to stop the vehicles if they reach his OP."

"Sounds good. Just remind him that we are number three in line and don't have an engine block to stop a round."

"Done and done, Hobo."

They continued on for another two minutes. Jake was starting to think on how far they'd come and how close Lupe's position must be when the jeep in front of them started pulling away.

Jake grinned as Grant let go of the grab bar, getting ready to point and tell him what he'd just seen. He mashed the accelerator, and Grant was pushed back into his seat.

"If they fire at anyone," Jake yelled into the wind. "Take out their driver's side tires!" He quickly caught up with the jeep, approaching its driver's side so both Grant and Danny could shoot. He made sure to stay well behind it with enough room to swerve back to the righthand lane when it rolled.

*

"Here they come!" Allen yelled from the far back of the Suburban.

Mitch saw them coming in his mirror. He feathered the brakes even as he started to speed up. In the glow of the brake lights, he had no problem seeing a silhouette of someone standing up in the jeep, hanging over the top of the roll bar. He couldn't make out a gun, but he couldn't think of another reason for someone to be in that position.

"Everybody down!" he yelled.

A bullet hammered into the back of the rig, accompanied by the sound of a single rifle shot. Mitch glanced at his side mirror as the jeep tried to come up on his side. He swerved to take the lane and smiled as the jeep dropped back. Yep, they wanted the Suburban intact. In Raton, someone would be able to feed a family for a year with the gas it carried.

Machine gun fire erupted, and he instinctively ducked. When he checked the mirror again, the jeep had flipped and was rolling down the freeway amidst a carpet of sparks. Something ignited in the back of it, then the whole thing came to a stop upside down in the middle of the freeway, burning. He slowly rolled to a stop.

"What the hell?" Clive was kneeling in his seat, facing backwards. "You hit them?"

"I didn't even fire," Allen yelled back.

"What happened?" Patrick spoke up from the back seat.

"Don't know, buddy" Mitch answered. "I think we just got lucky." He was thinking it must have been an argument of some sort within the jeep, or maybe they blew a tire. It was suddenly quiet in the Suburban. They'd made it, or at least some of them had.

"Mitch," Clive slapped him on the shoulder. "Let's get out of here."

"Yeah," he agreed. He very slowly got them back up to a sedate forty-five miles an hour. The sounds of the engine coming apart were muted at that speed, but he didn't think their stolen ride was going to make it much further.

"Just a few more miles and we'll stop and fix Patrick up."

"Noah too!" Sandra hissed.

"Yeah, him too." Mitch realized too late how he must have

sounded. But there was shit-all they could do for the kid. Selfishly, he wanted Patrick around to deal with Sandra when she figured that out.

Ten minutes later, they'd stopped and unloaded at the desert-facing edge of a broad dirt-and-gravel shoulder area. Mitch was working on Noah, or trying to, standing at the open driver-side back door. He had Noah laid out in the backseat and had nothing to work with besides fresh bandages that consisted of clean or relatively clean t-shirts. Two through-and-throughs made for a lot of holes to plug, and the kid had already lost a lot of blood.

He glanced up over the edge of the backseat and grinned as Patrick grunted and held back a scream that ended up sounding like a squeal. Allen had Patrick face down and spread-eagled across the rear compartment and was digging out the bird shot with a pair of tweezers, dousing his back with liberal amounts of his moonshine as he went.

Noah was unconscious, his heartbeat way too fast. The worst of the bleeding had stopped, but he figured that was probably due to there not being enough in him at this point. Noah needed an IV, a transfusion, or whatever the hell doctors did.

He heard a boot in the gravel behind him. "Hey, shine your flashlight in here, would you?"

The beam of light did as he asked, just as a gun barrel came around his torso and pressed against the underside of his chin.

"We are here to help you," the voice behind him said. "We've got somebody here with us that knows what the hell they are doing. Step away slowly and keep your arms out. Nobody is going to be hurt, but if you so much as twitch—"

"I won't." Mitch croaked.

"You won't what?" the voice asked.

"I won't... twitch."

Mitch backed away from the open door, glancing into the rear of the Suburban as he did. Two more guys, heavily armed, had everyone standing behind the tail gate covered. There was something familiar about them that he couldn't quite put a finger on. Seconds later, an ATV came flying into the pull off area, rolling almost silently from the desert west of the freeway. Four people jumped out. One of them was a middle-aged lady directing a man carrying a large duffel bag. They went straight past him to where he'd been working on Noah.

The gun momentarily pressed harder against his chin. "She's a doctor, or as close as we've got with us. We *are* here to help." He was quickly frisked and then the gun was pulled away. "Turn around."

Mitch was struck again with the sense that he should know these guys. The guy in front of him waved his gun conversationally. "You almost kill someone, and you don't even remember them?"

"What the hell are you tal…" and then recognition clicked. He'd been the guy that pounded on the hood after Patrick had almost run him over back in town.

"There it is." The soldier grinned.

"You!" Sharon Ballard yelled through the cab of the Suburban. "What's your name?"

"Allen."

"Allen, climb back in there and finish what you were doing with your friend. Smells like a distillery in here, so at least you're not an idiot. Grant—check on the lady and those two children for me."

One of the men holding a rifle almost jumped at the woman's voice.

"Sir?" the same soldier asked, looking for permission from the man who had pulled him away from the car.

"Do what your mom tells you. I think we're good here."

Mom? Mitch's head was spinning. "What the… who the hell are you guys?"

*

Chapter 8

Indonesian Archipelago, Island of Sulawesi—Chandra

"It's as fine a tool as any High Blood boat captain would carry." Amona described the compass using his best impression of the Junata jewelry makers hawking their wares in Portsmouth.

Some of the liberated Junata had created what the Edenites called a "cottage industry" focused on selling local wares to visitors from Eden. Rings, torcs, and pendants for Edenites—but what had struck him most about those entrepreneurial artisans was their ability to sell.

"Note the skill with which it is constructed," he continued.

They were a long way away from any Junata. The local clan here, on the other side of the world from Caledonia, called themselves the Tor'ami. As far as they'd been able to tell, the Tor'ami were the smaller of two ethnic groups scattered widely across what the Edenites and Jema called the Indonesian Archipelago. Amona had made a detailed study of Edenite maps and was still amazed that the world of his birth was so large and varied. Some of the islands in the chain were several times larger than all of Caledonia. This one was called *Sulawesi* in the Eden tongue, and parts of the sprawling and strangely shaped island were over 800 miles away from the beach he stood on.

"As you say," the local boat captain palmed the compass whose parts had been printed in a nano factory on Eden. The local turned in a tight circle, watching the needle as it held to magnetic north. "I can't argue the quality, but it would get me killed the first time a High Blood saw it and wanted it for himself. Where did you say you come from, friend?"

"From the mainland, far to the west and north." The now well-practiced lie rolled off Amona's tongue easier than it had a couple of days ago. This was the third coastal fishing village they had stopped at on their way towards the largest settlement on Sulawesi. In typical fashion, they'd given the large Kaerin-controlled plantation city an Edenite name: Makassar, named after the city on Earth that was in nearly the same location.

"Where is your boat?" There was no suspicion in the local's voice. The locals here seemed friendly, and to someone like him who had grown up under the eyes of the Kaerin, almost naïve. The question itself was more than natural. No one here went anywhere without a boat. It was a coastal culture, and the mountainous interior of the island was covered in thick, nearly impassable jungle.

"They are fishing," Amona replied truthfully. "We may be traders, but we must eat."

The local bobbed his head under a wide-brimmed straw hat in understanding. "We haven't had traders like you before."

The fisherman eyed the Jema scout Stant'ala and the Edenite Captain Nagy standing a short distance away on the beach—again, it was in confusion rather than suspicion. This village was at the outer edge of Kaerin control, built up around a small river outlet on the coast between steep, deep green hills.

"From a distance, I thought your men High Bloods, and you, their prisoner."

"Do the High Bloods come here often?" Amona asked.

The boat captain shook his head and pointed his chin inland, where mountainous jungle stretched unbroken for hundreds of miles. "Not unless they are hunting the hill people. We take our catch and many other goods to O'tees, to them. It is a two-day sail farther up the coast."

"Yes, we saw the lights of the city across the water a few nights ago."

They had already learned O'tees was the Kaerin name for Makassar.

"You were on the deep water at night?"

Amona nodded in explanation and pointed at the compass the local still hadn't returned. "We have other tools that make that easy for us. We were hoping to trade with your village before making our way up the coast to O'tees. Our clothes mark us as strangers—we could give you very good terms for some of yours."

"For clothes?"

Amona grimaced inwardly. The fisherman, a captain of one of the boats anchored in the calm waters of the lagoon behind him, displayed his first twinge of suspicion. This was their third attempt at this approach—during the first two, such suspicion had quickly devolved into accusation and threats.

"Yes, clothing—and if you have a fishing boat available, we would purchase it from you at a very good price. We have foodstuffs from the mainland, spices, tools, and nets to exchange… perhaps a gift or two for your personal assistance."

"Anything you need, they have in O'tees."

Amona shrugged in apology. "We look to do a big business in O'tees, but we would like to arrive there not looking like such strangers. The High Bloods, if they are suspicious, could take our whole cargo."

The local looked more confused. "They could do that no matter what clothes you wear."

"Ah." Amona wagged a finger. "They could, but why would they bother to look at our holds if we don't raise suspicion?"

Understanding dawned across the fisherman's face. "You are here without their permission?"

"We do a great deal of business without Kaerin permission."

The local's eyes darted between Amona and his two guards before settling back on his own. "I cannot put my village at risk."

Amona nodded in understanding. *Another dry hole.* It wasn't a complete loss. They were learning more with each conversation. They'd probably end up stealing a local boat. Probably from the village they'd tried yesterday. Breda would be ecstatic.

"We understand."

"You would need to speak to Fee'ada, our Krathik."

Amona bowed his head, hiding his surprise. "I would be honored to do so."

"Tonight, when your ship returns, you may anchor in our lagoon. Come into the village. I will see that you speak to Fee'ada. May I keep this until tonight?" The fisherman held out the compass. "To show to Fee'ada."

"No." Amona smiled and pulled another compass from his pocket. "You may keep that one for yourself, for your help. You should show him this one."

The fisherman smiled in understanding. "My name is Ed'wo, friend. Ask for me tonight. It is a small village." Ed'wo reached for the second compass. "I will show this to *her*. Our Krathik is a woman."

*

"I still say it would have been easier to steal a boat from the last village," Breda volunteered.

They'd shut down the outboards and paddled their RHIB into the lagoon with great difficulty after motoring across the breakwater in the darkness. They had just pushed up onto the sandy beach between outrigger canoes and small skiffs when Breda had started up.

"Or steal one of these." Breda pointed back into the lagoon where the local village's larger fishing boats were anchored for the night.

"Breda…" Rob Nagy growled in warning.

Rob was loving this assignment so far. After almost an entire year of Caledonian weather, the sunshine, beaches, and ocean air of the Java Sea were more than welcome. Amona was a natural at making friends, which, as far he figured it, was job one for a spook. Breda, on the other hand, was a work in progress and a general pain in his ass.

"Do not make me regret bringing you."

The darkness was broken by their lantern as they emerged from the beach to a flat, cleared shelf of land dominated by row upon row of bamboo fish-drying racks. They knew what they were looking for from their earlier visit. There was a beaten path paved in places with smooth river stones that gained a low plateau of cleared land given over to rice patties and planted gardens.

Rob paused the group. "Adams, you've got overwatch here. Don't hide—might be alarming if we are being watched. Just chill and keep an eye on the boat. We'll keep the comms open so you can hear what's going on."

"Yes, sir. Bring me some leftovers if you can."

The village fronted the far edge of the rice paddies, which acted like a quarter mile-wide moat around the settlement. A dozen or so large, well-built structures formed the center, surrounded by a number of smaller huts and sheds. Bamboo construction, thatched roofs, and torchlight—it reminded Rob of one of those vacation eco lodges that had been all the rage back on Earth before people had stopped traveling. There were a few locals on the packed dirt road bisecting the fields and leading into the village. He didn't want to think what was in the buckets being dumped into the paddies.

"Ok, Amona—you're up. Lead the way."

They didn't have to hunt for Ed'wo. The fisherman was waiting for them with a small boy of about seven or eight years at the entrance to the village. Father and son were both dressed in dark shorts and clean white shirts. Rob noted the two fighting-age men sitting close by. One was trying to look busy repairing a net, but the other wasn't even pretending and watched them closely.

Fair enough, he thought. They were strangers in a place that didn't get a lot of visitors. He wasn't too worried as he walked through the well-lit village behind Amona and his contact towards the largest structure. They'd watched the village all afternoon with the drone and hadn't seen any sort of preparations that had worried him.

Worrying about Breda was enough, he thought. He'd coaxed a promise out of the hothead that he'd keep his mouth shut in exchange for being allowed to come this evening. At their last village, he'd jumped into the middle of Amona's initial conversation and screwed the whole effort up. They'd been lucky to withdraw without having to hurt someone.

One entire end of the largest building was open on the ground floor. A massive teak table dominated the space—it had to be ten feet wide and close to thirty feet long. The table would have set back any corporate boardroom on Earth several hundred thousand dollars. It was set with large trays of sliced fruits, spiced rice balls, and what looked to him like sushi rolls. Beyond the far edge of the table was a firepit roasting a small boar or pig. He did his best not to smile at the prospect of some food that didn't live in its own pee.

A few locals were already present, all dressed in clean, bright white shirts like their guide. His first impression was one of general prosperity—at least far more than any subject settlement they'd seen on the mainland. He put it down to the limited Kaerin presence. It was night-and-day from their experience with Junata villages on Caledonia. There, the Junata had lived in abject fear with the Kaerin ordering their daily lives and driving them to produce. One glance at the smiling children ringing the perimeter of the interior, plates of food balanced in their laps and stuffing their faces—Rob couldn't help but worry that they weren't going to improve the lives of these people.

It became clear that they were expected to fill their plates themselves and eat in silence. It appeared at least that aspect of Kaerin culture held here as well. They followed the lead of their local host and walked the length of the table, loading up and then moving to the spitted pig where Ed'wo cut them each a slice of meat before indicating that they should sit at the low-hanging table.

Rob did his best to get a good look at the woman seated at the head. She was helping a small male child drive his plate with a pork rib in her other hand. She looked to be in her late forties, perhaps early fifties—about Amona's age. Dark-haired, she had a single streak of white atop her head that was so pronounced he wasn't sure it was natural. He'd been on Chandra long enough to know the woman was likely far younger than she looked.

That said, the locals looked healthy. They all seemed to have most of their teeth. The kids seemed happy, and among the dozen or so locals eating around the table with them, there were even a couple that could have stood to cut back on the calories. He didn't think he'd ever seen an overweight Junata.

Several men and women joined the feast soon after, and, following a head bow in the Krathik's direction, wordlessly filled their plates and took their places. One man went directly to the Krathik and whispered something in her ear. She offered no reaction beyond a slight nod. Rob did his best to take in as much as he could while stuffing his face. Of all the Kaerin customs that had been imprinted on this world, the habit of eating in silence before speaking fit him just fine. He'd grown up with two older brothers and it had usually been a race to see who could eat the fastest.

When he looked up again, the Krathik was cutting slices off a piece of fruit with a small knife and watching Amona closely. The other diners seemed to take the Krathik's fruit course as a signal that the meal portion of the dinner was close to finishing. As a group, they seemed to tuck into their plates and started wolfing down food with true purpose. He followed suit, popping two of the spiced rice balls into his mouth. It was a lot better than the four-day enforced diet of fresh fish and re-hydrated veggies that they'd been living on.

He couldn't help but watch as one of the local men held his plate up to his face and started shoveling. The villager offered a satisfied belch when he was done. Rob could appreciate the gesture even if no one else seemed to notice—perhaps the Tor'ami had grown up with brothers as well.

A minute later, the Krathik clapped her hands once. Several of the children hopped to their feet from around the edges of the chamber and walked around the table, collecting the plates. Others put out polished teak cups and filled them with what smelled like the rice wine they'd sampled at the last village.

"To our visitors—be welcome." The Krathik seemed pleasant enough. There was a slight stand-offish tone to her that wasn't exactly haughty—it seemed more polite disinterest.

Across the table from him, Amona held up his own cup. "Thank you, Krathik. For sharing a meal with us and your welcome. I am Amona."

The Krathik nodded in acceptance before taking a drink.

The rice wine was better than it had been in the last village. Chilled, it might have been almost drinkable. After sundown or not, it had to be close to ninety degrees Fahrenheit. "Room temperature" here in the tropics wasn't a good thing, and asking for some ice would probably just get them burned at the stake as some sort of lunatic. Rob swallowed hard and managed not to grimace. Fine time to be a wine snob.

"Amona," the Krathik repeated slowly. "That is a strange name. It matches your strange faces. I am Fee'ada, Krathik here for the past two years since my handfast perished at sea."

"We are honored, Krathik Fee'ada."

Rob couldn't have been more pleased with Amona's performance thus far. The man seemed perfectly at ease. No doubt a testament to the fact he had served high ranking Kaerin his entire adult life.

"Ed'wo tells me you are from the mainland." Fee'ada continued. "Yet you are not of the Tay'ang."

Rob recognized the clan name, although it was more of an ethnic description in Chandra's version of Asia. To the Kaerin, the word Tay'ang was generally used to refer to Asian ethnicity. Confusing the issue, there was also a large clan that referred to themselves as *the* Tay'ang in what he thought of as southern China and northern Vietnam. Listening to the Krathik, he was certain she meant the Asian mainland.

"No, Krathik. We come from the far west. Some of us, like myself, are from near the Kaerin Sea—at least originally. Others of us," Amona gestured towards him and Breda, "are from lands closer to the city of

Kaerus itself. We are all many moons' sail from where we started."

A low murmur broke out, punctuated by a genuine gasp of surprise from the food slurper. The Krathik herself took the news in stride.

"These are places I have heard of, though we have never seen traders from such lands." A look of what might have been confusion danced on her face for a brief moment. "For which clan do you trade?"

Amona glanced at Rob for a moment before turning fully around and facing the head of the room. "Home is where we lay our heads, Krathik. We are a free people. We stay on the move."

"You trade with the High Bloods? In their wares?"

"At times, Krathik. We do have High Blood goods to trade. If possible, we prefer to trade outside their reach, free of their... interference."

Fee'ada leaned back in genuine shock. She took a moment to shake her head in what Rob hoped was surprise and not anger. She leaned forward, leveling a finger at Ed'wo.

"Ed'wo? I expect more from a ship's Krathik. Explain yourself. Did you know this?"

The fisherman turned to face Amona, looking anything but happy. "I did not, Fee'ada—I knew only that they came from afar."

"What is it you people want here?" Fee'ada's suspicious tone was directed at Amona. Gone was the patina of disinterest—she suddenly had an intensity to her that left no doubt as to why she was the Krathik, dead husband or not.

"Captain," Amona whispered in English. "Perhaps now would be an appropriate time for the gift?"

"Should have started with it..." Breda couldn't really help himself, but the look Rob threw in his direction shut him up.

He unzipped the small backpack he'd brought with him and sat the small gift box on the table between him and Amona. The craftmanship was Junata, made of polished and lacquered Caledonian oak. It was a beautiful box, but it didn't hold a candle to the contents.

Everyone had sat up as he reached for the bag, and the expectant air increased when the heavy weight of the box was set down. He opened the lid and turned it in the direction of the Krathik. The two twenty-ounce bars of gold, mined from the Yukon, rested on a bed of single-ounce silver coins minted in New Seattle.

"We have business in O'tees," Amona explained, putting on a friendly smile that almost surprised Rob. The little man, as competent as he was, usually looked either worried or eager to please. "We wish to purchase one of your larger fishing boats. We would not cause you any more trouble—and humbly ask you to forgive us for any trouble we may have caused. We simply have a need to appear as local as we can when we sail to O'tees."

The Krathik looked at the small treasure for a just a moment in thought before growing suspicious. "Your own ship does not suffice? After bringing you all this way? As you said, 'many moons' sail' from the Kaerin's Middle Sea?"

"Krathik," Breda broke into the momentary silence. "Perhaps you would prefer to discuss this issue in a more private setting? You and your trusted officials."

Fee'ada's mien of suspicion changed in an instant to one of outright disgust. Rob was already turning on Breda when Amona's fist slammed down on the table between them. "Remove him from our presence."

Rob backhanded Breda across his chest, knocking him off his low bench and spilling him onto the rush-covered floor. He grabbed a fistful of Breda's tunic and belt, picked him up, carried him out the door like a bale of hay, and dropped him between two torches.

"Don't even think about coming back in here!" He hissed in English.

"But—"

"Shut it!"

When he walked back inside, it was hard to tell who was more shocked, the Krathik or Amona, whose eyes looked like dish saucers.

"Forgive our man's outburst," he announced to the Krathik before retaking his seat.

"Yes… please forgive us, Krathik." Amona recovered quickly. "We have dealt with many Krathik—many would not have chosen to have this discussion in public. We meant no offense."

Fee'ada regarded them both for a moment before shaking her head. "Your man tried to appeal to my greed. Now you try with my vanity. Why is it so important to have a local boat?"

Amona glanced at him in question. Rob decided to gamble—he liked this Krathik, and it was the first time he'd been able to say that—ever. At the end of the day, what was the worst that could happen? Were the Kaerin going to find out they were gunning for them? That secret was out.

"Go ahead, Amona. Like we discussed."

Amona again faced the head of the table. "Krathik, earlier I said we conduct our business outside of Kaerin control. I was speaking truthfully in that, and all else. In addition, I would say that there is not anything we do that would meet with Kaerin approval."

Fee'ada's brows climbed up her forehead before she snorted in what he hoped was laughter and not disgust. Rob wanted to smile, but none of the other locals at the table seemed the least bit amused.

"Now I understand you not having a home," the Krathik gave her head a slow nod.

"Ours *is* an interesting life, Krathik." Amona unleashed that smile again. If Rob didn't know Amona as someone married to his work, he would have sworn the man was infatuated.

"Interesting?" Her eyes grew large again in surprise before she smiled at both of them and started laughing. Most of those around the table joined her.

When the laughter died down, Fee'ada focused on the treasure box. "You could purchase a street of houses in O'tees for that sum, or this whole village, if you wished."

Fee'ada crossed her hands on the table in front of her, as if she were ready to negotiate. "Any one of our boats would be recognized, and all would know where it came from. Perhaps not the Kaerin—their gaze does not often fall this far from O'tees. If the Kaerin wished to know about the boat, or had reason to wonder... there are many who would tell them. Some villages would do so without being asked."

Amona gave a nod of acceptance. "We understand, and we appreciate you hearing our offer. We will seek other arrangements."

Rob's burgeoning enthusiasm faded. Those other arrangements meant stealing a boat from this village or another. They could use some help. The small RHIB that the *Party Favor* had left them with wasn't going to cut it.

Fee'ada held up a finger. "We do have a new boat under construction on the river. One that has not been seen before. My own boat, as it happens."

"Krathik?" The villager who had whispered in her ear upon arrival spoke up. "That boat's purpose is spoken for. We've already waited."

Fee'ada pointed at the treasure box. "We could build a fleet of ships to redeem our honor." She dismissed the man's concern with a twitch of her hand before turning back to them.

"Its sails have not been seen before, but it is of local construction and a fine ship besides. It may suit your needs."

"If its construction is as fine as those anchored in your lagoon," Amona gestured over his shoulder and nodded at several of the captains, "it would indeed."

"Then it can be yours," Fee'ada announced. "It will be finished in two ten-days. But first, I'd like to know how profitable your trade in O'tees will be."

Amona looked confused for a moment. Rob quickly came to the conclusion that, Krathik or not, they were dealing with a businesswoman.

"Offer her ten percent of the profits." He spoke softly in English, but the room was quiet enough that she'd heard him clearly.

"Is that a trader's tongue you speak?" Fee'ada raised her voice. "Which of you truly speaks for your crew?"

"It is, Krathik," Amona responded quickly. "As you say, it is a trader's tongue from our own lands. I speak for our crew on all matters ashore." Amona lifted a hand in his direction. "Master Rob is the crew's Krathik. I would not offer a portion of our profits without discussing it with him. He speaks for our crew. We meant no offense."

"None was given." She waved away the concern. "It is a boat Krathik's folly—often his last one—to sail where the crew would not."

The entire gathering seemed to nod in agreement with her words. Rob was reminded of Elisabeth's briefing on maritime cultures—she'd called them "high-trust cultures." She'd said the ones that succeeded were generally the most egalitarian. It certainly fit here.

"Krathik, we would be willing to give you one part in ten of our profits." Amona was a man of hidden talents, Rob thought. That, or he'd done this before on behalf of those he had served.

Fee'ada lifted a finger to the treasure box. "In addition to the boat's payment?"

"In addition to, yes."

"One and a half parts of ten," Fee'ada countered.

Rob struggled to keep the smile off his face as Amona threw up his hands and shook his head, rubbing at his bald scalp. "For that, we would need other help. Local clothing for our crew, provisions, and a local boat krathik who could assist us in these waters."

"This is acceptable," Fee'ada said with a smile pointed directly at Amona. "Yet the fact you don't have a clan whose honor you can swear by gives me pause. I would insist that you remain here until your trade is complete. As my guest."

Amona looked like he had just swallowed a bug, but Rob wasn't too worried. With what they needed to do in Makassar, Amona was baggage until he was needed to speak to the locals. In those cases, like now, the man was worth his weight in gold. Amona turned to look at him for direction, or maybe just for help.

"You're more useful here building relations than you are with a gun." Rob used English, but didn't try to hide it. "Also, tell her we have some skilled craftsman with us who could help with the boat. I don't want to wait twenty days."

Amona nodded to himself before turning back to Fee'ada. "This would be acceptable. I was also reminded that we have some skilled craftsman and useful tools. If allowed, we would like to assist you in finishing the construction of the boat."

"You would do this?" Fee'ada looked shocked. "After paying us for the work?"

"It would be our pleasure." Amona answered.

Fee'ada looked doubtful as she glanced at several of her ship captains. Rob figured boatbuilding here was a village affair. "This is acceptable." Fee'ada grinned in thought. "Though, if this is the skill with which you conduct trade, perhaps I should have asked for a larger share of whatever meager amount you will profit."

Rob and Amona laughed along with the rest of the villagers. Rob was already feeling relieved. With a local ship, and some local help, they could quit motoring around the coastline looking for the starting line.

*

"Say again, Rob."

Rob hadn't stuttered, and the sat comm connection was superb. He was making his daily report to Colonel Pretty, who was sitting back in Portsmouth.

"Pirates, Sir. We've teamed up with pirates."

"What are you basing that on?"

"Sir? Do you know what a corvus is? In the context of, say, ancient sea battles. Specifically, the Romans, according to Sergeant Adams."

"The heavily weighted plank thing that swings down from one ship into another?" Colonel Pretty sounded incredulous, but his explanation had matched Adam's. "It basically fixes an enemy ship and allows your boarders to cross to the other ship."

"Yeah, that's it, sir. Adams recognized it for what it was immediately. And after you knowing what it is, I'm beginning to question my public education. The locals were in the process of removing it when we got our first look at the ship. My take—it couldn't have any other function."

"Interesting... who are their prey?"

"Apparently, the Krathik we are dealing with lost her husband, the former Krathik, in a sea fight with a nearby village. Our ship had been planned to be the instrument of her revenge. It's that clan honor thing again—except here, it's a village thing. Probably started over fishing grounds, stands of teak trees, or who knows what else. Now it's just revenge and honor."

"Hard to believe the Kaerin would allow that type of unsanctioned conflict." Pretty had a good point, but he was sitting ten thousand miles away, a lot closer to where the Kaerin influenced and controlled everything.

"Not really, sir. Near as we can tell, the Kaerin probably don't even know it happens. They wouldn't notice, unless one of the warring parties missed a quota or a delivery date. The Kaerin don't seem to have pulled any of these people into a local clan militia. Hell, it would probably be too much trouble just to round them all up. No one here goes anywhere except by boat.

"The High Blood assholes stay in Makassar and collect the produce of the entire area. Regular Kaerin cargo ship traffic between Makassar and the mainland takes it all to where it gets used. The locals here are a lot better off than what we have typically seen, and their opinion of those unlucky enough to live in Makassar under the Kaerin thumb is extremely low."

"So, the pirate queen? She's somebody you think we can work with?"

Colonel Pretty couldn't see the smile on his face. He turned to look at Amona being walked around the shipbuilding site at Fee'ada's side. He had her laughing and smiling like a young girl.

"I think Amona has it well in hand, sir. They seem friendly enough."

"Friendly pirates?"

"Pirates is overdoing it, sir. It's local, honor-based warfare. For what it's worth, I'd put my money on our host. She's scary sharp, and so far, appears to be coin-operated. Though we watched her disperse our boat payment out to the whole village. My previous experience with a village Krathik is Arsolis, and she couldn't be more different." The last memory Rob had of Arsolis was the old man scratching at his crotch, hawking up a loogie, and spitting before asking how long it was going to be before he got one of the patrol boats the EDF Navy used.

"Arsolis is a pretty low bar." The colonel's laughter came through loud and clear.

"Seriously, sir. She's a good leader, good with her people, and they know it."

"How big is the village?"

"About four or five hundred here. They've got another small settlement in the hills, and another down the coast a few miles. But we haven't put eyes on either yet."

"You still holding to a week from now?" Pretty asked. Rob knew he was looking for a hard date to sail for Makassar.

"The boat will be ready, sir. We aren't provisioned yet, and I need to figure out a way to let our hosts know we aren't sailors. We are going to need more than just a local pilot. I still need to move our supplies from our cache into the village. We should be ready in a week, but I hope to have a better answer for you by tomorrow."

"Good enough, Rob. I'm only asking because Audy and Jake's assault force is anxious as hell. Audy has been asking every day. Frankly, you've moved more quickly than I thought you would."

"The credit goes to Amona, sir." He turned back around to catch their operative, and did it in time to see Fee'ada reach out and grasp Amona's hand down by the river's edge. "He's definitely got the situation in hand."

"Copy all, Rob. Pretty out."

He continued watching Amona and smiled. Yeah, Amona wasn't going to mind being held hostage here at all. *That sly dog...*

*

Chapter 9

Izmir, Chandra—Holding of Lord Oont'tal

The engines of Tima's airboat revved as it touched down with a hard bump and rolled roughly down the landing field. Out his window, the bright blue of the Middle Sea contrasted with the drab color of the surrounding hills in the distance. Between the water and the heights lay the city of Pagasta, the seat of Lord Oont'tal's Holding. Oont'tal was the single Kaerin Lord capable of challenging Prelate S'kaeda, and, by extension, Tima's own future. He didn't want to be here.

Nothing characterized these dangerous times more than the fact of his own apprehension. A set of stairs was being carried to where he waited at the airboat's open door by two of Oont'tal's Kayseri clan servants. Tima had time to look at what awaited him. He was the presumptive heir to the Kaerin Prelate. That still unofficial assumption relied entirely on where Lord Oont'tal stood on the matter. If his host was leaning towards challenging Lord Noka openly, he was, in all likelihood, a dead man.

As much as Lord Noka seemed amused by Lord Oont'tal's challenges and games, the threat was real. Tima didn't enjoy being a game piece. True, he had his own mission here, and the visit had even been his idea. But Lord Noka hadn't been able to resist using the visit to draw a line on the game board.

Tima couldn't fault the thinking. If Lord Oont'tal prevented him from leaving—or worse—the Prelate would have the excuse to end his rival's machinations once and for all. If Oont'tal took his visit as an offer for further cooperation with the Prelate, both current and future—it would be what the Edenite prisoner called "a win-win" for Lord Noka.

Lord Oont'tal's Gemendi Prelate, Yun'nay, was waiting at the edge of the landing strip flanked by two High-Blood warriors. The scene could have been taken as an indication of Yun'nay's status. Tima knew better—Yun'nay was a gifted Gemendi, particularly in all things maritime. The man's designs for ship-borne pivot cannons, as well as dozens of other shipbuilding improvements, were already being incorporated across Chandra. But Yun'nay was no Kaerin Lord. No, the warriors were there for him. Whether it was out of respect for his relatively new noble status, acknowledgement of his position as Lord Noka's heir, or purely as extra surveillance of his movements, would remain to be seen.

Tima nodded in return to Yun'nay's respectable bow, wondering if the warriors were a mistake on his host's part. He could have been watched more effectively—perhaps even lured into doing something suspicious—without the presence of guards. The pinch of it was, he did have a mission here that Yun'nay and his master could not learn of.

"Lord Tima Bre'jana," Yun'nay bowed again in greeting. "My Lord Oont'tal bids me to welcome you, and to assure you that you will have my, and my Gemendi's, full cooperation during your visit."

"That is good to hear, Gemendi Prelate Yun'nay. Your reputation in all things nautical is well known. Did your Lord advise you concerning my inquiry?"

"Only to say that the Lord Prelate's gift to him, the ancient boat, may hold some secret that could prove beneficial to us all."

"That is correct," Tima held out both hands in explanation. "It may be nothing. As you know, research and experimentation with new tools seldom occur in a straight line."

Yun'nay nodded knowingly with what might have been a smile

playing on his face. "These days, few things do, Lord Tima."

Yun'nay held out a hand to the motorized carriage. It had to be Lord Oont'tal's own. "Unless you'd like to refresh, we could go directly to our boat-works. We keep the ancient watercraft there. Lord Oont'tal himself may stop by if his schedule allows."

"By all means." Tima put on a brave face. "I look forward to meeting him."

It wasn't five minutes into the drive, with his two warrior-minders sitting silently in the front seats, when they rolled past an exercise field. Two complete War Fists of High Bloods stood at attention as the Bastelta, wearing the bright blue sash of House Oont'tal walked between the blocks of troops screaming words that Tima couldn't hear but would have recognized immediately. There were days when he missed his time serving the host.

"Two of our newly formed War Fists." Yun'nay pointed out the window. "Two of the ten we have formed in the last several moons."

Tima nodded in appreciation. Lord Noka and he were well aware of Oont'tal's expansion of his ground forces. Every Kaerin Lord was under writ to do the same, yet Oont'tal had clearly made a point of having him driven past the field. Was it to show him that he was doing as asked, or a demonstration that Oont'tal's power would soon extend beyond the waves where he was already the undisputed power? Neither he nor Lord Noka were concerned. No Kaerin Lord came close to the sixty—soon to be eighty—War Fists that the Kaerin Prelate could field. Yet his host was clearly fishing for a reaction.

"Tell me, Gemendi Yun'nay, are they all equipped with the new model firearms?"

"They will be very soon. The production tolerances of the ammunition are difficult, not to mention the extrusion process, but we are making progress."

"Good, because the Shareki and Jema forces went through three Fists of Lord Atan'tal's warriors on Irinas in a little more than a day."

"We had heard that." Yun'nay nodded. "But was not the majority of his force there Junata subjects? Not High-Bloods."

"You've been misinformed." Tima took little pleasure in correcting the Gemendi. "There were two High Blood Fists, and one Junata standing against the Shareki and their Jema dogs. Lord Atan'tal's two Fists lasted no longer against the Shareki than did the single Junata Fist."

Tima saw the two warriors in the front glance at each other in what was probably surprise. Yun'nay leaned across the seat towards him and, in a whisper, asked, "does Lord Oont'tal know this?"

"He does, of course. The High Council were all advised." Tima realized immediately that if Lord Oont'tal wanted to keep his troops in the dark as to what they were up against, the lives of the warriors in the front seat were probably forfeit after hearing the truth. It was certainly within Oont'tal's authority to do so.

Tima lifted his chin out Yun'nay's window. "They look like fine warriors. We will need every one of them."

Tima's secret mission was complete before he stepped out of the vehicle. The ancient Kaerin watercraft was under a shed, up on heavy blocks, and had been partially disassembled. There was a pile of the thick, shiny power conduits sitting off to the side. They were exactly the same as what sat in his office back in Kaerus, only longer.

"I see you've wasted no time in your research." Tima recovered quickly and gave Yun'nay a nod of appreciation over the roof of the vehicle. "I felt if anyone could pull something useful from this craft, it would be you."

"I haven't attained the success you credit me with, Lord." Yun'nay shrugged in defeat. "The panels that somehow collect impetus from sunlight are a complete mystery." Yun'nay pointed at the sleek hull. "At the moment, we are focused on trying to identify and catalogue the materials used in the hull to see if we can recreate the power generation. We have not had any success to date."

"We tried the same on Landing," Tima acknowledged. "I agree, it's the critical… piece." He'd almost used the Edenite word *technology* that he'd adopted from Ocheltree. He needed to be careful here. Yun'nay was every bit the Gemendi he was.

"But not the point of your visit?"

"No," Tima pointed at the stern of the craft their ancestors had built on the planet Kaerus. The ancient Kaerin technology was a source of mixed emotion for him. He'd long held the tools of the ancestors in high esteem only to learn that the Shareki's technological path had developed along the same lines. It was disconcerting.

He walked around the vehicle to the stern of the ancient boat and pulled a tarp off the propellor. "The source of the boat's impetus through the water."

"The water fan?" Yun'nay joined him. "Without the ability to power the craft's motors…"

Water fan? It was as good a name as propellor. "I'm not thinking about this craft, Yun'nay. Our ships' boilers turn the drive paddles of our boats. At any time, only four or five strakes of the paddle wheel are in the water, and are actually pushing the craft forward, yes?"

"Yes, the others are out of the water, coming back around."

"Doing nothing to drive the boat forward during that circuit." Tima circled a finger. "There is no efficiency in it, not to mention the obvious target the paddles present in a naval engagement, no matter how well-armored the paddle housing may be."

He pointed at Yun'nay's water fan. "Every turn of this fan pushes water throughout its revolution. Each of the three blades would be equally efficient at all times."

"But the speeds with which this craft's motors turn this water fan cannot be matched by our steam engines."

Tima arched an eyebrow and waited. "Can they not? I just flew here. An airboat's engine turns the blades at rates far faster than what would be needed in the water."

"Those are fuel powered engines, turning thin blades against air." Yun'nay shook his head. "Water is a far different medium, a ship far heavier. They might turn this water fan fast enough, but it would hardly move one of our ships. I know this for a fact. I tried to push, and then tow, one of our smaller frigates with this craft with a full charge on its batteries. It moved, but barely. The crew could have rowed faster. There was not enough power to move the weight."

"You do your reputation justice, Gemendi Yun'nay. That is precisely why I've come."

"My Lord?"

"One of our scout planes overflying Irinas survived," Tima began his well-rehearsed lie. "One of only two to attempt that mission and survive to report what they saw."

In truth, nothing approaching Irinas in the air survived long enough to spot the coast. It was as if the Shareki could see them coming, night or day, regardless of the weather. Ocheltree had explained radar to him in an extremely depressing conversation.

"Our airboat overflew the port at Irinas—the enemy has expanded it substantially. The enemy was building a large ship. We think it was a cargo ship of some sort. The vessel was in a building cradle, out of the water, and the crew of our airboat described the water fan at the stern. More importantly, they were able to describe its blades, all four of them."

Tima pointed down at Yun'nay's water fan on the ancient boat. "Shaped, as best as they could describe, just like this one. Though the fan had four blades, and was taller than a man from bottom to top. I knew I had seen the like before."

Tima watched as the Yun'nay's eyes suddenly lit up. "The amount of water such a fan could push, even at lower speeds... powered by our steam engines..."

"This is why I'm here."

Yun'nay knelt until the small propellor was level with his face. "The sweep of the angles is continuous, and difficult to duplicate." Yun'nay jerked upright, almost jumping. "But not impossible. Casting them would be difficult, but with some effort, we could just scale up from this model."

"Something easy to cast," Tima followed, nodding in agreement. He silently thanked Yun'nay for his jump in logic. The man was as sharp as his reputation, and he had no need to lead the man. "I was thinking of some combination of brass and bronze, like we use for small cannon. But metals are not my expertise," Tima added. "The airboat crew who spotted the Shareki vessel described the water fan as having a color that sounded like gold. I doubt even the Shareki would fashion a water fan from gold. My guess is some material the salt water won't corrode."

"That may work," Yun'nay was nodding himself. Tima recognized the look. The man was a hundred kamarks away, his Gemendi intellect seeing the possibilities, making the connections. He'd felt the same way every time he managed to get Ocheltree talking.

"There was one more thing of interest, Yun'nay."

"My Lord! I feel like you've just provided me with my life's work in these last few minutes."

"The Shareki boat, Yun'nay—it had two such water fans at the stern. Most of our larger boats already have two steam plants, each driving their own paddle wheel. Could we simply modify our existing ships, run the drive axles to the stern instead, and affix them to a water fan? Or fans?"

Yun'nay's jaw opened and then snapped shut. "Two?" The Gemendi nodded almost absently. "We might... it certainly..." The stunned Gemendi pivoted on one foot, jerking himself into a tight circle in three or four furtive steps as he mumbled to himself. "Yes, I see the... universe! Yes!" The Gemendi reached and grabbed him by the shoulders with both hands. "Lord Bre'jana, you are a man of rare ability."

Tima waited for the Gemendi to remember who he was, who he had a hold of. He wasn't offended. If anything, he was a bit jealous of the Gemendi's excitement. A part of him envied Yun'nay's simpler, more focused life, and the much safer waters of scientific inquiry.

"Forgive me! Lord Tima." Yun'nay released him and looked at his own hands in shock, as if they'd acted of their own accord. "I forget myself."

"No need to apologize, Gemendi Yun'nay. When I placed these pieces together in my own mind, I had much the same reaction."

"I will begin working on this problem immediately, without delay!"

"That's between you and your Lord," Tima reminded the man. "Lord Noka felt that if anyone could give us the benefit of this new knowledge, and actually make it work, they would be found here. I'll be happy to report that he was correct."

"Thank you for the confidence you put in us, my Lord—in me. I will be certain to tell Lord Oont'tal the same."

"He's not coming, is he?" Tima hadn't believed that was the case when Yun'nay had first alluded to it.

"Earlier, my Lord." Yun'nay looked embarrassed. "I may have misspoken. I will tell him what you have shared with us today. It was my impression that he would possibly meet with you later in the day."

Tima glanced back at the vehicle that had brought them from the landing field. The two warriors stood by the vehicle watching them, no doubt wondering why or even how their Gemendi Prelate could be so excited.

"I'll await his summons."

*

He'd been escorted to Lord Oont'tal's sprawling palace complex overlooking the long bay that held the city of Pagasta. It was an ancient city by Kaerin standards—one of the oldest on Chandra as it was on the Middle Sea, near the island of Landing. The Holding of Pagasta had been the Kaerin capital before their conquests had taken them so far from the water's edge. The palace itself was a historical marvel that—according to Lord Noka—Lord Oont'tal thought was just one more justification why he should lead the Kaerin.

Tima had yet to meet the Prelate's challenger in person and had no doubt that he'd be presented with the opportunity very soon. His perception of this place and the resultant feelings regarding Lord Oont'tal couldn't help but be flavored by what Lord Noka had told him.

Tima was anxious to form his own opinions. He'd been installed in a spacious suite with a high balcony from which he could look down upon the city and its harbor. The whole panorama stood in contrast to the capital of Kaerus, which was locked away behind its snow-capped mountain ranges. This was a Holding that looked outward. Its fleets of boats of every type and size formed much of the Kaerin's ability to link disparate lands and the Holdings of the Kaerin nobility together. Looking at it now and seeing the constant activity its commerce demanded, Tima couldn't help but wonder how different his people would be had this Holding remained the capital.

They would never know. That future had died long ago, and Tima could not help but wonder what else had been lost. He also wondered what other secrets this place held. The second beacon may very well be here. Perhaps it was sealed behind a false wall, as the one on Landing had been, or maybe it collected dust in some forgotten storeroom. At the end of the day, he had no way of asking. Certainly not until they had a better idea of where the Lord of this Holding stood on his understanding of the Kaerin's true history.

His suite was so large, and he was so lost in thought, leaning over the balustrade taking in the busy harbor below, that he hadn't heard the door open.

The warrior behind him coughed politely before speaking. "Lord Oont'tal would see you now, My Lord."

"Tell me, Teark." He recovered from his surprise. A simple push from the warrior, and Lord Noka would have needed a new heir. "The Shareki attack on this place—which island did it originate from?"

The warrior stepped to the edge of the balcony and pointed down to the easternmost island in the bay. It was given over to a vineyard and sat more than two kamarks from the edge of the city's waterfront.

"There, my Lord. They just appeared in a clap of thunder, carried out their attack, and disappeared the same way. Like ghosts, there was nothing remaining there when we landed our warriors. Only the strange tracks left in the soil by their gun vehicles."

"Motorized cannons?"

"Just so, my Lord."

Tima nodded. "Those same men and weapons attacked the Prelate's military base at Meldona the very next night. They left nothing behind there either, beyond the wreckage of one of our airboats that managed to get close."

"Will they ever choose to stand and fight us, my Lord?" The Teark would no doubt share their conversation with his superiors—and ultimately Lord Oont'tal—but in the moment, it was merely a Teark veteran asking a question of a former Bastelta.

"If I were them, I'd avoid a pitched battle with us like it was a plague. It will be up to us to force that battle."

The Teark nodded to himself in agreement and then remembered why he was here. "I'm to escort you to Lord Oont'tal."

"Lead the way, Teark."

It was nearly a ten-minute walk through the palace to get to Lord Oont'tal. If the master of this place chose the location to send a message, it worked, Tima thought. He was ushered into a cavernous wood-paneled room, where maps covered every wall panel, each dotted in pins and colored arrows. The floor was taken up by about twenty desks, whose occupants were hard at work updating forms behind towering stacks of reports.

Lord Oont'tal, trailing a single hulking warrior, held a hand up in greeting as Tima entered. Oont'tal said something to the official seated at the desk closest to him while pointing at something on the desk. The clerk nodded once and went back to work as Lord Oont'tal made a straight crossing between the desks towards him.

"Let's take this out in the hall. I don't want to disturb them." Oont'tal jerked a chin over his shoulders.

His host shut the door to the room the moment they were back in the hall. "Running a Holding with commercial and maritime interests spanning the world takes a Fist of officers whose attention to detail is matched only by their ability to get distracted."

"I understand, Lord." Tima bowed his head deeply. "I appreciate you taking the time to meet me."

Oont'tal was on the short side of average height and had shoulders as thick and wide as the door they'd just used. His blue eyes were focused on him with an intensity that Tima was sure could melt many of the people who called him Lord.

"I hadn't planned to; I'll have you know that." Oont'tal's delivery was blunt, but there was no hint as to why. The man's demeanor gave nothing away, other than leaving Tima with the feeling that the man didn't possess the depth of imagination needed to be half as devious as Lord Noka often accused him of. Difficult? Yes. Bluntly honest? Tima's first impression was yes. Lord Oont'tal seemed to be a hammer to Lord Noka's blades.

"I know your father from the Council, Lord. He is a good man, but his long association with Lord S'kaeda has no doubt left you with an appreciation for the Prelate's subtle ways. I don't play those games, Lord Bre'jana. Which is why I'm meeting you here and now, as one High Lord to another—nothing more. You understand what I'm saying?"

A hammer indeed. "Because Lord Noka has not officially named me his successor?"

Oont'tal jerked his chin once in agreement as if the movement caused him pain.

"Because our Prelate continues his practice of slow boiling anyone he considers a challenge to him. Every major decision the man has ever made is like a stone pushed slowly up a hill to its crest. Once at the peak, you must step in front of it to arrest its roll or be crushed by it."

Tima couldn't disagree with that assessment. Lord Noka often floated ideas as one would release a stalking horse when hunting wolves. All to gauge where other Lords of the High Council stood.

"In my case," Tima offered a grin. "I believe my recent close association with him had more to do with his own uncertainty. He does not act rashly. It is a decision he would be sure of."

Oont'tal shook his head. "It's not a decision until it is. This particular rock isn't to the top of the hill—nothing's been decided. Yet we are all expected to act as if it has been—the S'kaeda slow boil."

Tima could understand some of Oont'tal's frustration, if not the anger it produced. In front of him stood a man who seemed to view the world in very clear black and white. A man of honor, not even Lord Noka would dispute that. A man who would never be convinced of something he couldn't put his hands around...a dangerous man indeed. He immediately saw Oont'tal as less a challenger to Lord Noka and more of a direct opposite of the Prelate.

Tima held out his arm. "High Lord to High Lord, well met, Lord Oont'tal."

The grip on his forearm was as solid as the man himself. "Well met, Lord Tima Bre'jana. I expected you to defend the Prelate's practices, or worse, make excuses for him." Oont'tal gestured down the hallway. "Let's walk. I've been crouched over maps most of the day and will return to it when we are done."

Tima fell in next to him, aware for the first time of Oont'tal's slight limp. It was said he'd grown up shipboard, so probably a result of some accident.

"I won't defend the Prelate," Tima began. "He needs no assistance from me in that regard. As for excuses, he is the Prelate. He can direct the High Council as he sees fit."

"True enough. Don't mistake me, Lord. I only wish he'd dispense with his subtleties, misdirection, or trial policies. This is not the time for it. We are at war. He mistakes honest disagreement for treachery. To be clear, this is nothing I haven't said to his face in private numerous times. No one, least of all the Prelate, has cause to wonder where I stand."

True enough, Tima thought. Except on the issue of his own elevation to heir. There wasn't a Lord on the High Council who knew where Oont'tal stood on his being groomed to replace the Prelate. Tima decided on directness.

"There is one issue of which we have already spoken, my Lord, where your opinion among the Council is needed. As you have said, we are at war. A war that is not progressing to anyone's satisfaction to date. Stability is a prerequisite for any chance of success."

"He sent you to get my acquiescence?"

"I came to speak to your Gemendi Prelate, My Lord. I'd like to think I'm not one to waste an opportunity."

"I not going to weigh in on future possibilities. He wants to hand you the iron medallion or bequeath it to you upon his death—it's within his right to do it. I have no intention of being a part of his echo chamber in this matter or any other. He has enough voices for that."

"For myself," Tima bowed his head. "I appreciate your honesty."

"It's all he's ever gotten from me. If you follow him as Prelate, it's all you'll ever get from me." Oont'tal paused at the end of the hallway and turned them around. "Don't fall into the Prelate's own trap where he believes every Lord he doesn't own is a threat. I am a Kaerin Lord. I know what internal dissent or a power struggle would mean at this juncture. We already have our hands full with the Edenites."

"There's a wisdom in what you say that I will take pains to remember, Lord Oont'tal."

Oont'tal grinned himself. "I've formed a good initial opinion of you, Lord Tima. Don't change my mind now by licking my boots."

"I meant what I said." Tima was surprised just how much he had.

Oont'tal regarded him closely, as if to weigh the veracity of what he was saying. The nod to himself was clearly a decision. As to what, Tima had no hope of knowing.

"Gemendi Yun'nay is one whose opinion of you is not likely to diminish anytime soon," Oont'tal changed the subject in an instant. "He thinks you've provided a critical breakthrough that may just give us a chance at sea. I've long dreamed that our paddle wheels would be under the water, protected and out of sight." Oont'tal grinned with a dead shark's eyes, as if he could see the possibilities. "This water fan? His name for it? Or yours?"

"His, Lord. Gemendi Yun'nay made the leap in logic. There was no better place to bring what we have learned. The Prelate agreed."

The compliment of his Gemendi seemed to roll off of Oont'tal as did the Prelate's blessing of the decision. "As welcome as the breakthrough is, it will be moons before we can complete a retrofit on enough hulls to make a difference. But make a difference it will, no doubt. It will be Yun'nay's priority, and we will share everything we learn with every Lord who is building ships. No new construction now should begin until he finalizes a build plan. Conversions will be far more difficult than new construction."

Tima simply nodded in acceptance. Lord Oont'tal had already stated he didn't need empty pronouncements of agreement.

His host laughed to himself momentarily. It sounded almost like a deep cough. "I haven't seen Yun'nay this excited before. He's quite convinced his new naval pivot guns, in combination with armoring our ships and your water fans, will give us a fighting chance at sea."

"I understand his excitement—I felt the same when our scouts returned from Irinas with a detailed description of what they'd seen. I have no doubt your Gemendi would have put the pieces together far faster than I did given the same information. He's a credit to your House."

"Lord Noka did not bother to share with the Council that any of his air scouts sent to Irinas had returned successfully."

"No, we've held that information very tightly," Tima explained. "The Prelate holds the opinion, which I share, that the truth of how many airboats we have lost over the Irinas Channel would be very damaging should our air fleets come to know of it. As you can imagine, it would not be helpful should our airboat pilots learn just how easily the Edenites intercept and dispatch our craft."

"It's that daunting?"

"I doubt I can do the situation justice," Tima replied honestly. "The most stalwart air boat crew may come to prosecute their missions... differently should they come to think they have no chance of success. The mission that provided us the information, involved thirty airboats, launched from every landing field in range of Irinas. Each crew was told nothing of the others. Two airboats returned. One had reached Irinas," Tima finished, knowing only the last bit was a falsehood.

In fact, several of that type of mission had been launched. No one had returned with anything useful other than reports of enemy airboats that flew circles around them and shot them out of the sky with ease.

Oont'tal shook his head in dismay. "Why does the Prelate withhold this information from the High Council? Protecting the morale of our warriors, I can understand. Keeping other Lords in the dark as to what is being done, the results... it concerns me greatly."

"It was my hope," Tima replied, "and that of the Prelate, that my coming here immediately with what we have learned would allay some of that concern."

"I more than appreciate the fruits of your visit, Lord Tima. Be assured of that." Oont'tal paused his slow walk down the endless hallway and turned them back around. "Though, I can't help but wonder how many other information-gathering efforts he has withheld from the High Council."

Tima was worried about his guilty knowledge showing through. Could Oont'tal somehow know of the prisoner? He didn't doubt being caught in a lie by Lord Oont'tal was a deficit no one could work their way out of.

"I assure you, Lord, it is only out of concern for the morale of our warriors, and yes, even some of our Lords on the High Council, that Lord Noka has been circumspect. Surely your own naval crews are not fully aware of the power of the Edenite's boat-killing rockets? That they fall out of the sky, launched by those same cursed airboats of theirs to turn whole sections of our largest boats into floating kindling?"

"No..." Oont'tal agreed after a moment. "They do not. But I do not command one of my boats. I sit on the High Council."

"As I've said, Lord, the fact of my personal visit, its context, was meant to allay your concerns. The Prelate felt it important that I be the one to visit."

Oont'tal smiled for the first time. It was not a thing of warmth. If anything, it seemed a harbinger of violence. "I don't doubt that is at least partially the reason for your visit, Lord Bre'jana." The smile remained as Oont'tal stopped and faced him. "Speaking for myself, and for no other member of the High Council, I hope that this is not the last time I benefit from your insights and information gathering... efforts."

"A sentiment I share completely." Tima felt he managed to hide what he was thinking. He couldn't help but think Oont'tal knew about the prisoner. It might have been his guilty knowledge, but the man's smile said it was not.

"You will convey my regards and concerns to the Prelate?"

"Of course."

"Then for your own ears, Lord Bre'jana—words which I have already shared with the Prelate. I will not challenge his seat, nor will I challenge any Lord he appoints to replace him."

Tima bowed his head. "I will take those words with me, and I thank you for them."

"Don't thank me, Lord Bre'jana. If the war with the Edenites continues as it has, with us merely preparing for a battle the enemy seems very capable of avoiding—I won't have to challenge the Prelate. It will be done by others."

Tima smiled then. "If those others have a workable solution for defeating the Edenites, they—including you, My Lord—deserve the iron medallion, and they would have my support in seeking it. In the meantime, I don't believe complaints and criticism of the Prelate are a solution. Wouldn't you agree?"

Oont'tal nodded once very slowly in what might have been agreement. "I won't argue that point. I would only add that continued inaction has very little to recommend as a way forward."

*

Chapter 10

Patrick's back had almost stopped hurting, but the itching was driving him insane. There'd been an idiotic move this morning when he'd woken up in his sleeping bag drenched in sweat. He'd pulled his shirt off over his head before remembering not all the scabs on his back were bandaged. Mrs. Ballard, their host's medic, had cut out half a dozen pieces of shot that had gone deep. Those wounds had stitches and bandages, but even they didn't seem to hurt like they should.

He couldn't complain about how they'd been treated. These people had saved Noah's life—probably his own as well. He looked past the campfire and could see Sandra sitting at her brother's side in the aid tent. Noah was sitting up on his cot and talking. They'd been fed all they could eat, and he could already see a difference in everyone's faces after just three days. He didn't want to think how hungry they all must have looked to their rescuers, if that was actually what they were.

Since they'd been intercepted on the road, he still hadn't learned who these people really were. Their story of being some anti-government militia outfit had sounded to his ears like it had been pulled out of their ass. There was a lot they weren't being told—that much was clear. Two days ago—the first day he'd been up and about—their rescuers had loaded up everyone except Noah and Sandra and driven them back out to their vehicle to get their stuff. The spare clothes were nice, especially for the kids, but the whole expedition had felt orchestrated to get them out of camp.

When they'd returned, the militia group was half the size it had been. When he'd asked the driver of his four-wheeler where so many of their people had gone, the response had been "on patrol." It hadn't felt right to him. Half the tents were gone as well, and they hadn't been the kind you broke down and hiked out with. Their unused four-wheelers were still there, as well as two old pickup trucks. If they were patrolling, he couldn't imagine where they'd gone on foot. It wasn't like they were going to find a place in New Mexico to hit back at the government. This place was a prison, and the guards were all outside the fence line.

Patrick saw Allen's eyes flick upward at something behind him. A moment later, he heard the footsteps.

"Nice fire." It was one of the two brothers that Mitch had collectively named Dumb and Dumber.

"Evening," he replied, motioning at one of the empty camp chairs. "It's Josh, right?"

"Right-o, I'm the good-looking one. Can't stay. Captain Lassiter asked me to see if you were up to chatting."

"Sure. Just me? Or all of us?" He pointed at Allen and Mitch.

"Uh... you know, I probably should have asked."

"You go," Mitch gave him a nod. "If it's a recruitment pitch, it's probably safer for all of us if you're the one to say thanks, but fuck off."

Allen laughed as he nodded in agreement before lifting his chin in the direction of the big tent where Captains Lassiter and Bullock had disappeared into. "Be nice to know what they want to do with us. You got this."

Patrick, mindful of his back, stood slowly. "Lead the way."

Josh was patient enough to keep pace with him. This was a strange outfit they'd fallen in with. There was almost zero military formality, yet there was a definite chain of command. His and Noah's savior, Mrs. Ballard, was the mother of one man and had known Josh and his brother Danny all their lives. He hadn't seen a single salute since they'd been here and hadn't heard more than a couple of "yes, sirs." It left him feeling like they all been taken in by a group of friends out for an extended, very well armed, camping trip. That seemed to fit the whole group, except for Kyle, Jake, and Carlos, who everyone else seemed to take orders from.

"You guys must feel like the rabbit that fell down the hole."

Patrick glanced at his escort, wondering if the soldier had mangled the saying on purpose. Then again, after one night of playing cards with him and his brother, he knew that wasn't probably the case.

"You mean 'fell down the rabbit hole'? Like in the story?" Patrick tried.

"What story?" Josh looked at him like he expected more of an explanation.

Patrick already regretted this rabbit hole of his own making. "You said 'down the rabbit hole'—I thought you meant the story? About that girl, Alice?"

Josh's heavy eyebrows scrunched together. "You catch any of that bird shot in the head?"

"No, why?"

"Whatever." the soldier shook his head in confusion before pulling open the tent flap. "Here he is. Did you want just him, or the others too?"

The exasperation on Kyle's face was hard to miss. Patrick didn't think it was from the lack of decorum on Josh's part. Whatever they thought of Josh, the two men seated in the tent were definitely military—special forces, unless he missed his guess. Their national guard unit had always had more than a couple of veterans in it who had gotten out and settled down close to home. A few of them had that same no-one's-shooting-at-us-all's-good attitude that these two had.

"He'll do fine, Josh. Thanks." Kyle came to his feet and held out a hand as he spoke.

"How's the back?" Jake, the always smiling smart-ass who had "captured" them, didn't get up and just waved in greeting.

"Itches like crazy, but healing quick."

Both of them nodded in understanding before Kyle looked past him. "Thanks, Josh—that'll be all for now."

Patrick looked around the simple tent as he fell into the seat. Three cots and as many camp chairs arranged around a folding table covered with a map of New Mexico. Assault rifles and combat vests were laid out at the foot of each cot. He knew they shared the tent with Carlos whom he'd seen leave camp in an ATV a while ago.

"I'm not trying to be a dick." Patrick pointed at the tent's door. "But is he—"

"Dumber than a box of rocks?" Jake asked. "Oh yeah."

"He and his brother are both a lot brighter than they let on," Kyle smiled. "But I swear, sometimes…" Kyle made a strangling motion in his lap.

"I know the type," Patrick laughed along with them and then waited for the other shoe to drop.

"First off, I need to apologize for throwing you in the four-wheeler the day after you'd been shot," Kyle started. "That was my call. Operational security and all that. I needed you guys out of camp."

"About what we figured," Patrick nodded. "Not like we were in any position to complain."

"Still, it's not what I would have done if I'd had a choice."

Maybe it was bullshit, but Kyle sounded sincere. That, or he was just really good at this concerned neighbor routine.

"Hey, we're healthy, or on the mend. I'm not in a position to bitch—none of us are. You saved Noah's life when we were all pretty certain we'd end up burying him. Probably saved my life as well. Antibiotics are pretty hard to come by around here. If you could spare some supplies, we'll take our chances and be out of your hair as soon as Noah is on his feet."

"I'm afraid we won't be that long." Kyle gave his head a shake as if he too wished that was an option. "Mrs. Ballard says it will be a close to a month before he's in walking shape. I'm planning on leaving you one of those beaters out there, but even then… according to her, moving him at all for a week isn't a good idea."

"You do not want to make that woman angry," Jake added.

"Leave us enough supplies, and we could wait it out here." Patrick's mind was going a million miles an hour. He hadn't dared hope they'd leave them a ride.

"We could do that," Kyle agreed. "But we might have another option for you as well."

Patrick laughed to himself. It was just like he and Allen had figured. "My guys told me that if this was a recruitment offer, I was authorized to tell you to fuck off." He looked at both of them. "They didn't mean any offense by it, and I don't either.

"We've got kids with us," Patrick continued. "I'm not using that as a crutch. We are… spent. The last few days are the first in over a year that we haven't gone to sleep hungry. We aren't afraid of a fight. It's how we all ended up here."

They'd all been pumped for their story over the last few days. The questions had mainly focused on the tactical situation in and around Raton and throughout New Mexico, just as one would expect.

"We don't have anything to give you," he finished. "Besides." he stopped himself. These people had to know what they were up against.

"Besides?" Jake prompted.

Patrick smiled. "I have to admit, hiding from the Feds inside their own prison is the last place they'll look for you. But it's not like you're going to be able to take the fight to them here either."

"That's true enough," Kyle replied.

"Yeah, that's a really good point." Jake echoed, with a smile playing on his lips.

He looked back and forth at them. Neither one struck him as the crazy zealot type. He knew what that animal looked like. Raton was full of them. There was something else going on that none of them had been able to figure out, and their hosts didn't seem to want to share.

"Please tell me you're not some sort of ISS Unit pretending to play for the other side. One of my guys thinks everything is a conspiracy—that was his theory."

"Nah, we hate those dickheads." Jake answered.

"We are most definitely not any part of the USG," Kyle explained. "I'm not ready to explain who we are yet, but let me ask you something. If you had an opportunity to get yourself and your people away from this place, away from this war—out of the country and someplace safer—would you take it?"

Patrick couldn't help but laugh. "Six months ago, I would have said sure, give us a full citizenship package to Australia while you're at it." Patrick had dreamed about Australia for a long time. "But the UK, the Kiwis and the US have declared war on them. There's nowhere safe left."

Patrick would have had to have been blind not to see the reaction on both Kyle's and Jake's faces.

"Seriously?" Patrick was genuinely confused. "It's on the radio—the Fed's TV as well. We didn't get a lot of it, and we don't believe half the shit they say, but what chance is Australia going to have against the US and most of the NATO countries? How could you guys not have heard that?"

"We've been out on the pointy end for a long time," Jake answered. It was another knee-jerk, bullshit answer.

"How we didn't know might make more sense tomorrow." Kyle shook his head at Jake. "For now, do you feel up for a ride back into Raton tonight?"

"Why the hell would you guys want to go there?"

"Your girl Sandra has been in the ear of Mrs. Ballard," Jake responded. "So have the two kids, talking about how you all had to leave their grandparents behind. We aren't judging you. Sounds like they knew the score, stepped up, and did the right thing. Mrs. Ballard is busting our balls to go get them… and enough of us had a good look at Raton over the last week that the idea of leaving them behind is becoming a morale issue."

Patrick was beyond confused. A morale issue? What kind of military unit, good side or bad, would give two shits about Sandra's parents? "Who are you guys?"

"Could you guide us to them? We'll cut through the desert in the four-wheelers and avoid the roads until we get to town." Kyle asked, ignoring his question.

"Sure," he answered. "None of us wanted to leave them, but they stayed for a reason. They can't travel, and they know it. The elderly don't do well here. Sandra's mom is in pretty rough shape."

"So was her brother," Kyle answered. "My people would like to try to help them."

"When?" It was all he could think to say. If Sandra found out he'd said no, he'd be dead to her.

"We'll leave in about an hour," Jake answered.

"An hour?"

"Has to be tonight," Kyle responded. "Sunup is in nine hours. We are all leaving before then."

This time, Patrick was almost enjoying the ride out of Raton. Rescuing Sandra's parents had gone without a hitch. They'd rolled up to the edge of town just after midnight, and the only group they'd encountered hadn't wanted to stick around and ask questions. The group of men—no doubt out trying to steal something to eat—had taken one look at Jake and the three other heavily-armed soldiers and wanted no part of them. It wasn't like an armed patrol could have been mistaken for anything other than ISS in the middle of the night.

Jake was in the driver's seat across from him, driving slowly through the scrub brush south of town with night vision goggles in front of his eyes. Sandra was in the seat behind him next to her mother, who bore the ride in silence under a pile of blankets. Juan Orosco followed in another four-wheeler along with the three soldiers Jake had brought with them.

Patrick turned around to check on Sandra and could just make out the smile that she offered up. She'd been speechless at the offer to retrieve her parents. He felt her hand give his shoulder a squeeze that felt like a thank you. He couldn't take credit for this. Part of him was still in disbelief that a military unit of any flavor, especially one that had security concerns about telling them who they were, would have taken the risk.

"We're almost through this shit." Jake spoke up for the first time since they'd left the edge of Raton. The electric four-wheeler didn't make any more noise than his mother's old chevy Volt had. "I just want to stay off the freeway until we are well south of town."

Patrick flashed a thumb in response. "What happens when we get back?"

He could sense Jake shrugging in the dark. "I suppose you folks will have a decision to make."

What decision? He'd already told them that none of them were interested in joining up for whatever fight they were headed to.

"Please tell me we didn't just rescue Sandra's parents so you guys have some more leverage over us."

Jake shook his head and let out a long sigh. "That's some dark shit, right there. Seriously, if we were going that route, I would have thought the two rug rats would have been enough."

"Is that a no?"

Jake laughed. "You've got some real trust issues, don't you?"

"Given the last few years, can you blame us?"

"Hey." Jake turned to face him, the dim back glow of his NODs giving his cheeks a spectral look. "It's not like we're the Feds asking you to trust us again."

That was true enough, Patrick figured. Then again, Jake and his weird company of soldiers hadn't told them shit. Thinking back on his conversation with Kyle and Jake in the tent, he could at least be certain that Jake's people were being honest with them so far.

"I know that," he started. "We all do, but I don't think you people realize what this place does to people. You know that group you guys scared off tonight? If you hadn't been there, wearing your ninja outfits and carrying rifles, they'd have likely killed us on the chance we had some food or an extra meal chit. They were probably decent people before being sent here—at least I'd like to think so. But trust them? Now? No fucking way."

"I get it," Jake responded. "But you seriously need to stop worrying about us. If anything, I think we might just restore some of your faith in humanity."

Patrick felt his head shake almost of its own accord. He wasn't certain he could trust in his own humanity at this point. "Why can't you just tell us who the hell you are? Allen heard a couple of your folks speaking together this morning in the chow line in some language he didn't recognize. He's no dummy—his dad was in the Air Force and he grew up all over the world. Whatever it was, they shut the hell up the second they realized he was in earshot. Then there's those weird bowie-looking knives a lot of you carry, like you all went to the same ren fair or something."

Jake grunted out a short laugh. "There's a pretty cool story behind those knives. A lot of our people, including Kyle and myself, are—I guess you could say—honorary members of an alien race. They don't just hand those knives out to anybody, let me tell you."

"Aliens?" he asked, more surprised that he'd resisted telling Jake to fuck off than he was by the whole "aliens" joke.

"Not like big-eyed grays, or some sort of two-headed blob people— I mean, they're human, just like us." Jake stopped himself and shook his head. "Actually, not like us at all, except to look at. We met them on a different planet. That's where we live now."

"Oh, riiight." Patrick nodded as if it all made sense. "So, you guys are aliens too. Got it!"

Jake shook his head and muttered something to himself. "I'm no good at this shit. I told Kyle just to wait and show you. He thought it would be a good idea if I told you first."

"That you're aliens?" Patrick laughed to himself.

"We aren't aliens! I grew up in Louisiana, for fuck's sake. I said we met the aliens on a different planet. We just came back here to check out how things have been going."

"Right." Patrick shook his head. To hell with these people! The sooner they could be on their way, the better. He just hoped they stuck with their promise to leave them a truck. "Why didn't you just say so from the beginning?"

He couldn't help but like Jake. In a strange way, he seemed like a more talkative, and, without a doubt, more imaginative version of Mitch. Jake was every bit as much of an asshole as his friend.

Patrick couldn't tell if Jake's laughter was at his expense or not. If they had shit to hide, fine! They should have just said so, instead of spinning science fiction fairy tales.

Jake rolled them to a stop a few minutes later. Patrick could sense that the freeway's embankment was somewhere just ahead. Jake was speaking to whoever was controlling the drone that had been on overwatch, following their ingress and egress from Raton. He kept his mouth shut and just listened to Jake's side of the conversation.

"All clear," Jake announced, before digging through his thigh pocket. He held up a flask between them.

"Take a snort of this. It'll help."

"With what?" he asked as he took the flask.

Jake barked another laugh. "With just about anything."

They climbed up the embankment of the freeway slowly, glancing back at their passengers to check on them. Once they were on flat asphalt, Jake hit the accelerator and shot south on the freeway.

"Smells a bit like peaty scotch." At this point, he considered himself somewhat of a connoisseur of fine spirits—or at least of anything that could be mashed, fermented, and turned into alcohol.

"I thought so too," Jake added, sounding suddenly serious. "But it's not."

Patrick looked at the flask a moment and then at Jake before taking a slug. He coughed out of reflex and pounded on the forward grab bar as the liquid burned what felt like a new path to his gut. For a second, he thought the small aperture of the flask might have saved his life.

"Holy shit!" he managed, before coughing again. "What is this?"

"It's called jasaka." Jake snapped his fingers, reaching for the flask.

Patrick watched Jake take a snort and grimace like he'd just been punched in the chest. He handed the flask back.

"Those aliens I told you about distill the stuff. My buddy Audy says it's an old family recipe. Knowing him like I do, it's probably got some secret ingredient like toe jam or ear wax in it—you know? Just to fuck with me. But I have to admit, it's damned good."

"You're friends with an alien?"

"Dude! I married one."

Patrick took another, smaller sip of the jasaka and held it in his mouth, imagining it was dissolving the enamel of his teeth before swallowing. "You can't help it, can you?"

"Help what?"

"Being an asshole?"

"Not really," Jake admitted. "Doesn't mean I'm not being straight with you, though."

Patrick ignored the teaser and gave the flask a shake. "You should let Allen try this stuff. He built and ran our still back in town."

"He's the chemistry professor? Or the big guy that doesn't like me."

"He taught chemistry 101 at a community college—you ask him he'll tell you he's a distiller. And Mitch doesn't not like you, he just doesn't trust anybody he doesn't know well."

"Nothing wrong with that," Jake admitted.

Patrick held the flask back out.

"Keep it." Jake waved it off. "You're all going to need a drink here in a bit."

Patrick refused to take the bait and ask why. The miles flew by in the dark, and it seemed just minutes before they passed by a shadow that he knew was their abandoned Suburban. Jake started slowing and looking for the wide shoulder where a gravel road stretched out westward into the high desert towards the camp. The next thirty minutes passed slowly as Patrick worried over what came next.

He couldn't imagine that Kyle and Jake's command could or would part with enough supplies to see them through the next week while Noah continued to heal. It was probably just a matter of time before the inevitable happened and he'd be digging another grave for Sandra's mother. Even if the soldiers left them with a truck, he doubted there would be enough gas to get them very far.

They rolled over the crest of the last big hill before starting the descent into the natural bowl between the hills and the campsite.

"Made it in time," Jake announced, sounding like he was suppressing a yawn.

"In time for what?" Patrick asked the question out of reflex. He had no hope for a straight answer and wasn't disappointed or surprised when Jake's only response was a squirrely look and a short exhalation of laughter.

They came around the low hill that hid the camp from the poor excuse of a gravel road, and Patrick was struck by the stark absence of the tents. He'd seen enough bivouacs prepped for transport that he recognized it immediately. The resultant waist-high pile of gear was as wide as their four-wheeler and nearly twenty yards long. Most of the soldiers stood around the pile of gear, waiting. That was the part he couldn't figure. These guys were well-equipped enough that it seemed impossible they moved around without being spotted by the Feds.

Patrick spotted Mitch and Allen standing near the far end of the supply pile with the children. The relief he felt at seeing them safe made him feel stupid and guilty at the same time. Jake had been right—he had some serious trust issues. Jake aimed the buggy at the red lens of a flashlight wagging itself back and forth. Kyle, standing next to Mrs. Ballard, materialized out of the darkness. Patrick turned to watch as the medic helped Sandra get her mother out of the back. Kyle's hand dropped onto his shoulder.

"Can I talk to you and your guys for a second?" Kyle jerked his chin towards Mitch and Allen. "We're getting pressed for time."

"Sure," he answered, before glancing back at Sandra and her mom, who had been moved to a camp chair that had an IV bag hanging from a jury-rigged brace above it. Emilia Orosco was looking directly at him and offered up the first smile she'd ever given him. He wasn't the only person with trust issues.

Kyle was in a hurry, though Patrick still couldn't figure why. It was going to take several trucks to move this all shit and it wasn't like they'd seen anything like that on their way in. He spotted one of the beater trucks sitting off to the side by itself. The other was fully loaded and parked next to the pile of gear.

"You still going to leave us a truck?" he asked as he caught up to Kyle.

"If you want it, yes," Kyle answered, waving a hand in that direction as they approached Mitch and Allen. "There's something you all need to see first." Kyle nodded in greeting to his friends, before taking a knee in front of Erin and George as Jake joined them. Jake ruffled Erin's hair and waved in greeting as the young girl toed a desiccated cowpie toward her cousin's feet.

He watched as Kyle produced two small ziplocked bags holding compressible foam ear plugs. "You two can go say hi to your grandparents. Ask Mrs. Ballard to show you how to use these."

Patrick waited until Sandra's niece and nephew were out of earshot. "What's going on?"

Kyle stood and turned towards Jake. "You didn't tell him?"

"I tried," Jake said. "He thinks I'm full of shit."

Kyle rolled his eyes a little. "Can't imagine why."

"You going to give me some bullshit story about aliens on a different world?" Patrick couldn't help but shake his head at Jake, who stood there grinning.

"Aliens?" Allen almost shouted.

Kyle looked at the three of them in turn before checking his watch. "Nope, figured it was best to just show you."

"Pat?" Mitch asked. "What the fuck is he talking about?"

"Got me," he answered, jerking his chin at Jake. "This one says he's married to an alien from a different planet."

Kyle shook his head at Jake. "That's what you started with?"

Mitch snapped his head back in surprise before eyeing Jake. "You some kind of nutjob?"

Patrick knew how Mitch thought. He was probably thinking these guys weren't so tough, but Patrick didn't think his friend would stand a chance against either Kyle or Jake.

Jake just smiled back at him. "Depends who you ask. You think I'd make something like that up?"

"Gentlemen, this way." Kyle pointed up the short hill behind him and started walking before looking back over his shoulder. "Did any of you see that video that was going around a few years ago? Sir Geoffrey Carlisle? From the mountain in Colorado?"

"The one where those separatists blew themselves up?" It was Allen who spoke. Patrick wasn't surprised. Allen had been their resident conspiracy theorist long before their own government branded them insurrectionists.

"Yeah." Kyle barked out a short laugh. "That's the one. You've seen the video?"

"I did," Allen answered, sounding suspicious.

"What the fuck are they talking about, Allen?" Mitch asked as they reached the top of the hill and Kyle stopped them.

Patrick had seen the video as well. Somebody had brought it to a drill weekend on their laptop. He could remember thinking at the time that whatever had happened there, it was probably something different than the story they'd been told.

Kyle looked at them again as he rubbed an ear. "Well, I guess you could say we are those same separatists. We most definitely didn't blow ourselves up. What Sir Geoff relayed in that video was—is—true. We came here from a different world, a different earth."

"I knew it." Mitch was shaking his head. "They're all crazy."

Kyle looked like he was going to argue the point, but one of his soldiers near the pile of gear let out three quick blasts from an air horn. Kyle turned back towards the flat, low ground at the bottom of the hill and pointed into the dark. "In ten seconds, you'll want to plug your ears and keep your mouth open."

"What the hell?" Mitch spoke again.

Jake slapped his arm. Patrick looked up and Jake was staring at him, dropping a pair of goggles over his eyes and plugging his own ears. "I tried to tell you."

Patrick glanced at Kyle, who was pointing again. "Eyes front."

The faintest glow of the pre-dawn was visible behind the hills in the far distance. He and Allen exchanged a glance before shrugging and following suit.

"Seriously! What's the f—"

Mitch's outburst was cut off by a sharp crack. A bolt of lightning had hit a hill a hundred yards away from his camper once when Patrick was a kid. It felt like they were inside that clap of thunder. It was nothing compared to the wall of dirt and dust that followed. Even in the dim light, they could see the edge of the cloud racing towards them up the slope. It washed over them like a sudden gust front as he ducked down out of instinct. The wind was gone just as quick, followed by another gentle push from behind.

Patrick stood back up, coughing and spitting out the dirt he'd just eaten. They all were. Even Kyle was doubled over, shaking the New Mexico desert out of his hair. There was something out there in the bowl beneath their hill. A line of lights shimmered through the dust-filled air.

"What is that?" He heard Allen ask next to him as he wiped at his own eyes.

The flying bridge of a ship took shape above where he'd been looking. Blue- and amber-hued lights from inside it were enough to outline figures of people standing behind the windows. His eyes followed the small line of lights running horizontally well beneath the bridge. Whatever it was, it was huge—a football field long—and it most definitely hadn't been there a moment ago.

"The... fuck?" Mitch stood just beyond Allen, his mouth hanging open.

"That is our ride home," Kyle announced. "It's how we got here as well."

"Aliens?" Mitch took a quick step back and the big guy would have stumbled if Jake hadn't caught him.

"No," Kyle answered quickly. "We built that—it's called the *Door Knocker*. The aliens Jake was talking about are every bit as human as we are."

"Way to kill the suspense," Jake laughed and shook his head before raising a radio to his face. "Hobos to *Door Knocker*, we're secure here. Let's get the trucks rolling. Fifteen minutes and we are out of here."

Additional lights shone through the settling dust at one end of the ship as its bow ratcheted down loudly to crash into the desert floor. Three large trucks raced down the ramp and started up the same trail Patrick and Jake had used just minutes earlier. Their headlights were partially masked, and only a dim light showed on the sagebrush in front of them.

The line of small lights running the length of the ship's railings were becoming clearer. Most of them blinked off and all that was left was a few running lights, as if the thing was worried about running into another ship out here in the desert. What was left was the black outline of the vessel's hull, slightly darker than its background.

"A different world?" Allen asked.

Kyle turned back to face them. "Geographically speaking, it's just like Earth, except no people. Well, except us, that is. You're still welcome to the truck if you want it. We've left you all the extra gas we brought with us. It might be enough to get you where you're headed... or you can come with us."

"What the actual fuck?!" Mitch's hands were out in front of him as if he could push the image of the ship away. They all looked at Mitch for a moment as if they expected more, but the big guy just stood there shaking his head and staring down at what hadn't been there a moment ago.

Kyle ignored Mitch's outburst and focused on he and Allen. "If you still think trading one town for another in this hellhole is your best option, come with us." Kyle grinned and jerked a thumb over his shoulder behind him towards the ship. "We can get you there in a flash, and drop you off a day's walk from this Silver City you told us about."

"Guys?" Mitch almost whispered.

They all looked over to see Mitch pointing down at the ship. Something with a single light beneath a domed canopy of some sort was lifting off the massive, flat deck.

Kyle brought up his rifle, activated his IR pointer under the barrel, and started lassoing it above his head. "That would be our wives," Kyle explained. "They brought a couple of kids the same age as your little ones. We thought that it might help put them at ease."

"You too, for that matter," Jake offered, eyeing Mitch.

"You planned all this?" Patrick could barely speak, and it had nothing to do with his mouth full of dirt.

"More like made it up as we went." Kyl explained. "We've been honest with you. We came here to check up on how things had progressed on Earth. You all falling in our laps just happened."

Kyle pointed up at the… what the hell was that thing? Patrick could see the outlines of a bunch of heads inside the domed canopy, backlit by some interior lights. "We planned this when we sent you out of camp a couple of days ago. We thought we might be able to give you and your people a better option."

The craft flew past them, thirty feet off the ground and moving slowly. The whine of its fans would have drowned out anything he could have said, if he had had anything to say.

"That's a flying car!" Mitch yelled.

Patrick was still watching, and it did sort of look like an overstretched 1950s Corvette convertible with a plexiglass dome. They all watched the thing settle amidst another dust cloud down by the gear pile. Soldiers and other personnel were already loading the equipment.

The inside of the car lit up as the dome retracted. Across the front seat were three women, and in the back was a big guy seated next to two young boys.

"Not aliens." Mitch announced, sounding very relieved.

Patrick was less relieved by Jake's gentle chuckle next to him.

"Come on." Kyle waved them forward and started down the hill. "Introductions are in order."

The car's occupants were standing outside waiting for them by the time they made it down the hill. The first thing Patrick noticed was that they all looked clean and healthy, like they'd been eating regularly. Things like that stood out. Next, it was the big dude with a pommel of a longsword standing above his shoulder. You didn't see that every day.

"Gentleman, I'd like to introduce my wife, Elisabeth. She's from Earth, just like me and you. This is former US Army Captain Brittany Souza and her two boys—Matt and Craig. We thought they could talk with Sandra and her two charges. They were all being pursued by the ISS when we came across them almost two years ago."

Patrick's head was still spinning, so he relied on rote mechanical politeness. "Uh... nice to meet you both." He offered his hand to shake, aware that the guy with the sword and the third woman stood a little off to the side.

"They are right over there, with Sharon Ballard." Kyle pointed to the far side of the trucks.

"It's nice to meet you all," Elisabeth offered. "I hope to get to know all of you better."

The other woman, the former Army Captain, looked them up and down, smirking. Patrick could very easily believe this woman was used to command. "I hope you're smart enough to believe what you're being offered. I know it's a lot to swallow. Best decision me and my family ever made. Come on, boys."

Jake waved the other couple forward and reached out a hand to the woman. "This is my wife, Dere'dala. She's from a planet we call Chandra, it's just like Earth as well—but very full of people."

"A different... different Earth?" Allen sounded as confused as he felt.

"There's three that we know of," Kyle explained. "Earth where we stand, Eden where we come from, and Chandra—where Dere'dala hails from."

"You're…" Mitch was struggling to say what they were all thinking. "Aliens?"

"Not like from your movies," the big guy with the sword spoke up with a strange accent and a smirk playing across his face. "We're just people like you, from a different earth."

"Not so much like us," Jake laughed. "Guys, this is our friend Audrin'ochal. He goes by Audy. He's the one I was telling you about. He distilled the jasaka I gave you."

"Jasaka?" Allen and Mitch asked with near perfect timing.

Patrick pulled the flask from his pocket and took a small sip before handing it over to Mitch as the liquid burned its way down his throat.

"Careful." He managed a dry cough.

Mitch didn't even hesitate before tilting it back and taking a heavy pull from the flask. He looked at Audy and Dere'dala for a moment before an involuntary shudder seemed to pass through his body. He coughed once and gave his head a slow nod.

"Not aliens," he announced, almost to himself. Mitch held out his hand to Audy. "Seems like we have something in common."

*

"That could have gone a lot worse," Kyle admitted as he gave Elisabeth a hug. They were on board the *Door Knocker*, and the last of the trucks were coming up the bow ramp.

"She was easy to convince," Elisabeth lifted her chin towards the bow where Sandra Orosco stood next to her parents, still talking to Brittany Souza. All four of the young children had gone running past them a moment ago. The Souza twins had taken George and Erin Orosco under their wing and were playing tour guide. "She ended up convincing Patrick herself."

"I figured she might," Kyle whispered. "It was those two I was worried about."

Allen and Mitch stood talking with Jake, Dere'dala, and Audy a few feet away. They were close enough that they could hear Jake in full bullshit mode talking about the fishing on Eden.

Elisabeth cocked her head, listening for a moment before smiling. "You still think they might be willing to come back here and do a different kind of fishing?"

"I hope so." Kyle pulled her in a little closer and planted a kiss on her head. "We need them to, and not just because I don't want to come back. This place is unrecognizable to us—so are a lot of its... occupants. This group is solid, especially Patrick. He's a natural leader, but they've all been through hell. There's a bunch of people here, including former convicts that own the hell and are living la vida loca. Inside this place, they're more of a danger than the feds."

"Just show them Eden. I'll make sure Sandra and the kids get set up." Elisabeth smiled up at him. "Give them something to believe in."

The warning horn started beeping from the pilothouse. He grinned down at her. "You know what I believe in?"

She shook her head. "I really hope you're about to say a shower—you smell like a goat."

He was still laughing when the *Door Knocker* blinked.

*

Chapter 11

Tor'ami Village, Sulawesi—Chandra

Rob Nagy couldn't put his finger on it, but something felt off at the shipbuilding site this morning. Over the last ten days, they'd all pretty much lived here. The wide expanse of sand along the riverbank that flowed out of the jungle had been a perfect place to pitch their tents and keep a close eye on their investment—the Te'ru'asta. The ship had been named and christened—or whatever passed for that in this part of Chandra—long before they'd shown up.

They'd been told in no uncertain terms that the name of the ship could not be altered, not if Rob and his party of "traders" wanted one of the locals to ever step aboard. After the previous day's training session with some of Fee'ada's sailors, it had been very clear that they were going to need the locals to sail the boat.

Sergeant Adams and the two Earth-born EDF members he had with him had quickly dubbed the vessel the *Terrorist*. It was close enough phonetically that, with their already foreign 'Edenite' accents, the locals had stopped trying to correct their pronunciation. He could see Adams, Corporal Singh, and Private Mendoza chopping wood for the fires that would cook down the raw rubber latex until it made a watertight caulking material.

The Tor'ami work crew hadn't shown up yet, and they were usually here with the rising of the sun—that had been the first thing he had noticed. The second outlier was the half dozen spear and bow-wielding men he thought of as Fee'ada's pipe hitters watching them. There were two at the trailhead leading back towards the village and another two on the upriver path that led to the lumber camp in the hills. A third pair of the local warriors sat on a log near the saw pit. None of them seemed to be doing anything other than watching them.

Rob put two fingers to his lips and whistled shrilly, watching his men's heads come up from across the work site. A radio call would have been much easier, but he didn't want to risk it. Some of the villagers already thought the strange visitors were touched, as they'd been caught several times speaking into their mic pickups pinned to their collars. He held up two fingers and beckoned Adams with an arm.

"Something is wrong."

Rob almost came out of his boots. He turned around quickly and was surprised to see Breda standing behind him. The little shit could skulk with the best of them. Then again, snakes didn't make much noise. Rob had already formed an opinion that the mouthy shit should be assigned full time to Stant'ala's scouts when they got back. It wasn't like Jake Bullock would put up a fight for the guy. Then again, Stant'ala didn't like Breda any more than the rest of them.

"No shit." He replied as he watched Adams make his way across the clearing. "Make yourself busy doing something, and don't be looking around. I don't want to raise suspicion."

"Did Stant'ala go with Amona?" Breda asked as he knelt, fumbling around in one of their bags.

"Yeah, but right now I'm a little more worried about us than I am about him. He's with Fee'ada."

"Yes, but she had eight, maybe ten, warriors with her when they left."

He looked down at the back of Breda's head. "No, she dropped these six off here. I saw them leave them leave with her normal two-person escort."

"There were another eight or so that met them at the edge of the trail." Breda didn't look up, he just pointed towards the upriver trail.

"You saw them?"

"I was at the river's edge checking our prawn trap."

"Why didn't you say something?"

Breda stood up quickly and spun around red faced. Facing Rob— or the middle of his chest, as the case may be. He was half convinced that much of Breda's attitude flowed from the fact that the guy was more than a little vertically challenged.

"Each time I raise a concern or voice my opinion, I am told to shut up, be silent, or take a walk."

Rob couldn't argue that point. Maybe he'd been a little too rough on the guy. But damn if Breda couldn't get on his nerves. Like now, every word that left Breda's lips came out with a tone as if his manhood had somehow been insulted.

"This morning was worth mentioning—don't you think?" He asked, expecting another scathing comeback.

"What's with all the hairy eyeballs this morning?" Adams interrupted them the moment he was in earshot.

"We were just discussing that." Rob nodded. "You have any words with our minders? Where the hell is the work crew?"

"Mendoza asked them, real nice-like. You know, like 'Good morning, where's everybody else?' He didn't get anything more than a shrug. Then again, his Chandran is as bad as mine is."

"They are hiding something. We could take these guards easily." Breda was vibrating with excitement. Rob bit back on the "shut your pie-hole" that immediately sprang to mind. If Breda had been a puppy, Rob would have thrown him out the door before he peed on the carpet.

"Relax, Breda. That is an order. These are friends until we know they aren't. We need these people."

"I've got my Glock on me." Adams lifted a chin in the direction of Corporal Singh and Private Mendoza. "So do they. You want us to go back to work?"

"Boil the rubber." Breda's English made it sound like *roo-bar*. "Like we are still awaiting the work crew. When it is ready to apply, you will have reason to ask the warriors where the workers are once again, without raising suspicion."

Adams looked at him for confirmation. It was as good a plan as he had at the moment. Rob gave a quick nod. "Do it. Stay chill, but make sure your guys know the score. Nobody does anything unless I say so."

They watched Adams saunter back to his men, whistling the work song from the *Bridge on the River Kwai*.

"What about Amona?" Breda asked.

"I don't think Queen Fee'ada would let anything happen to her boyfriend."

*

Amona smiled at his escort. He was convinced Fee'ada didn't know what to make of him or what was developing between the two of them any more than he did. Which wouldn't take much. He was confused—his previous experience with the opposite sex had been limited to three different relationships with other staff members serving Lord Bik'mas, Lord Tima's predecessor on the island of Landing. Those relationships had been born of mutual need and convenience, and had been allowed because it hadn't detracted from their duties in service to the Gemendi Lord they served. This—whatever this was—was different. It was a difference he felt every time he looked at her, but it was nothing he had felt before.

She smiled back at him and reached out to take his hand. Fee'ada enjoyed walking, and it had been on a walk on the beach the night after meeting her when she'd first reached out for his hand. He hadn't known what to do at the time, or what significance to attach to the action. He'd figured it out very quickly as she'd invited him back to her private home upon returning to the village. Since then, even with not knowing what it all meant, it had been easier, and far more enjoyable, to spend time with Fee'ada than to put up with the good-natured ribbing and constant questions from his companions.

The Jema scout, Stant'ala walked twenty paces ahead of them, leading the way along the narrow, well-worn path through a forest of towering trees with a handful of Fee'ada's guards. Having been born and raised on a desert island, the trees were just one more thing he could never have imagined.

"This place has been a favorite of mine since I was a young girl." Fee'ada nodded up the trail. "My friends and I would come here a couple of times a year. We'd run the whole way from the village."

"You didn't have guards with you then?"

"Why would I?" Fee'ada shook her head. "My father was a simple ship Krathik—I was but one of his four children."

"I thought maybe we were headed someplace dangerous because of all the guards." He nodded ahead of them and then lifted his free hand to point behind him where another four warriors walked in single file.

"Oh… it's farther than I usually walk," she responded quickly. "And you are still strangers, with even stranger ways."

Something in her response hit him in the gut. He couldn't have said why, but he was certain she was lying. Ten days ago, it wouldn't have bothered him the least—she was the leader of her own people and had no reason to be truthful with him beyond courtesy. He knew enough of negotiations and diplomacy to understand that courtesy was a surface manifestation at best. But this was Fee'ada, and a lot had passed between them in that short span of time.

He fumbled for something to say. "I hope I'm something more than a stranger to you."

She squeezed his hand and smiled in silence, as if she didn't trust herself to speak. With the sudden unease, there came a realization that Stant'ala was outnumbered ten to one, and that they were a long way from anyone that could help them.

The trail opened up into a small clearing, allowing them to see the skyline for the first time in over an hour. In front of them was a spine of dark rock running up from the grassy clearing to form a ridgeline rising above the green canopy. A small waterfall poured from an outcropping of stone about halfway up.

"We are here." Fee'ada pointed upwards. "There's another waterfall on the back side of the rock that falls into a cave. From there, it comes out this side."

It *was* pretty, he thought. Then again, he thought anything green or wet was beautiful.

"Come." She pulled on his hand before dropping it. "We'll go on alone. You must see the cave."

"Krathik?" It was Tar'wo, Fee'ada's lead warrior, who spoke up. He'd overheard his boss. Tar'wo was a brother to Ed'wo, the first Tor'ami Amona had met. The younger brother unfortunately didn't possess any of Ed'wo's good nature. Rob had taken to referring to Tar'wo as "Sergeant Joy-kill."

Fee'ada smiled good-naturedly at Amona before turning to her warrior and patting the blade on her belt. "You needn't worry about me. We won't be long."

Fee'ada pulled Amona up the hill. He couldn't help but glance at Stant'ala as they passed. The Jema looked anything but happy and relaxed. Whatever was going on, the scout had probably picked up on it a lot sooner than he had.

The trail up to the cave was well-made and well-tended. Steps had been cut into the rock face where needed, but its width relegated him to following behind Fee'ada. He risked a glance back downward to check on Stant'ala before the whole party disappeared behind the curve of the hill. They were all there. The warriors had surrounded Stant'ala with spears leveled. He liked Stant'ala, and was well aware of the man's legend. His thoughts flashed between hoping the Jema would be alright and wondering how many Tor'ami Stant'ala would kill before he made an escape.

Fee'ada paused at the dark entrance of a cave, holding out her hand. "It's dark inside. Your eyes will take a moment to see, but I know the path well."

Wonderful. He forced a smile and grabbed her hand.

'Dark inside' didn't begin to describe the utter blackness. Within a few strides and one sharp turn, the glow from the entrance was gone. Amona was reduced to reaching out and placing a hand on Fee'ada's shoulder to keep his balance. Off to their left was the sound of running water—the output from the upper falls, he guessed—as Fee'ada slowed her pace to what felt like a well-practiced shuffle. They navigated another series of turns, and the sound of running water diminished quickly. He couldn't be certain, but it just felt as if they'd entered a large chamber of sorts. He bumped into Fee'ada, who had come to a sudden stop.

"Apologies," he said. "I can't see a thing."

"Wait a moment," Fee'ada whispered in his ear. "There's a pool just below us—it will glow." The edge of her blade was suddenly at his throat, maintaining a constant pressure. "I've been wanting to show you this place for days. It will be the last thing you see if you don't tell me who you people are—the truth this time."

"I don't understand, we've told—"

"Lies!" she hissed. The blade pressed a little bit harder. "You and your people would drown trying to sail one of our children's jukus out of the lagoon—let alone cross the open ocean—as you claim to have done. Who are you?"

The day before, Ed'wo and some of the other sailors planning to accompany them to O'tees had tried to acquaint them with the sails of the *Terrorist*. He had heard from Breda that the training had not gone well. Evidently, for the first time since he had known the man, Breda had under-emphasized something.

"We told you the truth of where we are from," he managed. "How we came to be here would be hard to explain."

"We all know you didn't get here with that strange paddle boat sitting on our beach. I asked who you are? And before you think of telling me another story, know that I will shed tears over your body. Do not doubt me. I must lead my people, and that means protecting them. I thought we were… more… a beginning of something I had not thought I'd find again."

"For me…" Amona swallowed. Was it just him, or could he almost see the outline of her arm? "It is something I have never felt before, for anyone."

The blade pressed harder. He felt the sting as the sweat on his neck ran into the shallow cut.

"Playing with my heart will not help you."

"Fee'ada… I'm not playing. The truth?" he raised his voice. "We are at war with the Kaerin. My friends, except Stant'ala and Breda, are from a different world. They have joined forces with the Jema—Stant'ala's clan—and Fee'ada, we will win. We are winning. Soon we will all be free from the Kaerin. We need your help to get to O'tees. We will destroy the Kaerin garrison there. Kaerin troop transports and the High Bloods will never darken your shores again. For my own part, what I feel for you is as real as your knife. If you use it, I only ask that you help my people. They want nothing for you except your freedom."

"The High Bloods will kill you all, and then they will come for us."

Amona resisted the urge to swallow, the knife was hard up against his throat. "I grew up under the Kaerin—lived as a slave my entire life to them. I know far better than you what they are capable of. My friends' people have destroyed an entire Kaerin host in a day. They come from a different world, the same way the Kaerin came to this world many centuries ago."

"The old stories?" Fee'ada moved the knife, and whether she meant to or not, he was cut again. "You believe them?"

"It is a well-known fact among the Kaerin themselves. They are not from this world."

"Your friends would rule us in their place?"

Amona couldn't help but laugh. "They are asked that often—they usually say that they don't rule anyone, even themselves, well enough to claim that right. They think people—all clans—should live as they want. I've lived among them for over a year, and I believe them. They are a good people."

"You would have me risk my people on a… story? Such as this?"

The slight bluish glow from the pooled water below was now bright enough that he could make out the outlines of her face. "No, not on a story. We can prove the truth of it, if you will let us. We thought it better if we could show you what we could do in O'tees first, then reveal the whole truth."

"How do I know it's not another lie? One to keep you and your friends breathing a day longer?"

"You may trust me," he said. "I'll never lie to you again, and I had hoped for more than another day with you. What I said about you, about us—it is the truth."

The knife was pulled away from his neck. "I spoke the truth as well." She reached up slowly and placed a hand against his cheek. "I would have wept over your body."

"Is that what this place is for?"

"No, I was being truthful when I said I wanted to show you this place." She bent over and picked something up at her feet.

Her sudden movement startled him. It was followed by the splash of a rock into the pool below them. The water itself erupted into a soft azure glow that filled the cavern.

She looked twenty years younger to him in the light. "This water sleeps until disturbed."

Amona wanted nothing more than to hold her in that moment. But he was already bleeding, and she still held her knife. He wouldn't risk whatever time she'd just allowed them by misjudging her again.

"If you are speaking the truth, would you leave here? After O'tees?" She turned away from the pool and back towards him.

"Yes." He nodded. "I have sworn to do all I can to free us, all of us, from the Kaerin. But you could come with me, or I could visit here."

"From a world away?" Fee'ada's lips pursed in disbelief.

"How we got here is how we can prove our story is true. My friends' manner of travel is… not something I can describe. You will need to see it for yourself."

She shook her head in confusion. "You are a strange people." She spoke softly before stepping in close against him. "You will have your chance to prove yourself. My heart is lightened that I did not kill you."

"And my friend outside?"

"The warrior will live as long as we leave the cave together."

Amona was suddenly more worried that Stant'ala might have done something to destroy whatever accommodation he'd just reached with Fee'ada. "We should go now," he said.

"My men were told to be patient." She pushed away from him. "They will not hurt him unless he forces them to act."

"I'm not worried about Stant'ala."

She shook her head again, as if she was talking to a crazy person. "There will be no more of you and I until I know you can be trusted. None of my people will sail the Te'ru'asta for you until I am convinced it will not put my people at risk."

"I understand," he said. "My friends will understand as well."

She stepped past him to start back the way they'd come. "Your friend is so powerful that he could overpower my warriors?"

Yes. He reached out for her hand and was relieved in more ways than one when she took it. "We all carry powerful weapons. We have carried them since we have arrived. Weapons we would not think of using unless we are threatened. That is why I am worried."

"Magic weapons? Carried by warriors from a different world who can't read the wind or raise a sail? I suppose this is one more thing I will have to see."

*

Chapter 12

On board the *Terrorist*

"Let me get this straight." Jake stood with Audy and Rob amidships, near the forward most of the *Terrorist*'s two masts. "Amona recruits the pirate queen, falls in love, then almost gets his throat cut until he convinces her to let him show off his magical friends from a different world?"

Rob was listening as he drained an iced-down bottle of beer that the *Door Knocker* had delivered along with Jake, Audy, and the first platoon of the joint EDF-Jema assault force that they'd been training up for the last six months.

He pulled the empty bottle away with a satisfied smile. "Yep, you're all caught up. The *Door Knocker* rings hello, and you know the rest. We started up the outboards on the RHIB before you arrived, showed them it wasn't a horribly designed row boat, and gave them all rides around the lagoon as a first act. I think the piece-of-shit fish finder on the RHIB was nearly as big a hit as your arrival."

It had taken half a day for Fee'ada or any of her warriors to come back out of the village after the *Door Knocker*'s concussive arrival on the beach. Even then, Fee'ada had sent Ed'wo out alone, as if she blamed him for the presence of the strangers and considered him expendable. A full day later, demonstrations including a few small arms and the hand-held radios had further swayed the locals. Fee'ada herself had been convinced more easily than some of her people, but they all knew that had been Amona's influence. He'd been the one explaining everything the locals were seeing.

Included in Amona's explanation had been the story of where the *Door Knocker* had come from. By the time the *Door Knocker* departed, blinking out of existence from the beach after offloading Jake and Audy's assault team, Fee'ada and her people were more than ready to help the strangers in any way they could.

Jake worried a little that the villagers were just acting out of fear, but figured that would change as the Tor'ami saw the newcomers had come to remove Kaerin authority, not to replace it. He knew Audy and the assault force couldn't wait to get started on that phase. Meanwhile, Amona was busy filling in the gaps for Fee'ada. He wasn't often the first to notice such things, but it was obvious they were a couple.

Amona, standing on the upper deck at the stern of the ship, had more than earned his keep. They had a locally crewed ship already on its way to the Kaerin garrison at Makassar, and, for the moment at least, Fee'ada seemed to believe they were on the side of the angels.

He grinned and shrugged at Rob. "Maybe you guys should just start with the *Door Knocker* next time—speed things up a bit."

Audy pointed with his chin in Amona's direction. "I think establishing some trust first worked well."

"It did here," Rob agreed. "We tried a few other villages first. They were far less friendly. Just showing up with the *Door Knocker* might have worked, but I figure they'd have just run for the hills—tough to say."

They'd been on the water for just under an hour, and Jake figured they were doing five or six knots in the mild but steady breeze. It would put them into O'tees sometime after sunup tomorrow, if they could convince their local crew to sail through the night. They hadn't seemed at all happy about that prospect. He was anxious to get to Makassar, deal with the Kaerin garrison, and establish a real base in this part of the world. Their previous recon had shown no more than twenty or thirty High Blood assholes, but the question of how the locals would react was still unanswered. At least there wasn't a local militia to deal with on the islands.

"How was New Mexico?" Rob asked as he fished through the ice chest for another beer.

"Ugly," he answered. "And surprisingly crowded. We brought a small group back with us. Kyle and his wife's team are busy giving them the dog and pony show back in New Seattle right now."

"Was it hard to convince them to come back with you?"

"Jake told them the Jema were aliens," Audy blurted out, shaking his head. "Like the kind from your old movies."

"Well, technically speaking, you are ETs." Rob gave Audy a big smile as he answered.

"Right?" Jake nodded, thankful for the support.

"'Technically speaking,'" Audy fired back, waving a hand around his head, "of us three, I'm the only one from this planet. By your own argument—you are the aliens."

Jake's sat phone started beeping loudly. He held up a finger in Audy's direction, trying to think of something to say.

Audy grinned, leaning forward and pointing to the phone on Jake's belt. "Phone home, Jake."

"I liked you better when you didn't speak English." Jake shook his head and stepped away, pulling the sat-phone from his belt.

*

"Your Krathik is speaking to his other world? Right now? On the ray-doe?" Fee'ada squeezed Amora's hand and nodded towards Jake, Rob, and Audy on the deck below them.

Amona had no idea how to describe the sat phone Jake was using, it had taken him some time to get used to the idea of a network of satellites now orbiting Chandra, put in place via translations from Eden. With all that had been revealed to Fee'ada in the last day and a half, satellites probably would have been pushing it.

"He's probably speaking to his Krathik in our homeland on this world—or possibly his handfast. Our devices do not allow for communication from one world to the next, at least not in the moment. Messages can be sent back and forth—the same way their ship came and went—but our radios only work with relatively short range. The one he is using works very long range."

"Still magic, but not gods?"

"Like magic," Amona had to admit. "But it is only what they call technology—it is their tools."

"Like High Blood airboats, long-talkers and their steam ships?"

"Yes, just more advanced. Far more advanced—and unlike the Kaerin, they will share their technology with you and your people."

Fee'ada went quiet, watching the scene on the deck below. Several groups of Jema and EDF assault force members stood near the railings, trying to stay out of the way of the *Terrorist*'s boat crew.

"And those men, they are of the same subject clan as that tall one who was arguing a moment ago with the one on the radio?"

He knew she was talking about Audrin'ochal. "Yes, many of the soldiers they brought—warriors, you would say—are Jema. A subject clan from the other side of this world. Like the Tor'ami, they were subject to the Kaerin until a short time ago. Also, they were not arguing. Those two are close friends. They enjoy giving each other what they call a 'hard time.'"

"Not so different from us." Fee'ada nodded to herself, as if that simple description had done more to convince her than everything else that had been described to her regarding Edenite-Jema relations over the last day.

She pointed directly at Jake. "And you said your Krathik is handfasted to one of these Jema?"

"She is from this world, but not a Jema—she is a Creight. In their lands, her people are much like your own hill tribes. They have made their own way for centuries, staying outside of Kaerin control. Many Edenites and Jema have joined hands. Stant'ala," Amona pointed at the Jema scout who was standing in the middle of a mixed group of soldiers and warriors across the deck from Audrin'ochal, "is handfasted with an Edenite. She was a healer who he met after being injured."

"Such a match is not forbidden?"

"No, why would they forbid such a thing? It is welcomed. It creates bonds even greater than what those soldiers have as they fight together."

Fee'ada squeezed his hand again, and he lost his train of thought. Surely, she hadn't meant him, not in that way. It had been about this time two days earlier when she had come close to cutting his throat.

He was saved as Jake was waving at him, coming across the deck with the sat phone still held up to his head.

"What has happened?" Fee'ada asked him as Jake climbed up the steep staircase to the rear deck.

"I don't know."

Jake held a finger up to forestall Amona's question, listening to whomever was on the other end of the call.

"Copy all. I'll get back to you in a few minutes." Jake hung the phone on his belt and looked at Amona for a moment before turning towards Fee'ada.

"Ma'am, our satellite just picked up a large Kaerin cargo ship steaming into O'tees. Do you or any of your people know how many Kaerin warriors they usually carry?"

"Who is sat-lite?"

"Right… sorry." Jake looked to him for help.

"We have someone watching O'tees," Amona explained. "They have seen the Kaerin steamship approach."

"A crew of maybe five full hands," Fee'ada splayed both of hers out. "Some ten perhaps would be Tay'ang warriors, with only a handful of High Bloods—if that many. It is perhaps early, but it is there to take collected cargo to the mainland."

"Fifty crew," Amona started.

"Yeah." Jake waved him off. "I got that. Ma'am? is there a place we could drop anchor? A cove or a place that would hide our final approach to O'tees? Still close though, no more than say… an hour's sail from the harbor?"

"What is ma'am?" Fee'ada questioned.

"It is a name of respect," Amona explained. "As he does not know you well enough to use your name."

Fee'ada nodded. "On this side of the great arm protecting O'tees harbor, there is such a place—many such places. Why would you stop? I thought you had nothing to fear from the Kaerin."

"We don't." Jake smiled. "My boss, sorry… my Krathik thinks it might be useful to have a Kaerin cargo ship of our own. We are planning our attack as we go. I'd like to get a close look at the ship and the harbor before we sail in."

"You can't see the harbor until you sail around the point of the arm."

Jake smiled at Fee'ada and then clapped an arm against Amona's shoulder. "We can. Amona can explain how." With that, Jake turned and went back down the steps.

"More tek…"

"Technology." Amona nodded in agreement, wondering how he should try to describe a drone. It would be easier to just wait and show her.

*

Red sky in the morning… Jake shook his head at the beautiful sunrise as he felt the *Terrorist* tug slightly against its anchor cable. He didn't finish the rest of the old saying. If it was even true in this part of the world, it wouldn't matter. They'd be ashore within a few hours.

A team of Jema had hand launched a small winged drone a few minutes ago and were gathered around the control unit held by a Jema whose name he didn't know. He knew it would be a few minutes before the bird climbed high enough to begin making its way over the harbor. Another drone launched earlier was circling high over the *Terrorist* and would act as a relay antenna to get the signal past the arm of land they hid behind. The Jema warriors operating the drones had come a long way, and he didn't doubt that at some point in the near future some of Fee'ada's people would be as familiar with their technology as the Jema were now.

They'd probably never be the soldiers that the Jema were, but then again, few Chandrians had the experience—let alone the tradition—the Jema had. The Special Assault Team (SAT) that he, Audy, and Jeff had spent so much time training over the last six months was the pinnacle of the joint Edenite-Jema EDF. The 1st platoon of A Company—four squads, each led by a sergeant—had made the trip with them. They were as good as training and their experience to date on Caledonia was going to make them.

With his and Jeff's experience as SEALs, and heavy input from Kyle and Colonel Pretty, the long-term plan was that the SAT would become a recruitment pool for an even more elite Special Operations Group. That would be a bit further down the road though.

Audy joined him and stood in silence, watching the SAT squad leaders as they hunched over the small screen showing the scout drone's feed. "A bottle of jasaka, it will be Baker."

"How's that a bet?" Jake asked. "You make the stuff. If I lose, I'll still have to find a bottle somewhere, or worse, buy it back in Portsmouth from one of your people in order to pay you."

Audy shrugged in response. "The odds work for me, I admit."

"He's too quiet." Jake shook his head, watching Justin Baker, the sole Edenite among the four squad leaders. The three Jema Tearks were arguing over what they were seeing, but Baker was listening to them and focused on the screen.

"Not quiet." Audy may have smiled. "He thinks before he speaks."

Jake flashed Audy the evil eye, figuring that had been a backhanded dig at his own style. Audy was either focused on the group or pointedly ignoring him. "The Tearks respect him… they listen to him."

"You guys have a plan yet?" Jake raised his voice loud enough to be heard across the deck.

They ignored him and he nodded in appreciation as they stayed focused on their discussion. Baker and Teark San'kar held hands up to forestall him. Baker was saying something, and he could see the other squad leaders nodding in agreement. He hated it when Audy was right.

"We start the assault on the cargo ship." Baker pointed at the screen. "Two squads to go up the boarding poles from the ocean-facing side as we pass by on our way to the quay that Tar'wo said they had to use. Once we have the ship, we'll come back down to the quay. Snipers will remain on the deck of the steamer to take advantage of the elevation. They'll have a line of sight the length of the quay. The rest of us come back down to the quay and join up with the two remaining squads on the *Terrorist* before moving towards shore."

"Good decision to take the ship first." Jake nodded in appreciation. "But too slow overall. Why have the other two squads holding their dicks waiting for you? Speed above all else."

"Two squads still on board… start up the quay as soon as they dock?" Baker asked. "Ship assault crew follows as soon as they are able."

"Sounds like a plan," Jake answered and looked in Audy's direction.

"Make certain the LAW rockets go with the squads on the quay," Audy added. "First priority is the radio tower. The Kaerin will definitely react to that. We'll try to track where they come from with the drone."

"You'll not be accompanying us, sir?" Teark San'kar asked.

"Do any of you think there is anything in this plan, or in the opposition, that you cannot handle?" Audy answered, maintaining his usual levelheaded calmness.

"No, sir," they all answered quickly.

"We've got our orders too," Jake added. And he didn't like them one bit. In Colonel Pretty's words, "You trained them. If they aren't ready, they aren't ready. If they are, you and Audy plant your asses on that boat and direct traffic. Your assault days are over."

Jake took the remote control of the drone from Baker. "Audy and I will stay with the *Terrorist* and direct you if needed. Sergeant Baker, you have command of the assault, which means your squad stays with the ship until it docks. Your call on who assaults the steamer."

"Nicely done," Jake admitted as the last of the squad members disappeared over the side of the Kaerin steamer as the *Terrorist* sailed slowly past, making its way towards the bow of the steamer. They'd already had to shoot one crewman who leaned over the railing of the steam-powered paddle-wheeler to shout down at them that they were "too close" and to "veer away."

Several suppressed shots had answered the shout, and the body had fallen into the bay just ahead of the *Terrorist's* passage. A moment later, the assault poles had extended, and the two squads had started up the side of the ship.

"Does she really need to be there?" Amona asked him.

Jake didn't have to follow Amona's glance. He knew he was worried about Fee'ada standing on the raised platform at the stern.

"Her own people said she needed to be standing on deck as we dock. We aren't going to let anything happen to her."

"You promise?"

He smiled down at Amona, the one person among them who had more experience with the Kaerin than any of them. "You asking for professional reasons or personal?"

"Would your answer be different?"

"No." Jake smiled. "I'm just razzing you. If it makes you feel better, when we hit the docks, you can try to get her and her people below. Although from what I've seen so far, the lady seems to want to watch. And this shit really has to go sideways for this boat to be involved at all."

"This is what has me worried."

Jake laughed. "So, personal then."

"Am I going to be in trouble? For my... relationship with her?"

"For what?!" Jake couldn't help but enjoy the look of panic on Amona's face even as he noted the suppressed barks of the boarding team's assault rifles. "Falling for a beautiful lady who happens to be an ally? Or soon to be ally—trust me on this, Amona, you're allowed to enjoy your job."

They were just starting to approach the bow of the steamer when another figure appeared above them, leaning outward with a Kaerin long rifle in his hands. Jake brought his gun up to his shoulder quickly, but at least three of Baker's team on the *Terrorist's* deck were quicker on the draw. The long rifle fell into the water, barely missing their own ship as the body slumped out of sight.

Amona was still staring upward at the sides of the steam ship, expecting more Kaerin or Tay'ang crewmen to appear, when Jake nudged him and nodded towards the *Terrorist's* stern as if nothing had happened.

"She's bound to have some questions about what's happening. Keep your earbud in." Jake tapped his own ear. "You can give her a play-by-play—channel four."

"Play-by-play?"

"Explain to her what is happening." Jake winked at him. "Play it up, score some points with her. I'll throw you a bone as we dock."

"I think I understand English better than you think I do, but I still have no idea what you are saying."

Jake clapped him on the shoulder. "You're a smart guy. You'll figure it out." With that, Jake moved to the steep ladder leading down into the ship's hold and disappeared as he joined the soldiers who had not gone up the side of the steamer.

Amona climbed the stairs to the upper deck as quickly as he could, trying not to appear as though he was scared out of his mind. He knew what those muted coughing sounds coming from the steamer's deck above him were. Fee'ada seemed far calmer than he felt.

"Their weapons are truly miraculous," she pointed at the gunwale of the steam ship nearly thirty feet above them as the *Terrorist* started to turn and crawl its way past the bow rising out of the water on their right. "They are all warriors? Your friends?"

"In truth, very few of them are warriors. They call themselves soldiers. They draw a sharp distinction between soldiers and warriors. To them, it is more of a calling or an occupation. Most of the Edenites, in fact, are what they call civilians, who possess no more warrior or soldierly experience than I do."

"But you are trusted." Fee'ada nodded towards the deck below them. The hatch cover had been removed and the heads of dozens of soldiers could be seen waiting to spring into action. "I saw their Krathik speaking to you."

"He felt it important that I stay with you to describe what is happening."

Fee'ada pointed up at the steamship as the *Terrorist* rounded the bow, slowly driven by a pair of long oars sprouting from either side of her teak hull. "I can see what is happening above us. Your friends are fighting scared Tay'ang slaves. What will happen when the High Bloods in the city are alerted?"

"The High Bloods will die." There was no bluster in his words. He had seen the EDF work before. He'd witnessed Jake, Kyle and Jeff in action personally when they had pulled him from the island of Landing.

Five minutes later the *Te'ru'asta* had crawled past the cargo ship and made its way to an open slot on the stone quay.

"Tor'ami to dock." Tar'wo, standing a few feet behind them at the steering yoke, gave a yell directed at the group of three well-dressed locals who stood watching them approach. Or at least one of them did—Amona could see the other two officials looking upward at the steamer docked at the end of the quay.

The sounds of muted gunfire, single shots for the most part, reached Amona. He recognized it as suppressed fire from the EDF's assault rifles. Most of it sounded as if it came from within the ship at this point.

A hundred feet away, amidst the creaking and bumping of a dozen ships tied up along the quay, the sounds emanating from the Kaerin cargo ship hadn't yet been recognized by the locals for what they were.

"That is a new boat!" The one dock official paying attention to them flicked a wrist in signal, and dock workers threw lines towards the ship and were caught by Fee'ada's sailors.

"The Tor'ami, you say? I've seen no requests or approvals for a new boat."

Amona panicked as Tar'wo stretched out and kicked him in the back of the leg. "What do I say now? These slaves should have never known about this ship."

"I have a writ of approval," Amona yelled back, patting his belt. He imagined he was back at the docks on Landing, screaming at Tarnesian or Morot boat masters who thought they had some modicum of authority. "The Kareel ordered this boat built personally. Go and fetch him from his morning meal, or help us dock so I can fulfill my writ and be about my business."

"Look at the balls on you." Amona's heart almost stopped, until he realized it was Jake speaking into his earbud.

"Tie them up!" The dock clerk, in a burst of efficiency, yelled at his dock workers. "Hurry! They are on High Blood business."

"We are all dead if this does not work." Fee'ada whispered next to him. "A writ! You dare claim a writ!"

"It won't matter in a moment." He answered loudly enough that Tar'wo could hear him as well.

A gunshot from a Kaerin long rifle on the deck of the steamer shattered the early morning calm of the harbor. Sea birds resting on the ropes and spars of the harbor's ships launched at once and coordinated their angry screeches.

The officious clerk said something to the two men behind him. One took off at a run down the quay towards the waterfront. The other moved more slowly towards the set of narrow stairs hanging down from the landward facing side of the steamship.

Amona clicked his talk button. "They sent a runner for help."

"No worries," Jake drawled. "Look down at me. Make sure your lady sees me looking."

"Who are you talking to?" Fee'ada's calm was quickly fading.

"Down there," he said and nodded toward the open hold. Jake was standing on the steps, his torso almost out.

"I want you to repeat after me, Amona. Say 'yes' if you understand." Jake sounded like he was struggling not to laugh. "My exact words."

"Yes."

Amona listened to Jake's words. Confusion reigned for a moment until he figured it out. This is what Jake had meant—this was the bone being thrown. Amona cleared his voice and glanced at Fee'ada, who was watching him closely. He felt himself stand a little taller. "I order you to initiate the attack. Report in as soon as you are able. Go now!"

The soldiers boiled up out of the hatch. Jake led the way, followed by Audrin'ochal. One of them, perhaps both—Amona could not tell—dropped the harbormaster with a short burst. Jake stayed on the *Te'ru'asta's* deck, his rifle up and pivoted in place until it was in line with the steamship. One shot rang out, and the harbormaster's assistant slumped over and rolled backwards down the steps.

"Snipers, you've got a runner on the quay. Let him go." Jake spoke calmly. He sounded almost bored. "The more Kaerin that show up at the same time and place, the better. I don't want to have to hunt them down."

Within seconds the only EDF still on the *Te'ru'asta* were Jake and Rob. Audy had jumped over but hadn't followed after the twenty soldiers racing down the quay towards the waterfront.

Amona turned to face Fee'ada who was looking at him in surprise. "They will let the messenger go to raise alarm with the High Bloods. The more of them that show up together, the better."

"You are their Krathik?" Fee'ada's eyes squinted at him, seemingly uninterested in Jake's play-by-play.

"No." He shook his head decisively. "Not close to that. I'm only here because I'm the most familiar with the Kaerin."

"You commanded them. I saw you."

He had promised he wouldn't lie to her again. In the moment, it seemed more important than scoring points, as Jake had suggested. "Jake, the Krathik of this... mission. He was doing me an honor." Amona smiled and shook his head. "I'm no warrior, but he thought to impress you."

"He did this to add to your authority?"

Amona couldn't help but laugh. "You'd have to know him better. To him, he was doing me a favor. I could not begin to tell you why."

Fee'ada reached out for and squeezed his hand. "I know the why of it. Thank you for being honest."

He was about to respond when two loud pops, followed by a swooshing sound filled the air. Two rocket plumes spiraled up and away from where the quay met the broad waterfront until the projectiles impacted the brick and bamboo structure underneath the Kaerin's long-talker antenna. It wasn't the largest building on the waterfront, but in typical Kaerin fashion, it was the best built. Fee'ada jerked back at the sight of the explosion and gave a surprised shriek when the sound reached them.

"We have destroyed the High Blood's ability to talk to the mainland. The Kaerin will not know what has happened here for some time."

"What was that?" Tar'wo, standing behind him, shouted the question.

"Those were rockets or missiles. I'm not sure which," he answered honestly. Breda probably knew which, as well as how to use the damned things, but his former colleague had gone up the quay with the soldiers.

"Your warriors return," Fee'ada spoke, almost whispering.

He looked up and could see the initial boarding party coming down the steamship's hanging stairway to the surface of the quay. He did a fast count as they rushed past. He only counted sixteen, then remembered that there were still four aboard acting as two separate sniper teams. That accounted for all of them.

Amona looked back up at the profile of the steamship, amazed at how many trees must have gone into building something so large, and immediately spotted the two sniper teams, their long-guns hanging over the gunwale. He pointed up and explained their presence to Fee'ada.

"No one can shoot that far!" Tar'wo overheard him.

"With a Kaerin rifle, you are correct. *Those* men are very capable of hitting targets farther away than the waterfront." Amona was surprised at the pride he heard in his own voice. At some point, he'd gone from bewilderment to pride at the Edenite's technology. In his own thinking, when it came to the Edenites, it was no longer them—it was us. He was one of them.

"He is not worried at all, is he?" Fee'ada pulled at Amona's hand until she was pointing at Jake, who was leaning against a Kaerin shipping crate on the quay with the drone's controller in both hands.

Amona was uncertain if anyone would ever know if Jake was worried about something or not. "He believes this to be a simple mission. Earlier when I asked him if we should be worried, he said this would be good training for his soldiers."

"Training?" Fee'ada's eyes went wide, and she shook her head, saying something to Tar'wo that he couldn't follow. Amona was focused on the radio tower as it collapsed through the roof into the burning shell of the radio shack.

Justin Baker ducked out of instinct, the wood board of the Kaerin packing crate shattering above his head. Those .48 caliber slugs were no joking matter.

"Baker—be advised you've got two groups of Kaerin incoming to your position."

Jake's voice in his ear was a welcome relief. This was his first real command since joining the EDF, and the last thing he wanted was to lose somebody because of a mistake he made.

"Approaching from the east—two blocks away. Coming up the roads either side of the radio shack."

Justin mashed his transmitter. "We've got at least one Kaerin rifle out there now, position unknown."

"Wait one," Jake responded. "Drone is coming back overhead."

Justin was transmitting the Kaerin's approach vector to the rest of his team as they bear crawled into position, when two distinct rifle shots split the air overhead. Evidently, the SAT's own snipers three hundred yards away had seen the enemy fire.

"Kaerin sniper is down," Jake reported. "He was in the building next to the radio shack—no movement visible."

They were spread out amidst the piled cargo that had probably been slated to be loaded aboard the cargo ship. Justin peeked around the edge of his crate. He could see a hundred yards up the cobblestone road running past the burning radio shack, but nothing yet.

"This is Alpha one—I've got eyes up the road on the left of the primary. Anybody have eyes on the other road?"

"Alpha, this is Bravo three. I have four—wait, one… I have eyes on six Kaerin rifles on the road to the right of the primary."

"Copy Bravo three—everyone holds for my order."

A pair of Kaerin appeared around the curve of the road Justin was watching as he gave the order. Within moments, there were eight Kaerin High Bloods, followed by what looked like a detachment of unarmed locals. All seemed to be focused on the pillar of smoke rising ahead of them. The locals kept coming, pulling a strange wheeled cart with what looked like an iron oil barrel laid on its side. It took him a moment to recognize it as the water pump it was. The canvas hoses coiled up on the cart should have been a dead giveaway.

"All—be advised. Kaerin are escorting a local fire brigade." Many of the large warehouse-looking structures at the waterfront had slate roofs, but most of the smaller buildings had the usual grass roof one would expect in this part of the world.

He reached for his radio to switch channels back to Jake and stopped himself. Jake and Audy wouldn't always be here, and his training had made it abundantly clear that he would be expected to act independently. He stayed on his local channel.

"All teams, we will proceed as planned. We wait for them. Wait for my signal and target all Kaerin. Try to avoid the locals and their pump unless threatened. Bravo three—advise when your targets are all visible."

"Alpha—Bravo Three, copy."

On his road, the enemy had slowed down and the Kaerin warriors were leading the way, pushing past the remains of the stone walls of the radio shack. He did the quick trigonometry in his head, noting the team on his left would have an angle on the whole group he was watching once they came around to the front of the building.

"Locals approaching water with hoses. We're going to be seen." There was no call sign used. Whoever it had been was getting nervous. He should have known they'd need to pull water from the harbor—it wasn't like they had fire hydrants.

"Alpha One—Bravo Three, six Kaerin visible."

"All units, go," Justin ordered, pushing his own rifle up over the lip of the crate as he did.

He focused on the nearest rifle-wielding target he could see. Most of his team fired before he did. Nearly thirty of the forty soldiers he had under his command had a good line of sight, as well as the element of surprise. It wasn't that different from their shoot house exercises—the only difference was the range.

Justin only managed to fire at two Kaerin, and he was pretty sure both had already been hit. The entire firefight lasted less than five seconds before forty assault rifles were panning back and forth across the stunned group of locals, looking for another target.

"Don't just stand there!" Breda screamed, waving his arms to get the locals focused on anything other than the carpet of dead Kaerin around them. "Put out the cursed fire! You will not be harmed!"

"May that be true," Fee'ada murmured. They'd all overheard Breda shouting from down the quay. "What will happen here now? What will your people do?"

"You will need to decide what it is you wish us to tell the locals."

Amona nodded to the city of nearly five thousand people who, until moments ago, had been slaves to the Kaerin's maritime supply depot. Not very different from the city he had grown up in on Landing—a city of slaves serving a specific purpose.

"Our people will use this place as a base of operations in the area—the first of many. Our reinforcements should be arriving sometime tomorrow. For our broader efforts here, we will need local leadership with whom to work. I cannot imagine anyone who is better suited for that than you."

"But you will return? You, I mean—to help us if the Kaerin come back. It's difficult to believe what I have just seen, yet it happened." Fee'ada stepped a little closer to him. "They will not let this stand—they cannot."

Amona pointed towards the waterfront, where the smoke from the destroyed buildings was turning darker as the pumped seawater hit the burning thatch.

He gave her hand a squeeze. "I will stay here to help as long as you will have me."

"Because of your oath to your people?"

"I have far more than that keeping me here... I think you know that."

"And the High Bloods?"

He smiled to himself and then at her. "The Kaerin have far more to worry about from us, in lands far more important to them."

*

Chapter 13

Kaerus, Chandra

"Everyone on the Council agreed with the decision!" Gasto Bre'jana, Tima's father, raised his voice and shook his fist at Lord Noka. Even in support of the Prelate, it was a gesture and tone few others could get away with. "They can't fault you for it now."

Yes, they can, Tima thought. And they will. As usual, his father played the role of moral support to Lord Noka.

"The Council?!" Noka's face colored. He looked as if he would have spit had they been outside. "They'd agree with me if I suggested they start marrying their daughters off to their local clan leaders."

Tima's father cocked his head to the side and gave a short grunt of laughter. "If you convinced them it was needed to defeat the Shareki—they just might."

"There will be some second guessing," Tima answered with something other than empty protestations meant to make the Prelate feel better. If there was one thing he had learned in the last year, very few people had the courage to tell the Lord Noka anything beyond what they thought he wanted to hear.

"It's to be expected," Tima continued. "If any of your detractors have the foresight to look at this latest move—considering what it may point to in the future—they should be worried."

His father was looking at him as if he'd grown a horn out of forehead.

Noka glared back at Tima and then turned to his old friend. "Gasto, you once warned me never to ask your son a question I didn't want the unpolished truth of, but there are times—"

"I think there is an opportunity here." Tima held his hands out to placate the two older men in the room. "Yes, the Shareki took a garrison in the Tay'ang Sea—and they did it without us even knowing they were in the area or had an interest in the region. We still wouldn't know it happened if we hadn't been fortunate that the local subject leader was able to escape on foot to a nearby village. He managed to sail to the next closest garrison at Sor'bat. It was their long-talker that made the report to the mainland."

"We know what happened, Tima. How is this an opportunity?" His father was no longer the man who raised him, but a member of the council. Gasto Bre'jana was his own seat at that table, and one whose policy inclinations were far more conservative than his own.

"The shipbuilding effort which has so divided the council," he answered. "Will any of them be unable to see the thrust of the Edenite's strategy? It's clear they aim to strip of us of any holding we can't threaten with our hosts. As long as the enemy controls the seas, there's little we can do to stop them in that strategy. We should use that to emphasize the policy you have already put forward, My Lord. We must build our capability at sea until we can retake Irinas—it's their seat of power. Everything they do on this world begins and ends there."

"That will make Lord Oont'tal puff up like a damned bird!" His father spoke out again.

"Good," Tima answered, striving to put his father in place without offering offense. "The more so, the better. We need Oont'tal, his ships, and his people's expertise on the water far more than any other five Lords' war hosts that we can't get to the fight."

Lord Noka almost choked on a short laugh. "Tima was quite taken by Lord Oont'tal. I sent him there for a specific purpose, and he returned with stories of how impressed he was."

"He and his people's understanding of all things nautical is the very

best of what we have in that arena. He should be commended for that."
Tima was speaking to his father—he'd already shared his opinion of
Lord Oont'tal with Lord Noka.

"We need him, his ships, and his leadership for the naval effort."

His father's face went white, looking from him to Lord Noka. "The
boy's gone mad." His father shook his head and nearly came out of his
seat, leaning across the table towards him. "If Oont'tal succeeds, he
will be unstoppable."

Noka remained seated, but looked at Tima across the table and
offered a slim smile. "He's right, Tima—and your head would roll on
the ground next to mine."

Tima held up both hands. "There's no denying that," he agreed. "I
was impressed by Lord Oont'tal, true. We need his support desperately.
I also believe he is a threat to the Kaerin in this struggle. The man has
the imagination of a rock. He can't conceive of an enemy that doesn't
think in the same terms he does. He's about order, efficiency, and
control."

Tima was toeing a dangerous line. Lord Noka was more similar to
Oont'tal in disposition and make-up than he would ever admit. It was
in large part the reason for their enmity. He could deliver more than
one message here.

"You're talking with two tongues here!" his father yelled as he fell
back into his seat in exasperation. "Either he succeeds and wins all, or
he fails and we all lose."

Tima nodded in agreement, but looked across the table at Lord
Noka. "Lord Oont'tal has to win."

"Explain yourself." Lord Noka's dead shark eyes made an
appearance. It was as if every story told of the S'kaeda family flowed to
the surface of his face in an instant.

"If we don't win at sea, we cannot win. He is our best hope to do
that."

His father stopped his glass halfway to his lips. "And if he loses,
he's done for! That's what you're saying, right?"

"No—that is not what I'm saying. If he loses, we are all lost. There will be no stopping the Shareki—we should do everything in our collective power to ensure Lord Oont'tal can defeat them on the water."

"And if he does?" Lord Noka shook his head.

"Lord Noka, father—I ask you both, what is the true purpose of defeating them on the water?"

"You said it yourself!" his father yelled. "If we don't, they'll surround us, choking off Holdings one at a time."

Tima ignored the outburst and kept his eyes focused on Lord Noka. The light was slow to come on in those dead eyes, but the realization of what he was saying flashed in an instant. Noka S'kaeda had a laugh that was said to make Kaerin Lords shake in their boots. Tima could half believe it in that instant. He smiled, half in relief as Lord Noka pounded the table once with his fist and then patted him on the shoulder.

"The purpose of defeating them on the sea, Gasto," Noka leaned forward to speak to his oldest friend directly. "Is that it will allow me to land however many millions of warriors it takes to grind the Edenites into the mud of Irinas. In victory, who will have the power? The warriors that defeated the Shareki, at sword point if need be? Or the ferryman that carried them across the channel?"

"He wins at sea," Tima reiterated, "so we can win the true battle— failing either, I am at a loss as to how we stop them. Time is not our ally."

"I think I chose well in my successor." Lord Noka beamed, lifting his glass in salute to Tima's father, and lifted a chin in Tima's direction. "Your son may be your crowning achievement, Gasto. Did you see it? He can discuss our potential undoing and our victory in one breath."

"Heh!" his father waved the backhanded compliment away. "Living with Oont'tal's pride in the meantime may not be worth it."

"If I can do it," Noka grimaced. "It is a certainty, old friend—that you will as well."

Tima wasn't entirely at ease. The ability to defeat the Shareki on land might be every bit as difficult as what they were asking Oont'tal to do on the sea. There were nearly weekly reports of engagements at sea. Most were one-sided affairs where a stupid boat master wandered too close to Irinas and was sunk by one of the speedy Shareki boats—or worse, by one of the cursed airboats that would dive out of the clouds and launch those wretched guided rockets.

Tima listened in silence, nodding politely at the conversation of the old men. He was amazed at how neither of them could even conceive of the Kaerin losing on land. By any measure, they had very little information to truly judge the Edenite's strength on land. Reports from the Strema survivors from the disastrous invasion of Eden, or from the High Blood women survivors of Irinas, were precious little to go on. His prisoner, Ocheltree, was their best source of information, but the man raised as many questions as he answered.

"When could Oont'tal be ready?" His father asked him directly.

"He needs another half year," Tima answered. "But only if he's given full control of the entire shipbuilding program and full command of the attack."

"We've been leveling forests and cooking iron for boat building that long already." His father was as impatient as Lord Noka was calculating. "Another half year?"

"It will coincide with our world gate being active," Lord Noka answered for him. "We will be sending a subject host to their own world at the same time. The Shareki will, for once, be forced to choose what world they wish to fight us on."

"You don't worry we'll just be giving them another subject clan to subvert to their own purposes?" His father still didn't grasp what was at stake.

Noka shook his head slowly. "Gasto, if we don't win here, and soon—what will it matter what happens to another slave race we send to their world? We'll be fighting our subjects here."

His father was near speechless and leaned back in his chair. Tima picked up movement amongst the guards standing at the far end of the room. Teark Ban'are met his eyes and took half step forward, signaling his intention but waiting for permission. Tima waved at him to approach. He could guess at the news by the look on the warrior's face. Tima had asked for the status of the garrison at Sor'bat that morning. It was near midnight now, and even half a world away, he'd expected an answer hours ago.

Ban'are handed him a small piece of paper.

"What is it?" His father asked.

"Is it as you feared?" Lord Noka leaned forward.

Tima nodded once. "Our garrison at Sor'bat is not responding. It seems the enemy has wasted no time in expanding their attack in the southern seas."

"They'd been alerted," Lord Noka explained to his father. "Those island garrisons are small—most are no more than a Fist or an Arm of warriors."

"That cursed land-ship, no doubt." Gasto breathed out. "What did you say they call it? The *Door Breaker*?"

"The *Door Knocker*." Tima shrugged. "A strange name, but one our prisoner is certain of. It's an advantage we can't hope to match. We have to remove them from this world before they control more of it than we do."

*

18 hours earlier... New Seattle Waterfront, Eden

Newly promoted captain of the E.N. *Bolivar*, Sajay Pratha was half wishing that his old ship the E.N. *Constitution* and his first captain, Amelia Harper, had gotten the nod for this mission. But the *Constitution* and his old crew were already on Chandra patrolling in the Jema Channel and North Sea.

Unlike the *Independence* and the *Constitution,* which had both undergone final assembly on Chandra, the *Bolivar* was the first of four warships of the same class built and fully assembled on Eden. More pressing was the fact that his brand-new ship and first command would be the first to attempt a wholesale portal to Chandra—while afloat.

"Captain, you look like I just asked you to eat a dead cat." Dr. David Jensen patted him on the shoulder as he squeezed past him on the bridge. "I'm here to allay any concerns and put you at ease. You need to relax—we've tested this. It works. If it didn't, we'd still be assembling these patrol boats on Chandra."

"You tested it on a bass boat and a RHIB—and I saw what happened to the bass boat."

"It's not the size of the boat, Captain..." Jensen grinned. "It's getting the volume of water surrounding your hull right." Jensen manipulated his hands in three dimensions. "We're going to send a shoebox-shaped volume of our Pacific Ocean to Chandra along with you. That way, your hull won't get folded in half by the reciprocal concussion of the water you'll be entering. The portal effect will form a vacuum—or negative space—as usual, and the shoebox of water around your boat—"

"Ship," Sajay corrected.

"Around your *ship* will go with you and fit right into that negative space on the other side. The real trick was figuring out a way to shape the block of water that goes with you—lots of high math there, not to mention the engineering needed to design the floating portal generators. Nothing to worry about though, they are anchored to the harbor floor six ways to Sunday—they aren't going to float out of position."

Sajay glanced out at the sloped ballistic glass wrapping around the front of his sleek patrol boat's bridge. A box-shaped parking slot framed by anchored buoys lay just ahead of his ship, which was two hundred yards off New Seattle's waterfront. A crowd had gathered to see them off. *Wonderful.*

"What happens if they do?" he asked.

Jensen smiled back at him. "They won't."

Something in his face must gave convinced Jensen that he actually wanted an answer to the question. "Relax, Captain. There's over a dozen LIDAR sensors measuring your ship's position inside and on top of that volume of water. The computer won't initiate the translation until it's sure you and your water are all perfectly lined up. Sometimes it finds a solution real quick. During one of the tests, it took almost fifteen minutes—wind, tide and all that. Don't get worried if nothing happens for a minute or so."

"In the meantime, we just stay in our lane and rely on the station keeping jets?"

"Exactly." Jensen clapped him on the back and started moving. "I should get back shore-side and monitor from there. You're going to leave a decent-sized hole in the water here when you leave. We're hoping for a pretty water show at this end for the crowd when it fills back in."

Sajay couldn't bring himself to care what kind of water show there would be at *this* end. He and his ten-person crew wouldn't be here. All he could think of was Captain Harper's words to him when he got the nod to captain his own ship: "They're going to ask you to do some weird shit. Your job is to get it done, but your first priority is your crew."

Translating a ship this size was no big deal. The *Door Knocker* was hundreds of times more massive, but doing it while it was afloat, along with all the water around it, was pushing the bounds of weird shit and bumping up against crazy. The fact was, they now had a base in Chandra's Java Sea without any real ships in the area to take advantage of it. They didn't have any ship afloat on Chandra with the range to get to Makassar. So here he was, getting ready to take his ship through a wormhole, or whatever the translation effect was.

He shook hands with Jensen. "I hope the water show stays at this end."

"It should, it really should." Jensen nodded to himself. "That said, report back as soon as you are able. Jake Bullock, Audy, and the team will be on the air with Portsmouth as you arrive in Makassar to let us know how it went. I know you're on the hook for a mission as soon as you get there, but I'd like your impressions of the entry and any secondary effects that we might have missed. Should go fine unless we totally missed something."

"Dr. Jensen, no offense, but you really suck at this whole putting me at ease thing."

*

Sor'bat—Kaerin Garrison, Chandra (Surabaya)

"It is just one ship, a small one." Dadus Par'och, standing next to him, was gazing out to sea with the telescope. The Shareki boat was already close enough that Teark Dur'ret didn't need the scope. The boat was growing larger by the second—its sleek, almost-spearhead shape made it appear as a weapon itself. How could anything move so fast on the water? No sails, no water paddles—it just flew across the surface.

"We had enough warriors to defend this place." Par'och was angry, and Dur'ret couldn't blame him for it.

The Teark turned and looked east across the narrow straight of water separating Sor'bat from the next closest island. Most of his garrison's warriors had already been sent across with Teark Mar'laka in command. They had orders to observe what happened here and then make their way across the island to where they could report. His own writ was to defend Sor'bat with the ten warriors left to him. They'd been told of what had already occurred in O'tees, but he could hardly believe it.

His writ had come from far-off Kaerus, down the chain of long-talker stations, originating from the seat of the Prelate himself. *That* had convinced him the rumors of these Shareki and their advanced weapons that they'd been hearing about for the past several moons were true. Seeing the strange vessel approaching, propelled at such speed by what he couldn't imagine, his doubts were gone. He'd been ordered to defend this garrison with a third of his original detachment and, for the first time in his life as a warrior, he was asking himself why.

Dur'ret was a warrior of nearly forty. His battle experience had been gained in wars on the mainland against a handful of different Tay'ang Clans that had been scheduled for culling. Most of that fighting was carried out by one subject clan against the other, but Kaerin troops had always led those efforts. He was as experienced as any Teark in his War Fist, and he thought in terms of numbers. Par'och may not have his experience, but he wasn't wrong—how many warriors could a ship of that size carry?

"They aren't slowing." Par'och stated the obvious.

If anything, the enemy craft had just accelerated. Its bow lifted further out of the water as a rooster tail of churned water shot out from behind its stern.

"Signal the cannon. They are to fire when they have the range."

He leaned forward on the railing of the bamboo tower that supported their signal antenna above him. Par'och was waving the red and white checkered flag at the shore battery below him, a pair of cannons that had been installed just four moons ago. At the time, he hadn't understood the need for them and he hadn't been told. So much of what had been happening of late suddenly made sense.

*

"Captain Pratha, signal flag spotted on the radio tower—the platform two thirds of the way up." Ensign Haruki Mikada's voice sounded muted against the growl of the twin diesels that had the *Bolivar* vibrating. It was a comforting feeling. At this speed, it would be a damned lucky shot for one of the shore cannons to hit them—but the odds weren't lottery stupid. The asshole Kaerin on the tower could wait.

"I saw it. Stay on course. WEPs—ready the Grenade launchers. Swing us through, Grady. Target an arc from the radio shack at the bottom of the tower to the shore battery. Circle back out immediately,

190

rinse and repeat until we are sure the guns are knocked out."

"We have word that there is only a skeleton force left here." Sajay had been so focused on his target that he'd forgotten that *the* Audrin'ochal was standing behind his own seat. "These Kaerin are aware of what happened at Makassar."

His first instinct was to tell the Jema to go back below with his team, that this was his bridge—his ship—and he didn't need a backseat driver from the ground pounders he was transporting. But this was Audy, and everyone knew who Audy was. No one in their right mind told any high-ranking Jema officer anything—especially when said ship captain doubted whether Audy understood that a ship's captain was in charge of everything on a ship.

Instead, annoyed, "how could you know that?"

"We've had a scout team watching this place for a moon. The Kaerin evacuated most of the garrison to that island across the strait yesterday."

Sajay looked up and followed Audy's pointing. "I just received a satellite call from their team leader," Audy continued. "Hyrika will have been certain. She would not be mistaken in this."

"My orders are to deliver you to this garrison here and help you secure it. When we are done, if you want a ride over there, I'll see what we can do. In the meantime, it would be really helpful if you could go back below with your team."

"Of course."

"Grady, drop us down to thirty knots as you start the run across the wharf. Just like we practiced. Watch the stone quays if you would."

"Aye, sir." Grady pulled back on the throttle as the ship bit deeper into the water and started leaning into its sweeping turn through the harbor. "Avoiding stone quays."

Sajay grinned. Grady was as much a smart-ass as he was, but he could flat out make the *Bolivar* dance when he needed to.

"WEPs—weapons free as they bear." They'd practiced strafing runs with this type of mission in mind for weeks. The bow- and stern-mounted automatic grenade launchers would fire almost continuously as they blew past the waterfront. Their targeting was based on some very good photographs of the place, which he now knew was thanks to some Jema scout named Hyrika.

"Grenade launchers are hot." His weapons officer Haruki had a serious manner and was a somber counterpoint to Grady—her boyfriend. The personal relationship between his two officers was something he practiced ignoring. Just as Captain Harper had ignored his relationship with Stephanie, the other ensign aboard the *Constitution*. Stephanie had been given command of the *Lafayette* and was undergoing sea-trials in the Puget Sound. If this war lasted another year and Eden kept building ships, Haruki and Grady's relationship would get reduced to e-mail as well.

"Firing... now."

The rapid pop-pop-pop of the grenade launchers from inside the insulated bridge and over the sound of the diesels sounded like a rapid cough. He checked their path through the harbor, and Grady was on top of it. They'd miss the end of the quay by a good thirty yards before starting their path away from the waterfront. He switched his view landward, noting his Jema passenger hadn't moved at all.

None of their 40 mm grenades had landed yet, and both launchers were still shooting. A trough of foam appeared off the starboard stern as he noted that the cannon ball had missed them by several hundred yards. With any luck, the land-based cannons wouldn't get a chance to reload.

He grabbed his binoculars and squeezed past Audy as he made for the passage at the rear of the bridge. "Don't mind me..."

He wanted to see the impacts, and they were already coming around to head back out of the harbor as the grenade launchers emptied their ammo cans. Between the two launchers, they'd just laid 96 grenades in a pattern, starting a hundred yards back from the water.

He stopped at the door and shouted back. "WEPs—get the reloads moving! Stay on plan, Grady."

Audy followed closely behind him to the deck hatch, where he stood on the bottom step of the ladder. Sajay swallowed his annoyance at his unwanted shadow and focused on the shoreline. The first half dozen or so grenades had just impacted, and he was having to lean out in order to see around the rear half of the *Bolivar's* superstructure. The grenades were exploding with little or no effect until a large secondary explosion a hundred yards east of the radio tower cooked off. He continued to watch as the airborne fan of grenades fell in a concentric but wider arc to the ship's passage. The grenades were sailing over the waterfront, landing well inland. Two bamboo shacks came apart, fires started, and a few luckless locals could be seen running further inland.

*

"It is shooting at us! What are those?" Par'och was pointing out to sea, high above the enemy boat.

Dur'ret could see the projectiles as well. Small rapid puffs from the strange-looking weapons mounted at the bow and stern of the craft were shooting small dark objects that stood out against the bright blue sky. Especially when they slowed at the top of their trajectory and seemed to hover for an instant before beginning their fall to the ground.

"They won't be rocks," he answered. "Get off the tower, Par'och—now!"

"And you, Teark?"

"Go!" he yelled and reached for his rifle. He may die up here today, but he liked the view. At his age, with his knees, he saw no need to die on the ground.

The Dadus wasted no time moving down the circular staircase. The first few grenades landed just as Dur'ret heard the younger man's voice shouting back at him, asking why he wasn't following. He flinched as the line of explosions walked ever closer to the base of his tower. Dur'ret took a knee and laid his long barrel on the cross tie of the platform's railing. He could see a single Shareki's head and shoulders standing up at the side of the boat. He was almost relieved that there was a person, no doubt several, inside the unbelievable craft. People could bleed and die.

An explosion somewhere beneath him rattled the tower just as he squeezed the trigger. He whispered a curse as he reached for another shell. Bamboo cracking, exploding under the weight it held reached him. A second later, a sense of vertigo washed over him as the observation deck was suddenly moving through space. He let go his rifle and gripped the railing. It seemed he would beat Par'och to the ground after all.

Chapter 14

New Mexico (Earth)

"This is so fucking wrong." Mitch Bennet didn't make much of an effort to keep his muttering under his breath. Kyle heard him, and so did his fellow former Missouri National Guardsmen.

"Hey, no one is making you go." Kyle played it cool. He knew none of them were excited to go back to New Mexico. Hell, he wasn't excited about it. But after a little trust had been established with Patrick and the others—particularly with Patrick's girlfriend and soon to be in-laws—the whole group had relaxed a little and opened up. They'd shared everything they knew and had learned during their internment. All of it led Kyle to believe pulling people in from their involuntary exile would be easier than they had once thought.

On the other side, Patrick and his motley crew, once the wow factor had worn off, had warmed up to Eden in a big way. Again, it was Patrick's girlfriend, Sandra, and the children they were both responsible for that had convinced Patrick. Sandra's seal of approval was all Patrick had needed in the end. Kyle wouldn't swear to it, but where Mitch was concerned, the credit might all be due to the New World Pub and its wide selection of beer.

As for Allen Okamura, the former college professor had announced that he was "home." Hot showers, flying cars and the ability to distill and sell his liquor without having to answer to anyone had been all he'd needed. If his first recruits were any fair measure of what the place had to offer, Kyle was even more convinced New Mexico was more than worth the risk.

"He's going," Patrick answered for Mitch before turning on his friend. "What else you going to do? Stay here and get fat again?"

"Screw you! I've never been fat."

Allen snorted in laughter. "Yeah, and you didn't personally float that keg at the pub last night either."

Mitch waved away the comments while looking at him, as if he thought Kyle cared one way or another. "I've always been big boned."

Kyle tried to get them to focus, waving his gloved hand in front of his face. "Remember, keep this button wired to your glove mashed as we translate. Most of the potential side effects are harmless. A couple of them really suck though."

"Space spiders!" Mitch agreed. "Heard about that one at the pub." He turned to Allen. "Not just drinking. I've been listening as much as I can to make sure this one," Mitch jerked his chin in Kyle's direction, "isn't full of shit."

"What's the verdict?" Kyle asked.

Mitch's heavy eyebrows popped halfway up his forehead in surprise. "I'm here, ain't I?"

Patrick leaned in close to Kyle. "That's as close to approval as you're going to get with him."

"That's fine." Kyle smiled back at Mitch. "I'm not looking for salutes, 'yes sirs,' or any of that horseshit. But while we are on the ground in New Mexico, if I ask you to do something, take it as an order you not only agree with, but are personally invested in." Kyle pulled his compad out of its holster and waved it in Mitch's direction.

"Because you are. If you piss me off, I'll make sure when the rest of us pop back here, you'll be left standing in the desert, dick in hand, smart-ass comment on the tip of your tongue, wondering what just happened. If I don't come back, nobody comes back, so—"

"So, you've got three bodyguards?" Allen interrupted him.

"Works for me." Kyle grinned.

"That work for you, Mitch?" Patrick asked.

Mitch gave a grunt and shrugged. "Simple orders I can understand… I can work with that."

They translated at night, based on intel provided by Patrick and company. The group had been trying to get to Silver City, a town in southwest corner of the state. Local prison rumor indicated it had been able to maintain some semblance of order and control. There were people in charge—hard people, it was said—but supposedly it wasn't the ongoing game of survivor between wannabe warlords that most towns and cities in the former state had devolved into. Sandra Orosco believed it, and so did Okamura. Neither Patrick nor Mitch would believe anything they couldn't put their hands on.

Kyle held them back as the small security detachment, led by Carlos, drove two of the all-terrain four-wheelers down the bow ramp of the Door Knocker. His eyes adjusted further, and he was able to pick up on the glow cast behind the mountains from Silver City's lights.

"They've got the power on." Patrick had noted the light as well.

"Hell, Raton had power," Mitch countered. "At least most nights."

"This is the Gila National Forest. We're thirty miles northwest of the town," Kyle noted, pointing into the darkness. "There should be a creek, the Pinos Altos, on the far side of this closest ridge. We can follow it all the way into town. Two days' easy hike."

"Why'd we bring the four-wheelers if we're going to walk?" Patrick asked.

Kyle had expected the question from Mitch, but the larger man just had a confused look on his face. "My Spanish isn't so good, but the Tall Penis? Really?!"

"High Pines, genius." Patrick shook his head in disgust.

"Right." Mitch nodded. "That makes so much more sense, except the part about a two-day walk."

Kyle couldn't bring himself to care about what made sense and what didn't to his new *team*. But he was hopefully going to be in a position to leave them to their own devices soon. He needed them thinking right and making good judgement calls.

"The moon buggies are our quick reaction force. They'll come in a hurry if we need them." Kyle thumbed the dark tactical gear they were all wearing. "These outfits don't exactly scream US military—if anything, they look ISS hit squad. If we get stopped by anyone that qualifies as a prison guard or part of the administration of this shitshow, that's exactly who we'll say we are. Our helo went down, and we are hiking out to the nearest town, following the creek downstream."

"And if the locals find us?" Allen was at least paying attention.

"Same story we fed you guys," Kyle answered. "At least to start, until we know we are dealing with somebody we can trust. Remember, we are here to assess if Silver City actually has its shit together. If it does, we'll try to recruit their leadership—and along the way, figure out if any of them are playing both sides and are chummy with the warden."

"We talked about this," Patrick jumped in. "At least I explained it to your wife in my debriefing. I know how the ISS thinks about this place—the NCWA too, if they are here. Any camp that has kept its order and civility won't be seen as a success story in their book. The government actively wants chaos here. I was told point blank that reformation is not the goal."

"Have to give them credit where it's due," Mitch added. "They've got their chaos. Prisoners are killing each other off every day."

"Understood," Kyle replied. Elisabeth had shared Patrick's debrief with him. It was nice to hear the opinion repeated. "Call me cynical, but I have a tough time believing the Feds would allow a city or internment location to thrive without some sort of ulterior motive."

"Man, you're starting to sound like me," Allen noted.

Wonderful. "Let's help get this camp set up. We should all be able to get a few hours of sleep before we kick off tomorrow."

"Walking?" Mitch repeated.

"Big-boned guy like you?" Kyle slapped Mitch on the shoulder. "Exercise will do you some good."

*

"Yeah, they're locals," Mitch grunted from behind the binoculars. "Looks like two hunting rifles and a pump shotgun. All three of them are carrying sidearms. I'm betting they don't have more than a few rounds each for any of it."

Kyle listened through his earpiece from a position a hundred yards closer to the three-person roadblock the locals seemed to have thrown up on the county road leading into Silver City from the northwest. The rest of his team had been keeping eyes on as he continued to move closer. He could go no further without actively sneaking around them, and, at the end of the day, the men at the roadblock were probably associated with the people they were here to try to meet.

"They look at all edgy? Or nervous?"

"They look bored," Patrick answered this time, sounding just as bored.

Kyle knew his three compatriots thought he was overly paranoid. They still didn't seem to grasp what was at stake if whoever went for the national authority these days learned of Eden.

"All right, I'm headed in. I'll leave my mic open, but I'm hiding my earpiece."

"Good luck," Patrick radioed back.

Kyle climbed through the snow pack up to the roadway. There'd been some truck traffic on the road since the last storm, and there were two packed troughs of snow that made walking at once easier and far more slippery. He only had to go about forty yards before he rounded a corner and could see the two parked cars partially blocking the road into town. All three guards were standing around an oil barrel that had been converted into a burn barrel. From the looks of it, it had been there for some time. He couldn't blame them for that—he was cold, and he'd been walking all morning. He lifted his rifle and held it above his head with both hands.

"Hey there!" Heads came up, and the guns were all swung in his direction. "Don't shoot! I'm friendly! Just hoping I can warm up at your fire a bit."

He could see them discussing something until the one armed with a shotgun took a step forward. "Who are you? And where in the hell did you come from?"

Kyle kept both hands over his head but took one off his rifle and pointed back at them towards them and their fire. "It's a long story. If I'm going to get shot, could I at least warm up first?"

More discussion, but again it was the short stocky fellow with the shotgun that seemed to end it.

"Turn around and put your weapon on the ground."

He paused. Who the hell would do that? "If I wanted to shoot at you, I could have done it an hour ago. I'll drop the mag and open the bolt—good enough?"

"Not hardly!" the lead guard shouted back. "Who are you with?"

"I'm not Army or ISS, if that's what you are worried about!" he shouted. "We're a militia group. Most of us started up in Colorado. We've been working our way south to Mexico, and figured going through New Mexico might mean fewer run-ins with the feds or the Army. It turned out to be the smart thing to do, except some of the towns and camps here aren't any better than the ISS—maybe worse, in some ways. We heard good things about Silver City from some folks in Raton."

"Who the hell is 'we'?"

Kyle hit the mag release. From their faces, they all recognized the sound of a full magazine hitting the packed snow roadway at his feet. He adjusted his grip on the M4 very slowly until he could cycle the bolt and eject the chambered round. From the looks on their faces, the spinning brass cartridge might have been gold as it caught the overhead sun. It looked like Mitch might have been right about the ammunition situation, but it only took one round of anything to ruin his day. He took a step forward, and when he didn't get shot, he took another.

"My arms are getting tired." Kyle raised his voice. "I can't shoot you unless I go for another magazine or draw my pistol—either way, I'd guess you guys would win that race. I'm not an idiot. Can I come in?"

"Real slow, partner," the leader relented. "Like your life depended on it."

No shit. Kyle tried to put on his best smile. It was hard—a training Sergeant at Fort Bragg had once told a young butter-bar lieutenant, "Having guns pointed at you by nervous men of unknown or dubious training is never a calm'-inducing input."

Ten minutes later, Kyle felt a little better. He thought he'd convinced the guards he wasn't ISS or with the army. The problem was, they were not at all impressed by the story of being part of a militia outfit. He was pretty sure they believed the story—they just didn't seem to care one way or another.

"Don't care who you are." The lead guard shook his head. "We don't take in stray groups—never have. Strays sure, we do it all the time—especially if they have a skill we can use or don't represent a threat. I don't mean to give offense, but your skills probably all point in the direction of being a threat. Am I wrong?"

"Yeah… I can see your point," Kyle admitted, ignoring the deep truth in that statement. "Unless you have other threats you're worried about. In that case, I could easily see how we might be of use to you."

The other two locals standing behind the leader shared a look. Kyle jumped back in before the leader could shoot him down. "But I get it. I don't blame you. You're personally responsible for a lot of people. That's a lot to ride on your shoulders."

"You seem mighty understanding for somebody with an empty gun surrounded by loaded ones." The man with the shotgun was one of those guys that needed to be in charge. Kyle had picked up on that immediately and had done everything since trying to put the man at ease.

He jerked his chin back into the hills north of the roadblock. "You don't think I'd walk in here with an empty gun unless my people had you all covered, do you?"

The leader chuckled to himself as the other two backed away to move further behind a rusted-out Crown Vic that had to have been close to thirty years old.

"I've played a lot of poker, mister." The leader puffed up and hooked both thumbs into his belt. "You're doing a lot of bluffing without any cards. If there was any more of you, you would have moved on us."

"If we meant you harm, you're right." Kyle held out both hands close to the burn barrel in an attempt to put him at ease. "We would have. We aren't that sort—we really just want to talk to your people in charge. I promise you, we're the good guys."

"You're full of shit, and right now, you're dealing with me."

"Hey, maybe we should throw this up the chain." One of the other guards, a teenager, finally spoke up.

"Maybe you should shut your trap and follow orders," the leader fired back.

"Give my guys a target," Kyle spoke calmly. "Something that won't get me shot, so you'll at least know I'm telling you the truth."

The leader laughed, but something in his face took on a look of doubt, maybe even fear. Fear was never a good thing—people did stupid shit when they were scared.

"Fine." The leader pointed his shot gun at the stop sign where a cross street into a rural neighborhood met the county road. "That stop sign there."

"The stop sign, to my right—one round only."

"What the hell? Who are you talking to?"

"His radio is on," the young guard spoke up again.

"Be funny as hell if we just left Captain America's smart-ass hanging in the wind for a bit." Mitch laughed as he adjusted the 30.06 hunting rifle slightly to bring the stop sign into his scope's picture.

"Don't be a dick. Shoot the fucking sign," Patrick ordered. "I'm tired of laying in the snow."

"Nobody says 'please' anymore."

"Mitch…"

All three of the guards flinched a little at the rifle's booming report—so did he. Kyle had just started wondering what the hell was taking so long when the shot rang out. The stop sign was still quivering from the impact.

"You have my word. We're the good guys."

The leader's attention was focused out onto the hills, as if he was going to spot where the shot had come from.

"If he's willing to leave his weapons and ammo here, I'll take him into town—just him," The young guard who had been shouted down offered.

"Shut it, Max!" the leader yelled. "Let me think."

"Works for me." Kyle ignored the leader, who seemed suddenly very much out of his depth.

A second later, the leader spun towards him. "Dumbshit here is half-right, except all your people can come in and give up their guns. Then we'll take just you into town."

"Not going to happen," Kyle responded as calmly as he could. "I'm not going to give them an order they wouldn't follow, and you'd better get that shotgun out of my face before you're the next demonstration target."

The shotgun's barrel dropped away quickly before the leader seemed to realize it made him look weak. He started to raise it again, hesitated, and then backed away.

"All your guns and ammo." Max, who couldn't have been older than eighteen or nineteen, stepped forward and pointed at the ground. "Your radio too."

"Fine," Kyle agreed. "Patrick—move Carlos and team up to you. If I'm not back standing in one piece at this spot in four hours—he'll know what to do. Give me one more shot to let us all know we're on the same page."

He didn't have to wait nearly as long for the next shot. The stop sign took another hit, and he started pulling his mags from his vest and dropping them next to where he'd grounded his rifle.

The young guard, who looked like he should have been finishing up high school, watched the growing pile of gear, shaking his head. When Kyle pulled the fat-handled Glock 26 that he'd been carrying in a belly holster and dropped it on the pile, he stepped back. "That's everything."

"All you guys this well-supplied?" Max pointed a finger at the pile of gear and jerked a chin into the distance behind Kyle.

"More or less," Kyle spoke truthfully. "Wasn't like I was going to approach you guys carrying the SAW."

"What's a SAW?" Max asked. "I mean, I know what a *saw* is. Why do I think you mean something different?"

"It's a machine gun." Kyle grinned. "A good bit heavier than our assault rifles, a Squad Automatic Weapon—"

"More bullshit!" The leader barked. "Get him out of here, and make sure you tell anybody that will listen he needs to be back here quick, right?"

"Right." Max turned and lifted a thumb over his shoulder. "It's about an hour's walk each direction. You first."

Kyle smiled and nodded in agreement as he started walking. "Take me to your leader... clock's ticking."

They'd only been walking ten minutes or so in the bright midday sun, their breath standing out as puffs of steam, when Kyle spotted a truck coming towards them from the direction of town.

"Somebody probably heard the shooting," Max offered before he could ask.

"Does that change anything?"

"Shouldn't," Max ventured after a second as he stopped walking. "Unless you do something stupid."

"I won't," he promised. "I've been straight with you."

"This road you came up on," Max stamped his feet as they waited for the approaching truck. "It kind of peters out up in the hills. You expect us to believe you guys came across the Gila wilderness in that storm?"

"Seemed like the thing to do at the time," Kyle answered. He knew there was a network of logging roads through the forest, and some of them connected to larger state highways on the western side of the mountainous wilderness area. "We take pains to avoid the Feds."

"You all should have just skirted around us too." The kid shook his head and jerked his chin towards the approaching truck. "'Bout three months ago, a whole new team of ISS bureaucratic types were dropped into here. They didn't like how Marion was running things. Been a little weird lately."

"This Marion, she still running things? We were led to believe the Feds left this place alone, it's why we are reaching out to you."

"Him," the kid corrected and nodded at the approaching truck. "Marion Smallstone—he was a deputy sheriff here. He'd just retired when all this crap went down."

Kyle could see three guys sitting across the front of the truck's cab. The individual behind the wheel was every bit as big as Hans Van Slyke and looked to be hunched over so he could see out the front window.

"That him driving?" Kyle asked as the truck's wheels crunched to a stop in the snow twenty feet away.

Max coughed, as if the idea were crazy. "Uh… no."

The driver just sat there, scrunched over and staring at him. The passenger side door popped open with a squeal of metal on metal. The guy riding shotgun hopped out and kept himself behind the door. Another guard, Kyle figured.

The middle passenger slid slowly across the seat and came around the open door. Marion Small-Stone, Kyle corrected internally. The former sheriff's deputy was clearly a good part Native American. He was on the short side, heavily built, and kept his long hair in a graying ponytail that came out the back of an old cowboy hat.

"Max? All good?" The man asked.

"All good," his guard answered. "The shots you heard were this man's friends, just letting us know he didn't walk in alone."

The former sheriff's deputy looked behind Kyle. "You walked out of the Gila?"

"It's a long story, but yes."

"How many are there of you?"

"Just shy of thirty in my group." Kyle couldn't think of a reason to lie. "A lot more elsewhere."

"They are packing some real gear - M16s, lots of ammo, sidearms too."

"M4's," Kyle corrected the kid. "We are working our way down to Mexico and decided to use New Mexico as our route. We figured the Army wouldn't expect we'd be dumb enough to travel through their prison. So far, I think we've made the right call."

"We'll see about that. For now, you two hop into the back of the truck." Small-stone came to a decision abruptly and leveled a finger at him. "You either lose that gear you're wearing, or lay down in the bed—you'll stand out like a freaking ninja."

Kyle smiled to himself and nodded in agreement.

"Marion," Max spoke up. "His people need to see him back at the guard post in three hours," he checked his watch, "and thirty-eight minutes."

"Or what?" Small-Stone was looking directly at him.

"It's just sign of life," Kyle answered, holding out both hands, palms out. "We're all strangers here. And the guy running your guard post wasn't listening to what I was saying."

Small-Stone nodded once to himself. "That's why I've got him out here guarding a road nobody in their right might would use this time of year."

The kid, who had seemed on the ball to Kyle, jerked his head back. "You had me out there too!"

"Had to have someone with a brain out there," Small-Stone patted the kid on the shoulder, before looking at Kyle. "Hop in back with Max. I'll make sure to have you back in time."

*

It was clear Small-Stone's office doubled as his home. It was the former Silver City Museum. Long before that, it had been the home of some local mining magnate, so it had been a residence at least once before.

"Sit." Small-Stone directed Kyle to the chair at the front of his desk and continued past to throw some fuel into the creaking wood stove that seemed to have nearly gone out. Max stood across the room, near the back door they'd snuck into after parking in a garage.

Kyle did a quick scan of Small-Stone's office, which doubled as part of the old mining town exhibit. It was a strange mash-up of museum display and dwelling. Unless he missed his guess, Small-Stone wasn't the only one living here.

"I don't want anybody to see you, if you're wondering." Small-Stone sat down slowly, pain playing across the weathered face as he carefully leaned back into his reclining wooden chair.

"I understand." Kyle nodded. "Max there said your town recently got a new team of overlords. Things changing?"

"Oh yeah," Small-Stone grimaced. "The last guy they had here was weak-sauce—he rarely left his office. Stayed out of our way. I think if you'd asked him, he probably felt he'd been sent to prison too."

"And word eventually got out that some locals kept their shit together?" Kyle hazarded. "They can't have that."

Small-Stone regarded him with a face made for poker. "Things are in flux. We had people in homes for the most part, with some overflow to the dorms of the small college in town. But this new ISS team doesn't look kindly on any sort of comfort. They've got a lot of our people building a new trailer park south of town. The trailers are scheduled to arrive in about a month. Supposedly, it will make it easier for them to control us if we're all living in a refugee camp."

"I'm sorry. Your reputation had made it as far as Raton. That's where we heard about you."

"Huh... when was that?"

Kyle quickly did some math in his head. How long would it have taken to walk here, making trouble to avoid notice? "Early fall."

He saw the corner of Small-Stone's lip twitch upward. "That's the first time I felt you've lied to me." The guy was good.

"It was," Kyle admitted. "We were there about two weeks ago. Some of the people I have with me now are from there—well, were interned there. Former National Guardsmen from Missouri. They had heard about Silver City."

"So, you've got wheels, and gas?" Small-Stone almost squinted at him. "What could you possibly want from us?"

"To give you all a place to go. Some place the Feds aren't going to put you into FEMA trailers."

"FEMA would be a godsend." Small-Stone laughed. "They always went away when the cameras did. I'd be happy if it was the old Bureau of Indian Affairs—that's how bad it's going to get here. But if you think Mexico is better, you aren't up on your current events. It's an absolute shitshow."

"Better than Mexico, for all your people." Kyle smiled. "I'm not asking you to take me on my word. I can show you and have you back here before you're missed." Kyle felt like the gamble of going off script was worth it. Small-Stone exuded a quiet competence that was refreshing. He couldn't have said why, but he trusted the man immediately.

"Alberta? Alaska?" Small-Stone shook his head. "I've got nearly twenty thousand people here. A fifth of them are kids younger than Max there. There's nowhere you could take us that wouldn't bring the Army back down on us. Anyone crosses that border, they call in one of those airplanes with all the guns on it. I've seen the results myself. They tried it one night—they might as well have thrown themselves into a blender."

"A gun ship, an AC-130 probably."

"Whatever." Small-Stone shrugged. "But it begs the question - how did you manage to cross the DMZ they've set up at the border? You fly in? Cause you're sure as shit not going to walk out. Besides, the free zones in Alberta fell a year ago. Nobody's heard shit about Alaska in forever. You'd know that if you were the militia you say you are. In the interest of time, which I gather is important to you and your people, why don't you just tell me who the hell you people are?"

An hour and a pot of watery herbal tea later, Small-Stone looked up from the empty coffee mug he'd been playing with. "When you started that story, I figured nut-job straight away, full-blown window-licker." The leader of Silver City looked over at Max, who had pulled up a chair next to him five minutes into Kyle's sales pitch.

"Mister," Small-Stone continued, "I don't believe anyone is crazy enough to pull a story like that out of their ass—at least on short notice—and you clearly believe it." He glanced at Max. "And I can tell Max here wants to believe it as much as I do."

"You asked me to come clean," Kyle replied. "It's the truth."

He'd deviated so far from Elisabeth's protocols and Pretty's timetable that Kyle figured this would be his last trip to New Mexico. So be it. It was easy to see why Small-Stone led these people. Kyle trusted him.

"And you said you can prove it?" Small-Stone didn't look convinced.

"I can. I'd suggest taking you personally, if you can be missed for 24 hours."

"I'll go." Max was nearly vibrating with excitement.

Small-Stone gave his head a shake in frustration. "Max, you don't breathe a freaking word of this, you hear me? Not to a soul." His mark looked across the antique desk at him. "I think I might be coming down with something. I figure I wouldn't be missed for a day. But you're going to have to figure out a way to explain to my guards why I'm leaving with you. Nothing I could say to them will make any sense."

"Not a problem." Kyle sat forward and pointed at the street map of Silver City under glass atop the old desk. "You just drop me off back at the guard post as planned. I'll walk out the way I came in. You pick a place somewhere on the northwest side of town you can get to—say by midnight—without being seen. We'll come get you."

"And me," the teenager added.

"And you, Max," Small-Stone relented.

"One thing," Kyle added. "Not tonight. Our team is kind of on a hard schedule. I won't have the means to prove it to you tonight—has to be tomorrow night."

"For the trans-dimensional boat-thing to show up?" Max asked.

"Yeah," Kyle apologized—not for the delay, but for how crazy it still sounded to his own ears. "I can't contact them to show early. It doesn't work like that. They are due tomorrow."

Small-Stone started laughing. "Mister, If I were you, I wouldn't give me more time to think about this."

*

Chapter 15

Silver City, New Mexico—Earth

"These people aren't going to be mad that I'm a surprise guest?" Victoria Newell was bundled up in a heavy coat, scarf, and wool cap. In the dark, she looked like the profile of a very short Michelin man.

"If they are," Marion looked at her and then to where Max hid with his rifle in the upper deck of the unused backyard playhouse across the street, "I guess that's an answer too."

"But you wouldn't have asked me here if you didn't think it was safe, right?"

"The guy I spoke to," he let out with a frustrated sigh that had nothing to do with Victoria's question and everything with the fact that his visitor was almost thirty minutes late. He was unused to explaining himself and wasn't the most talkative guy in the world to begin with—being worried just made things worse. "He seemed like a straight shooter."

"You mean besides the part about interdimensional travel?" Victoria snorted in what might have been laughter.

"You still think he was making it up?"

He'd brought her along because she was, hands down, the smartest person in Silver City. She'd been some sort of research scientist out at Los Alamos and, to hear her tell her story, she'd gotten a little too loud when questioning why the government was acting outside the constitution.

She hadn't been the only one, and a whole busload of the scientists had been shipped off to one camp or another. Victoria had landed in Silver City, and it was her ingenuity that had designed the new power station that ran on a network of dispersed wind, solar, and hydro in addition to a small coal-fired plant. It was just one of the things the new ISS crew was probably going to shut down.

"Without a doubt." She sounded sure. "Sorry, I know you'd like it to be true. Bells! I'd like it to be true. If such an extra-dimensional framework existed—and it's only been theorized really—the idea that this other universe or dimension would be a mirror of our own… that would be like trying to win the big Powerball lottery every day for a decade. Beyond mathematically remote—its non-existence is a near statistical certainty."

Victoria, on the other hand, *could* talk, and it all fired forth in a rapid staccato delivery that made his head hurt. "So, he's full of shit?"

"I don't know what his story is." Victoria shook her head. "I'm just saying his story is a fairytale. You're the one that met with him. Why do you believe him?"

"I've spent a career being lied to." He chuckled to himself. "I know bullshit when I hear it. He believed his own story."

"That just makes him a whack job, Sheriff." Victoria didn't quite look down her nose at him, but it was dark enough that he wouldn't have been able to see it if she had. He could hear it in her voice. "Not trustworthy. Besides, it's not like he's trying to pass off a fake ID."

"You're probably right." He wasn't going to argue with her. He'd probably lose, and he was too tired to try.

"You have some sort of sixth sense about it? A Native American gift telling you it's true?"

It took all he had not to laugh. Smart people could convince themselves of anything. "My ancestors talking to me, you mean? Telling me his story is true? *That* you could believe? Before you'd believe his story?"

"There's data to support the spiritual aspect of some Native

American legends." She sounded defensive, and he figured she'd probably seen something on television or read about it.

Sure, there was, he thought. He'd even seen and witnessed a few things that he'd never be able to explain that would fall into Victoria's bucket of spirituality. He also knew the mescaline in peyote, or the psilocybin found in some mushrooms was the fuel behind the "ghost walks" in his people's past. Some of the rich kids he'd gone to school with in Albuquerque at the university had considered it tripping. One group used it in a spiritual sense, the other for escapism. During his career he'd responded to a handful of bad trips. He could remember one particular woman that had become convinced she was a badger—she'd nearly asphyxiated herself trying to drive her face through the ground.

"You hear that?" he asked, looking past her in the dark. Max was across the dark road somewhere as insurance. Maybe the kid was calling it quits. He was definitely making noise.

"I didn't hear any—"

He held up a hand, stopping her. "Quiet."

"Max!" he yelled. "That you?"

"Nope, it's me—Kyle Lassiter. Max is here with me. Say hi, Max."

"I'm okay." Max's voice came out of the dark, sounding closer. A second later, the two of them emerged out of the shadows.

Marion couldn't recognize Kyle until the soldier flipped the night vision goggles covering the top half of his face up. "We saw three of you, and one," the soldier nudged Max, "who looked like he was trying to get the drop on us."

"My idea," Marion pointed out. "Seemed like a good one at the time."

"I can understand that." The stranger seemed oddly at ease. "If you would, please keep your hand away from that cannon in your holster. I'm not alone here." Kyle pointed at something behind him.

Marion turned to look, afraid of what he might find. He wasn't worried about himself, but he'd promised Max's dad to look after him.

There was nothing in the darkness until the headlights of a small vehicle flashed. It was a lot closer than he could believe something could have gotten without him hearing it.

"It's electric," the soldier explained. "Very quiet. We didn't know what to think when we saw three of you."

Right… "This is Victoria Newell." He held out his hand. "She's a scientist from Los Alamos. Victoria was interred here with one of the first busloads we were told to take in."

"Miss Newell." The soldier bowed his head slightly. "It's a pleasure to meet you."

"It's Doctor Newell." Victoria laid it out there like she was challenging the stranger to a fight. "I have a PhD in physics."

"Victoria here," he interrupted, "has my trust. She's probably the smartest person I've ever met. Admittedly, I didn't run with a lot of folks that have letters after their names on their business cards—or who had business cards, for that matter. Point is, she says your story can't be true—scientifically, that is."

"She wouldn't be the first to say it," the soldier answered. "And like I said earlier, I'm not the guy to try to explain it. I can show you, but we need to go back up the valley a bit for me to do that. We were only expecting the two of you. Max here is going to have to stand on the back and hang on."

"I can do that," Max answered immediately. "Not a problem."

"How far up the valley?" Marion asked.

"How far do we have to go?" The soldier spoke into his collar as he held up a finger, asking them to wait. He turned back to them. "It's an old hayfield. The mailbox on the ranch's driveway says Lemon… something."

"The Lemontier place. That's about eight miles."

The soldier may have shrugged. "If you say so. We really need to get going though. Like I explained earlier, this show runs on a schedule."

Marion exchanged a look with Victoria, who smirked and rolled her eyes. Even in the dark, the soldier couldn't have missed it. A small part of him wanted her to be wrong, just to see her reaction.

"Alright, let's go."

"It's a truly wonderful hayfield." Victoria pointed out for the second time, sounding even more cynical than she had the first. The moon had finally risen, and they could all see a little better.

Marion was ignoring her and focusing on the men and women, all kitted out as soldiers, who seemed to materialize out of the darkness. Some had arrived on another four-wheeler just after they had. Others had clearly been here waiting for them to arrive.

So far, Kyle hadn't been bullshitting him. He'd counted twenty-five of them so far, all of them heavily armed, and it only made sense that there were more of them out there that he hadn't seen.

Kyle leaned in close to him. "She's going to keep that up, isn't she?"

Marion grinned back at the soldier and shrugged. "Yes, but I'm about to start in myself."

Kyle checked his watch and pointed out into the darkness of the field. "One minute."

Something was definitely up. The soldiers all had pretty much stopped whatever they were doing and were checking their own watches as they all seemed to orient themselves towards the open field.

"No one lives out this way?" Kyle asked him conversationally.

Marion shook his head. "Couple of months ago I wouldn't have been able to say for certain. The ISS has started forcing everyone into town in the last couple of months. I wouldn't be surprised if there aren't some folks ignoring it, but the Lemontier family have been gone since the beginning."

"Good, going to be real loud here in a moment."

He was about to ask why, but the soldier started shouting. "Thirty seconds! Ear plugs or fingers." Kyle turned to the three of them. "Stick your fingers in your ears. There's quite a concussive shockwave when our transport arrives."

"You mean something large just materializes here?" Victoria asked, sounding doubtful.

Kyle looked straight at her and placed fingers in his own ears before glancing at him and Max to be certain they had followed suit. "Ma'am, that's exactly what I'm saying. I'm being straight with you. Please cover your ears."

Marion, with fingers stuck in his own ears, turned to Victoria. "Nobody is going to look more a fool than me. You can say 'I told you so' later."

Everyone around them seemed to be on edge, and when one of the soldiers behind them yelled, "five seconds!" Marion saw a few of the soldiers turn their backs to the hayfield.

Five seconds came and went. He glanced at Kyle, who hadn't moved.

"Still a hayfie—"

Victoria's comment was cut off by her high-pitched shriek that was in turn drowned out by a bone-shaking *boom*. A moment later, they were all dipping their shoulders into an unseen wall of wind that washed over them and was gone just as quickly as it had appeared.

Marion's mind had a what-the-hell moment as it framed the reality of the three-hundred-foot-long ship that had just appeared before them. He stood there numbly for a moment before looking over at Kyle, who had turned in Victoria's direction. The scientist was just staring at the ship with her mouth hanging open and pieces of hay caught in her wool cap.

"That's the *Door Knocker* in your hayfield, Doctor." The soldier addressed Victoria directly with a smile. "We use it to jump, portal, or translate between worlds, realities, universes, or dimensions— whatever they are. Every time I've overheard a debate between our physicists, it has always turned into an argument. Whatever it is, whatever we do when we go from one place to another - that's how we do it."

"Not..." Victoria struggled to speak. "That's... impossible."

Marion shrugged to himself and glanced back at what clearly hadn't been there a moment ago. He had no idea what had just happened, but *impossible* wasn't the word he would have chosen.

"That is so cool. When do we leave?" Max couldn't stand still and was tugging on Marion's jacket like a five-year-old.

"Five minutes." Kyle grinned and pointed out towards the ship where his soldiers were already carrying loads of gear towards it. A pickup truck shot down the bow ramp of the ship and drove over to a stacked pile of equipment. Kyle turned back to him. "Decision time; come with us, or be another crazy that saw a UFO land in a field."

Marion had been thinking along the same lines. He turned to Victoria, but she was already moving towards the ship. Max took it as permission, and he was already a step ahead of her.

"I think that's a yes."

Kyle held out a hand in the direction of the ship. "I'll have you back here in 24 hours—or sooner if you want."

*

Marion was in a hurry to leave and return to the Earth he had known his whole life—it just wasn't for the reason he would have imagined a day ago when they had climbed aboard the Door Knocker for the first time. A small part of him wanted to stay with Victoria on Eden, no matter the responsibility weighing on him to go back and convince as many people as he could that there was a place for them to go – where here was. He'd already stayed half a day longer than they'd planned.

That first jump to New Seattle had been terrifying, at least for him and Victoria. Max had faced the whole affair like a carnival ride. Once the fact of Eden's existence had been irrefutably established in Victoria's mind, she'd had a chance to sit down and speak to someone who spoke the language of quantum physics. She wouldn't be going back with him and Max. Neither Victoria, nor the people in Kyle's Program that she had been talking to about the whole multi-world thing, thought it was a good idea for someone who had the wherewithal to explain the phenomena to be walking around an ISS-controlled internment camp.

After a tour around New Seattle, they'd gone to yet another world—to a Portsmouth, in an England that didn't exist on a world they called Chandra. He'd met so many people, his head had started to hurt. But what he'd really seen was disparate groups of people trying to find their way in a place that allowed them to live however the hell they wanted to. It was more than a selling point with him, especially with how he knew Silver City was going to change in the very near future.

He turned away from the sunrise fighting its way over the mountains to the east and faced Kyle. "What would you have done if Victoria hadn't been willing to stay?"

His new friend—he was confident he would be able to call Kyle a friend now—shrugged. "I was playing tour guide with you and the kid, so I don't know what conversations she had with Doc Jensen. I don't imagine he would have said anything substantive until he had her agreement to stay. You can understand that, right?"

"I can," he responded.

"She'll be here waiting for you, as safe as any of us," Kyle added.

"It's not like that." He shook his head. "The woman drives me nuts, but she is a friend."

"I understand." Kyle gestured to the door of what they referred to as "the translation station," smiling as if he didn't believe him. From where they were standing outside, a ramp led down into the building where hangar-like doors were pulling apart. Beyond, the stainless steel of the translation chamber they'd already used to go to Portsmouth was visible.

"I'll be back your way in ten days, and we can start planning your people's disappearance." Kyle handed him a radio. "In the meantime, we dropped repeaters on the way into Silver City when we picked you all up. They should give you a decent connection to the small team I left in the hills. Their only job is to listen for you in the event you need help. Don't hesitate to use it. We're only a planet away, and you've seen how fast we can get there."

"Real fast," Max added.

Marion gave the radio a waggle. "Channel?"

"It's locked in."

He hooked his chin in Max's direction. "Max? give Mr. Lassiter and me a second."

He waited until Max was out of earshot and on his way down the ramp, shaking his head when he realized he was going to step in there to be zapped back to Earth. Marion didn't know what was crazier—that, or the fact he wasn't on Earth right now. He'd spent a lot of time talking to Kyle and coming up with a plan of how to pull this off, and as much as that plan worried him, there was one piece to it that truly scared him.

"Second thoughts?" Kyle asked.

"Not for me, no—or for him." he nodded in Max's direction. "It's these Kaerin folks you told me about. Am I going to get my people out of prison just to throw them into a war?"

"We *are* in a fight," Kyle answered him. "We aren't trying to hide that. Our people aren't being drafted to fight, and yours won't be either. We are desperate for people. You've seen the Creight and the Jema in Portsmouth. The Jema *only* fight, and the Creight are a generation away from understanding our technology isn't magic. We need more people who at least understand our level of technology. Our success depends on integrating them and others like them as fast as we can."

He had visited Chandra; seen Portsmouth; met Jema, Junata, and even a few Creight during the trip. One of Kyle's friends was married to one of them, and there hadn't been any of the second-class citizen bullshit that he'd felt he had every reason to worry about.

"I think I just needed to hear you say that again." Marion couldn't help but chuckle to himself. "I made a personal decision a long time ago to not live in the past, but you understand this isn't the first time someone in my family has been told life will be better where we're going."

Kyle nodded in what Marion took as understanding. "Yeah, I get that. I wondered if it might be an issue. To be honest, it's why I wanted to introduce you to Jake's wife Dere'dala and for you to meet Jomra, the leader of the Jema. None of that is an issue here—lack of people is our problem."

Marion held out his hand to shake. "Just be sure your guys stay close to their radio. I have no idea what I'm doing."

"Welcome to the club." Kyle shook his hand.

*

Chapter 16

Silver City, Earth

"Fun police just rolled up," Dale Bronski called out from where he stood next to the office window overlooking the street.

Here we go. "Let me do the talking," Marion replied from his desk.

Rick Benoit, the only other person in the room who had been a local cop in town before the shitstorm had started, just grunted in acceptance before smiling back at him.

"I'm still not sure you haven't gone crazy, Marion." Dale lifted his chin out the window. "You sure that's the right track?"

Marion figured Dale was only half joking. He'd told Dale and Rick about where he'd been and Victoria still was. It had taken Max's word to convince them that he hadn't lost it, but that didn't mean they weren't going to give him shit over it.

"Looks like the high potentate himself," Dale reported before turning away from the window and taking a seat at his own desk.

"Wonderful," Rick moaned as he put another stick of wood into the stove. "I wonder what they'll have us tearing down today? Sewer treatment plant, maybe? I mean, who needs flush toilets, really? Maybe the grocery store? I know they want to put us all into the food chit program."

"Rick…" Marion warned.

"I know." Rick made a motion of zipping his lips. "You do the talking. Wouldn't trust myself to say anything to the jellyfish anyway."

Marion watched Michael Tormina, flanked by four heavily armed ISS-security types, walk past Dale's desk on the other side of the front window. The middle-aged, overweight bureaucrat walked like he had bad knees, or maybe it was just the fact he didn't get out from behind his desk much. He was still learning his way around Tormina, but from the evidence so far—the Washington bureaucrat wielded his authority like a crown. Full of ego, and with an attitude that his dictates, or Washington's, were all being pursued for the internee's best interests.

As an individual, Silver City's new Secretary of the ISS-administered district had an almost an almost inhuman ability to speak exclusively in terms of policies, goals, programs, and methods. Not once had he heard the man refer to the people who lived here as people. Marion's attention flicked to the security escort through the window, and he resisted the urge to roll his eyes.

Max and the young man's friends referred to the ISS security troops as 'Storm Troopers'. It was an analogy that he couldn't find much fault with beyond the color of their dark uniforms. Only one of the goons came through the front door with Tormina. It was 'Flat-top'—none of the ISS goons wore name tags, and the man's haircut had defined him in the month or since his arrival. Marion wondered if the lack of name tags was some sort of programmatically approved admission that what they were doing was wrong—not to mention illegal—or would have been illegal back in the days before the suspension of all the most important parts of the constitution.

Flat-top never said a word to anyone. Marion had a myriad of interactions with the ISS force—this one and the previous team—as part of his job. He had yet to share a single word with Flat-top. As far as he knew, none of his people had. He couldn't help but worry Flat-top had been assigned here for a specific reason that would be aided by an extra layer of separation from the people he supposedly guarded.

Marion stood up behind his desk before speaking. "Secretary Tormina."

"Good evening, Sheriff."

Why Tormina insisted on calling him Sheriff was beyond him. He'd explained that he'd never been elected Sheriff, and as to his current position in Silver City, Mayor was the official title, which had no more official authority than what Tormina allowed.

"If you gentlemen would excuse me, I'd like to speak to Sheriff Small-Stone alone." Tormina didn't bother looking at either Rick or Dale as he spoke, he just kept coming across the room and took the time to glance at the glass-topped display case of old mining pans and pickaxes as if it held some interest for him. Flat-top held the door open, signaling his two deputies out.

"Sit, sit." Tormina motioned across Marion's desk after he had seated himself. "I hope you're feeling up to this. I was told you'd been under the weather."

"Definitely felt a little under the weather," he replied, rubbing at his face. "Bad sinuses, always been a thing with me. How can I help you, Secretary Tormina?"

"Where to start?" Tormina looked around the room as if he expected to be offered a cup of coffee or a stiff drink.

The cup of coffee Marion had on Eden had been the first he'd tasted in over a year, and although alcohol could be had in Silver City, it didn't come cheap and was more useful as barter than for consumption, in his opinion. He wasn't about to share the bottle in his desk with Tormina.

"Right… I suppose I should start with a bit of history to make this easier." Tormina crossed his legs and sat back. "When the ISS set up the first internment camps around Santa Fe and Albuquerque, they had a protocol, or a game plan the administrators were told to use to explain what was happening, and why. Two months later, when the Internment Act was passed and New Mexico was selected as the Federal holding area, a lot of towns like Silver City were simply annexed into the internment area."

"I remember."

"I'm sure you do," Tormina agreed. "You can certainly remember the mass transfer of internees in and the flow of citizens out. The prisoner population was brought in from a myriad of holding facilities across the country to places like Silver City, and, in many cases, that initial protocol I spoke of earlier... I guess it's safe to say it took a back seat to the massive effort of the transfer itself. Not to mention the security measures that were put in place at the state border. In my opinion—shared by many others in Washington—it probably could have been done more efficiently. But you'll remember, with so many areas at the time still under active revolt, the priority was relocation and getting the internees to the hundreds of camps."

"Hundreds? I had no idea there were so many," Marion lied. He tried to sound sympathetic to the frazzled bureaucrat who had played a role in the exile and internment of millions of people—including children when the parents were lucky enough not have been separated from them.

"Seven hundred and twenty-three camps." Tormina's eyebrows went up. "Most were preexisting towns or cities such as this camp, but a few were purpose-built." Tormina leaned forward, as if he risked being overheard. "Between you, me, and the walls—those places are horrible. You have it much better here."

"I don't doubt it." He nodded as if he didn't know of the first camps built by the ISS. There was one some fifty-odd miles south of them, outside of what had been Deming. Now it was just Internment Camp 4.

"At any rate," Tormina seemed to recall what he'd been talking about, "you remember the influx—the administrative challenge of setting up a federal penal reservation of this size."

"I do," he responded, wondering if human trauma, severe emotional dislocation, and everyday violence were somehow now categorized as "administrative challenges" by the government. He'd been a psych major with a minor in criminology. He couldn't recall ever seeing an entry for "administrative challenge" in the DSM - the psychiatric bible for mental disorders.

Tormina seemed shocked for a moment. One hand flew to his lips. It was the best acting performance he'd seen Tormina pull off, but it was still an act. "My apologies, I didn't mean to say that."

"I'm sorry?" Marion played stupid. The government might not have a problem with locking up a good portion of its people, but to refer to a *reservation* as the accepted-upon solution? In the presence of an actual Native American, *that* bordered on offensive in the bureaucrat's world.

"The transfer was a challenge, to the say the least," Tormina recovered.

Marion got the distinct impression the man had been fishing for a reaction.

"I lived it," Marion agreed. "To your point, it was chaos."

He wished the spineless dick would just get to the point. It was an understatement of the highest order. Millions of people uprooted and thrown into camps after being deemed enemies of the state. A good portion of them had just been unfortunate enough to be caught up in the sweeps of one problem area or another. If anything, the government had actively created as many discontents as they had arrested. He was in that boat himself. He'd dealt with the influx as best as he could.

"We were one of those camps," Marion added. "I'm tracking."

"Silver City is not the only camp that was allowed a high degree of self-governance—whether because of your exceptional leadership, or the fact the prisoners here did not cause problems—the status quo was not questioned by my predecessor during his tour here."

He knew there was a "but" coming. Every conversation he'd had with Tormina in the last month had turned on a "but." *The local pre-school seemed to be working well, but... The local effort to relocate the elderly infirm and care for them was admirable, but...* The list was endless. They were going to tear it all down.

"I'm not assigning any guilt or wrongdoing in my predecessor's direction," Tormina assured him with a palm against his chest. "I promise you, if he was still here, he'd be having this same conversation with you."

"What conversation are we having?"

Tormina acted as if he hadn't spoken. Marion was certain this whole affair would be more efficient if the asshole had just posted a public notice.

"I understand why he administered this internment district the way he did... but there is a new set of protocols nationwide. The ISS believes that some areas, like Silver City, run a risk of developing an unacceptable level of autonomy."

"Autonomy? We're just barely hanging on here."

"Precisely. Because you're attempting a degree of self-sufficiency that is deemed inappropriate for internees."

He'd heard this setup before. "By inappropriate... you mean it will no longer be allowed."

"Yes... yes, I'm afraid that's exactly what the new guidelines mean."

"What specifically are we talking about?"

Tormina made a show of patting at his sport coat's pockets before coming up with a single piece of tri-folded paper. It was pristine white. These days, the only time he saw paper like that was when he was being handed something from the ISS Admin Office.

"Here is a list of several new policies that you and your team have two weeks to implement for the entire camp. Failing that, I'll direct my security team to enforce the changes. Item number one is the priority— the rest you can deal with in any order you see fit."

Marion scanned the list quickly, getting more pissed off as he went along. It would lead to deaths—not potentially, in actuality. Silver City would cease being whatever made it livable and become just another camp.

"This will lead to a great deal of unnecessary suffering. You're giving free license for the strong to feed off the weak."

"What I'm giving you, Sheriff, is a chance to maintain your position and influence."

He'd never cared one way or another about position or influence. If there were any right to the world, he'd be truly retired and dragging his trailer from one fishing hole to another.

He focused on Tormina's priority. "I already account for every weapon and every round of ammunition. How do you expect my men to keep the peace if we turn all the guns in? The only guns you'll collect are those held by law-abiding citizens. The rest, you'll just drive underground."

"Not citizens, Sheriff. Internees." Tormina seemed pleased with the distinction. "After the deadline, my security team will deal with anyone found in possession of a firearm decisively."

He'd long suspected the gun confiscation was coming. It was already a fact in other camps he'd had word of. Hadn't worked there either. In truth, it didn't bother him near as much as the forced closure of the K-6 school. They'd never been allowed to start up a junior high or high school, but the elementary school had been something everyone had liked and taken some pride in. It was probably why it was on the list.

Marion laid the paper out on his desk. "I don't see much reason for my position after this."

"Don't take it like that, Sheriff. I need you to do this, and do it well. I'd like to get you on the rehab list. We are going to start one here." Tormina swelled with pride as he said it. "You'd still do your time, of course, and you'd need to enroll in some extra educational opportunities. But you could earn your release in eight to ten, and be allowed to live wherever you want."

"I like it here." He tried to make light of the insulting offer. Besides, he'd be sixty-two in a decade. What were they going to do to him if he told them to fuck off? Put him in prison?

"I can appreciate your frustration, Sheriff." Tormina sounded almost sincere. "I'll need an answer from you by noon tomorrow. If I need to rely on my security team to enforce that list, there are preparations I need to make."

Marion pushed back from his desk and stood up slowly, hopeful that it would be an end to the meeting. "No need, I'll do it."

Tormina had just handed him the excuse he needed to do a little proselytizing. He'd been worried about how he was going to manage to talk to so many people without raising suspicion.

"I expected more resistance, I'll be honest."

"If your security force has to make these changes, a lot of people will get unnecessarily hurt—or worse." He glanced at Flat-top still standing at the door behind his boss. The man hadn't moved, and stood with his hands clasped in front of him. The soldier gave him the slightest nod of what Marion took as appreciation. He didn't know if it was in thanks for taking the task off his and his men's hands, or something else. The interaction was far enough out of character that he was taken by surprise.

It must have registered on his face as Tormina came to his own feet and looked back at his guard for a moment before facing him again. "Sheriff, I appreciate you and your people leaning into this effort. The ISS security force is in no way designed or expected to act as a police force. I see no need to use a hammer to put in place a few common-sense limits on the internee's activities."

*

Chapter 17

Prelate's Estate, Kaerus

Senior Gemendi Wal'asta had served the Prelate's Office for nearly thirty years. He had been one of six chief administrators of the Prelate's Office of Order and Communications for the last decade, and he'd long since ceased drafting orders that flowed to every vestige of Kaerin-controlled Chandra—whether by long-talker, horseback, boat, or airboat. He and his select group of senior Gemendi now simply approved writs composed by an army of Gemendi supporting House S'kaeda.

"We need to take a closer look at this cadre of Gemendi supporting Lord Tima." Wal'asta looked up from the draft of the writ he was checking and directed his comment at his colleague, Gemendi Daker'as.

"Careful, he'll be our Prelate soon—we all know it." Daker'as didn't bother to look up from the accounting sheet he was pouring over.

This war was eating up every bit of free resources the Kaerin produced. The only good thing to be said about that was the fact that the added industrial capacity would still be there when the war had run its course.

"Word has it he hand-picked most of the Gemendi supporting him. They all act like no one else understands what they are doing," he continued.

Wal'asta grunted to himself. He didn't need to be told the obvious. He and Daker'as had shared their distaste for Lord Tima's favored

Gemendi before. "Can I read you something they want to put out?"

Daker'as sighed from across the massive table they shared, separated by stacks of paper. "If you must."

"Relax, old friend, you'll see what I'm talking about." Wal'asta took the opportunity to stand up and stretch his legs. It would be another three hours before their day ended. "This is from Lord Tima's office and already carries the Prelate's seal."

"So approve it and send it along." Daker'as waved back at him. "Clearly, the Prelate's staff agrees with it. You're not suggesting to send it back for clarification to Gemendi Casm'ara? I'd hate to have to break in a new work partner after all these years."

"No, of course not. But this is yet another instance where the Prelate's seal predates the actual writ. My issue is with how the writ is worded, and that is clearly the fault of Lord Tima's cadre. It's the new shipbuilding orders from Lord Oont'tal. It was passed through the Prelate's office, then on to Lord Tima's Office. There's a part here that is so watered down, I hesitate to classify it as a writ."

Daker'as shook his head. "Bad enough that Lord Oont'tal's monkeys are drafting writs for the Prelate's seal—perhaps the poor wording came from them."

"No, those consist primarily of technical drawings. The script chamber has been turning out copies of them for the last moon. Could you imagine having to redraw hundreds of technical construction instructions? Over and over for a moon or more?"

"I would welcome anything beyond numbers at this point." Daker'as smiled, leaning back. "What does Lord Tima's writ say?"

"All current boat construction will immediately utilize the attached construction plans detailing the technical changes."

"Sounds pretty clear to me," Daker'as responded.

"It does indeed," Wal'asta agreed. "Particularly in light of all that precedes it, which is basically the standard justification statement detailing the Shareki threat and the need for whatever follows in the respective document."

"There's another clause, I take it?"

Wal'asta shook his head and held up a finger as he read out loud. "Where possible, any boat or boat hull not yet in a state ready for delivery should be considered a candidate for conversion. Final decision is left to the discretion of the senior Gemendi officers at each location."

"'*Should be* considered a candidate for conversion?' Universe!" Daker'as grimaced. "Can you imagine the needless traffic that will generate? They'll all have questions—not to mention how much work those boatbuilding facilities will try to get out of. Orders like that... there won't be a single ship converted. I agree, send it back."

"It's marked 'Immediate.'" Wal'asta shrugged. "Once again, I'll just do their job for them and make an actual writ out of what would otherwise be a suggestion."

He bent over the desk and crossed out the second clause, adding one with his own wording: *to include any ship not yet delivered.* He nodded to himself in congratulations. "Words that even a hayseed Gemendi building skiffs in Aster'apol could understand."

"We should really have a talk with Lord Tima's Gemendi." Daker'as nodded in agreement. "This kind of watered-down direction keeps up? Every writ the Prelate puts out will be end up being questioned."

*

Port City of Ler'atta, Chandra

Gemendi Badj'tek had served House S'kaeda his entire life—first as a warrior, and subsequently as Teark for ten years. According to his father, he'd always had ambition beyond his skills. He'd submitted to and passed the rigorous examinations required to be admitted into the Gemendi cadre. Once he'd acquired the prefix 'Gemendi', he'd assumed his career serving the Prelate's house would progress without interruption. He'd been wrong—and there had been many times where he wondered if his father had been wiser than he'd credited. He'd found himself one of the thousands of Gemendi that it took to support the more technical and specialized fields required by a House headed by the sitting Prelate.

There were always select Gemendi who had some special skill or knowledge related to the natural sciences who could potentially make a name for themselves. The infamous Lord Tima was proof enough of that, though Badj'tek was of the opinion that Lord Tima's elevation was almost certainly more a result of his father's relationship with the Prelate than anything the former Gemendi had accomplished on the island of Landing. After all, the Gemendi pavilion had been destroyed on his watch, yet the man now walked at Lord Noka's side.

There were no High Council members in Badj'tek's family. His father had died a retired Teark just like his father before him, and so on. The far more mundane work of administration, accounting, logistics, and construction fell to Gemendi like him who kept the House running and the Prelate himself able to maintain a House that was the envy of all others. So it had gone for the last eight years. Badj'tek had advanced to become the second-highest-ranking Gemendi in the Office of Naval Supply at the port of Ler'atta on the northern shore of the Middle Sea.

House S'kaeda had never dedicated many resources to its naval force. While unmatched on land, House S'kaeda could always call on the resources and capabilities of any other House if they needed maritime support. As a result, being the number two Gemendi in all things related to maritime construction and supply at Ler'atta had relegated him to a life not very different from the sackless drones who shuffled mountains of paper in Kaerus. That is, until the Shareki had arrived, brought to Chandra by the honorless Jema. In the last year, his work had taken on an importance and urgency that he could not have imagined, even in his most ambitious dreams. Then his superior at the shipyards, Gemendi Ner'ama, had died.

The old man had dropped dead a ten-day past of a weak heart, under the stress of a workload that none of them could have imagined a short time ago. Overnight, he was no longer addressed as simply "Gemendi," but "Gemendi Badj'tek." He now had two hundred nameless Gemendi under his direct control, as well as nearly fifty thousand subjects working the dockyards and manufactories that had transformed the waterfront of Ler'atta over the last year and a half. He would prove his father wrong. His name would mean something to his two sons when they needed it.

He looked down at the construction plans for the new warships that had arrived from Lord Oont'tal's renowned Maritime Design Center in Pagasta. In the new design, the steam engines would drive two shafts that ran to the stern of the craft. Then they would pass through a gearbox before protruding out the stern. There was not a lot new to the build itself—though the new design drastically shifted the components and arranged them differently. The driving force behind the change was what attached to the shafts at the stern of the ship. The strange, almost petal-shaped strakes of a fan—one attached to each of the drive shafts— terminated inside a newly designed and much expanded rudder system.

His first question was how the thing would be steered without being able to alter the power going to one or the other widely separated paddle wheels that existed on their current ships. But then he surmised the new rudder itself might do the work, if those fans could push enough water. He couldn't imagine they would—as large as they were, they weren't nearly as substantial as the massive paddle wheels on existing warships.

Not his problem, he realized. If the nature of the design was faulty, he would only be following his writ, and his writ was spelled out in very clear, uncompromising terms. All current ship production at Ler'atta— and he assumed every other Kaerin shipbuilding facility—had received the same and was to integrate the new design parameters as quickly as possible. Fine, that was a problem that he could work. It was far from the only design change in the last year. It was the next line of the writ that gave him pause: *to include the conversion of any ship not yet delivered.* Were they mad?

He knew his concern would matter little in the end. The writ had arrived by a courier airboat that morning and had been stamped with the seal of the Prelate's office— it was law at this point. The voluminous construction plans had been accompanied by a written explanation from Lord Tima Bre'jana in Kaerus of why these construction alterations were necessary and the critical importance that Prelate S'kaeda placed on them.

The threat of the Shareki, he understood. The value of the new plans, he took on faith—but someone wasn't thinking this through. You just couldn't take an already built boat's guts apart and then put it back together. Technically, he supposed one could, but he doubted if anyone had ever tried. Getting to those engineering spaces was hard enough while the ship was under construction. Doing so with a completed hull was not anything he would have ever considered. But someone had… and it was now part of his writ.

He'd gone back and reread the document several times. The words did not lend themselves to confusion. Still, he'd taken the writ to Gemendi Ast'oroa for an outside opinion, and hopefully a sympathetic reading that might lead to permission to ask for clarification. Ast'oroa wasn't a specialist in naval construction, but he was the overall highest-ranking Gemendi in Ler'atta.

Badj'tek had left Ast'oroa's office, in his superior's words, "fortunate to still have his position." In his anger, the old man had gone so far as to question the decision to replace the recently deceased Ner'ama with a Gemendi that couldn't interpret a clearly stated writ. He'd returned to his own office, staring back and forth from the conversion plans on his desk to the eleven construction shipways lining his end of the harbor. His eyes didn't want to look past them, out to the water, where three completed hulls floated in various stages of their final fitting out and provisioning—but critically - *not yet delivered.*

He had his writ, so he started writing out tomorrow's work orders. Today's, he corrected himself as he glanced out the windows at the lightening horizon. He knew full well the questions his own writ would generate, as well as how it would reflect on him in the opinion of the hundreds of lower-ranking Gemendi that now reported to him and managed Ler'atta's work crews. If enough of that—or any of it—reached Ast'oroa's ears, he might very well lose his newly gained position.

There was only one way to prevent that from happening. He added the writ from Kaerus, word-for-word to his own. His own Gemendi wouldn't dare complain about orders from the Prelate. He glanced out at the completed boats anchored in the calm water of the bay. Hull 87 was the farthest along in fitting out and was perhaps only a ten-day from taking on its crew and disappearing over the horizon. It would be the most difficult boat by far to convert. Hulls 88 and 89 had been launched from the shipway together almost a full moon later and were the obvious choices for conversion.

Or were they? He only had one dry dock open and available for this insane project. Hull 87, if the work improved impossible, provided a built-in excuse for how difficult a process this was going to be. Always ambitious, his mind grasped to find another step on the ladder. If he and his facility were somehow able to successfully convert a nearly complete ship, they'd have a template for the process that could be shared out across Chandra. The thousands of ships that had been built in the last year could all be converted. Credit would fall to him, to his facility, and to House S'kaeda directly. Those arrogant Gemendi shit-heels in Pagasta would end up working off *his* building plans.

He wrote quickly, ordering hull number 87 to be pulled from its anchorage back into dry dock. The work of tearing her deck off, sawing through the rivets of the iron hull cladding, and accessing the engineering spaces would be underway by this afternoon. There was an opportunity here, he was sure of it. His value to House S'kaeda, his name, and the future of his children could only benefit.

*

"Someone's gone mad up there." Junior Gemendi Wim'las jerked his chin up at the windowed fourth story of the construction dock's control building as a swarm of Jehavian and Tarnesian workers went up ladders, across catwalks, and swarmed under the still dripping hull 87. The catwalks had fallen in place even before the dry dock had finished pumping out. Crews had been at the heavy wood deck with saws for an hour.

"Careful Wim," Junior Gemendi Sel'tag muttered. "You saw where the writ came from."

Wim'las shook his head. "This beast already has its new gun turret, and the only crane we have that can pull those is all the way back down at number two shipway. It'll be three days to get it taken down, moved, and reassembled here."

"Crane's your problem." Sel'tag smiled. "As soon as we get some holes cut into it, I have to unload the damn thing and figure out where we're going to store everything we've spent the last month putting aboard. Warehouses are near bursting."

"Why wasn't it unloaded first?" Wim'las opened both hands at the ship across the narrow gap between the dock where they stood and the steep drop-off into the stone and brick tub that held the vessel. The boat looked like a big beetle overcome by fire ants.

"I report to Rost'las." Sel'tag shrugged. "He thought the cargo clearance would be more efficient after we get through the deck. Otherwise, my work gangs would be going single file in the holds and passageways right in the middle of all that."

"What could Rost'las know of shipbuilding?" Wim'las spat. "The old man spent a career managing a cattle herd."

Sel'tag just looked back at him. "Seniority…" It explained how the Gemendi worked. For junior Gemendi, it was a curse that would hopefully become a blessing at some point in their future.

"Terk'ama's crew has some work ahead of them getting that protective belt off." Wim'las pointed at the four inches of steel plating that ran from the gunwales to about a span below the waterline.

"All of it," Sel'tag agreed. "I got a good look at the plans." He waved a hand from midship, near where they stood, towards the stern almost two hundred feet away. "From the boilers on back, both sides of the ship. Do you have any idea how hard it is to unload fire rock? We can all be glad the powder stores are still empty."

Wim'las almost convulsed at the comment. "Please tell me you have more than Rost'las' word on that."

"I just deal with the consumables," Sel'tag pointed out. "He's got Par'chas to handle the powder and ordnance… hey! Where are you going?"

Wim'las ran for the air horn. The alarm would bring all work to a halt, but it was located on the other side of the dry dock up against the control building's entrance. He scrambled across the catwalk onto the deck of the boat, weaving his way between teams of subject workers who wouldn't dare bar his passage. Suddenly all he could hear were the steam-powered saw's metal blades whirring against the ship's decking. Somewhere deeper within the tub of the dry dock, down against the metal hull of the ship, other steam powered saws and power chisels were already at work on the steel plating.

Wim'las never learned that he'd almost made it to the alarm. He never knew that it wouldn't have mattered. Sparks from the saws had already landed on the stacked linen bags of pre weighed gunpowder. Specks of the powder on the outside of a bag had tried to flare and already gone out several times in the nearly airless number four port side powder hold.

The Tarnesian man working under the unforgiving gaze of his Kaerin master finished his cut and moved out of the way to make room for the two men running the steam chisel.

Five minutes later, a sheet of steel the size of a large pillow fell away, ringing like a cymbal against the stone bottom of the dry dock. This was going to take forever, he thought, as he moved back in place with his saw on the scaffolding. He opened the steam valve that pushed his saw blade into motion and leaned into the next cut.

Wim'las was knocked off his feet from the initial explosion. His mind hadn't even registered what had happened when the flaming shock wave ran through the ship and set off every powder store and ammunition hold on board. They had all been full, awaiting ignition and the fresh air that was now more than plentiful.

High above the dry dock, Gemendi Badj'tek had been watching the afternoon's work out of his wall of windows with pride. He had no warning. His life, and everyone else's within a quarter of a mile, was snuffed out by the blast. The parts of his brick office building that weren't vaporized were turned into shrapnel.

To those miles away across the bay, it looked like a volcano had just erupted out of Ler'atta's waterfront—the stone pit of the dry dock had directed most of the blast upward. Most of it—the sea gates of the two nearest dry docks on either side of hull 87 were torn free from their mounts or bent so badly that the harbor water rushed in, helping to put out the fires on the shattered hulls. The buildings and warehouses of the harbor weren't so lucky.

A quarter of a mile inland, two water towers were toppled as they were hit with the shock wave. The water from the largest one rushed across the floor of a steel forge in a deluge until it met the newly designed blast furnace. That explosion leveled a solid square block of Ler'atta, and the fires were just getting started.

*

Kaerus, Chandra

In the ten-day that followed the incident at Ler'atta's docks, Tima had more than a few moments of doubt about whether his people could fight and win against this enemy, especially when the means to win was at the bleeding edge of what his society could produce. In his heart, he knew the problem resided as much in their culture as it did their tool set. He looked across the chessboard at his opponent and resisted the urge to drive a pawn—no, a rook, which was better suited in terms of length—into Ocheltree's brain.

How could a culture that produced men such as his prisoner, even rewarded them with some modicum of authority, be threatening to the Kaerin? Was Kaerin culture so ill-suited for these new ways—modernity or a technological society, as Ocheltree called it—that there really was no hope?

"It sounds like a horrible industrial accident. There's nothing worse." Ocheltree fingered his knight, and then ended up moving a pawn in nothing but an effort to buy time. Tima would have the man in check within six or seven moves.

"Your people suffer these as well?"

"Not so much these days, but in our past—especially during our industrial revolution—they were quite common. Some were horrific."

"And this was many years ago?"

"God, yes… started centuries ago for us. We've come through the digital revolution much more recently, and I guess we now claim to be in the information age—it has its problems too, mind you. Mainly in how it affects people's minds, especially our young people. Far less dangerous physically, but probably more of a problem in the long run."

Yes, he thought. The rook, held tightly, could reach the man's brain pan. "The accident happened under a writ I wrote."

Ocheltree never talked to another soul, and if Tima couldn't bare his soul here, to the one man that might be able to help him, why waste the time?

"You can't blame yourself." Ocheltree knew he was in a bad temper and had been trying to placate him. "You told me what occurred. The orders, those writs of yours, you say they are law as soon as they are issued. Somebody changed the wording of yours with catastrophic results."

"This would never have happened in your culture?"

"Not now." Ocheltree shook his head. "Anybody working in a technical field, especially one involving potential explosions…" Ocheltree paused, as if asking himself whether his one remaining friend in the world could be assuaged by what he was saying.

"Please, do not worry about upsetting me. I really am trying to get to the root cause of this. To save lives in the future," he added, playing to what he knew drove his prisoner.

Tima had already removed some of the root causes. Two Senior Gemendi from the palace had been executed three days ago. The Senior Gemendi in Ler'atta—two days ago, after having admitted under questioning that one of his Gemendi had asked for permission to question the writ.

"Fine." Ocheltree paused and looked down at the chessboard. "Shall we call this one a draw?"

Tima struggled to maintain his smile. Graciousness in victory wasn't a Kaerin trait. "If you'd like."

Ocheltree wasn't half as sharp as he thought he was. Not for the first time, Tima wondered how he'd been thought of among his peers before betraying them.

"The writ you issued is not to blame." Ocheltree at least had the honor to tip over *his* king. "It's your system of command and authority. I know it is ingrained in your very culture, and I'm not trying to make a value judgement here."

"Continue… please."

"Do you remember the discussion we had about my planet's history—Earth, not Eden?"

"Of course, I found it fascinating." Tima was still surprised at the truth of that statement.

"It all comes down to competition. When our industrial revolution first began, Earth was ruled by monarchs. Wars soon took on a scope and scale that formerly would have been unthinkable—besides being beyond the scope of any kingdom to pay for. The monarchies, over time, were replaced by governments which, to varying degrees, allowed for the citizens to participate. It created the wealth that nation-states could call upon in times of war.

"I don't want to give you the impression that our society evolved in lock-step as part of some grand plan. The people living through those changes didn't even have the concepts to explain what was happening. I have the advantage of having paid attention in my history classes. It was incredibly haphazard—fits and starts, wars, revolutions, counterrevolutions, etc."

"I know you aren't calling for a revolution here," Tima pressed. "Continue."

"The new economic systems relied, to varying degrees, on an educated populace, and so did the new political structures. Gradually capitalism, our economic system, became the most efficient way for a nation to harness the energy and spirit of its people. An individual with a great idea could become rich and powerful—good ideas were rewarded by the system itself. Bad ones would die on the vine. The problems started when the rich and powerful became the political leaders—too many laws and rules were created to protect the status quo, and it was no longer good idea versus bad, but which idea had the backing of the powers that be—"

"Stop." Tima held out a hand. "You are getting off into your recent history—the reason for your people leaving Earth and going to Eden. I'm less interested in that, and more in weighing your Earth's development against that of my world. Why is this development prevented by our culture?"

Ocheltree shrugged and pointed a finger at him. "You yourself have complained to me how hard it is to get others to even consider a new way of thinking. People have to be free to bring new ideas forward. If all you have is dedication to authority, you really are limited to the creativity and genius of your leaders."

Ocheltree held a palm out. "You are one of the sharpest minds I've ever met, Lord Tima, but you are one man. Why is it on you to come up with every new idea? Or why must you rely on only your Gemendi's for this kind of progress or development? From what I gather from you, most of them are what I'd consider clerks and bureaucrats... uh, paper pushers."

Paper pushers indeed, Tima thought. In the end, what Ocheltree was talking about *would* require a revolution. One that would be the end of the Kaerin. He grinned. "Paper pushers?"

Ocheltree's face drained of color. "I assure you, I meant only the non-technical Gemendi, not the scientists like yourself."

"I've long held similar concerns myself." Tima waved away the worry on the prisoner's face.

He could remember telling Lord Noka much the same on Landing during that first week following his entitlement. He knew the Prelate had assumed he'd been advocating for the gradual extermination of the subject clans—rather than a way forward where their potential could be harnessed. That gradual path of reform was no longer an option. The Edenites—he refused to think of them as Shareki—had moved up the schedule. Defeating them was the only option the Kaerin had left.

*

Chapter 18

"Is it the kid?" Allen asked at his shoulder.

Patrick lowered the binoculars. "Yeah, it's him."

"Max," Mitch called out from a few feet away. "His name's Max."

"What's he doing out here?" Allen asked what they were all wondering.

The kid was walking down the last few hundred yards of blacktop before the road went to gravel and started climbing into the hills beyond where they had waited for more than a week.

Nothing good. "They have the radio Kyle gave the Sheriff." Patrick removed his wool cap and scratched at his scalp, seeking some relief. They'd been waiting here for some signal for eight days, and they all could use one of the hot showers in New Seattle. "Something must have happened."

"Won't be good news, that's for sure." Mitch seemed to agree with his assessment.

"I'll go get him," Allen volunteered. "Kid's been walking awhile."

"Yeah, do that," Patrick agreed. "Mitch, take that hunting rifle and move back a hundred yards or so. If he was followed out here or is working for those assholes, they'll be right behind him."

"He's a good kid," Mitch complained. Patrick didn't know if Mitch was standing up for the kid or just didn't want to move.

"I'm not saying he isn't, but the sheriff isn't here and we haven't had a radio call. Let's be smart about this." Besides, he thought, they wouldn't have any help coming for another two days.

Mitch came to his feet with a groan and moved off with the rifle, mumbling as he went. "Be smart? Wrong fucking team for that."

*

It had been eight days of camping without a problem—unless one counted Mitch's snoring. The camp food, which included bacon and fresh eggs, was more plentiful and tastier than what they'd grown used to in Raton. Even the MREs they'd been left with were better than before. They had a tent, warm sleeping bags, and even a bottle of jasaka that Kyle had left behind. Patrick had spent a lot of their time here thinking. Sandra and the kids, the future they might have on Eden... the future had eaten up a lot of his cycles as his psyche slowly got used to recognizing the concept of hope once again.

They'd almost made it the ten days until Kyle returned with their replacements, but the kid, Max, had just turned that shit on its head. Small-Stone had been arrested, and over a dozen of Silver City's citizens had been killed—gunned down in the street, according to Max.

"They put it on Marion to enforce all of their new rules." Max was worked up. The kid looked like he was about to cry, and Patrick could tell it was from pure anger mixed with powerlessness.

"He said he knew what it was they were doing," Max continued. "Trying to get the people pissed off at him and all his deputies. It didn't work though. People started marching in front of the ISS office and then somebody burned down the NCWA center they had us building. That's when they started shooting people."

"How many ISS troops in town?" Patrick had already made his decision to do what he could. He couldn't watch this happen, not again. These people were so close to getting out after having made the best of an impossible situation for the last two years.

"Twenty." Max wiped at his eyes. "But only nineteen now, because somebody beat up one of them pretty bad two nights ago. The story is he may not make it."

"How many internees still have guns and would be willing to help?" Patrick asked. He knew there was a snowball's chance in hell all the guns had been turned in.

"Wait just a second there, hoss," Mitch broke in. "We were just supposed to sit here and wait for a call and arrange a place for the sheriff to meet Kyle when he gets back—not go into town, guns blazing."

Patrick turned and glared at Mitch. "Fine, you can sit out here around the campfire while they kill Small-Stone. I'm done being helpless and watching this shitshow play out."

"I'm in," Allen chimed immediately.

Mitch just glared back at him in anger. Mitch's concept of "us" was limited to the three of them. His friends' definition of people he didn't give a shit about? That, could generally be relied upon for its inclusiveness.

"We have a chance to get out," Patrick continued. "I think it comes with a price—and I want to be able to look at myself in the mirror. So do you, I think."

Mitch's grip on his rifle was turning his knuckles white, but after a moment, he jerked his head up and down once. "You might be right... maybe. But I swear to God, if this gets us killed, I'll haunt your ass." Mitch's head swiveled towards Allen. "Yours too, Professor."

"Deal." Patrick smiled.

"You'll help?" Max looked from one face to another.

Mitch maneuvered forward on his knees until he was part of the circle and started drawing in the dirt with a stick. "Okay kid, how many people are going to be willing to help us, and where are they?"

*

Marion Small-Stone sat on the edge of a piss-stained cot in a cell of the city's old courthouse. The two-story space had been the ISS security team's headquarters since they'd arrived. At the end of the hall, at a small desk, the office's only other occupant was Flat-top. The soldier seemed to be as upset about what had happened earlier in the day as he was. That was not anything he would have guessed at a day ago.

"You know the kids in town call you Flat-top? You have to have a real name."

Flat-top looked up from the newspaper spread out across the desk. He seemed to nod in confirmation after staring back at Marion for a moment, but an answer wasn't forthcoming. Marion had been doing this for a long time—he just had to get the suspect talking, and it didn't look like either one of them was going anywhere for the moment.

"I saw you out there when your colleagues opened up." Marion tried again. "You tried to stop it. I thought I'd at least ask your name." He waited a moment for some acknowledgement, but it was like the guy was deaf.

"Hey!" He tried raising his voice. "It's not like I'm going to live long enough to tell anyone—it can't be worse than Marion Small-Stone." He laughed to himself. "Kids can be mean. They used to tease me—joked that I had small nuts."

Flat-top shook his head in annoyance before looking up at him. "Well, they'd be wrong, wouldn't they? If they'd said you were stupid, they'd have been a lot closer to the truth. What the hell were you thinking, agreeing to do Tormina's job for him? How'd you think this was going to end?"

"Figured there would be less blood if I carried the bad news."

"Nothing's going to stop the blood from flowing here—or anywhere else, for that matter."

"How'd you get here?" Marion changed tones. "Most of the guys I used to work with—some of my own family—did time in the service. You do a shitty job of hiding the fact you used to be a soldier. You don't have much in common with the rest of Tormina's rent-a-thugs. How does a man like you wind up working for the ISS?"

It was clear he had touched a nerve. Marion waited for a response, but the enigma that was Flat-top went back to his newspaper. It was clear he wasn't reading it. The man's eyes weren't moving, focused instead on something he was clearly trying to forget.

Marion let him stew in silence, going back to staring at his own feet, until the soldier's chair slammed back against the wall as he stood quickly and disappeared into the squad room. Didn't matter, Marion figured. Guys like Flat-top were going to do what they were told, even if they didn't like the orders.

A minute later, the soldier came back in carrying two Styrofoam cups. He'd been smelling the coffee—real coffee—since they'd brought him in here earlier in the afternoon. He stood to accept the offering between the bars.

"Thank you."

He meant it. He'd almost given himself an ulcer drinking so much coffee back in the day. Going cold turkey had been tough, and he didn't suppose there'd be any more of it after this. Flat-top nodded and backed away until he was leaning against the bars of the opposite cell, sipping at his own. Marion stayed quiet. Sometimes you had to let the suspect answer the questions in his own head before the dam would break.

"Ganz, First Sergeant Timothy Ganz."

"Good to meet you, Sergeant Ganz." Marion lifted his cup in greeting, but said no more.

"Tormina didn't trust any of the other guys to watch you. He says you're too damn likable, and the townspeople will probably try to spring you. He thinks they're scared of me."

"He's not wrong." Marion smiled. "About them being scared of you, that is. As for the other, my fan club isn't what it was." He'd lost some friends in the goat-fuck out in the street, not far from here. Old man Simpson had been one of those guys in town that would do anything to help anybody, whether he knew you or not. He'd been at the front of the group that had been fired on. So had Charlotte Guterres. He'd seen the woman who managed the community garden and greenhouses take two rounds in the chest.

"This whole idea of New Mexico is fucked up." Ganz spoke up. "They want to send you people here? Fine. I can accept that, especially if it means the Army doesn't have to fight Americans out there. But they should just fence the shit in and leave you alone. Why they want to keep screwing with you is beyond me."

"Is that what happened to you?" Marion asked. "Have you been involved in some of the fighting?"

Ganz stared back at him for a moment without answering. He took another sip of coffee and grimaced as he swallowed. "I was a good soldier. I just focused on keeping my guys alive—I guess I didn't think too much about who we were fighting. When your platoon is pinned down by snipers and the locals are dropping Molotov cocktails on you from the apartment balconies above, it doesn't really matter if you are in Minneapolis or Tabriz—and I've been in both. You just..." Ganz couldn't finish, and looked away.

"You just do your job?" Marion whispered.

"Yeah." Ganz turned back to him. "Did it so well I got a commendation and was seconded to the ISS to help professionalize their security teams. You believe that shit?"

Marion tried to smile. "From where I sit, they could use some. Firing into a group of hungry, helpless people who have had everything taken from them because they dared to try to make their situation a little better—doesn't strike me as anything other than evil."

Ganz wouldn't look at him. What he'd taken for an angry, quiet soldier looked like a sad, broken man.

Ganz shook his head slowly before he looked up. "Like I said, nothing is going to stop what's going to happen here. I'd stop it, if I could."

Marion regarded the soldier for a moment. Yeah... he believed him.

"Do you mean that?"

An hour later, Ganz had retreated back to a desk in the squad room and seemed to fall asleep. Marion couldn't be sure—all he could see through the open door at the end of the hall were Ganz's crossed boots thrown up on a desk. The dead clock above the door between them had stopped at five minutes till two o'clock at some point. Marion guessed that the clock was close to being correct in this moment. Somehow it felt like some sort of surrender to fall asleep on what he'd already decided was his last night on Earth.

The muted tat-tat-tat of machine gun fire was so muted that it didn't even register at first. The second burst went on for a few seconds. He felt sick to his stomach as he knew the targets were the same people that had entrusted him to keep them safe.

"What the hell is going on?" Ganz was suddenly standing under the clock.

"You tell me!" he fired back. "Those are your people out there."

Ganz had his head tilted to the side with a finger pointed at the ceiling next to his ear. "You hear that? That's a SAW, Sheriff. A Squad Automatic Weapon, and our heavy weapons are locked up here." Ganz fished something out from around his neck. They were close enough that Marion could see a big steel key on the chain next to the man's dog tags.

"No one around here has anything like that," Marion countered.

Or did they? He knew some people who did, but they weren't due back for another two days. He hadn't been able to get to the radio Kyle had given him before he'd been arrested, and he'd hidden it well enough at the museum that no one else was going to find it.

Another round of firing seemed to interrupt whatever Ganz was about to say. The sound of other weapons joined the battle, and all of it sounded a lot closer than it had a moment ago.

Ganz was at his cell door in four quick strides, pulling a set of keys from his pocket. "I think I gotta call bullshit on that."

"I'm being straight with you," he answered. "That can't be us. What are you doing?"

Ganz swung the door to the cell open and waved him out with his sidearm. "I'm not going to be a party to this."

"What does that mean?"

Ganz reversed his Glock 17 and held it out to him. "Those rent-a-cops will be headed back here to get at the weapons locker. You can help me make sure that doesn't happen. We don't let them up to the second floor."

The sound of tires squealing to a stop outside jolted him to action. His people sure as hell didn't have any wheels at this point. It would be the ISS team.

"What do you want me to do?" Marion wasn't a soldier—he'd never thought of himself as anything remotely close to one.

"Come on." Ganz turned and ran back into the squad room, which took up the majority of the second floor of the building. Marion checked that the Glock had a round chambered and followed. Ganz's radio, lying atop a desk, was going crazy as several voices stepped on each other, cutting off the transmissions. The one voice he recognized was Tormina's, ordering the entire ISS team back to his office. Another voice, perhaps trying to respond, was drowned out by automatic rifle fire that sounded like it was just outside their building.

"Get down, behind a desk!" Ganz shouted at him over his shoulder as he accessed the old evidence room. Marion caught a glimpse of the weapons stacked within as the heavy metal door swung open.

He heard shotguns, a hunting rifle, and more automatic rifle fire that sounded like it was coming from the street just below the windows across the room. Ganz walked back into the room with an M4, shrugging on a vest stuffed with magazines.

"Anybody but me comes up these stairs," Ganz didn't look back, but pointed at the stairs with his rifle, "don't hesitate."

Gunfire and the sound of breaking glass from the lobby below reached them, just as Ganz was about to start down the stairs.

"Peters!" Ganz yelled. "That you?"

"He's dead. They fucking shot him!" a voice called back. "Help me with Chan—he's messed up bad."

"Bring him up," Ganz shouted back down the stairs.

"I can't carry him! I need some help, dammit! They're right behind us."

Ganz turned to look at him. Marion was on his knees with his head up over the edge of a turned-over desk. Ganz held up a hand to him, asking him to wait, before heading down the stairs.

There were more gunshots farther away in town that broke the silence, and Marion was again caught up in the guilt of his friends dying because he'd been arrested.

"They came out of nowhere, man," a frantic voice reached him. "Started just like yesterday's protest—all of a sudden, these guys opened up with machine guns from the fucking crowd. Peters, Johnny, and Olski were dead where they fell."

Marion peeked around the corner—Ganz and another man were dragging a third up the stairs between them.

"Chan and I made it as far as here—but they followed us, man! Followed us! I thought we took all their wheels. How'd they follow us? They're right outside, dude!"

"Chan's gone." Ganz's voice was a steady calm in contrast to the staccato drumbeat of the frantic soldier.

"He's not gone. He was just talking a minute ago. Check him again."

"TJ!" Ganz shook the young man by the shoulders. "He's gone."

Marion did his best to watch while staying out of sight. TJ had been tagged with the nickname Skittish by Max and his friends before all this happened. The young man was a wreck, coming apart as he begged Ganz to fix his friend.

"Boss, the convicts ain't supposed to have machine guns. We're the top dogs here. This can't happen—it ain't fair."

"You're in the wrong place for fair." Ganz's voice sounded sad.

The young man was on his knees, looking down at his friend. Marion couldn't help but feel bad for the kid. He'd probably been recruited into the ISS out of some NCWA work program. Then again, he wondered how many of his friends and fellow *convicts* he'd lost tonight.

A bright flash of light at the bottom of the stairwell was accompanied by a concussive explosion that rang his ears painfully. He shook his head, trying to clear the buzzing. The next thing he was aware of was Ganz at his side, pulling him to his feet and screaming something that he could barely hear.

"Your people! Talk to them!"

*

"This is Timothy Ganz—security code Motel 3-8-7 Bravo 1-2. Reporting on behalf of Secretary Tormina. Situation at Internment district four one six, Silver City, is nominal."

"Confirmed Bravo One -Two. The administrative file has one message tagged for you. The trailers you have requested will be delayed. ETA on the delivery plus five days. Snow storms have slowed everything down. Nothing else to relay."

"Copy all, Denver." Ganz looked up at the gathered faces crowded into the radio room. A couple of them had guns not quite pointed at him. "Ganz—out."

"How do we know there wasn't some sort of alert signal in all that bullshit?"

The big guy named Mitch was sneering at Ganz, after voicing his concern.

Marion could admit that he'd wondered the same thing. He waved the concern away. "If he wanted to send a signal, all he had to do - was not tell us somebody had to report in every morning." He faced Ganz. "Right?"

"Yeah," Ganz answered him and glared back at Mitch. "A report has to be made every 24 hours. Barring that, I think you'd be looking at an ISS security platoon. A real one, not mall cops."

Mitch grinned. "You look like a mall cop to me."

Marion had to separate them. His personal rescuer, and the three men who had led the assault that had saved Silver City, at least for the time being. Those three had been waiting for Kyle to return, just as he had been. They'd been internees themselves and had no reason to trust Ganz any farther than they could throw him.

"Dale, Rick." He turned to face his two deputies. Rick's arm was in a sling, as he'd caught a ricochet during the previous night's fighting. Another seven civilians had been killed in the fight, as well as the entire ISS security team, including Secretary Tormina.

The only two that were left alive were Ganz and the young guard named TJ, who was locked away in the same cell he'd been in. "Give me a second with these guys, would you?"

"You sure?" Rick asked.

"I'm sure." He nodded.

The door to the radio room shut behind them, and, with a nod, Marion looked to Patrick for some help in controlling his colleague. For his part, Ganz just sat there at the radio as if he didn't care what Mitch did to him. Then again, maybe he was tough enough that he didn't have to care.

"Sit down." He raised his voice. "All of you."

"Mitch…" Patrick, the nominal leader of this group that Kyle had left behind to help him if needed, slapped his colleague on the arm. "Give it a rest."

"I'm as much an internee as you three," Marion started. "More than that, I was interned *here*. This is my community… as much as I have to thank you three for your help last night, I know I have a better idea than you of what the ISS has done here. I certainly have a better idea of what they *wanted* to do here, as I was the tool that volunteered to help them do it while we waited for our new friends to return." He pointed at Ganz. "I know what this man did last night. He didn't have to—but he helped me."

"You think he'd have helped you if we hadn't gotten the jump on the assholes?" It was Mitch again. "What if his side had been winning?"

Marion took two steps to stand in front of Mitch. "He let me go and gave me a weapon long before we had any idea who was 'winning.' If you can call the fact that we spent the morning digging more graves for my friends winning."

"Why?" Patrick asked suddenly. He turned, but it was clear Patrick was asking Ganz himself.

Ganz shrugged. "What does it matter? If I were you, I wouldn't believe anything I could say."

"Try me." Patrick held a hand out, almost in Mitch's face, that stopped him from saying something.

"I didn't want to be part of what was going to happen," Ganz jerked his chin in Marion's direction. "To the sheriff, or to his people if they fought back. I've seen my last massacre."

"But you've played your role in the past, I'll bet." Mitch wasn't going to be shut up.

"I was a soldier," Ganz replied. "Green Beret out of Fifth Group. We didn't get used for that shit—we were only sent to active fronts. Crowd control, enforcing martial law, and dealing with prisoners was left to Guard-types like you guys."

"That didn't go over so well with us," Patrick countered.

"Bullshit!" Ganz smiled. "I'm willing to bet you would have done anything you were ordered to do as long as it wasn't actually shooting civilians. I'm guessing that's what happened to you guys? You get ordered to light somebody up?"

"Yeah," Patrick answered. "ISS killed our CO for it. We killed them."

Ganz's slow nod was one of approval. "As you should have. Look, why do you think they have New Mexico?" Ganz shook his head. "They can starve people to death that hold out—that doesn't seem to bother them much. But the idea of actually rounding up and shooting civilians? Only groups I've ever heard of actually doing that were in the aftermath of Boston. You think the government wants a civil war against its own military? Cause that's what they'd have. As long as they are using us to enforce their stupid laws and dictates, the military brass will salute and follow orders—or most of them will—and that's all they need."

"But here you are," the quiet Asian of the trio spoke up. Marion didn't think he'd yet heard the guy open his mouth. "All dressed up in ISS Gestapo gear. What gives?"

"I was seconded to the ISS—a bunch of us were—there's a program to work with the ISS and professionalize their security detachments. Officially, I'm still Army."

"It was big Army that chewed us up in Texas," Mitch broke in, reminding the others who was in the room with them.

Ganz got a funny look on his face for a moment. "You guys were that Missouri Guard unit?"

"You heard about it?" Patrick asked, surprised.

Ganz just nodded. "The colonel... it was the 10th Mountain, wasn't it?"

"Yeah, that was them." Patrick confirmed.

"Relieved of duty, reduced in rank, and probably in charge of some emotional wellness program on base back in New York."

"Is that supposed to make us feel better about what happened?"

Ganz leaned forward, his forearms resting on the desktop. "I'm not trying to make you feel better—I'm just telling you what happened. We all have to live with the shit we've done." Ganz turned and looked at all three of them. "Or would have done, had some ass-clown of an officer not ordered his dumb as shit Bradley commanders to fire on troops. Spare me the sermon—we are all in a world of shit. Nobody's clean."

"I have my reasons for trusting Sergeant Ganz," Marion said after a moment of uncomfortable silence. "I'll talk to Kyle about it when he gets here. For now, I believe he left orders that you three are to render any assistance I may need."

"He did." Patrick waited. He thought he knew where Small-Stone was headed.

"Well, I need the four of you to stay out of sight. You all look like ISS to most of the people out there. My folks who were involved in the fighting last night are spreading the word that we had help—but it's not like we can put out a news broadcast. It'll take time—during which

I'd like to not have to worry about you going after each other."

He glanced in turn at each of them and got a nod from all, even Mitch.

"You've got the AM radio station," Ganz pointed out. "It's low enough in power that the edge of town doesn't even get a signal. Use it to organize your people—they have to be scared."

Scared didn't begin to describe what he was dealing with, but the comment was another point in Ganz's favor, as far as he was concerned.

"That's a good idea. I'll do that."

"What about the other one we have locked up?" Patrick asked.

Marion knew they meant TJ. Last night, Ganz had eventually leveled his weapon at and disarmed his former ISS colleague.

"He's just a scared kid," Ganz stated.

"Call it protective custody for now." Marion agreed. It was one more decision he could offload on Kyle when he got here.

"Who's this guy that's coming?" Ganz asked.

The rest of them just looked at each other. Mitch started laughing to himself until it turned into a full-blown belly laugh. When he stopped, his eyes were watering, and he was grinning. "I'd like to tell you just to see the look on your smug face, but I'm not sure I believe it myself."

Patrick nodded in agreement as he looked at Ganz. "Yeah, I don't think that's our story to tell."

"Agreed," Marion replied.

*

Chapter 19

"So, how mad was he?" Carlos asked as they walked down the loading ramp leading into the translation vault of the facility at Whidbey Island. Another trip to Earth's New Mexico was in the offing, and a four-wheeler awaited them inside the steel chamber.

"You're going to need to be more specific." Kyle laughed. He figured Carlos meant Colonel Pretty, but he'd made enough people angry in the last weeks that he had several options to choose from.

"Colonel Pretty..." Carlos' eyebrows darted upward in question.

"I think Hank is just more annoyed that this recruiting program is pulling me away from Portsmouth and the raft of shit we have to do to prepare for what we know is coming. Stephens, on the other the hand, was truly pissed. He threatened to revoke my translation privileges."

"Privileges?!" It was Carlos' turn to laugh. "Like you wouldn't rather be home, or in Portsmouth playing with your kid, and spending some time with Elisabeth."

"Yeah." Kyle cocked his head. "Elisabeth pretty much took Stephens' side on this one too." *Maybe even more so.* "Neither of them thinks I fully understand the risks and moved way too quick—which I probably did. But it was an opportunity I wasn't going to pass on."

"I wasn't there." Carlos shrugged as he inserted a magazine into his assault rifle and tightened the sling. "But I met this sheriff when you brought him over for sightseeing. He seemed like the perfect recruiter, and he's got a whole town to work on. Plus, we don't have to be there to help him do it."

Kyle grunted to himself. It was fairly close to what he'd told Stephens.

Three EDF soldiers were coming down the ramp towards them. Waddling more like, as they were so loaded down with gear.

"You know any of these dudes?" Carlos asked as he dropped into the passenger seat.

Kyle glanced up. "I think I've met that Teark somewhere before. The others… no." He'd thought it before—heading into a war and having enough soldiers that you didn't know each of them personally wasn't necessarily a bad problem to have. "Looks like recent trainees."

"You guys don't have to carry all that. Drop it in the back or throw it on the roof," Carlos directed the security team.

The soldiers would wait and secure the insertion site while the two of them snuck into town to meet up with Small-Stone. One of the land yachts would translate over to retrieve them in twelve hours.

"How far out from town are we landing?" Carlos asked him.

"About eight miles. The last four or so are rural-suburban, turning over to neighborhoods, so lots of cover." Kyle knew what Carlos was digging for and smiled in response, slapping the steering wheel. "We'll drive in as far as we can."

Carlos laughed to himself. "Hey, I'm the last guy in the world to question the tactical decisions on the ground—you're the boss."

Kyle had to smile. "Too bad others don't seem to realize that."

The door to the translation chamber dropped quickly, and somebody in the control booth initiated the ten-second countdown. Kyle's last thought before the quantum squirt that pulled them back to Earth was that Paul Stephens, his wife, and even Colonel Pretty should have cut him a little slack in how he handled Patrick's group from Raton and then-Sheriff Small-Stone's off-the-cuff initiation into Eden. He was the guy on the ground, after all.

"Contact!" The shout from one of the EDF troopers behind them focused his attention out of the head-spinning arrival. By the time he turned around to look, the EDF security team was on one knee at the rear of the ATV with guns leveled at several hundred people. Some of the people had guns—no uniforms though. He spotted Mitch Bennett standing a head above everyone else near the center of the loose arc of people.

"Hold!" he shouted.

"This is bad, amigo. Who the hell are these people?" Carlos asked, the barrel of his assault rifle laid over the top of his headrest as he knelt in his seat, facing the gathered crowd. "No bueno, man. No bueno."

Next to Mitch, he spotted Sheriff Small-Stone and Patrick Loukanis standing at ease, but several people in the crowd seemed to be getting over the shock of seeing them materialize in the empty field and were starting to notice the guns pointing at them.

"Everybody! Guns down, stand easy." Kyle gave the order and watched all three of his soldiers comply. He knew just how close they'd come to firing—he'd been there himself.

"Holy shit, who are all these people?" Kyle echoed Carlos, speaking half to himself, already wondering how he was going to explain this. Small-Stone and Patrick's group started across the field towards them.

Carlos started laughing. "I don't think I've ever said this before, but I really want to sit in on your after-action report."

"What the hell?" Kyle asked as soon as the four-person group was in earshot.

Nobody answered until they were all standing before him and Carlos.

"My fault," Small-Stone started.

Kyle listened to their story, doing his best to ignore the shit-eating grin on Carlos' face.

"How long before the authorities figure this out?" he asked, at once relieved that the ISS crackdown and Small-Stone's arrest seemed entirely unrelated to anything they had divulged to Small-Stone, but at the same time, trying to come to terms with the hundreds of people that had just seen them translate in.

"We got that covered," Mitch spoke up. "One of the ISS guards told us somebody had to contact their higher ups for a daily check-in. He seems to be a decent guy—I mean, for a goose-stepping ISS thug."

Kyle couldn't have missed the strange look Small-Stone, Patrick, and Allen all gave their giant friend. But it was the news that an ISS trooper had been allowed to report in that felt like a gut punch.

"And you believed him?" He looked at each of them.

"I did," Small-Stone spoke calmly. Kyle already knew the sheriff well enough to believe he was smarter than that. "Same way I believed you. I trusted my gut. And I might add," Small-Stone gave Mitch a harsh look, "he's made that check-in call twice now. Nobody's shown up yet."

"And all these people?" Carlos asked, pointing at the gathered crowd behind the sheriff.

"People willing to go right now." Small-Stone nodded. "They just needed some proof."

"You realize they don't have a choice about that now," Carlos said out loud what Kyle had already been thinking.

"I think I do, but I wouldn't recommend taking that approach with them. They're all feeling the first taste of freedom they've had in a while—it wouldn't go over well."

"I can vouch for that sentiment," Patrick chimed in.

"Take these people back with you," Small-Stone continued, jerking his chin over his shoulder. "Show them what you showed me. Then, if you're willing, let those that think they can convince others to make the trip come back and do so."

Kyle shook his head. "I can't promise that."

"But you would be willing to try?" Small-Stone asked.

"I can try," Kyle agreed after a moment.

Carlos let a chuckle escape in his amusement. "You are so going to get your ass chewed."

His sudden headache was worse than if he hadn't worn the finger shocker during their translation. He glanced at Carlos, wanting to say something, anything, that would wipe the grin off his friend's face. Nothing came to mind and Carlos wasn't wrong. He turned back to face Small-Stone.

"Why do you sound like you aren't coming with us?"

The Sheriff smiled. "I will go, but there are a lot more folks here I can talk to that would probably jump at the chance." He waved at those standing behind him. "These are the people I knew well enough I could convince to walk out here on my word."

"That's a lot of people," Carlos added needlessly.

"A lot of people that don't have a choice at this point." Kyle made the decision easily. "Our ride won't be here for twelve hours." He pointed at Patrick and his crew. "Don't be obvious about it, but I want you between these people and the town. Nobody leaks back."

"We can do that," Patrick concured.

Kyle turned to look at Small-Stone. "Do you have some people that can help out with that?"

Small-Stone nodded. "I do, and I'm sorry, I wasn't trying to get you in trouble, but I've a got a city full of people scared over what comes next. I think almost all of them are going to want to go, given half a chance."

Kyle couldn't argue that point, but Small-Stone still didn't get it. "It's not the numbers that are the issue. It's what the people who stay end up knowing about where you all went."

"That's what he said," Small-Stone nodded in Patrick's direction. "Anyone who asked was told this group was going to try and walk up to Bear Mountain Campground and the cabins up there. No one wants to be here when the word gets out that the inmates have taken over. On that score, the whole town knows we are on borrowed time. There's another internment camp in Deming forty minutes away, and I can't say if officials will or won't show up for one reason or another. Best we can hope for is about another ten days—a whole building crew is due to arrive to finish building out our new trailer park area."

Kyle's headache wasn't going to let up. "Alright, I want to meet this guard who is being so helpful all of a sudden." He nodded at Small-Stone. "I'd like you there for that." He glanced at Carlos. "You too, amigo."

With the ISS presence in Silver City eliminated, the trip into town went quickly. They drove nearly the entire way until Small-Stone directed them down some back alleys and they reached the museum-cum-office where Kyle had been taken on his first visit.

"We should leave your golf cart." Small-Stone pointed through the alley's fence into the backyard. "Park it in there. It's a short walk to the old courthouse that the ISS were using as a base."

"So, he's under guard?" Carlos asked, leaning forward from the backseat. Small-Stone had filled them in on everything he knew about Sergeant Ganz during the drive.

Small Stone waffled his hand back and forth. "I've got someone setting on him, but the truth is, he's hiding as much as we are. Anybody here finds out he's alive—I doubt I'd be able to stop the lynching."

"Hadn't thought of that side of it," Kyle admitted. Special Forces out of Fort Liberty - there was a small chance he might actually know the guy, although the name Ganz hadn't rung any bells for him.

"I know him," Carlos said under his breath as they reached the top of the stairs of the old municipal courthouse, having passed the evidence of the town's firefight during the walk from Small-Stone's house. "Can't say from where."

The stocky, average-height soldier was facing the stairway when they reached the landing. He looked relieved at seeing Small-Stone, and so did the man holding a gun sitting at an adjacent desk.

Small-Stone waved. "Dale, take the chance to stretch your legs and give us a moment, will you?"

"Sure thing." The local stood and gave him and Kyle a close inspection. "These the... uh... friends?"

"Yeah," Small-Stone grunted and then waved towards the stairwell. "Stay close, will you?"

"No problem." The Deputy grinned. "Bastards have actual coffee here."

Small-Stone waited until his man disappeared down the stairs before approaching Ganz.

"Sergeant, this is—"

"Marine Staff Sergeant Delgado, winner of the SOC Sniper competition in twenty-eight." Ganz spoke up with a wave of his hand. "My team finished fourth—behind the French and the Czechs—but hey, we beat the SEALS, so it was a win as far as I was concerned."

"I thought I recognized you." Carlos crossed his arms.

Ganz was quiet for a moment and then shook his head. "So, what? You went insurgent? And you're hiding out inside the enemy's prison? Or did you get interred?"

Carlos offered nothing more than a non-committal shrug in response. "And you went to work for the Nazis?"

"Not hardly," Ganz answered.

Carlos looked in Kyle's direction. "This is your show, brother. I'm going to sit down."

Wonderful. "Let's start with these radio checks you've been doing." Kyle said, thinking he had to start somewhere. He was trying hard to forget that the last ISS soldiers he'd interacted with had come very close to killing him.

*

Whidbey Island, Eden

"Uh... sir? What the hell? Oh damn! Sir?!!"

Hank was almost able to ignore the voice at the edge of his awareness. He'd just eaten a late lunch in Portsmouth before translating back to Eden to meet Kyle and Carlos for their scheduled early morning return to Whidbey Island. His attention was buried in his compad, reading a series of intel reports that were coming in from recon teams all over Chandra. The Kaerin were gearing up in a big way, and it was becoming clearer by the day that they weren't going to wait much longer. He'd heard the concussive boom of the *Party Favor's* arrival, but hadn't even looked up. Seen one translation arrival, you'd seen them all.

"Sir!" The young woman manning the observation station raised her voice an octave. "You're going to want to see this, sir!"

He was almost afraid to look, it was more 'sirs' than he'd heard in one sentence in a long time. Looking up from his compad, he had a short-lived moment of cognitive dissonance before his blood pressure seemed to double.

From the height of the tower, he could see down on much of the *Party Favor's* open deck. It was full of people. A lot of people. There was a flurry of sudden movement as he could see a dozen or more running for the rails. Some of them even made it before emptying their stomachs. It was clear that a lot more hadn't, and gaps appeared as people backed away from others who had fallen to the deck and were thrashing about as the legendary Space Spiders made a return. *Shit.* Kyle's phone number was at the top of his favorites list.

Kyle and Carlos stood near the pilothouse on the deck of the *Party Favor,* watching sheer pandemonium break out post arrival as at least three people fell to the deck screaming and clawing at their clothes. The *Party Favor* had shown up with a grand total of six extra finger buzzers to hand out. The crowd hadn't acted as if they believed the warnings of what they might experience. Kyle was certain they did now.

"I think that's your phone ringing," Carlos deadpanned as he pointed up at the observation deck eighty yards away, just outside the orange safety bollards. "Isn't that Colonel Pretty up there? I got a dollar says it's him."

Kyle waved at Hank as he reached for his compad. "I'm so screwed…"

Carlos couldn't hold it in any longer and started laughing. "Put it on speaker, please!"

Six hours later, Kyle was in New Seattle in the conference room down the hall from Paul Stephens' office. Part of him felt like the school admins had called for a parent conference to discuss a problem child, and the other half of him almost hoped they took that approach.

Stephens hadn't yet said a word to him and sat at the head of the table, reading the report he'd spent most of his time working on since returning. Elisabeth and Hank Pretty flanked him. Jomra sat as still as a totem across from him, and Doc Jensen sat to his left. Probably there to tackle him if he tried to make a run for it.

If he had a friend in the room right now—his wife included—it was probably Jensen. The surly brainiac had just smiled and gave his head a slight shake as he'd walked in.

"Everyone had a chance to read this?" Stephens looked at everyone at the table but him.

"I was given a summation by Colonel Pretty," Jomra spoke up.

"I skipped a lot of it," Jensen admitted. "But I gather the recruitment effort moved at a faster pace than we envisioned?"

"Just a skosh." Elisabeth folded her hands on the table and stared at him, a smile playing at the corner of her mouth.

"That's not a real word." He tried a little charm and added a smile for his wife, but she was having none of it.

"It is a word," Stephens cut in. "But not the one I'd use. What the hell were you thinking? You, of all people, understand the risk involved with visiting Earth."

"I do," Kyle answered. He lifted a finger towards the printed version of his report. "We quarantined the area. Everybody there, with the exception of Small-Stone himself and our own people, made the trip back with us."

"Two hundred and thirty-six?" Jomra asked.

Kyle nodded. "Yes."

"Such numbers are not worth the risks as I understand them." Jomra was logical, if anything, and pragmatic to a maddening degree.

"You are correct," Kyle spoke formally, knowing in Jomra's mind this was an official meeting, and not the let's-yell-at-Kyle-so-it-doesn't-happen-again session that he suspected it was.

"That said," he addressed the entire table, "there's just shy of another twenty-one thousand people there. Small-Stone believes all but one or two thousand would come. He thinks he can have as many as another five-hundred convinced by tomorrow. A lot more—perhaps the majority of those willing to come—within three or four days if we can take a few recruiters back with us."

"From this group that just arrived, you mean?" David Jensen seemed to come awake. "I don't like that part. How would you prevent losing some of them?"

"Two options," Kyle answered. He and Small-Stone had given this a lot of thought. "Hostages… we only take back a few, and only chose people with family or loved ones that remain here."

He could tell from the look on his wife's face how she felt about that. "What's the other option?" Elisabeth asked.

"Same thing his team would have already done," Hank spoke up, "had any of this group tried to run away."

Kyle owed Hank a huge thank you. He hadn't wanted to answer Elisabeth's question. As much as she could understand the need, there were contingencies associated with this effort that she managed to do a good job of pretending didn't exist.

"As it was," he added. "Small-Stone took pains to get an accurate headcount—they all made the trip. Willingly, I might add. Those that remain there aren't going to stay in town forever. Many are already in the process of bugging out with what they can carry. No one wants to be there when the ISS discovers their guard force lost a battle for the town. One more reason we need to move quickly."

"Where are they?" Elisabeth asked.

"I ordered them held at Whidbey's cafeteria," Hank answered. "Not much of a choice out there for a place to hold them. As a group, they were more than taken with the food."

"That speaks for how hungry they are," Doc Jensen joked. "The food out there sucks ass." Even Jomra added a smile in agreement.

"I don't see how you maintain any semblance of control over the knowledge of Eden's existence." Paul Stephens was rubbing at his temples with both hands. "This whole effort is too risky. People just don't disappear from prison."

"It's more of a fenced-in game park than a prison," Kyle answered. "That entire town was controlled by two squads' worth of ISS rent-a-cops. It's a free-range system. As an internee, if you don't want to starve, or happen to be addicted to potable water—you stay put. If you want to wander the roads, you can. No one but the road gangs are going to stop you. And they would. It's one more reason people stay put. The real security is on the outside."

Doc Jensen broke in, "Until the ISS sends a construction team to your town and discovers the inmates are running the asylum." Jensen was proving to be less of a friend in the room than he had hoped.

"I thought you said you skipped most of it." Kyle had to turn to face Jensen.

Jensen's eyebrows crawled up his head. "*That* part kind of stood out to me."

"It's the biggest reason we need to move fast," Kyle admitted. "There won't be any explaining away the ISS absence."

"They've probably got uniforms." Jensen held both hands up in explanation, sounding almost bored.

"I think you just lost us, David." Stephens beat Kyle to the punch.

"You've already got one ISS guard already helping you," Jensen barked, and stood up to go. He made it to the door before turning back to the confused faces.

"Seriously? Get twenty prisoners from town, or hell, some of your knuckle draggers to volunteer to play dress up. Any ISS construction detail would never know the difference, and in the meantime, you can take the time to actually vet these people."

Jensen grinned and leveled a finger at Kyle. "Something you should have done with these first volunteers, young man. I expected better from you." Jensen winked at him and looked like he was about to laugh. "If I can be excused, I've got a raft of shit to do in Portsmouth. We're arranging a Kaerin boat barbeque."

"That might actually work." Hank was leaning down the table, looking at him for an answer.

"Yeah." Kyle shrugged, glancing at the frosted glass door that Doc Jensen had just used. "I should have thought of it myself."

*

Chapter 20

Portsmouth, Chandra

"Biggest difference is your altitude." Doc Jensen pointed at the flight line of Wolverines out the briefing room window. "You want to pickle those things at about five hundred feet for the optimal bomblet dispersion. The launch vector was all programmed into the simulators, so all of you should have a feel for this by now."

Jeremy Ocheltree made a motion of taking notes. He'd practiced this mission two dozen times in the simulator—his whole squadron had. His squadron, as of yesterday. Callie Hurd was heading up the new squadron outside of New Aberdeen in the far north of Caledonia. As everywhere else under Kaerin control—the coast of Norway and its hundreds of miles of protected fjords—were busy building ships. It was clear that the Kaerin were going to try and overwhelm Caledonia's defenses as soon as they thought they had the numbers. The Kaerin naval build up was global in scope, and enemy ships were already pre-positioning between Gibraltar and the Gulf of Finland.

By this time, the Kaerin had to know their strategy wasn't anything close to a secret. In a strange way, the brutal math of it made sense to Jeremy. He knew how many anti-ship missiles his turbo-prop could carry—not enough. He also knew how many missiles a patrol boat could carry—again, not enough, and their reload times were a lot longer than his were. Jeremy had a rough idea of how many shore-based missile batteries they had. The back-of-a-napkin math he and the others had done over beers didn't paint a rosy picture. The Kaerin had a shit-ton of ships, and nothing they'd seen over the last year seemed to indicate that they gave a rat's ass about how many they lost.

The portals on Eden were effective in delivering ordnance, but were much better-suited for stationary targets. If there was a practicable and repeatable way to track a mobile target, get the data back to Portsmouth, port the target data to Eden, program the target coordinates, and then deliver the ordnance in time to hit something besides open water—they hadn't figured it out.

As happy as Jeremy was regarding his promotion, a large part of him wished Callie was still here. E-mail and phone calls weren't going to replace what had developed between them—not by a long-shot. The weight of responsibility he was feeling for his fellow pilots was worse than he had imagined it would be. He felt like he'd already proven himself, in light of what his father had done. That was a different kind of pressure. Worrying about others to this degree was going to take some getting used to.

Dee Tipton sat in the folding chair in front of him. She was methodical and flew like a surgeon managing the operating room. Next to Jeremy was Arto Harjala, wearing that glazed look in his eyes that signaled he was somewhere else and feigning politeness, because after all, this was Dr. David Jensen who was briefing them.

Arto was the best pilot he'd ever met, and that had been very hard for him to admit. Arto, who had become a good friend, had the reflexes of a cat, and vision so good it wasn't fair to the rest of them. In front of Arto was the one person in his squadron he did worry about. Milo'rana was the first Jema pilot in the EDF Air Force, and it wasn't the older man's skills that worried him. It was that the Jema pilot carried his people's single-minded aggressiveness into the cockpit. They'd all joked that should the EDF ever employ kamikaze missions, Milo would be the first to volunteer—and Milo not understanding the humor hadn't disagreed.

He knew how important it was to Jema leadership that they have their own pilots. Milo had been the first who hadn't washed out of the training program. That same political pressure was why he'd been told by Colonel Pretty that Milo was going to fly this first port-strike mission—the first of what promised to be many. They would have started earlier, but it had taken Doc Jensen and the eggheads a minute to engineer a hybrid version of two old weapon systems—the cluster bomb and a phosphorous napalm mix. It was the perfect weapon against the wooden-hulled ships that were stacked bow to stern at nearly every harbor or river estuary in Europe—if it worked.

The majority of the Kaerin marshaling areas were out of range of his aircraft, but that didn't mean they shouldn't burn them in place where they could. Every ship they destroyed before the Kaerin Armada set sail was one less missile they might not have when the day came.

"Any questions?" Jensen's tone didn't lend itself to inquiry.

Jensen turned directly to him. "Lieutenant Ocheltree?"

"We're ready, sir." He snapped his notebook shut to hide his doodles.

*

Jeremy had paid attention in history classes. He knew he was flying the same route British pilots had in WWII, though prior to D-Day, they would have been playing defense against German bombers coming north from the continent.

They had climbed to ten thousand feet. He and Arto were two miles ahead of Dee and Milo, flying southeast towards what one of his six display panels showed as Le Havre, France. He knew the Kaerin had a different name for it, but the mapping software loaded into the Wolverine's computers called it Le Havre. To him, it was just a big Kaerin anchorage of nearly complete ships well within range of their turbo-prop attack planes.

He glanced at his radar screen because he'd been trained to do so. Enemy aircraft were the least of his worries. Kaerin planes, or airboats came in two varieties—a single engine reconnaissance platform, and a big four-engine bomber that could be used as a transport as well. Both were slow, constructed of wood, and possessed zero air-to-air capability. Why would they? It wasn't as if anybody else on this planet had been challenging them for air superiority. At not until now.

They'd all been told to be on the lookout for a new model of Kaerin fighter since he'd started patrolling the channel almost a year ago. He didn't know if that was based on some sort of intelligence or just a commonsense assumption that the enemy would innovate. To date, there'd been nothing to report on that score.

"Tiger Lead to Tiger Flight—scope is clear—no bogeys. Arto—confirm."

"Arto to Tiger Flight—clear scope here."

Jeremy's navigation told him he was thirty miles from the target, and they had no reason to maintain a fuel-efficient altitude when it was so close.

"Dropping to Angels 1, let's not give them dots in the sky to look at."

He waited for the conformations to come back before giving his fly-by-wire system joystick a nudge. The Wolverine didn't hold a candle to the four F-35s that the EDF had, but they now had forty of these aircraft and were turning them out faster than they were pilots. The Wolverine might have been prop-driven, but the modern turbo-charged engine turned out 1600 horsepower, and the composite airframe included a wholly modern avionic and targeting system. Best of all, each Wolverine had seven hard points to mount weapons on its underside. For this mission, each of the six underwing hard points mounted one of Doc Jensen's new Vulcan bombs. Named after the Roman God of Fire, they were designed to burn—just like Kaerin wooden ships.

"Tiger Squadron," he called out on the radio as the dark shape of the northern coast of "France" began to take shape in the distance. "Activate the video trackers—they want good pictures of this."

"No pressure, right?" Dee's voice sounded cynical.

"No pressure," he called back. Right... no one else's father had defected to the Kaerin.

"Bandit at two-nine-zero," Arto's voice broke into his personal musings, and Jeremy mentally kicked himself. He needed to get out of his own head with this shit about his dad, but it seemed to creep into his attention on every mission.

"Confirmed," he answered after a glance at his own radar.

It was a weak signal, well ahead of them and moving away even though the range was decreasing given the disparity in airspeed. The enemy aircraft didn't present a threat and wouldn't have if it was coming right at them. May that long be the case, he thought.

"Tiger Lead to Tiger Flight, we are Charlie-Mike." *Continue Mission*—it was their standard operating procedure to catalog each threat and reassess at every step of their mission. No one believed the enemy was stupid. One way or another, they were going to learn.

They flew on in silence for the next ten minutes until the knuckle of land that made up the stubby peninsula protecting the harbor from the ravages of the channel resolved itself.

"Tiger Flight, come to course heading 215 and drop to five hundred feet."

Jeremy checked out his window. In the morning's light, he could clearly see Arto give him a thumbs up. The Wolverine reminded him of the venerable P-51 Mustang of WWII fame. Its airframe was different, but it had the same basic shape. That was where the similarities ended. The Wolverine had originally been designed and built on Earth with the sole purpose of providing a light ground attack and ISR platform that wouldn't break the bank. It was perfect for what this mission called for, and as the war progressed, he didn't doubt that they'd soon be supporting EDF troops on the ground.

One glance at his navigation monitor told him they had two minutes and forty seconds at this heading before they'd be able to turn into their attack run. He could just make out the anchorage in the distance off his port side wing tip. It was fair to assume that if someone down there was looking—or listening, for that matter—they probably knew they were coming at this point.

His eyes traveled in the familiar clockwise pattern: radar screen, engine readouts, navigation, window—rinse and repeat. The mission plan was programmed into the navigation computer, and technically he could have flown this route in the dark. The GPS network, thanks to Doc Jensen and his minions, was every bit as good here as it had been on Earth. He waited until the small carat on his navigation display representing his aircraft reached the terminal approach turn.

"Tiger Lead for Tiger Flight—turning to attack run on course three-one-five. Video tracking active. We are go for weapons release—package lights are green."

"Tiger Two—Copy all—I'm turning in and have all green as well."

"Tiger Three—Copy all—forty seconds behind you. I'm all green."

"Tiger Four—Copy all and understood. I have green indicators as well. Please leave some for me."

"Will do, Tiger Four. Fly safe everyone."

Jeremy shook his head. He'd felt like he'd needed to say something charismatic or memorable, and "fly safe" didn't cut it. He clearly needed to come up with something better than that. Milo was probably having doubts concerning his flight leader at this point, and he'd no doubt get a great reenactment with an impression from Dee as soon as they got back to base.

The target formation of ships was growing quickly in front of him, and his targeting computer began projecting a red chevron on the small heads-up display at the top of his cockpit's dash. One more circuit check of everything else, and then he put all of his focus on lining up his aircraft with this first row of ships tied together in a double line three hundred yards offshore. Arto, somewhere off to his right, was forgotten. All he cared about were his targets. There was a little bit of wind that tried to nudge his aircraft landward, but he added some rudder, overcorrecting on purpose to allow for the wind to bring him back in line in time.

His mental calculus was off, but only slightly. He ended up toggling the release of three-hundred-pound Vulcan bombs a second late. The targeting computer did the rest, and a pair of bombs fell free, followed by another pair a second and a half later, and the third pair after that. Even with the fly-by-wire system built into his joystick and the relatively small bomb load, his aircraft suddenly felt lighter, and he advanced the throttle to the stops to clear the area.

He resisted the urge to look back, but still caught the flash of an explosion from Arto's attack in the small rearview mirror on the right side of his cockpit. He focused on passing over the rest of the ships, and with his video camera in mind, aimed for the shipyard area at the far end.

"Good hits, Tiger One and Two."

Dee's voice in his helmet brought a smile to his lips. He hadn't missed. That was the trouble with Vulcans—their individual bomblets burned instead of exploding. There wasn't the immediate feedback of watching a missile go in or the massive concussion of five hundred pounds of explosive tritonal in the JDAMs he'd dropped before. It would take a few minutes to assess the damage as the fires caught, and they weren't going to be around for that.

What he first took as a massive water or fuel tank at the waterfront docks caught his attention as he screamed past, pulling back on his stick and arcing up to 1500 feet in a few seconds. Then his brain caught up—the water tank had been floating, tethered to the dock, and rising.

"Tiger Flight, beware—they've got a tethered balloon going up above the docks."

"We see it," Dee came back instantly. "Manned platform hanging beneath the balloon. Milo—mind the wires."

Jeremy knew Dee and Milo's attack run terminated at the harbor just as his had done, and it made no sense for the Kaerin to put unarmed observers in a gondola. They already knew they were being attacked.

"Milo—continue your attack run," he ordered. "Dee, drop your load! Get in there ahead of him and take out the balloon."

"Copy, Tiger One," Dee replied quickly. "Wasting very good bombs."

Jeremy put his aircraft into a slow turn back to land even as he kept climbing to get a view of the balloon. He was surprised at how fast the tethered blimp had gained altitude. When he looked back out to sea for Dee and Milo, at first all he could see were the burning ships from his and Arto's run and the billowing clouds of hot white smoke. His eyes went to movement, and he spotted the black eagle silhouette on Milo's tail as the Jema was approaching his release point. Jeremy tracked ahead of that point and spotted Dee's Wolverine racing ahead.

He was too far away to see her four .50 caliber machine guns fire, but he saw the tracer rounds flash against the dark blue water of the harbor. The Kaerin balloon seemed to convert to an expanding fireball as he watched. Hydrogen—not helium—the back of his brain was telling him. He picked out Dee's aircraft as she turned sharply and climbed out towards him.

Looking back, Milo was climbing out of his attack run and leaving another half dozen ships in the early stages of a conflagration that wasn't going to go out. He let out a breath he hadn't been aware he was holding.

"That's our first kill! Way to go, Dee!" Arto's voice came over the radio. "I got it on camera."

"Well done, Lieutenant Tipton." Milo sounded excited, but as formal as always.

"Tiger Three, to Tiger Flight." Dee's voice came over the circuit, sounding like there was a lot of static. "I'm hit."

"Say again, Three," he called out. "Where are you hit?" He turned his aircraft sharply to bring her Wolverine into view. It was still climbing out, and no smoke was visible.

"In the shoulder," Dee's voice sounded ragged. "Machine guns… in the gondola…right through the canopy. It's barely holding together, and I think they… caught my prop—low power."

"Tiger Two and Four—head for home," Jeremy ordered. "Dee,

slow down as you need to. I'm dropping down to escort you. Can you make it? We've got two patrol boats out in the channel if you need to bail or ditch."

Dee took a moment to answer and the sound of air whistling in her cockpit was audible for a long moment before she was. "Going to try to make it. Autopilot... on. Air speed 160 knots."

Shit. She didn't sound good. It took almost a minute to drop in behind her and slow his approach. He strained to get a look at her through the bubble canopy as he crawled past. The entire front of her flight suit was the wrong color, and the cracks in her canopy made getting a good view difficult.

"Dee, I want you to ditch while you can. Do you have Mother Duck One on your scope? It's fifteen miles ahead."

There was no response and no movement within her cockpit.

"Tiger Lead to Tiger Three—come back."

"Dee?"

He was waiting for a response that he knew wasn't going to come. He swung slowly underneath her and came up on her port side. He got a better look through this side of her canopy. Her helmeted head was slumped down against her chest. Her left shoulder was mostly gone. She'd been hit more than once. The skin of her neck was ghostly white. He flew on next to her for a few minutes before trying the radio again. She didn't stir, and suddenly the realization that he had ordered her to her death hit him like a hammer in the gut.

"Tiger Lead, to Tiger Flight—Dee is gone. Tiger Three is a dead stick. I'm going to stay with her as long as I can. Advise Portsmouth Airfield."

*

Chapter 21

Silver City, Earth

"I have to say, these convicts look better off than most we've seen." Terry Goulet, the ISS-contracted engineer in charge of the just-arrived thirty-vehicle construction convoy, was speaking to Sergeant Ganz. Kyle, acting in the guise of ISS District Administrator Michael Tormina and dressed in khakis, a white button down, and an ISS wind breaker—listened in with feigned interest.

"We like to keep them busy," Ganz answered. "If they want to work growing their own food, we let them."

"Huh." Goulet responded with what might have been surprise. Kyle thought the engineer looked the part of a typical work crew foreman.

"We've passed through a handful of other camps on the way here—a couple of them looked like it was full of scarecrows, I shit you not. I'm not sure why it makes sense to put them all in trailers with all this extra housing just going to waste. You ask me? I think you guys may be on to something."

"I wouldn't share that opinion too widely, Mr. Goulet," Kyle cut in. "ISS headquarters has pretty much told us we've been coddling these prisoners. It's the main reason we are going to start putting them in trailers. When do those arrive, by the way?"

"First tranche is due in three days—forty units." Goulet paused, looking beyond them at several groups of internees who kept their distance across the street. None of them looked too friendly, and despite their preparations for Goulet's construction crew, Kyle just assumed that many of the internees were still armed. He wasn't about to start blaming them for that.

"But don't worry," Goulet continued. "We'll dig the plumbing and water lines for all three hundred pads. I have no idea when the rest will show up—not my rice bowl—but I wouldn't hold my breath. Rumor has it that the NCWA had first dibs on the new trailers, and they are moving a lot of workers to where they need them all across the country."

"How long will your work take?" Ganz asked.

"We've scheduled three weeks." Goulet shrugged. "The area's already been graded, and the mains were laid in last year—so it's mostly a trench-digging and plumbing job for us."

"You'll let us know if we can be of any help?" Kyle asked before waving an arm behind him in the direction of the city center. "Labor's cheap around here."

Goulet offered what Kyle thought of as a forced smile. "I don't doubt that. If you gentlemen will excuse me, I'd like to get my people started."

"By all means," Kyle agreed.

He watched the engineer move away, screaming orders into his walkie-talkie.

"Too much?" Kyle asked.

Ganz shook his head. "Nope, I could almost picture Tormina saying that."

Kyle nodded in Goulet's direction. "He didn't sound like a huge supporter of what's happening here."

"You mean New Mexico?" Ganz turned to look at him.

"Yeah."

"No one outside the ISS who's seen New Mexico likes what's happening here." Ganz answered. "It's one reason the fences are so high at the border. This is one place the Feds aren't going to let the news crews into. Doesn't mean anyone has a mind to lift a finger. The Feds have everyone cowed for now. People want to eat, have jobs, and send their kids to school. In the end, it's all the sheeple really need. It'll take a while longer for them to regrow a spine."

Kyle shook his head. He couldn't help but like Ganz. There was something comforting in the soldier's matter-of-fact manner. "I'm going to start calling you Eeyore."

Ganz grunted in what was probably a laugh. "Call me whatever you want, but I've been out there these last two years. The fighting is all but over. The recent additions to New Mexico are the politically unreliable—or the poor bastards unlucky enough to have been caught up in the actual fighting. Wrong place, wrong time."

"Bound to happen." Kyle nodded. "Leftist revolutions always start eating their own at some point."

Ganz shrugged. "All I'm saying—the ones doing the eating don't have much to worry about at this point."

Yeah... Eeyore fit. Ganz's attitude went beyond taciturn. He was pessimistic to the point Kyle assumed there was some depression at play. He wasn't surprised—he'd gone through some himself after being taken out of the field to do a worthless, supposedly-career-enhancing tour at the Pentagon. The military had seconded Ganz to the ISS as part of some politically motivated scheme to professionalize the ISS. Kyle doubted if Ganz had been asked for his opinion on the transfer.

"Yeah, I get that," Kyle admitted, starting back to the SUV that until very recently had been the personal vehicle of Michael Tormina.

Tormina was now buried five miles out of town, along with the rest of Ganz's former ISS unit. Hopefully no one from the construction crew was going to notice the bullet holes on the far side of the vehicle, or the fact that the driver's window had been shot out.

Ganz played his role well and went so far as to open the back door for Kyle.

"Seriously?"

"Never know who's watching," Ganz replied before walking around to the driver's door. He crawled in, started the engine, and sat there for a long moment. Kyle could sense what was coming.

"Your people figure out what to do with me yet? It's been a week."

"I know," Kyle responded. "For now, we need you to help maintain the image that ISS is still running this place. If it means anything, you've got my vote."

"What the fuck does that mean?" Ganz turned halfway around to face him. "I see the way your guys follow you. You're an officer if I've ever seen one, but half the guys you have with you look like they've seen a war movie or two. Don't get me wrong, they're better trained than the rent-a-cops whose uniforms they're wearing at the moment, but that's mostly a degree of attitude—and probably character. You and I both know they aren't soldiers."

Ganz seemed to pause, giving him a chance to say something. When he didn't, the soldier shook his head. "And where the hell did all those people go? One minute they were headed north into the woods, the next Small-Stone is back here with you and we're all playing make-believe. If you have someplace to go, why delay here with all the playacting?"

"It's complicated," Kyle admitted.

"That part I can believe." Ganz sighed. "But it's not like I have anywhere to go, and it's just a matter of time before one of these people in town decides to shoot me on principle."

"They've all been told what you're doing for them," Kyle explained. He could feel Ganz's frustration. The man wanted to know where he stood—and, more importantly, how it was going to affect his immediate future. He knew Ganz well enough at this point to know Ganz would also want to know why.

This world—any world for that matter—could all use more people who asked that simple question. They needed Ganz to pull this off. Small-Stone and his team of trusted recruiters were taking another five hundred people to Eden this evening, the third such haul in as many days.

"Everyone has been told you're the reason the ISS hasn't fallen on this place like a hammer."

"Wonderful, I'm sure that's going to stop some of the hard cases in town. As I've said repeatedly, sooner or later the real Tormina is going to get an e-mail ordering his dead-and-buried ass to a meeting in Denver or LA—or worse, a video conference. I think maybe you are half full of shit, but you are not a good enough actor to pull that off... sir."

Kyle couldn't help but laugh. Ganz didn't look happy. "Can you give me until tomorrow? I'll try to get approval to show you what we're about."

"It's truly not your call?"

"Like I said, you've got my vote—but no, it's not up to me alone."

Kyle had already started this particular conversation with Hank. Ganz didn't have anything tying him to Earth. His parents were both deceased, and his one brother hadn't spoken to him in over a decade.

Ganz turned back around and put the vehicle in gear. "Fine. Just between us, I'm going to keep on pretending I don't know the sheriff has been sneaking folks out of town. I am not going to be left here holding my dick in a windstorm."

"Good to know." Kyle gave up on fighting his grin. Ganz was a wicked-smart combat veteran—in the best and worst possible way. He didn't miss anything. If they couldn't find a way to trust him and earn some reciprocal trust in turn, they'd probably have to either deal with him here or maroon him on Eden against his will.

"Take me over to Small-Stone's office," Kyle ordered. "I'll need him to take a message back for me. I'll see if I can get you an answer by tomorrow."

"I know he's taking another group out tonight," Ganz added with a shrug. "These folks in town flap their cake holes like troops just out of basic. I also know Small-Stone will be back by morning, so wherever he's going, it can't be that far. Why do you have to wait until tomorrow to get approval to tell me what the fuck is going on?"

Kyle rubbed the bridge of his nose, wanting to just tell the man the truth. But he'd promised. "It's—"

"Complicated? Yeah, you already said that. Fuck me."

*

The next afternoon, Kyle had Ganz drive him and Carlos out to the hayfield north of town. Small-Stone had passed his request along to Hank Pretty and returned with a thumbs up.

Ganz was his usual quiet self until they were almost there. "You two planning on burying me out here?"

Carlos, sitting in the front passenger seat, just laughed. "Nah dude, we could have done that back in town. Not like the citizens of town would have complained."

Ganz grunted in response. "Point."

"We're headed to our base," Kyle spoke up from the back seat. "Take the next right." It was a mile further down the gravel road before they made the turn at the mailbox for the Lemontier ranch.

"Any place along this field works."

Ganz looked out into the overgrown hayfield, parts of which were still spotted with snow, as he rolled to a stop. "Seriously, you made me drive all the way out here? You could have just capped me in the back of the head after you took my sidearm."

Carlos gave a short laugh. "Where's the trust?"

Ganz pointed at the empty field. "I've seen this movie!"

"Let's hop out." Kyle ignored him. "We've got a few minutes before they get here."

It was several minutes later when Ganz spun around and looked back at them. He looked like he'd almost convinced himself he wasn't going to be shot. "Radar coverage is pretty tight. How have you managed to get helos in here?"

Kyle looked over at Carlos and shrugged. "Tell him."

"Seriously?" Carlos faced Ganz and gave his head a shake. "Seems even stranger if I have to say it out loud."

"Don't I know it," Kyle agreed.

Carlos faced an expectant Ganz and scratched at his head. "We've been living on a different planet. We travel back and forth through some sort of quantum cosmic asshole that I'm not going to try and explain. It's where Small-Stone has been taking his people."

Ganz glanced back and forth between the two of them before shaking his head in disgust and managing a short laugh.

"It's true," Kyle intoned. "Not exactly a scientific explanation, but I can't do much better."

Ganz looked disappointed. "I think you're going to have to. I was at least hoping for some militia—maybe a chance at a little redemption doing the only thing I've ever been any good at."

Kyle checked his watch and pointed out into the hayfield. "Any second now. Plug your ears."

Ganz didn't turn around until he had looked back and forth at them a few times, just standing there with their fingers in their ears.

Finally, he turned around and plugged his own. "I hope you jackasses are enjoying this."

Kyle couldn't help but grin, but he was starting to wonder if Hank had changed his mind—or had it changed by others.

BOOM!

Doc Jensen's *Phone Booth* appeared a hundred yards out into the field.

"What the..." Ganz was frozen, fingers still in his ears.

"They didn't send the *Door Knocker*?" Carlos sounded disappointed and jumped the small irrigation ditch at the edge of the field. He started walking towards the jury-rigged *Phone Booth*, which had started as a CONEX shipping container.

"This wasn't exactly on the schedule," Kyle answered Carlos as he followed. "The colonel probably had to sell a favor to Jensen."

Kyle stopped and looked back at Ganz. "You coming?"

"What... what the actual fuck is that?" Guys like Ganz were generally unflappable. He almost looked pale at the moment.

"Parts of a couple of CONEX containers welded together," Kyle answered calmly. "What were you expecting?"

As they got closer, Doc Jensen himself was standing at the open door looking pissed off—but then again, it was a Wednesday. "This the new recruit?"

"We hope so," Kyle called out. "Sergeant Ganz, meet Doctor David Jensen – we call him Doc."

Jensen nodded in greeting towards Ganz and lifted a hand, pointing around the hayfield behind them. "Sergeant, I'll bet these two had you thinking there was a shallow grave waiting for you here. Am I right?"

"Uh… yeah, maybe a little bit."

"Well, we can do better than that." Jensen grinned and turned to Kyle. "Hank thought it best we port into New Seattle. You can get lost in the crowd at the bar and still show him around. Just be back at Whidbey by midnight. The *Door Knocker* is making tonight's run."

"*New* Seattle?" Ganz leaned forward, peeking into the reinforced container.

Kyle held out an arm, indicating the insides of the *Phone Booth*. Someone, he didn't have to guess who, had spray painted "Space Spiders - 2 Danny - 0" on the back wall.

Carlos pulled out finger shockers from a bin mounted to the wall. "You'll need to put this on… like this." He demonstrated the thimble-looking finger cap on his own thumb.

"Why?" Ganz asked.

Carlos pointed at the graffiti. "Because space spiders are real."

The look on Ganz's face was priceless. A second later, everyone but him was laughing.

Two hours later, at a back table in New Seattle's New World Pub, Ganz was finally starting to come to grips with his expanded reality. It had taken the soldier about twenty minutes on Eden before he'd turned to them both and announced, "I'm in."

Kyle had just finished refilling their mugs explaining their overall situation and the existence of Chandra.

"A third world?" Ganz's eyebrows went up.

"You want to get your war on?" Carlos asked. "It's there, every day."

Ganz took another big pull on his beer and set it down carefully, looking between them until he settled on Kyle. "I've told you I'm in. Why do you look like you're readying the other shoe?"

"Truth is, we need you on Earth right now far more than we need another shooter, even a 'real shooter,' to use your words."

"You're going to make me go back? Or hell, let me go back? After showing me all this?"

"We can't make you go back," Kyle started. "I mean we could—we could just dart your ass and send you back at any time. I don't have to explain why Small-Stone needs your help." Kyle leaned forward with his elbows on the table. "Most people I report to would think we are committing some kind of crime to allow you to go back at all. They'd vote for keeping you here, even if it was against your will."

Ganz nodded to himself. "Me being here, getting 'read in' for lack of a better term—your people aren't supportive of the idea?"

"Not all of them," Kyle admitted. "Not at this point. Doc Jensen and a few others trust my judgement. I think I can trust you. Carlos likes you, and *that* list is shorter than my trust list."

"I said he was a good troop," Carlos corrected him with a grin, before turning to Ganz. "I never said I liked you."

Ganz smiled, nodding in understanding. "Noted."

The former ISS soldier sat quietly for a moment, slowly turning his beer mug on the ring-stained table. "I have your word that after Small-Stone gets his people out, I can come here for good?"

"That, we will insist on." Kyle portioned out the last of the pitcher to each of them. "One way or another. But it's not as simple as just Silver City. Small-Stone has a pretty good plan to target some other internment sites in New Mexico, and we don't have anyone who knows how the ISS works better than you. Silver City isn't going to be our only recruitment venture."

Ganz rubbed at his face. "I can't argue with that. But if I'm going to be responsible for keeping Small-Stone and his—what are you calling them… recruiters? — alive, I need to be in charge, and he needs to know it."

Kyle smiled. "You just committed a mistake that I thought a sergeant of your experience would have avoided."

"What?"

"You just volunteered for the job I thought I was going to have to talk you into. Most of it was Small-Stone's idea."

Ganz looked at both of them for a moment before grunting in acceptance. "Fuck me."

*

Chapter 22

Portsmouth, Chandra (5 Months Later)

His first Friday night at home in three weeks and the promise of uninterrupted time with Elisabeth and Sophie was already in danger of slipping away. Even worse, it was Elisabeth's fault and she'd been complaining that he needed some downtime.

"All I'm asking is that you talk to him." Elisabeth reached out without looking, using her mom reflexes to steer Sophie away from her cup of tea on the table between them. The sixteen-month-old toddler goo-gooed, changed directions with a jerk towards him, and came on with a happy squeal. Her hands were outstretched because she just knew someone would be there to catch her.

"Last time I talked to someone in that family," Kyle swooped his daughter up, put her on his knee, and added a gentle bounce, "I think I might have convinced him to defect."

Elisabeth waffled a hand back and forth. "I know you do, but his dad was always a little strange. Jeremy is a good kid. His commanding officer is one of those German F-35 pilots up at Dumfries. A great pilot, I'm sure, but he's a little short on the warm and fuzzy. He has the personality of a compad."

"We do have a chain of command for these things, and I'm more than a few links above him—both of them—for that matter."

The look on Elisabeth's face let him know that he'd just stepped in it. "Would it help if I said it's not my idea?"

"Why would that help?" he responded quickly. "I trust you." He thought he might have regained some goodwill with that one.

"Okay, I tried." Elisabeth threw a hand up. "Give her to me. She needs a bath."

He lifted Sophie off his knee and pulled her close, out of his wife's reach. He knew what she was doing. Elisabeth knew, he knew.

"Alright, whose idea was it?"

"If you're just going to say no, why is that important?"

"I like the kid too," he admitted. Jeremy had been the very first person he'd met on Eden, a jealous, pimple-faced teenager at the time. The fact the same 'kid' now led his own fighter squadron said a lot for how far they'd all come. "Who was it?"

"Amelia Harper."

"Amelia?" He came up with nothing, and the look of disappointment on Elisabeth's face sent his brain into overdrive. "Wait! The boat captain? How is she involved in this?"

Elisabeth's eyes narrowed dangerously. "If you bring up your stupid chain of command again, bath time is on you."

"Fine, I'll talk to him." And he'd been thinking that he might actually get a full weekend without having to deal with other people's shit.

The Kaerin's bi-annual portal season would start in another week—and no one could think of a legitimate reason why the enemy would wait another six months to launch their attacks, especially with the hundreds of warships the Kaerin now had reinforcing far more cargo ships. This was probably going to be the last real weekend they had for a while. Colonel Pretty had ordered everyone to take a break. If they weren't ready at this point, another two or three days wasn't going to make a difference. Elisabeth and Sophie were headed back to Eden as soon as he went back to work on Monday.

"Just talk to him." Elisabeth's voice went up an octave. She'd clearly bought into the idea that this was something he could fix. "He doesn't have anybody else out here to talk to besides the other pilots in his squadron. He doesn't need to be yelled at."

"And I do?" he deadpanned back at her.

"No." She pursed her lips. "You don't. You're right, and I'm sorry." She offered a sly smile. "You just need the occasional reminder that I'm the next link up from you in your so-called chain of command."

He bit down on the smart-ass reply that came to mind. He couldn't help it. It was something having to do with a ball attached to said chain, but he didn't dare finish the thought. He'd been working closely with Jake, Audy, and the rest of the knuckle-draggers on a near continuous basis for the last four months trying to get ready for this fight. In that environment, if it wasn't sarcastic or a demeaning one-liner, things often just went unspoken.

"You look like maybe you have something to say?" Elisabeth waited a moment, smiling expectantly, before slapping both her legs and getting to her feet. "Good. I'll go run her bath."

Kyle plopped his daughter down on his lap as Elisabeth moved out of earshot. Sophie looked at him expectantly, three slobbery fingers in her mouth, ready to be entertained.

"She's not the boss of me," he explained. His daughter didn't look at all convinced.

*

"I'm looking for Lieutenant Ocheltree."

Kyle was wearing shorts, flip-flops, and an old sweatshirt that read Wayne's Bait Shop. His sweat-stained Cubs cap was so old it was starting to come apart on him. Putting it on a few hours ago, he realized that he had very few items of clothing left from his life on Earth. At some point, if it hadn't already happened, an enterprising somebody was going to start collecting the stuff, and it might be worth something at some point.

"Civilians can't be in here." The EDF private manning the front desk of the squadron operations building almost shouted the words as he shot to his feet.

"Relax, private." He reached out and pressed a thumb against the biometric scanner on the security officer's desk. It immediately blinked green, and the private's eyes went the size of saucers as the readout confirmed that indeed he could be here.

"Sir, sorry about that, sir."

"No worries, private." He thumbed his sweatshirt. "Not an official visit. The lieutenant?"

"I believe he's in hangar one." The private pointed back out the door he'd just come through. "I can wheel you down there myself as soon as I get a relief here."

Kyle nodded out the door at the golf cart-looking run-about. "Thanks, I can drive myself."

The young man tilted his head as if unsure of how to respond. "Uh, sir, I'm not supposed to allow anyone outside the squadron officers or their designees drive the carts. Those jer... I mean, people from the Navy base have swiped that one twice."

Kyle nodded knowingly. Eden's economy was close to breaking. They'd been focused on turning out enough supplies and munitions for the coming fight for more than a year. Shortages in strictly non-military items, like civilian run-abouts for instance, were becoming a thing. There were only so many nano-production facilities running, but they didn't create usable goods out of thin air. They required inputs, a lot of them. The last time he'd met up with Jason Morales, the economist-trained manager of Eden's economy had looked in desperate need of sleep.

He dropped the pleasant attitude and stared down the young man, almost feeling sorry for him. "I'll bring it back. If I don't, you can report me to your commanding officer. The same person I'm going to go see. If you want to go above him, you could CC the wing commander, Captain Gerhard Adelmein, up in Dumfries. Above him, the message would probably land on my own desk, and I really hate dealing with administrative bullshit that should have been dealt with six levels before I ever heard of it. It really ruins my day, corporal. On second thought, if I don't bring it back—feel free to shoot me. It would probably be safer for you."

"Uh..." The corporal dug around the front desk for a fast second and held out a set of keys to him. "On second thought, sir, I don't think our policy had people of your rank in mind." The young man pointed out the glass doors. "Head that way until you come to the runway, then go left. Hangar one is at the far end."

"Thanks." Kyle tipped his cap. He knew they, humans that is, couldn't help it. Move into the cave, start a clan, build a city, or God forbid create a military force—the bureaucracy was going to follow like worms after a summer rain. It didn't matter how hard they tried to kill it—and they were all actively trying to kill it at every step. They weren't going to repeat the mistakes of the past, at least not without a fight.

He spotted Jeremy Ocheltree as he drove up. The young lieutenant had his back to him, standing atop the tracks of the hangar's sliding doors and watching a maintenance crew as they climbed around the two aggressive-looking aircraft within. He waved as Jeremy did a double-take at the beach bum character driving his squadron's golf cart.

"Captain Lassiter?" Jeremy came to attention and gave a very sharp salute, considering they were both in civilian clothes.

"Relax Jeremy, this is a social call." He pointed at the aircraft within. "I understood all the pilots were ordered to stand down this weekend. What are you doing working?"

"We are, sir – stood down that is." Jeremy pointed back at the airplanes. "Hardly seemed fair that these guys had to work. I just brought them out some real coffee from town. Seeing how they keep us alive, it seemed the least I could do."

Kyle smiled to himself, knowing full well that there were already a few officers in the EDF that could have figured out how to do less. "Can I get a look? I haven't seen one of the Wolverines up close."

"Sure thing." Jeremy beamed. For a second, the young officer with the worry of the world on his shoulders disappeared, replaced by a proud teenager. "What brings you to the airfield? You guys have another special op in mind?"

More than a few. He grinned. "Always, but I was serious. This is a social call—I'm just delivering an invite."

The crew stopped working as the spotted their commanding officer and a big guy with two days of beard and flip-flops walked up to the plane.

"Guys, this is Captain Lassiter," Jeremy announced. "*The* Captain Lassiter."

"Holy shit, Lieutenant!" One of the mechanics, standing at the aircraft's engine with its cowling removed, came to attention. "If we knew you were tight with royalty, we'd have made sure to tighten *all* the bolts."

"That's Chief Bowman," Jeremy explained. "He's the squadron's official comedian."

Kyle couldn't help but laugh. Apparently, respect for authority and military decorum were as lax in the EDF's airforce as it was in the ground forces. It didn't matter in a military where morale was as high as it was. Everyone knew what was at stake, and it was a rare thing when a problem child wasn't handled at the working level before an officer became aware of the situation.

"At ease, please." Kyle pointed at the plane. "I just wanted a look at one of these things." It reminded him of the P-51 Mustang he'd seen in museums. "I had no idea it was a two-seater."

"It's usually not," Jeremy explained. "At least for us. Back-seaters are the one thing we have fewer of than pilots—hasn't been a priority as the pilot can handle everything. Not like we have an air-to-air threat to worry about yet."

"Give the Kaerin time," Chief Bowman called out as he walked forward, "and they'll get something in the air that can fight."

The chief mechanic slapped the side of the Wolverine underneath a blanket of mission stickers. "The Lieutenant's bird has more missions than any other plane in the EDF. We have to keep this one flying. Even if it means that the cap on the hydraulic fluid reservoir get locked on, isn't that right, Airman Dukes?"

"Yes, Sergeant." An unseen voice called back from the other side of the plane.

The crew chief faced him and smiled. "It's one mistake that won't happen again."

"Is that a bad thing?" Kyle asked Jeremy.

"Could have been, but they found it on the pre-flight check. They're the best."

Kyle didn't doubt it. Chief Bowman was glowing with pride. He glanced at the hash mark stickers and did a quick count. Fifty-eight missions. That was a lot of flying. Others were shaped like ships broken in half.

"Ships sunk?"

"We get a sticker for every five ships," Jeremy answered. "If we can get through the balloons and deliver the incendiaries, they usually burn, and with luck, take a few others with them. But they've learned. They aren't roped together in their anchorages any more, and their machine guns protecting the building sites and harbors are the real deal."

Still, it was a lot of ships that wouldn't be carrying High Blood Warriors across the channel. "I take it you've switched up to the stand-off missiles?"

"We could," Jeremy agreed. "But we've been stockpiling those for when they attack. Those and the rocket pods." Jeremy pointed to a dolly holding an oil drum-sized pod with holes for the rockets sitting a few feet away. "We'll fly with one under each wing—eighteen laser-guided rockets per pod—or with the hellfires, or a variant of the copperhead the egg heads have come with. The targets will be underway by then, and much harder to hit with gravity bombs.

"Up to now, we've just been hitting every shore concentration of building material or men we can, as well as any anchorage in range. Not to mention doing real-time spotting for portal-delivered penetrators. It's something to watch—one of those armored telephone poles just appears at a thousand feet, plunges through the deck of a ship, and just keeps going all the way to the bottom."

"I've seen it." Kyle smiled in agreement. "You fly boys aren't the only ones that have been providing those target packages."

"Then you know they've started keeping their ships in their marshaling areas on the move? Makes trying to take them out with the portal almost not worth the trouble, and if we have to be there providing real-time targeting data, we might as well be raining fire ourselves. They've got a shitload of ships, sir."

"Don't I know it." Kyle was very much aware of how many ships would sail against them.

"Can I ask you something, sir? Just tell me if I'm overstepping." Jeremy steered him away from the plane and the maintenance crew towards the hangar's door.

"Always," Kyle answered.

"When it comes to stopping the Armada," Jeremy smiled, "that's what we call it—our biggest concern in the air is that we have a safe place to land, refuel, and rearm. Portsmouth has to be their primary target, sir. And this base is, well, it's half a mile away from the water, two miles from the harbor and we have a lot of munitions stored here. Any thought of moving some more of it to the secondary fields north of the city?"

"Those have been fully stocked." Kyle nodded. "I get your concern, but we are going to have days of warning as the most distant part of their...armada sets sail." He grinned. "You and your squadron are going to have a target-rich environment for days. My guess is, you'll shoot through this base's stockpile and be operating out of Winchester or Horsham before they have a chance to concentrate their force near here. Don't forget you'll have our navy out there as well, and the Jema manning the shore, praying that some Kaerin make it that far. For what's it's worth, they are pretty damned good with our shore-based batteries—it won't be just you out there—or up there."

"Where are you going to be, sir? If I can ask?"

"Let's just say the Kaerin won't be the only ones playing offense."

Jeremy's face cracked in a huge smile. "That is very good to hear, sir."

"Look, the reason I'm here is that Elisabeth and I wanted to invite you and Lieutenant Hurd to a barbeque tonight. Our place, about seven—or whenever you can get there."

"I appreciate that, sir, but Callie—I mean, Lieutenant Hurd's—leave this weekend keeps her within twenty miles of her squadron's base at New Castle."

Kyle smiled. "I'd double check that if I were you. I'd heard that due to the tempo of air operations, all the squadrons were going to get a few extra days of mandatory stand-down. I think Elisabeth mentioned that she had already made sure Callie had a portal pass to get here." He checked his watch. "She's probably in town already."

Jeremy's face brightened in surprise, but quickly changed to something looking like suspicion. "Did Captain Harper say something to you, sir?"

"She said something to Elisabeth," Kyle admitted. He wasn't about to lie to the kid who was clearly sharp enough to have figured out what was happening. "I have no idea about what, but yes, Elisabeth was concerned enough that she asked me to talk to you."

"I should have never said anything."

"All I know," Kyle replied, "is that Captain Harper voiced an opinion that it wasn't fair or healthy that we've put someone in a position of responsibility so far removed from their chain of command, with no peers around to vent to. That is something I whole-heartedly agree with. I've got several people next to me at almost every turn that I can vent or bitch to."

He laughed a little. "Not that anything ever comes of it, but it does help. Especially when we lose somebody." He'd read Jeremy's own report of the mission that had killed his fellow pilot, as well as the addendum from Jeremy's CO, Captain Adelmein. There hadn't been anything in the file to suggest that Jeremy had done anything wrong.

"Eventually, we all lose people," Kyle finished.

Jeremy looked him in the eye and shook his head. "That's what you think Captain Harper was worried about?"

Kyle shrugged. "Jeremy, I'm flying blind here. I wasn't bullshitting you. I do not have any idea what you discussed with Captain Harper. But Elisabeth is very good at her job, scary good. She says you needed somebody to vent to, unofficially, and out of channels." He thumbed his sweatshirt. "Who am I to argue?"

Jeremy just watched him a moment before nodding. "I got past what happened to Lieutenant Tipton. The rest of the squadron helped with that. A lot. But it wasn't what happened that has me so pissed off - it was why it happened."

"That's a question that rarely gets answered in any way that helps."

"Sir, I know why. It was my dad. He had to give them the ideas for the siege balloons. We've got a Jema pilot. He'd never seen the Kaerin employ something like that. My own dad is helping them! Helping the Kaerin kill my squadron, and God only knows what else."

"Not willingly," Kyle answered. "I don't think anybody thinks that." Kaerin torture tactics weren't a secret. The Jema didn't try to keep those kinds of secrets.

"He went over to them willingly!" Jeremy's anger came to the surface. "I know," Jeremy wiped at his eyes, "intellectually, that I'm not responsible. But I feel like doing something about it. I dream of shooting him, sir! My own father... it's fucked up."

There was no denying the kid was right. Worry over Daryl Ocheltree kept a lot of them up at night. Steps had been taken to make sure no one blamed Jeremy or his mom, and even though they'd been worried about the Jema reaction at one point, it turned out that their ally's code of honor didn't attach a father's glory or shame to a child. After all, every Jema alive had been labeled a traitor by the Kaerin, unworthy of honor for what their parent's generation had done.

"Maybe," Kyle agreed. "But certainly understandable. You can't beat yourself up over it. Your dad's situation is something on all our radars. We'll do what we can, and I'm sure you'll understand when I say—what we have to."

"No worries on that account, sir."

"Drop the sir, Jeremy. This is just me talking."

Jeremy's compad started beeping.

"That's Callie." His face brightened. "She just arrived at the portal station."

Kyle waved at the golf cart. "Let's go. You can drop me at my house on the way, as long as you swing by your ops center first and let the duty station know you have it. I had to threaten a private to let me snag it."

"Good." Jeremy smiled. "Freaking Navy pukes have been eyeing it like it's a new boat."

"We'll see you tonight? Both of you?"

"The invite was for real?"

Kyle had to laugh. "Yes, most definitely for real."

"Tell Elisabeth we'll try." The kid's face turned three colors of crimson before he shrugged in submission. "We haven't seen each other in a couple of months."

Kyle laughed again. "Understood. It's going to be a party though, the last one for a good while."

Chapter 23

Pagasta, Chandra "Izmir"

"We'll sail the length of the Middle Sea." Lord Oont'tal was answering Tima's question but was clearly addressing Lord S'kaeda as he did. "We'll call out each fleet by long-talker as we proceed. By the time we pass the Taram Forts at the straight and refuel, we'll be in three waves of almost three hundred ships each. We'll proceed north to the Irinas Channel and land your troops."

"What of the hundreds of ships in our northern ports?" Prelate S'kaeda asked directly. "Will they time their attack with your own?"

"Some will," Lord Oont'tal replied gravely. "But I assume most will have been destroyed by then. We lose nothing there. They'll be carrying conscripted local clan warriors on deck—and only enough to make them look fully loaded. The enemy's weapons are complex. They can't be endless as well."

That comment struck Tima as pure assumption. Still, he was distracted enough by Lord Oont'tal's respectful and professional demeanor in the face of his rival as he was by anything the short and stocky Kaerin Lord said. On the other side of that exchange, the Prelate was showing Oont'tal the deference he thought he deserved. It was a thin patina of respect between the two men, but everyone present knew how much it was needed.

Tima had worked for days to convince Prelate S'kaeda to make this trip with him. The Prelate's health had continued to decline. For two years, the old man had slept too little, drank too much wine, and eaten sparingly. But he had made this trip and was doing a fine job of helping convince Oont'tal how important he was to all of them.

"We'll make a landing on Irinas," Oont'tal declared, "if I have to drive my ships ashore."

"We'll be ready," S'kaeda returned in his deep voice. "We've been husbanding our air transports. We'll put troops ashore inland and make certain the enemy is kept busy. Three subject war hosts are waiting outside of Kaerus to make the gate trip and attack Eden directly, starting in six days. They will have to decide which world is more important to them. We'll either succeed or fail in this together."

Oont'tal's grin was not a thing that improved his haggard face. "That is as it should be, Prelate." The Lord of Pagasta bowed to his Prelate with a back wholly unused to the action. Inwardly, Tima let out a breath of relief. This whole plan could have been destroyed by either one of these two men's egos, right here at the wharf before Oont'tal's fleet even sailed. So far, so good.

"If I may," Lord Oont'tal gestured down the hills lined with terraces and stone stairs towards the water, "I'd like to show you what your support has built."

Prelate S'kaeda opened both arms towards the water. The harbor was in motion as nearly fifty warships, including a double handful of the newly designed war ships being driven by stern-mounted propellers, circled the bay awaiting the departure of their flagship. The blue dagger of water that reached inland to form the bay was crosshatched with wakes from paddle-wheeled cargo ships and more than a few sail-driven frigates as well.

Prelate S'kaeda beamed with pride. "I can see what we've built, and I have some idea of the numbers of ships that await to join you. Lord Oont'tal, not since our landing have the Kaerin Lords been under such a writ. I know full well the weight of command in this struggle and I am... relieved that it is you I share the burden with. Let this be an example of what we can accomplish as a race under one banner. Victory to the Kaerin."

Tima watched Lord Oont'tal's face for a reaction after that pronouncement. The manner in which Oont'tal seemed to swell with pride, left Tima wondering if the fleet below them would change out their banners from House S'kaeda to that of House Oont'tal?

"Well said, Prelate S'kaeda. We alone can limit our power. Victory to the Kaerin."

The battle-cry was repeated by the gathered crowd, and shouted by a few.

Lord Noka turned to him. "Go, Lord Tima, view the flagship. My old bones would only slow you down."

Lord Oont'tal was not one for drawn-out ceremony. He bowed curtly once more to the Prelate and turned to head down the stairs, Tima struggling to catch up.

"He does not look well." Lord Oont'tal spoke quietly the moment they were out of earshot. "I wouldn't be surprised if you are wearing the iron medallion before this battle is over."

"Travel taxes him," Tima explained needlessly, wondering what Oont'tal was driving at.

Oont'tal glared back at him without breaking his pace down the stairs. "If that event *were* to happen, on your honor, you'll continue with his plans to support my invasion fleet?"

"I should think so. As I'm sure you are aware, it was my plan." Tima answered. Oont'tal was clearly wanting more. "On my honor, you'll have every measure of support we have to give. If we don't expel them from Eden now, I worry that word of their presence will spread even further among the subject clans. We would be foolish to think their image of this world won't spread among the subject clans. Time is not on our side."

"Agreed," Oont'tal barked and seemed to grin at the same moment. "You must be prepared for significant losses. The price we are about to pay will be high. You, more than any of us, cannot lose faith in the Kaerin. I will ensure our success."

Tima was swayed by the man's devotion. He may not like him, nor trust him entirely—but Oont'tal was a Kaerin Lord in the old mold.

"Make certain you are there to see our victory, Lord. Our people will need you."

Oont'tal shook his head gravely. "In the end, none of us may be here to see this victory, Lord Tima. I disagree with you on one point, though. Time *is* on our side."

It struck him as a very strange thing to say, particularly in light of Oont'tal's earlier agreement with him.

"There." Oont'tal stopped him at the last staircase landing above the stone wharf and pointed down at his steel behemoth flagship. "The *Bel'lasstor.*"

The old word had several meanings: "messenger" and "herald" among them. It was more of a nuanced moniker for Oont'tal's flagship than he would have credited the man for.

"Impressive."

Tima didn't have to feign a reaction. The massive steel warship had a structure in the middle that reminded him more of a building with multiple balconies than it did a raised deck. Unlike most of the new construction steel ships, which were built around a single powerful revolving gun turret, the *Bel'lasstor* had two of the double-barreled turrets—one fore and one aft of the bridge structure.

"I'd heard it was larger than any warship we had ever built," he said. "I had no idea it would be so large. Will the structure standing amidships not act as a sail you can't adjust?"

Oont'tal grinned and shook his head. "I forget you are a Gemendi of some renown. You are correct—it's a windbreak that does slow us down, unless we are fortunate enough to have the wind behind us. But the height of the bridge and observation decks allows our lookouts to scan the horizon up to ten kamarks on a clear day. It's worth the cost in extra fire-rock we burn. Still, we can make up to sixteen kamarks an hour, which is faster than most of those side-wheelers out there."

Tima almost caved to the impulse to tell Oont'tal about the enemy's radar. That had been a piece of information that Ocheltree had given up while talking about some ancient war the people of Eden had fought over the Irinas Channel in their past. Like the information he kept from their pilots, he saw no reason to tell Oont'tal that the enemy would see him coming long before he reached the battle. They would either overwhelm the enemy with numbers or they would not.

"And the guns themselves?" Tima asked.

"They fire an exploding projectile of eleven-and-a-half marks. I doubt one of the enemy's guided rocket boats could survive a hit from even one. It is the same gun turret possessed by all of our new ships, though this is the only vessel large enough to carry two. We've added the same model of cannon to many of our older ships as well, though without a turret. The turrets are simply too heavy to be supported by the older timber framing."

For a moment, Tima almost let himself get carried away by Oont'tal's enthusiastic description of the *Bel'lasstor* before the enemy's capabilities came to mind. This was all a giant leap forward in capability for the Kaerin. His prisoner had shared a concept with him not long ago that seemed more than fitting - "necessity was the mother of invention." Ocheltree's words rung more than true. They explained why Kaerin development had stagnated for so long—there had been no challenge, no need to innovate. Now, they were beyond need.

"Lord," he asked. "How do you propose to close with the enemy? They are so fast and nimble, and their guided rockets have a great range."

Oont'tal gestured out to the vessels pacing up and down the length of the bay. "We will lose a great many of our boats getting these guns in range—but the enemy has to come out and meet us or we will land warriors in their lap. It will be a battle of attrition, Lord Tima, not unlike two lines of warriors blasting away at each other across a field until one side is no more." Oont'tal's frown was the first time Tima had seen what could be taken for regret in the man. "Until I see different, I have to believe we have more ships than they have rockets."

Tima couldn't help but nod in agreement. If that weren't the case, then this effort would signal the beginning of the end for the Kaerin. *That* was what he believed. He spotted something on the deck of the *Bel'lasstor* that grabbed at his attention. Even under a tarp, it was hard to miss the arrowhead shape of the ancient Kaerin water craft.

"You are taking the ancient boat with you?"

Oont'tal's grin was feral. "It may have a use after all."

For a moment, Tima's paranoia almost got the better of him. That ancient vessel possessed more than one potential use, and Oont'tal *had* said, "none of us may be here to see the final victory."

No! He stepped on his paranoia. If Oont'tal did indeed have the second beacon, his Gemendi would still have had to make an extraordinary leap to conceptually combine it with the solar-charging attributes of the ancient watercraft. Even then, if all that had indeed occurred, why would the man take it to sea with him?

He realized Oont'tal was watching him, awaiting an answer. "It would be fitting if it found an enemy warship packed with explosives."

"I think you might have missed your calling, Lord Tima," Oont'tal responded with a grin.

He shook his head. "No, the sea is no place for me. Put me on a field with an enemy facing me—that's all I hope for."

"We will get you to *your* battlefield, Lord Tima." Oont'tal offered him a slight bow. Tima took the rare gesture as the signal it was meant to convey. The Lord of Pagasta would accept him as Prelate.

"You honor me, Lord Oont'tal."

"Honor us all." The Kaerin Sea-Lord gestured at his fleet, waiting beyond. "There is a heavy price due, and they will pay it."

*

Portsmouth, Chandra

"They've started moving." Hank looked up from his compad and updated the large map on the screen behind him. Multiple red lines lancing outward into the Mediterranean from every harbor and bay along its coastline converged at Gibraltar and the pair of fortifications the Kaerin referred to as the Taram Forts. From there, no one doubted which direction the enemy fleet would turn. "Satellite reconnaissance confirms the direct observations from several of our recon teams."

Kyle's hangover was one of the worst of his life. The party at his house had turned into an all-night affair, and he'd paid the price yesterday. Thirty-six hours later, he was just now beginning to feel human. They'd all needed it. Frankly, he remembered Hank being in even worse shape than him—but if the Colonel was still feeling the effects, he hid it well.

"Any movement from the northern ports?" Captain Jack Harper, of the *Independence,* sat further down the table and was out of sight unless Kyle leaned way back, which he didn't trust himself to do.

"Not yet," Hank answered. "But troop formations—Kaerin and subject clan both—are in place at anchorages from the Gulf of Finland to Brest. Not to mention the Norwegian, Swedish, and northern Spanish coastlines."

"Ship counts from our remote recon stations are confirming our estimates on their numbers," Hank continued. "A little less than nine hundred vessels coming from the Med, and another three to four hundred from ports farther north. Their newer prop-powered vessels are all in the fleets moving from the Mediterranean."

"Least they won't be hard to find." Captain Harper tried to make light of the situation.

Doc Jensen did even better. "For fuck's sake, with that many ships, they could build a bridge in the channel and just walk their troops across."

Kyle was only half listening. This wasn't a fight that would be over quick or even start all at once. Given the range with which their own ships and planes could begin to attack the Kaerin Armada, it was a battle that was going to last days. He and the guys would start the ball rolling even sooner.

He glared across the table at Jake with a jealousy approaching hate. His friend and stepbrother-in-law—if that was a thing—was nodding along with the briefing, a bag of heavily garlicked Creight jerky in his lap. Jake was tearing into the meat with abandon and occasionally flashed Kyle a smile, knowing that the smell of the stuff made him want to gag on a good day—one of those when he had a functioning stomach lining.

Jake leaned forward quickly, his chair slamming its front legs back to the ground with a bang that produced lights behind Kyle's eyes. "I still think we should just nuke them from orbit—only way to be sure."

Hank, who still looked a little green, stood slowly and walked up behind Jake while the rest of the room was still laughing at the classical military reference. Colonel Pretty reached down, grabbed the bag of jerky, and pushed open the conference room door before tossing the bag out into the hallway.

Evidently, Kyle hadn't been the only one bothered by the smell of the stuff.

"Thank you, Ripley." Hank didn't miss a beat.

Jake nodded in appreciation at the quick reply and then leaned over to Audy. "I'll explain later."

"We will stick with the plan." Hank took a deep breath. "The air strikes will begin in about six hours. No more dropping incendiaries." Hank grinned. "It's a battle of attrition, and that has to start now. F-35s and the Ospreys will get in on it as well. Targeting data will be updated as often as we can, but we are sticking to the plan to target ships we have confirmed are carrying Kaerin warriors. It might mean—" Hank paused. "It *will* mean that when ships get through, we want them carrying local clans to the greatest extent possible. Anything that manages to get through our fence will hopefully be targeted by portal strikes as they are offloading."

"The coastal watch teams are ready," Doc Jensen spoke up. "Our locals have gotten better at calling in coordinates."

"I hope so," Jomra responded. "During the last exercise, there were two simulated strikes on the heads of our own soldiers—not the enemy."

Jensen nodded and gave a shrug that was as close to apologizing as anything Kyle had ever seen from the mad scientist. "There were several lessons learned in that exercise. We've since teamed Edenite volunteers with the coastal watch effort. Whether Junata or Creight, most will have an Edenite with them who will be responsible for collecting and transmitting the coordinates back to Dumfries for immediate translation to Eden and our portals."

Jomra nodded solemnly. "A wise measure."

Hank took a moment to look at each of them in expectation, giving them all an opportunity to jump in. When there was nothing, he walked back towards the head of the table. "Anything we haven't covered?" The room was quiet. "Anybody have anything they want to say?"

They'd all prepped for this fight for a long time. Personally, Kyle was tired of waiting. He could only assume from the somber silence that he wasn't alone in that sentiment. Audy looked to be somewhere else. Jomra was still giving Jensen the eyebrow middle finger. Jake was worrying at something with a toothpick.

"Okay, out of respect to our navy," Hank announced, "I'm going to wrap this up. They've got the longest travel times. If any of us don't know what we're about by now, we've got bigger problems than the hangover most of us are dealing with."

There were a lot of nods around the table. The weekend's insanity hadn't been confined to Kyle's house. Not by a longshot—Portsmouth, the whole EDF, Junata, and Creight population on the island knew what was coming, as well as the expected timing. Everyone knew what the next week would entail.

"We've known the Kaerin would have to try this for over a year." Hank stood with his hands clasped behind his back. "We've prepared for it. We've trained for it. I believe we are ready. Godspeed to you all."

*

Chapter 24

Kyle adjusted the Eden-built sub-machine gun under his Kaerin tunic. The captured Kaerin-produced and reverse-engineered M4 variant they were all going to carry openly were, in his considered opinion, literal pieces of shit. The Kaerin rifles would generally work for a magazine's worth of shots before they started to jam. But even then, the quality of the stamped metal pieces reminded him of the cheap-ass Bulgarian knock-off AKs or SKSs that he'd used in the distant past—without their overall reliability and general indestructible nature.

Kaerin ammunition production was for shit. The lack of standardization of the cartridges and the poor quality of the powder were the main culprits, but many of the Kaerin weapons they'd collected from one skirmish or another over the last six months were so poorly machined they didn't work as anything more than a club. The captured weapons would however help them look like Kaerin.

"My team is ready."

Audy's voice in his ear brought his head up. Audy was standing across the entry ramp leading down into the Whidbey Island portal facility. Standing behind him were two squads of EDF Assault Force soldiers, all dressed up as Kaerin High Bloods. Audy had a red sash tied at an angle across his chest like a bandolier, signaling that he was the Bastelta in charge of this formation.

"Okay!" he shouted, glancing over at Jake, who was kitted out just as he was. Jake stood close by their "prisoners." They were all volunteers, and Junata who had joined the EDF. They were dressed in everything from work overalls to the clothes they'd been wearing when they'd been liberated a year earlier.

The one exception was the shortest of the prisoners. Breda, the former Subject Gemendi, was a Jehavian by birth and had grown up in the city of Kaerus. They'd be relying on him to help them navigate through the Kaerin capital city.

"You guys ready?" Kyle yelled.

"We're ready!" Jake shouted back, clapping Breda on the shoulder. "Just missing the garbage bags and something to spear the trash with."

Kyle rolled his eyes. He was pretty sure that, besides him and Jake, there were probably no more than half a dozen EDF troopers from Eden who got the joke.

"Kyle—this is Jeff." The voice in his ear startled him.

"Go, Jeff."

Jeff was in command of the Quick Reaction Force for this mission. The QRF would also be the guys that came and got them when it was time for the exfil. Jeff and his troops were standing by, ready to drop in where needed with both the *Door Knocker* and the *Party Favor*.

"We just wanted to make sure you guys remembered to charge your sat phones."

"Topped off," Kyle replied. "And I dumped my extra battery into Jake's pack."

Jake had his back turned away, adjusting something under one of the prisoner's tunics. He raised a defiant middle finger in the air without turning to look.

"You guys be careful," Carlos broke in on the same channel. "Would suck to lose you on the first day of the war—even Jake."

"Noted." Kyle smiled as the warning beep started and the doors to the translation chamber below them opened. "Gotta go, door's opening—when we do call...don't be late!"

The portal deposited them on the slopes of a meadowed hillside, surrounded by a stand of trees that was still visible in the fading light. In a first that would be remembered for all time, one of the EDF troopers had come through the quantum tunnel and translated directly into a physical space already occupied by another living being.

In this particular case, by a full a grown cow. The sound of the animal hitting the ground in two wet halves was nothing compared to the scream of terror from the unlucky soldier. It started as a surprised squeal and built into a scream until the man simply passed out from lack of oxygen, falling over into the remains of the cow.

The rest of them stayed on track and quickly set up a perimeter. Once he was sure their arrival in the alpine meadow hadn't alerted anyone, Kyle turned to go back and check on the soldier.

Jake was already there, standing outside the circle of hell, shaking his head as the soldier began stirring and muttering in Chandrian. He came to his knees and tried to focus on his situation.

"I'm alive?" The soldier asked in Chandrian.

"Yes, you're alive," Kyle answered. "Are you okay?"

The Jema shook his head slowly but raised an upturned thumb as a length of intestine slid off his arm. "I'm... I think."

"Well," Jake started. "You all were wondering what to put on your unit patch. I think we have a winner. You just made history, corporal."

Kyle couldn't help but smile as the Jema thought about it for a moment as he wiped his face with his sleeve, only making things worse. Still, the soldier's grin was hard to miss. "They will tell this story for years."

"No doubt," Kyle agreed. "Come on, there's a stream at the bottom of this hill. You can walk your clothes dry—we've got a long hike ahead of us."

The Jema corporal came to his feet just as Audy ran up and slid to a stop on the wet grass. He looked back and forth from the soldier's face to the pile of offal he was standing in.

"I'm sorry for the delay, Kareel." The unlucky Jema was suddenly embarrassed in Audy's presence.

"Yes…" Audy looked like he was about to lose his lunch. "I think you can be forgiven, corporal."

They watched the soldier stagger off down the hill in the company of two his buddies, who kept a close eye on him but otherwise maintained their distance.

"That may be the most horrible thing I have ever seen," Audy said after a moment.

Kyle just nodded in agreement.

"Cow killers?" Jake whispered. "For the unit patch, I mean. That guy will never have to buy another drink in his life."

"Let's go." Kyle started backing away, thinking that he wanted all these guys to have an opportunity for a free drink. For now, they had nearly twenty miles to hike to get down to the nearest road leading into the Kaerin capital city. "Time to move."

*

Pagasta, (Izmir) Chandra

Lord Noka delayed their return to Kaerus. The Prelate wanted to take the opportunity to speak to some of the minor Lords local to Pagasta without the pressure of having Lord Oont'tal hovering nearby. They'd had an update from the fleet during the night. Lord Oont'tal's contingent had already been joined by several other flotillas. It would only grow as it traveled to Irinas, and Tima felt a growing confidence that had been lacking for a long while.

Some of that was due to his talk with Lord Oont'tal, but in the main it was a result of the fact that they were finally dictating the war. From now on, the enemy would be reacting to them. Like a chess game, they could dictate the time and place of the battle and force the enemy to react to them and their sheer numbers.

Tima had begged off attending Lord Noka's meetings. He wanted to put his mind at ease regarding the missing beacon and speak to Gemendi Yun'nay directly. If Lord Oont'tal did have the beacon device with him, Yun'nay would know.

The shipyard foundries of Pagasta were ringing with the heavy stamp of steam-powered hammers on orange-hot plates of steel. Amidst the ever-present shriek of cooling metal and releasing steam, it took him several minutes to locate somebody who looked like they were giving orders.

"Lord Tima!" The Gemendi bowed several times in rapid succession. The man's reaction surprised him, and the only explanation Tima could think of was that this Gemendi must have been of high enough rank to have been present at the previous day's ceremony.

"I'm looking for Gemendi Yun'nay!" he shouted over the ambient noise.

The Gemendi's look of confusion was complete as he glanced around for someone of a higher rank to speak to the Prelate's deputy.

Tima grabbed the man by the elbow and steered him towards the nearest exit, which lowered the noise level to something that wasn't painful. Once outside, he watched as the Gemendi pulled two fingers of cotton from his ears.

"You're looking for Gemendi Prelate Yun'nay, my Lord?" The man yelled as if he was hard of hearing.

"Yes, I just wanted to congratulate him on all he's accomplished."

"Apologies, Lord. He's not here. He sailed with our Lord Oont'tal."

Tima's heart skipped a beat. He could think of several reasons to have somebody of Yun'nay's ability along on such a voyage, and one of them chilled him to the core. Further, Yun'nay hadn't been there during the previous day's ceremony. Oont'tal must have already put the man aboard.

"He sailed on the *Bel'lastor* with your Lord?"

"He did, my Lord."

"I see." Tima strived to remove the terror he was feeling from his face and voice. He forced a warm smile. "I assume Gemendi Yun'nay is there to operate the ancient device personally?"

The Gemendi in front of him bowed his head in what he took as shame mixed with more than a little terror of his own. "My Lord—"

"I assure you, I'm aware of the device. Gemendi Yun'nay and I were working closely on the project together."

"Lord, you would know better than I. We were instructed not to ask. One of my colleagues involved in the breakdown of the ancient boat asked about it—the device, I mean to say. He was… removed."

Tima, his mind racing, took the time to form his words carefully. "We are talking about the small device of ancient design? The size and shape of an elongated small barrel?" He held his hands apart, drawing the shape of the beacon in the air.

"My Lord, I never saw it, I swear. It was crated. But the size you describe, it fits."

"I thank you." Tima nodded his dismissal and watched the man walk back into the foundry, stuffing his ears.

His thoughts swirled faster than he could keep up. He forced himself to take a deep breath as he weighed the facts. Lord Oont'tal was in a position to call forth an ancient enemy and operating under the impression it would mean their salvation. Tima could not imagine another Kaerin Lord who would be more determined to follow through on a decided course of action than Oont'tal.

If they stopped his ship, confronted him, and revealed to him the truth of Kaerin history, Oont'tal wouldn't believe them. To do so, Oont'tal would have to disregard the very foundation of Kaerin history on this world and turn his back on what he thought it meant to be Kaerin. They might as well ask the man to surrender to the Edenites before firing a shot—it simply wouldn't happen. *Universe!* Oont'tal had as much admitted to him what he was going to do: *none of us may live to see our victory.* He'd been listening with the wrong ear.

The only thing thicker than Oont'tal's neck was his pride. The man believed he could defeat the Edenites. Why else would he take the device to war, if not to activate it in the event the Edenites proved too powerful?

Tima dismissed the notion of telling Lord Noka. There was nothing the Prelate could do to stop Oont'tal that wouldn't destroy their chances of winning this fight outright, and it might just force Oont'tal to lift the cover and toggle the button. Tima thought there might be another option, but it wasn't one the Kaerin Prelate would ever countenance. Tima had trouble coming to terms with it himself.

He and Lord Noka would depart Pagasta for Kaerus within the hour. Tima, in a first for him, needed something beyond intelligence from the prisoner Ocheltree. He needed advice.

*

E.N. *Constitution*, off the coast of Normandy, Chandra

Captain Amelia Harper was going over her orders in her head, keeping one eye on the radar plot of the Kaerin vessels as they surged forth from Saint-Malo. The Kaerin base had a Kaerin name, but if she'd ever heard it, she'd dismissed it then and there. The *Constitution* and her crew—strike that, her old crew—knew these waters well. Every one of her original crew were now either captaining their own ship or acting as an XO.

"Captain, Task Force Nest reports that their drone has three hours loiter time," Ensign Pauley spoke from the weapons station where she was monitoring the communications link with the EDF detachment.

The EDF had translated onto the island of Jersey two days before. Amelia's own radar plot was being transmitted from that same drone.

"Understood," she answered. "Thank you, Monica."

This battle would be joined in thirty minutes. If it was still going an hour past that, they were in very big trouble. Saint-Malo had twenty-seven ships loaded with warriors, and it was just one of a dozen harbors on the channel sprouting ships aimed at them. They'd finish here and sprint back to home for reloads.

Why the Kaerin hadn't manned or fortified the island of Jersey like they had Guernsey made no sense to her. But the island was now home to three separate laser-guided Hurricane missile batteries. The

Constitution's job was to stay on the move and paint the targets for the missile batteries who would be firing the Eden-developed anti-ship missile with a five-hundred-pound warhead and a fifteen-mile range. It was a heavier version of the same missile that the aircraft of the EAF would be firing, and it had been specifically designed for this fight.

They didn't need standoff weapons with the ranges in the hundreds of miles, they just needed to stay out of Kaerin cannon range. It meant smaller missiles that could be carried by aircraft, transported by small ships like the *Constitution*, or fired from land-based launchers that could be translated in and set up relatively quickly. It was exactly what the EDF had done on Jersey.

She'd helped test the Hurricanes and had come away impressed by what the high-explosive warhead did to one of their captured Kaerin transport ships—even through the armor they'd added for the test.

It was widely hoped and prayed for that the Hurricanes would deliver a one-shot kill. If they didn't, the EDF guarding the coasts of Caledonia were going to end up engaging the invasion fleet with artillery. Some of that was going to be laser-guided as well—something called copperhead rounds—but it wasn't her rice bowl. Her job was to stop as many ships as possible, as far away from their target as possible.

"Helm, hold station," she ordered. "Stay behind the island. We want them all in open water before we show ourselves and light them up."

"Aye, aye, Ma'am."

Ensign Andrew Calderon was young enough to be her son. He had been released by his parents from finishing high school until this fight was over. It was the same story as Ensign Pauley, but at least she'd started college in New Seattle before enlisting. Everyone was putting their life on hold to secure Chandra, and she counted herself among them.

She couldn't wait to turn the command of the *Constitution* over to someone who actually wanted a career in the Navy. For the last year-and-a-half, she'd been a training stop for young officers, and at this point, heading into a war, she knew most of the young captains in the fleet far better than she wanted to.

"Captain, twenty-six enemy ships have passed the point," Ensign Pauley reported, breaking the silence on the bridge that had held for too long. "Looks like someone miscounted, or one of the enemy had engine trouble."

"Fine," she answered, looking at the radar returns. "What's our best guess as to the length of their train, lead ship to caboose?"

It took her new weapons officer a moment to answer, which bothered her not at all. They'd all learned by now that she valued accuracy over speed any day.

"Between four and five miles, Captain."

She'd guessed five just looking at the radar picture, but that took practice.

"Okay, monitor that spread and update as needed. We'll move out when their tail is twelve miles from Jersey. None of them get to change their mind and go home."

The last hour had crept by, broken only by a call from the Jema-manned battery on Jersey, telling them that they could see the lead ship from their observation point. Amelia had ordered them to wait, and they had.

It wasn't like the EDF missile battery had a choice. They couldn't laze the targets themselves—at least until the range closed considerably. She doubted they were any happier waiting than she was.

Ensign Pauley removed her earbud. It was the signal Amelia had been waiting for.

"Captain, the last enemy ship is now within twelve miles of Jersey's south coast."

"Thank you, Monica. Andrew, time to say hello. Give it a gentle kick in the behind and move us out from behind this rock. Stay on a track east of their line approach—like we are headed back to their base.

Maintain a mile and half separation from their line."

"Aye Captain."

Andrew's throttle was similar to that of jet fighter and and she watched the ensign push the stick forward in a slow steady motion as the *Constitution* dug in at the stern and pushed them all back in their seats while they cut a path out from behind the easternmost point of the island.

"Monica, tell TF Nest we are beginning our run. We should have the first target in—" She paused, checked the radar track, and did the quick math in her head. "Call it five minutes."

She listened in on the outgoing comms, heard the reply, and then waited as their ship slowly came up on a plane. It truly started flying with the growl of the twin diesels, sending a tremor through the insulated bridge.

"What were you listening to before, Monica?" She asked the suddenly quiet bridge.

"Not really sure, Captain." Ensign Pauley answered, not taking her eyes off her targeting display. "A bunch of classical stuff my parents listen to. I used to hate the stuff, but now it's not so bad."

Amelia smiled to herself knowingly. "We get through this, I'll let you pipe it through the bridge."

The distance closed quickly. Two miles away from the lead ship in the Kaerin flotilla, Ensign Pauley brought up three monitors across the top of her dash. Each had a reticle in the middle of it that was slaved to targeting lasers mounted on a gimbal atop their flying bridge.

"Targeting system is in acquisition mode."

Amelia only had to turn her head slightly to see the ensign's monitors. The first two locked in quickly, the third locking onto the lead ship as well. She was impressed by how quickly her ensign broke the lock and reengaged the third ship in the line with just a joystick controlling the lasers.

"*Constitution* to TF Nest, we have three good targets: Alpha, Bravo, and Charlie signals."

The *Constitution* had a fourth laser, operating at a slightly different frequency designated as Delta. In this case, they were only feeding three launchers, and each one would fire missiles slaved to a particular frequency.

"Firing now." The response came back immediately.

Amelia unbelted from her chair and carefully made her way to the gangway leading out to the narrow walkway around their small superstructure. There was a small window facing aft, and it was in line with one of the missile launches. The ball of white smoke and the trailing tail of exhaust were hard to miss. Her curiosity satisfied, she got back into her chair and strapped in before the first missile slammed into the Kaerin's lead ship.

Even at their standoff distance of over two miles, the explosion would have been impossible to miss. The missile had plunged down at the unarmored deck of the troop transport and struck forward of the raised deckhouse in the middle of the three-hundred-foot cargo vessel. The ship's keel snapped a second later, and in moments it was in two halves—both burning and dipping towards the open decks as water flowed in. Amelia stared at the small figures jumping overboard, while in her peripheral vision the other two missiles of the salvo found their respective targets.

By the time she looked up, the second and third targets were still whole, but burning brightly against the dark water and slate gray sky. Smoke from both was being driven to the southeast by the wind, already obscuring their view of the next ships in line.

"Captain, lasers are having trouble getting—"

"Helm," she interrupted her weapons officer. "Bring us back up to flank, cross the bow of the next target, and put us on the upwind side of their formation. I should have thought about the smoke. My mistake."

"Weapons, notify TF Nest that we are repositioning. And if you get a lock on the new lead ship as we are approaching—put one of our own missiles into it." Tests were all fine and good, but they needed to know how effective the Hurricanes were going to be when fired from their own launcher cells.

Ensign Calderon sat forward with his binoculars up. "Enemy is firing, Captain."

The *Constitution* had a damned good long-range optical set up, and she immediately zoomed in on their target ship. Its single cannon was swung to the side, pointing in their direction. The splash of the enemy's first shot skipped harmlessly across the water a half mile off their port side. Most Kaerin transports didn't have the armored turrets that some of the new Kaerin warships sported, but their open-air deck cannons were mounted on some sort of turntable that allowed it to turn. It was certainly a bigger gun than the small three-inch jobs that their captured transports had carried—with a lot more range.

She wasn't worried about being hit at this speed by anything other than a one-in-a-million shot, but she couldn't think of a reason not to make it harder. She could see the enemy deck crew servicing the large muzzle loader cannon. They wouldn't manage more than one shot every two minutes at that rate. By then the *Constitution* would be passing beneath her bow. The ships farther back in line though…

"Monica, get a laser lock on the next three behind this target the moment we pass her bow."

"Aye, Captain."

"Andrew, maintain our course until we are a mile and a half past their line, then come back to a reciprocal course line, maintaining a mile and half separation."

"Aye Captain."

"We have a missile lock," Monica announced.

"Fire."

A Hurricane launched from one of their launchers mounted on their rear deck. The missile whooshed out past them on the port side of the bridge. Unlike those fired from land, this one followed the *Constitution's* own heading, and in seconds hit the side of the transport, just forward of its starboard paddle wheel.

They knew the paddle-wheel housing and the hull to either side of it were the most heavily armored part of a Kaerin ship, and that was before the extra armor that had become a more recent trend. None of it helped. By the time the fireball dissipated, they were close enough to see a hole in the side of the ship that the *Constitution* could have passed through. The near side paddle wheel and its housing were gone. Within the hull breach, the interior of the ship was dark, now emitting a thick oily smoke. At the waterline, the dark channel was flowing into the ship as if through a sluice. A few moments later, the ship was listing noticeably towards them.

"Nice shooting, Weps."

Amelia praised Monica as she kept her eyes glued on the approaching ship, its deck suddenly more visible with the pronounced list. Warriors packed tight on deck were scrambling for the far gunwales, but she knew that would only be a delaying tactic. They screamed by, much closer than they needed to, and she focused on those doomed warriors. Kaerin ships didn't generally carry lifeboats beyond one or two large row boats they used to ferry troops or supplies from shore. She paused and raised her binoculars. They weren't Kaerin warriors, that much was clear—no long swords. Some looked to be wearing nothing but the work overalls most subject races lived in.

She felt bile rising at the bottom of her throat. These were sacrificial lambs sent by the Kaerin who knew they'd have to be dealt with. She could remember the Junata dead around Portsmouth. They'd fought to the end because the Kaerin had control of their families. These poor souls wouldn't be any different. Kaerin or not, they had to be stopped.

The *Constitution* slowed as it separated once again from the staggered line of ships and reestablished its range. "TF Nest, we have three targets locked."

"Firing!" The Jema on the other end of that communication sounded excited.

Three more ships were hit twenty seconds later. On their third salvo, one of the missiles lost its lock and impacted the sea a mile long of the target. It was three salvos later before they had another miss, and by then, the Kaerin fleet was trying to scatter. But against the nimble *Constitution* and its targeting lasers, the old paddle-wheelers didn't stand a chance.

They stayed on station long enough to confirm all the ships had either sunk outright, as at least five of them had seemed to do, or were dead in the water and either sinking or burning—it was usually both. A Cessna knock-off—an EAF spotter plane out of Portsmouth—overflew the area, collecting intel a lot more efficiently from the air than they could do on the water.

"Helm, set our course for patrol station Bravo, no need for re-arm." They'd only fired one of their eight missiles. They could take up their new patrol station forty miles to the northeast, directly between Portsmouth and Le Havre and hopefully do this again.

"Aye, Captain. Course set—ETA eighty-five minutes at this speed."

"Okay, I'm going to be on the radio reporting in." She unclipped from her seat restraints and stood, stretching her back, which was as tight as a drum.

"Captain?" Monica piped up. "Is it weird that we didn't have one secondary explosion? I would have thought we'd have had at least a couple of magazines cook off."

"That black-hulled ship at the end cooked off," Andrew answered Monica directly.

"That was a steam explosion," Amelia explained, before turning to her weapons officer. "I don't think these ships were carrying anything more than enough local clan warriors to force us to burn up a missile at them."

"That's... that's sick, Captain."

"Yes, it is. Welcome to war with the Kaerin." She spoke before turning to go down the steps at the back of the bridge, heading to her tiny captain's birth for a sat-call to her husband. She wanted to know if he'd seen the same thing off the coast of Norway.

*

Chapter 25

Coast of Norway, Chandra

"I wish Arne could have been here for this," Dom Majeski was lying on his stomach, binoculars up to his face, watching the narrow inlet of the fjord south of what was Bergen back on Earth. "This was his country—sort of I mean."

"Ja," Hans grunted next to him. "I wish he was here, period."

"Yes, that too," Dom agreed.

The Kaerin's largest naval facility, on what the EDF considered Norway's west coast, was in a massive natural fjord called Troldhaugen. The Kaerin would have been smarter to have built their largest base in the location of Bergen, ten miles further north. It would have offered their ships several outlets to the North Sea. Troldhaugen's massive fjord was accessed by a single, narrow straight of relatively shallow water at a place called Nordasstraumen – or at least that had been its name on Earth.

"He would have at least been able to read the names on this map," Dom commented from behind his binoculars.

"True," Hans agreed. "What are they doing?"

"They are coming. That iron-clad paddled frigate is leading the way. I count forty-six transports behind it in a line."

"Is there a worse job than being a Kaerin sailor?" Hans asked.

Dom thought about that for a moment. "A subject warrior forced at gunpoint to climb aboard a Kaerin ship?"

"Ja, that would be worse." Hans agreed.

"Maybe those Junata who worked on the sewers underneath Portsmouth," Dom suggested. "That might be just as bad."

Han's laugh was that of a braying donkey. "Yes, that is worse, but at least they could go home at night and have a beer."

"These warriors might get the chance to go home tonight too," Dom added after a moment. "Not like they are going anywhere on those ships."

"Not the sailors on the warship," Hans pointed out.

"No," Dom agreed. "Those guys are screwed."

"Sideways," Hans added.

Twenty minutes later, triggered by a remote Hans held, six large, tethered mines released themselves from their weighted anchors at the bottom of the Nordasstraumen strait. They were buoyant enough that they floated upward towards the keel of the warship passing overhead. Only three managed to contact the hull and explode. The other three detonated a split second later in sympathetic explosions a feet away. Dom and Hans would later swear that the entire ship came out of the water for a moment. It was undoubtedly an optical illusion, but by the time it settled to the bottom of the narrow passageway, the only part of the vessel still visible was the top of its superstructure and radio tower.

They were amazed to see dozens of warriors alive and floating in the water. Some looked like they were good enough swimmers they might make it to the nearby banks. The next ship in line was backing its paddle wheels furiously to avoid running into the stern of the grounded ship blocking the fjord's narrow exit. They almost made it. The crunch and snapping of timber was audible from where they hid five hundred yards away. Behind it were almost four dozen trapped Kaerin transports that wouldn't be going anywhere.

*

Kaerus—Kaerin Capital, Chandra

"Any of this look familiar to you?" Kyle asked Audy in a whisper as he marched next to him.

Following close behind were Audy's hand-picked Jema 'High Bloods' wearing Kaerin uniforms and carrying Kaerin weapons. Behind them, their pretend prisoners marched, including Breda. This was a problem—while Audy was leading the formation, the only person who knew where they were going was forty feet behind him without a radio. Breda, all five feet of him on a good day in boots couldn't have passed for Kaerin.

"No," Audy wasn't one for emotion, but Kyle had no problem picking up on the anxiety in his friend's voice. The city of Kaerus reminded him of a centuries-old European city center, such as Prague or Vienna. Cobblestone streets, brick and stone buildings that topped out at four or five stories. There were a few main streets—broad, tree-lined affairs that were lit by gas lamps on tall poles. One block to either side of those lit thoroughfares, the darkness was near complete. That was all to the good, but it made navigating by memory from maps drawn from satellite photos damned hard.

"No," Audy repeated, turning his head. "Bring him up here."

Him was Breda, and so far, the little guy had gotten them into the city through a secondary gate where the presence of an armed patrol hadn't raised an eyebrow. Audy hadn't had to do anything more than wave his golden stick and show the fake writ he carried for the gate's guards to wave them through.

"Jake, bring the little guy up here."

"I heard him," Jake replied. "On our way."

A moment later, the party of Jema warriors parted way behind him as Jake escorted Breda forward and Audy thankfully slowed their pace. They'd been walking all day and had entered the city an hour before dark.

"This is why I wanted a radio," Breda started. He glared up at Jake.

"I've been telling this one for the last hour that we are on the wrong road."

Jake looked down at the much smaller man. "You said you didn't know where we were!"

"Which way should we be going?" Kyle asked before Breda exploded.

"Reverse direction," Breda hissed. "Go back to the main road—the last one we passed with the lights. We need to go left there, but we also need to get across it. We proceed three, maybe four, city squares, then we bear right onto the angled road on the right. Not a square corner, a thirty-degree road at an angle. It will take us to the base of the hills at the city's northern edge."

"Audy, you get all that?" Kyle asked.

"Yes."

Jake jerked his chin at Breda, "Come on—back in line."

"Just give me a radio," Breda was still complaining when his voice faded.

"We were headed in the right direction," Audy whispered once he'd shouted them all to a halt and led them in a course reversal. "But getting further away with each step. I thought we were already on the angled road."

"Relax," Kyle whispered back. "We busted ass getting here—we're good on time." Just barely, he thought. They'd probably just eaten up most of their buffer, but Audy didn't need to be dwelling on that.

An hour or more later, they arrived at their destination, officially a few minutes behind schedule. They were nearly a mile away from a large stone building that both Audy and Breda agreed held many of the offices of the Kaerin Prelate's military staff. Much closer, the parklike area they had just entered was lined to the south with High Blood barracks buildings, and they had no idea how early the Kaerin got up to start morning PT.

Audy had recognized the HQS building immediately. It was the same one he had entered years before, prior to being escorted through a series of tunnels to the Kaerin gate room somewhere beneath them.

No area on Chandra had gotten as much attention from their

satellite reconnaissance as the narrow greenbelt they stood upon. It separated the outskirts of the city proper from an abrupt line of limestone cliffs.

Kyle took in the three parallel lines of ventilation shafts stretching out into the darkness, each capped with grilled, witch hat shaped covers. There was something under their feet that needed air—a lot of it. This had to be it.

"What else could this be?" Audy asked him, pointing at the closest line of air ducts.

"Yeah." Kyle nodded in agreement and bent his ear down next to the slitted openings on the top of the pipe. He fumbled on the ground and found a marble-sized rock, dropping it between the slats and listening. It was several seconds before he heard it hit something. He tapped the mic pickup on his throat.

"Jake—this is it. Drop the beacons."

Jake just clicked back once. The orders spread quickly as their "prisoners" and "High Blood warriors" worked together to get the caps off the vents. Some unscrewed easily, others needed some encouragement, and there were a lot of them. Kyle was trying to create a mental picture of how many warriors could be stuffed into a chamber as large as the area covered by the acres of ventilation pipes.

*

"What is that noise?" Bastelta Juas'sart yelled down the chamber at his nearest Teark, who was standing thirty feet away, staring up at an air vent over his own head. As honored as they were to be here, they were completely unfamiliar with this place. Its very existence had, for him, until a day earlier, been nothing but rumor.

In a few days' time, an entire Rukii clan war host would be gathered in this chamber to be sent to another world. It was an honor to be asked to the guard chamber on behalf of his clan's host, even if the place made him uncomfortable. He'd been told the skin-itching and hair-raising power in the room would only grow in strength. At the moment, it was but an annoyance. The noise coming through the vents above though, that was new.

"It's coming from above, Bastelta!" His Teark yelled back.

He rubbed at the bridge of his nose. Universe, he knew that already. His ears worked.

"Walk farther down the line." He waved. "Determine if it is happening everywhere."

Juas'sart felt better at having given an order, but was now wondering if the noise warranted the long walk to the opposite end of the chamber and up the steps to the High Blood barracks. He glanced at his Teark, who was doing as he'd been ordered, and then stared overhead at the grilled cover of the air shaft. Nothing.

He took two steps away, when suddenly something solid and heavy landed against the grill closest to him. He jumped in surprise, and the noise was repeated twenty feet away. It happened again until it sounded like someone was hammering at the stone ceiling.

"Teark! Come here!" he shouted as he moved under the closest grill. It was too high for him to reach. He dropped his rifle and removed his weapons belt.

"Lift me up on your shoulders," he directed as his Teark ran up.

The grill was made of some sort of soft metal, but it was thick enough he couldn't spread the wires.

"Pass me up your knife, Red'dast."

He discovered something resting on the far side of the grate long before he'd bent enough of the grill to remove it. Finally, he was able to pull it through. "I have it. Let me down."

"What is it, Bastelta?" His Teark clearly didn't recognize the round metallic ball any more than he did.

"I have no idea, but I'm taking it above. You will lead here until I return."

Teark Red'dast swelled up with pride. "Yes, Bastelta."

*

"Movement! High Blood Squad, inbound from the city side."

Kyle had been observing the egg drops as best he could in the darkness from the middle of the green space. Crowned in the middle to handle runoff, the area sloped downward to both sides. As a group, their force was spread out so that some of Jake's "prisoners" were nearly four hundred yards away and out of sight in the darkness. He would have killed to have some night vision along, but they'd all been overburdened as it was.

"Everyone! Fall back to the north edge, towards the hills!" Kyle shouted, moving himself and trying to put as much darkness between them and whoever was coming. "Then move to the west end where we came in!"

The Kaerin patrol was either closer than he'd thought or just had really good eyesight. Several of their long-guns went off behind him and to his right as he was moving away. The EDF troopers opened up from half a dozen positions. He stopped, looking for a target. Seeing nothing, he kept going until he came up against two troopers following the brush line to the west as they'd been ordered.

"How many more behind you?"

"Audy, and three or four more."

"Right." Kyle slapped them on the shoulder. "I'll wait. You guys go and keep everyone moving back to the road entrance we came from."

He took a knee. "Audy, where are you?" he radioed.

"Almost to you." The response was followed by movement off to his left.

"Targets down," someone reported in over the radio. "Lights coming on in the barracks building."

Audy pulled up to a stop next to him. "They've been alerted. We will not make the egress point."

"No shit—I'm thinking plan B. There's room."

"Room for what?" There was enough light for him see Audy launch an eyebrow in question.

Kyle pulled the sat phone from his pocket and dialed Doc Jensen. He didn't trust anyone else to get this right.

"Why are you calling me?" Jensen was annoyed. *Shocker.* "I'm getting good signals from the beacons—we're ready."

"Hold!" Kyle yelled. "We are sitting on top of them. We need the QRF here, this location—one ship only. It's tight. It needs to translate in, oriented along the tops of the beacons—can you set that up? There's a steep hill along the northern edge. If you hit that, you'll catch us in the shockwave and the landslide might bury the ship."

"Hold on," Jensen said amicably enough, but he immediately heard the man screaming at someone in the background.

It was nearly a minute before Jensen came back on. "I've got a satellite photo—you've got buildings in a line running east-west on the south side of the clearing—correct?"

"That's correct—full of High Bloods that are in the process of waking up."

"Hmm." Jensen's sound effects made him seem distantly interested.

"Tangos, at the west end," someone reported in Kyle's ear just before more gunfire—Kaerin and EDF—erupted to the west.

"Doc?"

"Was that gunfire?" Jensen asked.

"Yes, it was." Kyle bit down on what he wanted to say.

"How tall are those barracks buildings along the south edge of the green space?"

"Two stories, I think."

"Are you sure? Two might work—three stories and there might be rubble high enough that it could damage the *Party Favor's* field emitters."

Kyle thought back—he'd remembered thinking they didn't look very different from the old-school troop barracks from his time in the US Army.

"Two stories."

"We don't dare land on top of the translation chamber, Kyle. It's a cave system underneath—it could collapse, and there's no telling what the quantum potential is in there. My guess, it's already building and might play havoc with my targeting."

"Doc!" Kyle shouted. "Can you do it, or are we back to plan A?"

"Not so fast," Jensen barked back at him. "The computer is chewing on it."

"Copy." Kyle looked at Audy, who was shaking his head in annoyance, an eyebrow giving him the middle finger as more gunfire broke out, most of it sounding like their own.

"Kyle, I'll make it work." Jensen sounded sure of himself. "I'm sending a solution to the QRF on Eden now. Get your people as far north as they can go—chew into that hillside if you can. Call it three minutes, give or take."

"Thanks, Doc!"

Audy grabbed him by the shoulders and turned him to the west the second he ended the call. "We must go! Jake reports a Kaerin firing line is forming up outside their barracks."

"How many?"

"Too many," Audy replied.

"Hold on." Kyle gave Audy a warning as he came to a stop and activated his mic. "All units, *Door Knocker* is inbound this location in two minutes—hug the hill, get as far north as possible. Landing site is the courtyard between the clearing and the enemy barracks. Alert everyone!"

They hadn't issued radios to the soldiers acting as prisoners—they'd already been weighed down with hidden weapons and Kaerin-style satchel bags full of Doc Jensen's beacons. Wearing something that would raise questions, like an earbud for instance, hadn't been worth the risk.

Kyle glanced up the slope of the green space. All he could see above the horizon of the crown was the peak of the barracks' rooftops. There were a lot of EDF soldiers gathered at the west end, exchanging fire with what sounded like a smaller number of Kaerin rifles. That, he wouldn't worry about for the moment. There was no way Jake should be able to see down into the barracks courtyard, unless...

"Jake, where are you?"

"Middle of the strip," Jake radioed back. "Just waiting on them to finish dressing their ranks—"

"Jake, get the hell off that field!"

"Copy all, wait one—" Jake might have yawned. "Seems like we got them out of bed and there's a couple of very angry Tearks down there screaming at their people. It's rifles and jock straps for most of them."

"Jake!"

"I got this, Kyle. We'll come running, don't you worry."

"Fuck!" Kyle didn't know if he'd released his talk button or not, and he didn't care.

"He knows he has some time." Audy sounded as if he was trying to convince himself.

"I know."

"Jensen's message must be portaled to Eden," Audy explained needlessly. "Relayed to the land-ship, coordinates changed from our original extraction point."

"Audy, I know."

"Sergeant Baker here," Kyle's radio went off in his ear. "Enemy at the west gate have been dealt with. Should we move to support Captain Bullock?"

"Negative, Baker. Hold there and get your people as far north as you can. Heads down!"

He'd just finished speaking when Jake and his party opened up with a full salvo from the center of the clearing. There were at least half a dozen guys up there with him. They fired until their magazines ran dry. The loud, sharp cracks of Kaerin rifles split the air. Kyle ducked instinctively as a wall of lead flew well overhead and smacked into the exposed limestone above them.

"Moving!" Jake's voice was clear.

It was perhaps sixty yards from where he and Audy were kneeling at the treeline fronting the cliff face to the middle of the grassy strip. Come on, he thought to himself. Run!

A figure came sprinting out of the darkness and ran past them, sliding to a stop and flopping to his stomach. Another shadowed figure appeared further away and disappeared into the treeline.

Suddenly, the entire horizon was backlit by a momentary flash of light. He'd seen the *Door Knocker* arrive at night before, but he'd never seen it produce anything approaching this strobe-light effect. Then again, he'd never seen in pop into the space occupied by buildings before either. It momentarily backlit half a dozen figures coming towards them, some directly at them. Some threw themselves forward in a headfirst dive just as the darkness descended, only to be replaced in an instant by the bright glow from the *Door Knocker's* spotlights.

The sound wave from the arrival hit them just a split second before the southern horizon blurred from the shockwave—full of turf, dust, a lot of Kaerin warriors, and pieces of their barracks. From his kneeling position, Kyle was bowled over backwards just as he saw the silhouette of a childlike body fly screaming overhead before being caught by the top of a pine tree. He knew it was Breda in an instant. Kyle turned around in time to hear the body falling through successive branches on its way to the ground.

Breda landed hard less than ten feet from them. He was alive and moaning incoherently. The next thing Kyle was aware of was Audy's face above his own and the chainsaw tempo of the *brrrppp* from the *Door Knocker's* mini-guns.

"Are you injured?"

"I'm good." Kyle grunted as he came up on his knees, listening to the mini-guns and the barking *wumpf* from the ship's auto mortars firing.

He pushed his mic. "Jake?"

"I'm here." The sound of his friend's groan in his ear was welcome, but he still wanted to strangle him.

"This is the QRF." Jeff's voice came through his radio. "You guys call for a taxi? The local talent is down, but there's a lot more coming. And, by the way, there is going to be a surcharge for this area of town."

"On our way," Kyle replied. "Send down a couple of trucks—we have wounded." He switched channels. "All units, gather up our people, get a head count."

He paused, shaking his head. This mission had been a must, and it wouldn't be a success until the portal facilities on Eden started translating bombs on top of the beacons they'd dropped. They had to remove the Kaerin's ability to attack Eden directly.

"Move fast, people. Evac team is sending out transports. Use your IR illuminators if you can't move. Everybody goes home."

*

Kaerus, Chandra

His mind afire, Tima made his way across the interior courtyard of the Prelate's estate, trying to come to terms with the only option left to him. Many of the windows he passed were cracked, some were missing. The early morning arrival of the enemy's land-ship had awoken him from just over a kamark away. He'd been dressed and on his way to Lord Noka's chambers when the explosions in the gate caverns had shaken the foundations of the estate, as well as any remaining optimism he'd developed over the last few days.

"They could just as easily have come here!" The Prelate had screamed at him, as if there was something he could or should have done to prevent the attack—or the next one. Lord Noka had raged until he'd nearly driven himself hoarse and waved him away in exhaustion. The reports coming from the first wave of naval attacks out of their northern ports were depressing, but they'd been almost forgotten in the aftermath of the night attack on Kaerus itself.

Their northern feint, as Lord Oont'tal had called it, was turning out to be a failure. So many ships had been destroyed upon leaving their harbors by some sort of floating or underwater bombs, that Lord Oont'tal's mission to force the enemy to use up its missiles seemed foolhardy. Not a single troop ship launched from northern ports had gotten within sight of Irinas, let alone landed troops. Oont'tal's own fleets were still days away from their target, and instead of a battle of exhaustion, the enemy was now, in all likelihood, waiting for them, rested and prepared.

Tima himself was due to leave for the channel coast later in the day, but now found himself headed to the prisoner's quarters. He was still uncertain what he would do when he got there. He was worried Lord Noka would order Ocheltree scourged—killed slowly in an attempt at a futile revenge for what the enemy had been able to inflict on them. There would be no invasion of the enemy's home world. The world gate was inaccessible, buried in tons of rubble and rock.

The result was far more practical. The enemy could now focus their entire strength on Chandra. Tima was beginning to doubt there was anything—short of what Lord Oont'tal held in his quiver—that could stop the Edenites. That particular solution would likely see the Kaerin killed or enslaved right along with them, however.

No one, least of all him, could be certain of who was now in control of Kaerus, the world of his people's birth. The only thing that he knew for certain was that his ancestors had lost a terrible civil war. In victory, he doubted if the victorious Torpun Clans would have mellowed enough to allow an old enemy or a potential adversary to reconstitute its strength. Change was not something any Kaerin welcomed.

It was unlikely that any allies were listening for Oont'tal's beacon, only the same ancient enemy that had beaten the Kaerin in battle and forced their ancestors to run. They had wound up here on Chandra, marooned and surrounded by a world of enemies. He needed to decide who he feared more: the Edenites who would dispossess the Kaerin of everything they had on Chandra, or the people of his homeworld who, if they had not changed, would end them all.

"Daryl," he spoke slowly. English was easy to learn to a basic level, but it seemed to get more complicated the more he learned. "Good day to you." He had to step around a tray of food that was spilled across the floor near the heavy door. "Your morning meal was... not to your liking?"

Ocheltree looked scared. He hadn't seen that look from the prisoner in a long time.

"My guards," Ocheltree answered in explanation. "They seemed upset with me this morning."

Tima nodded knowingly. His own sense of Kaerin invincibility hadn't been the only one shaken this morning. The unthinkable had happened and there was no hiding it. The air above the capital was still full of dust from the massive explosions.

"I'll make certain to have another meal brought. Did you feel the attack here as well?"

"It was an attack?"

"Oh yes, from your people. They came in their land-ship, planted explosives—a lot of explosives as it turns out—above the caverns that... keep? house? What is the word? Our world gate. We don't know how they would manage to do this in such a short time."

"Bombs," the prisoner answered. "Like they did on their attack on Irinas."

"No, the caverns are—were—a hundred or more spans underground. Through solid rock. It is now a massive ravine at the edge of the city."

"The bombs were translated in." The prisoner shrugged. "Underground. If they knew the location, they could adjust for depth."

"I see."

Conversations with Ocheltree never left him feeling confident. This one would be no different. He hadn't considered that, but then would they send a land-ship at all?

"I didn't mean to anger you. I'm not gloating."

"You did not anger me." Tima paused. "What is gloating?"

"Uh... It is similar to being proud of something, maybe too prideful, for too little of an accomplishment, or at someone else's expense or loss."

"I see." Tima nodded. "No, Daryl, I have never seen you gloat."

Ocheltree stared up at the narrow window near his ceiling for a long moment before turning back to him. "If you are losing, is my usefulness to you at an end?"

"No, Daryl." Tima wasn't sure it was the truth or not. "I'm still playing chess with my counterparts among your people—there are many moves left."

Ocheltree regarded him for a long moment before shrugging in what he took for an apology. "They aren't chess players, Lord Tima— you'd have been better off if I'd taught you to play poker."

It took a great deal of control to keep still. He took a deep breath. "What is poker? You said the kings of your world used chess to learn strategy."

"And they do, or did. It's an ancient game. On our home world, as I've explained, many of our countries enacted their foreign policies as if they were playing chess. Strategies were devised over the long term to bring about a diplomatic, or at times, a military solution."

"Thinking ahead, shaping the field? Like in chess?" Tima tried not to raise his voice.

"Just so," Ocheltree nodded.

"Finish what you were saying about your leaders."

"I doubt many of them even play chess," Ocheltree offered. "My own country of origin—the same as the military leaders on Eden— matured at a different time than many of our world's polities, or nations. Our diplomacy throughout our relatively short history could best be characterized by poker—a card game that has nothing in common with chess. It's been theorized that this difference led to many misunderstandings in the dealings we had with other countries. In poker, you can lose with a winning hand, or win with the weaker hand. Poker is gambling. I've heard it said that good players don't play the cards they are dealt—they play the other players at the table."

Tima regarded the prisoner in silence. The man wasn't quite smiling—the nerves in his face didn't work well anymore in that regard—but his eyes were bright in a way he hadn't seen before. Ocheltree had known what he was doing with chess all along.

"Lord Tima, you never asked me if *my* people played a lot of chess."

"A mistake on my part," Tima answered, as the struggle to remain seated waged within him. Intentional or not, the prisoner had… *played him.*

"Lord Tima, I think you have it in you to be a good man. I say this in all honesty—the Kaerin can't win this fight, not over the long term. You are up against an entire world's desire to live free of Kaerin control—or soon will be. I came here to save your lives as much as those of my people."

Tima had already come to terms with this himself. That didn't mean he was prepared to hear this particular truth from an honorless traitor, and his anger burned through.

"Your people's victory will be short-lived, Daryll. There's an enemy coming that will destroy or enslave whoever is left standing on this cursed planet. Kaerin and Edenite alike—I'm not. . . gloating, Daryl. I just wanted you to hear what awaits your people—your son. Your people have driven us to this."

Daryl was quiet for a long moment, looking at him as if to determine whether or not he was lying.

"How?" Ocheltree looked confused. "Why would you condemn your own people out of spite? The Kaerin are losing a war to a people that you could learn to live with."

"*I* perhaps would choose a different way. But it's out of my hands."

Tima kept talking, knowing this conversation would never leave the room. He explained the beacon, the world his people had come from, and who undoubtedly still controlled it. When he had finished, he took pleasure in the fact that he could still scare the prisoner. Not physically—the man had come to terms with his fate. What awaited his people, his family, was a different matter.

Ocheltree was silent for a long time, staring at the scars on his forearm. "I meant what I said, Lord Tima. I think you have it in you to be a good man. A decent human being. Choose the right side."

The right side? Tima wasn't entirely certain one existed. What he was considering doing, in the eyes of many Kaerin would make him no better than this pathetic traitor shivering in front of him.

"Your people listen to our long… radio signals?"

"They do," Ocheltree answered. "I've been honest about that."

Tima stood up slowly. "In a strange way, you have taught me much, Daryl Ocheltree." He held out his hand. "I thank you for that."

The prisoner squirmed to get his legs underneath him before coming to his feet. "Do the right thing." The prisoner's words held strength that his enfeebled, broken grip could not.

Tima's left hand went to the knife at his back. In a flash, he thrust it upward under the ribs and into Ocheltree's heart, lifting him up onto his toes. "I will try."

There was no surprise in Ocheltree's eyes. It was a quick death, more than a traitor deserved. With luck, there were people among the Edenites who understood honor.

*

Chapter 26

Bay of Biscay, Chandra

Lord Oont'tal read the reports of the first few days of the battle with growing dread. Each of the short messages was a product of long-talker communications from the mainland as he and his fleet crawled northward through the great bite off the coast of Lord Atan'tal's holding.

He had not expected any great success on the part of the Kaerin flotillas sailing from northern ports, but he had not thought so many ships could be destroyed without any apparent action on the part of the enemy. The submerged bombs fencing the exit routes from their anchorages were a tactic that made so much sense, he was angry that he had not thought of it himself.

There was also another wrinkle in the enemy's strategy that he found equally surprising. The transports seemed to take priority in the enemy's targeting—they seemed to ignore the few ironclad, new-style warships that had been produced in the north—at least until all the transports they'd been escorting had been destroyed or disabled.

His own fleet, built in more secure ports in the middle sea, possessed enough stern-driven ironclads that the enemy wouldn't be able to ignore them. Across the three flotillas of his own combined fleet, he had nearly eighty new ships—all stern-driven, all with rotating, armored turrets— and they were much faster than the large paddle-driven transports they were escorting. That fact presented him with options.

"Has there been confirmation from Kaerus that the world gate invasion has begun?" he asked no one in particular—there were half a dozen of his best officers around his flagship's map table. Each of them had a team in support.

"Nothing since last night's communications, Lord."

"Send a query. Ask Lord Tima directly." Lord Tima Bre'jana was the only Lord in Kaerus he held in any manner of esteem.

Oont'tal stared at the map spread out across the table, silently calculating the rate at which the new model warships burned through fire-rock. The one thing he missed from the much wider-beamed old style paddle-wheelers were the size of their fire-rock lockers.

He could surge all his newer ships ahead, force a battle, and make the enemy expend its missiles, all the while the transports would continue their approach behind them. Some of the new warships, especially those in the flotilla south of his position in the middle of the fleet, would run the risk of burning through their fire-rock in the process, but at least they'd get into position to do what they'd been built for.

"Also," he called out. "Confirm with Lord Tima that our airboat attacks will commence tomorrow as scheduled."

"Yes, my Lord."

*

Portsmouth, Chandra

"Your plane's ready, sir." Chief Bowman stuck his head through the office door, not caring what or who he was interrupting. In this case, it was just Jeremy and Arto staring at the latest satellite photos taken of enemy airfields across the channel. Dozens of them that, until a few hours ago, had been thought to be farms. Or *only* farms, he reminded himself. Those were real crops planted next to the large barns that had hidden a bomber force.

"How long before the others are prepped, Chief?"

Bowman nodded in Arto's direction. "Lieutenant Harjala's will be ready in another twenty minutes."

"Thanks, Chief. Switch half the planes for air-to-air, and keep the other half loaded out for anti-ship. Once they return from their strike in the morning, switch them all to air-to-air as well—at least until HQ lets us know we can go back to sinking ships."

"Sir, how in the hell did they manage to hide so many planes?" Bowman's question was *the* question of the moment.

"By not flying them, Chief," Jeremy answered. "Our guess is they were delivered in pieces and assembled in those barns. We know about them now though."

"Right, sir." Bowman sounded satisfied. "Navy still going to be able to sink all those ships with you guys up there swatting big bi-planes?'"

"Not our problem, Chief." Jeremy had been wondering the same thing himself.

Arto looked at him across his desk. "We've got enough light left to get an airfield strike in," his friend pointed at two dots on the map, "here or here. Normandy—it's close. They're just lined up, nose to rudder, no balloon cover."

Jeremy stood up. "Let's hit them both—we'll each take one. Hit them while they're on the ground and we won't have to deal with them tomorrow in the air."

Kaerin communications had been intercepted earlier in the day, throwing their attack schedule on the approaching fleet into disarray. The enemy would be launching hundreds of bombers—or worse, troop planes—that no one had realized they had. Bombs were being portaled from Eden, targeted at every big barn in Northern Europe. It was a lot of targets.

"Okay," Arto agreed. "What about Commander Adelmein's rule about no solo runs? Maybe we should coordinate with somebody."

Jeremy shook his head. "He can yell at us later."

Arto laughed. "Technically, we'll only be apart for about five minutes." His hands pantomimed the separation of their two planes.

It was Jeremy's turn to laugh. "In that case, I'm sure Adelmein will be alright with it." Sure, the commander might fly one of their two F-35s, but the guy had a serious stick up his ass when it came to rules.

It had stormed across the North Sea and the Channel most of the day, but the next couple of days promised to be clear. Jeremy held his plane steady at seven thousand feet as the coastline of "France" came into view.

"Dropping down," he radioed, knowing Arto would follow.

One thing they'd learned over the last few months was that the Kaerin operated a robust coast-watcher system that was backed up with long-talkers. Approaching a land-based target totally unawares was getting harder. Given warning, the Kaerin would float their balloons and man their machine gun emplacements.

He pulled out a hundred feet over the channel and then nudged his plane lower until he was forty feet above the water. "Stay low until we separate." He was just making conversation—they'd gone over the plan on the way to their planes. "I have us four minutes out."

"I see the river," Arto said a minute later.

"Take the lead, Arto," he ordered. "You'll break off first."

"Copy."

"Breaking off," Arto called out a couple of minutes later and flared upward to the right. Jeremy had another thirty seconds before he'd go left and eastward.

"Good hunting, Arto. See you at Angels 8 for return to base."

"Angels 8, for RTB." Arto called back.

A small riverside village was his visual reference, and it passed by Jeremy's port wing in a flash. He added power, pulled back on the stick, and climbed quickly to 1500 feet. The sun would set in minutes, but the collection of large hangar-barns were clearly visible about three miles ahead. The big, ungainly bi-plane bomber transports were out in the open, six of them lined up in two rows of three. He could see the dark shapes of warriors running for cover.

He lined up on the first row, suddenly wishing that he'd kept a laser-guided rocket pod loaded. His four .50 caliber machine guns would have to suffice. His approach was all about the angle of attack. The art was in preserving enough altitude to give him sufficient time over the target with his nose angled down, bringing his guns to bear. The challenge with a nose-down attitude was that he'd be flying at the ground.

The crosshairs on his heads-up display lined up with his row of targets, even as the collision avoidance system started beeping in his helmet. He pulled the trigger on his stick and felt his plane shudder as it spit out a storm of lead. One of the transport planes burst into flames, but he was certain he'd scored solid, repeated hits on all three.

He climbed sharply and went right for ten seconds before rolling over and pulling back on his stick to whip into a sharp left-hand turn. Too sharp, he realized as he reacquired his targets. The fire looked to have spread already, and at least two planes in the first row were burning.

He began firing too late on this pass, but he was pretty sure he'd nailed the last plane in the line. He climbed out and turned his plane in time to catch an explosion. Seconds later, they were all burning.

"Arto, this is Lead. Headed back to the channel. Targets destroyed."

"Mine too," Arto crowed. "Dumbasses learned a lesson the hard way."

"I see you, Lead," Arto came back a few minutes later. "Joining you on your port side."

Of course, he sees me. Jeremy shook his head. He'd been trying very hard to spot Arto first.

A mile away from the Kaerin's burning flight line, hidden in a thick stand of trees, First Sergeant Timothy Ganz—formerly of the US Army's 5th Group and the ISS in New Mexico on Earth—spun to face the other members of his strike team. The two Jema warriors looked as pissed off as he was. The three other EDF troopers were too green to realize what had just happened.

"Fucking Air Force!" Ganz wanted to hit something. "Doesn't matter what planet you're on. They're always fucking things up!"

He wanted an answer or a little commiseration from his squad, but the faces looking back at him had nothing. Someone had thought this target was important enough to put his team here via the portal in order to take out those planes.

"Who the fuck were those guys?" he asked.

"Our planes," one of the Jema answered him needlessly. "From Portsmouth."

No shit! "Who's got the fucking sat phone?" Different planet, same old shit.

Two minutes later, he ended the call. "Well, I got bad news and good news. Who wants what first?"

"Bad news," the two Jema warriors answered together, as if they had one brain.

"There's another of these dirt airfields, eight miles that way." He pointed off into the dark. "We have a new target."

"Is that not the good news?" One of the Jema warriors asked. He liked these Jema—they lived to fight, and they were hungry.

Ganz smiled to himself. "Not compared to the fact that two asshole pilots are about to get their asses chewed."

"So, what is good news?" The other Jema's English wasn't nearly as good, and he looked confused. One of the Edenites explained it to him in rapid fire Chandrian—it would at some point be Ganz's third foreign language, but he had a long way to go.

The Jema who had asked for clarification grinned back at him. "That *is* good."

"Won't matter," Ganz mumbled to himself as grabbed up his gear. "The fly-boys will probably have their green fees doubled or some shit." He ignored the confused faces looking back at him and shook his head. "Let's get moving—it's a long walk."

*

EDF Operations Center—Portsmouth, Chandra

Hank was staring at the wall of large screen monitors, kicking himself that the Kaerin had managed to prepare an entire vector of attack without alerting them to it. He stared at the radar tracks of the multi-engine bomber transports taking off across a wide arc running from the Jutland Peninsula to Brest in the extreme northwest of what would always be France in his head. The Kaerin had to have shipped the planes in pieces and assembled them under the cover of what they had taken for barns, on what was clearly farmland that could double as a landing field—or a rough runway. Good enough for one takeoff, which was all they'd been concerned with.

Hank had always assumed something would go wrong and decisions would need to be made on the fly during the invasion—but he'd assumed those moments would arise from some mistake, not from complete surprise. Not so much—EDF attack planes that would have launched their first sorties against the still-distant main Kaerin invasion in a few hours would now be engaged in an air battle to prevent the Kaerin from landing troops inland.

He shook his head in disgust at the display. There was an old saying in the front of his brain: history didn't repeat—but it did rhyme. He doubted if the guy who had coined the phrase had envisioned historical events on one world repeating on another—but here they were. As if the similarity with the Spanish Armada wasn't sufficient, he was now looking at a repeat of an air-war over the "English" Channel.

"Damn, those things are slow." One of the radar techs behind him spoke up. "The computer says one hundred and ten miles an hour. If we don't get them inbound, our planes will have time to re-arm and catch them on the way home."

Hank took his time turning around to address the room. He waved an arm in greeting as he spotted Kyle entering at the back of the room. His staff could be forgiven. Most of those present had been stuck at their monitors for the last six hours and had missed much of the frenzied preparation taking place in the city outside and across all of Caledonia.

"I want everyone's attention here," he called out. "This is not a bombing attack. Those planes double as transports. We have multiple teams on the ground who have confirmed they are loaded with Kaerin warriors. Whether we catch them in the air or not, this is a one-way trip for them.

"You all have friends or family outside. They are armed and preparing themselves as best they can in the event one of those planes manages to unload Kaerin warriors. As you all know, in preparation for the expected naval landings, we've got reaction teams pre-staged at every portal facility on Eden. They are going to get used earlier than we had anticipated, and potentially in a lot more widely varied locations than we had envisioned."

He held a thumb up over his shoulder, indicating the screen behind him. "We will not get all of them in the air." He paused and let that sink in. "We work the problem. It is our job to limit the number of leakers. Communication is key. We've got a lot of EDF already here on the island that were prepped to portal to Eden in response to a potential Kaerin translation event. Those units are now available to you for dispatch—make every effort to determine the size of the Kaerin unit before forwarding the QRF request to Captain Nagy or Lieutenant Delgado." He pointed to his reinforcements off to the side.

"If needed, they'll bring the issue to me. Keep in mind, given the portal, we can dispatch troops a lot faster than we can recollect and re-stage them. We don't want full companies responding to a squad of enemy warriors. Once they portal, it could be hours before we can collect them and get them back to a portal here. If the distance is practical, and there is local transport available here on Caledonia—try to dispatch local resources. Questions?"

One hand went up immediately, and the mouth it was attached to didn't wait to be called on. "Sir, a good portion of our attack planes that were stationed at the airfield in New Castle have been moved to bases farther south. There's going to be a lot of leakers coming from Norway headed to the north."

He knew that the decision had already been made to focus the air defense closer to the shores, where the Kaerin fleet would eventually try to land. Those areas couldn't be fighting airborne Kaerin warriors at the same time.

"We know. The Creight leadership has assured us they will have no issue in evading small groups of Kaerin warriors, and those who can't are a lot better armed than they have ever been before.

"These enemy transports carry ten to twelve personnel each. We aren't looking at what you think of when you picture military transports, and we don't believe they have any parachute capability. They need a place to land, and the terrain up north doesn't have the number of cleared fields or natural meadows that we have down this way. The north can wait—our units up there have been advised to not engage unless they are confidant of success."

He waited a moment for another question. "Godspeed everyone. Let's put our people where they can do the most damage."

Kyle walked up to him and faced the monitor, shaking his head. "Does this remind you—"

"Yes, it does," Hank interrupted. "Been freaking me out all morning."

Kyle grunted in what sounded like acceptance. "Had a professor at the academy that said the historical theory that geography determined history was bullshit… he'd have a hard time explaining this."

It was Hank's turn to grunt in amusement. "Yes, he would." He faced Kyle. "Did you get your scream on?"

Kyle shook his head and grinned. "I think the kid had been yelled at enough by his own chain of command by the time I got there. I ended up telling him to forget about it, that we appreciated the initiative, and to move on. He and his co-pilot did manage to destroy their targets without putting Ganz and his team at risk."

Hank smiled knowingly. "Ganz was a good find. His team managed to hit their secondary target about ninety minutes ago. Caught a dozen transports on the ground."

Kyle agreed with the assessment. In his mind, Ganz was built from the same mold as Jeff Krouse—they'd both probably had mothers that would have been at home among the Jema.

"Lightning One—approaching targets," someone called out behind them.

A blue diamond-shaped carat was crossing the channel north to south at a speed that made the yellow arrows denoting enemy aircraft look like they were stationary.

"That's Adelmein," Hank noted.

"I hope he's a better pilot than he is a leader," Kyle whispered. "He wanted Jeremy and his wingman grounded."

Hank rolled his eyes in disbelief. "You, Jake, Audy, and Jeff have local QRF teams, right?"

"Yeah, Jiro's going to be my chauffeur in a Harpy."

"Keep your head down." He jerked a chin at the screen. "This is going to be some serious-ass pain, but it's a nuisance attack at best. You are going to have bigger fish to fry than chasing down individual Kaerin squads that are going to be shot at by every Junata shopkeeper and farmer they encounter."

"Lightning One—painting targets now." Adelmein's voice sounded bored over the loudspeaker.

"Good luck, Colonel." Kyle shook his hand. "You've got my number."

*

Northern Coast of France, Chandra

Captain Gerhard Adelmein shook his helmeted head in disgust at the radar picture coming back at his flying computer, aka the F-35. He'd been trained to fly this plane—albeit a different variant—for Germany and NATO in an era, and on a planet, where radar signature was literally a matter of life or death. The enemy planes on his screen had the radar cross section of a house, and he was rapidly closing in on an entire neighborhood spread across six miles of air space in no particular order or formation.

If the enemy had radar, his aircraft wouldn't have looked any different. They didn't, of course, which was why his aircraft was loaded out in "beast mode" and carrying sixteen air-to-air to missiles—fourteen radar-guided, and two heat seekers. They were all curious if the shitty radial engines on the Kaerin transports would put out enough of a heat signature to allow the heat-seekers to get a missile lock. He'd soon find out, he thought, as he lined up his first salvo of four radar-guided missiles, assigning a separate target to each.

"First salvo away," he spoke calmly, watching the radar track of the enemy that was just starting to step out over the channel. The Kaerin weren't flying in formation. They'd had no reason to adopt that sort of tactic. He had to reorient the nose of his fighter to paint three more targets that the internal radar receiver within the missiles could see. "Second salvo, three missiles, away."

He was closing too fast. He slowed drastically—his plane's own radar blasting at full power, at its widest possible aperture—to paint the targets. Three of the first four missiles found their targets, and all three of the second salvo scored. He didn't react other than to say a silent prayer for their occupants. This was child's play.

He blew past the line of enemy aircraft three thousand feet over their heads and slowed further. Counting to ten slowly, he turned in a wide, casual arc that put his nose back on their tail. He doubted if they'd even seen him yet, but they knew something was out there hunting them as the Kaerin aircraft started weaving back and forth. At a closing speed closer to 250 knots, rather than the 500 it had been on his initial run, he had more time and could launch his remaining seven radar-guided missiles. They all scored hits, but two of the missiles had gotten crossed and hammered the same unlucky aircraft.

Adelmein had some travel time as he identified two more targets that would serve to test the heat-seekers. He came up directly behind them slowly, trying to get a tone from the seeker head on the missiles mounted on the underside of his wingtips. They'd chirp, recognizing the heat source, but the biplane's engines weren't hot enough to maintain a lock.

"Negative on heat-seeker lock," he reported in. "Wait one, going to try something."

He peeled off, circling back farther behind the target and shed a couple of thousand feet of altitude until he was well beneath the enemy planes. He came up behind the target and went nose up trying to stay slow enough to follow it. He was trying to give the heat-seeker a chance to find the Kaerin's engine heat against the colder background of the high-altitude air above the transport.

It worked almost immediately, and he toggled the missile the second he had a sustained tone. The missile dropped away and streaked out past his nose, straight into one of the starboard engines. The aircraft's wing separated, and in an instant, the aircraft became a tumbling brick.

He nodded in self-congratulation. At least the last one had required some flying on his part. "Inform all squadrons heat-seekers need to be employed from below target, oriented up at colder background air."

Having just taken off, Jeremy listened in on Adelmein's running weapons test. His commanding officer might be a frozen cardboard cutout of a human, but he knew what he was doing in the cockpit. Forty seconds later, Adelmein's missile racks were empty, and he was going to guns. The F-35 carried 220 rounds of 25 mm cannon rounds fired from multi-barreled Gatling-style gun. At three thousand rounds a minute, Adelmein had about four seconds' worth of trigger time.

Jeremy wouldn't have traded any of that heavy armament for all the ammo his four .50 caliber machine guns could put out. He had nearly twenty-one seconds of trigger time before he would run dry, and they'd all been practicing with short bursts.

"Falcon Flight, come to heading of 120. Fifty-eight targets at five thousand feet, just going feet wet. Range 43 miles. Repeat five eight targets." The intercept control office at the Operations center sounded harried.

"You heard them, Falcon Flight. On me." At least there were enough targets to go around.

*

Firth of Forth, Chandra

"This is all your fault." Mitch pointed a finger at Allen. They could all see the trio of four-engine bi-planes approaching out of the east across the North Sea. The distant dots looked to be headed right at them.

"How would this be my fault?" Allen lowered his binoculars.

"You were all fat and happy, crowing about how none of those ships we were supposed to be watching for got through. Couldn't just leave well enough alone, could you? Now we got this shit to deal with."

"We have no idea where they're headed." Patrick felt the same unease as the rest of them but could tell Mitch was spinning up.

"What the hell are they doing then?" Mitch pointed at the squad of Creight warriors they were nominally in charge of. Nominally, because none of them spoke Chandrian, unless you counted Mitch's recently learned ability to order a beer, and only one of the local tribesmen spoke enough English to make the idea of control anything but laughable. "They are acting like they know where they're headed. Stupid bastards can't wait to stick their nose in."

Patrick could see the group of eight tribesmen stowing their kit back in their bags and checking their weapons. He felt like he should do something other than radio the enemy's approach to higher, which he'd already done. Besides their rifles, they had one Javelin-stye missile and shoulder-mounted launcher between them. They'd been issued the thing in the event one of Kaerin paddle-wheelers made it to them.

He'd asked what he was supposed to do in the event more than one ship approached. The answer to "radio for support" hadn't made him feel any better. Still, he'd wanted to do his part. They all did, even Mitch, once he stopped complaining.

Patrick pointed out at the gray water of the bay. "They won't be landing out there, that's for sure. Let's get inland."

*

Chapter 27

Normandy, Chandra

Tima listened to the reports from the communication officers as they reported to him one-by-one. He'd wanted to be here to witness the attack as close as possible. If it succeeded, he'd be ready to lead the S'kaeda host across the channel. He'd traveled from Kaerus by airboat, and the reports of the air attack had started before he'd landed. The long-talker operators, all Gemendi, were housed in separate tents, operating on different channels, and in contact with one each of the airboats leading a wave of attack. They were under writ not to speak to one another. Which, as he listened to another report, was turning out to have been a wise policy.

Their airboats were being blown out of the air out over the channel. Still, he maintained hope that some planes would make landfall on the other side. There were a lot of them, and the last group he'd received a report on had been destroyed with the coast of Irinas in sight. They were getting closer.

"Will that be all, Lord?" The Gemendi bowed his head and waited.

Would it? He would not have a better opportunity than now to at least open up communications. He'd already lied to Lord Oont'tal. The maritime invasion force was proceeding as planned in the belief that the Edenites had their hands full on their own cursed planet.

His falsehood had been a short message transmitted by a radio.

World gate invasion has begun. If the Edenites had managed to intercept the message, they'd probably be confused.

"No, Gemendi," he answered. "Take me to your long-talker. I have my own report to make."

"Of course, my Lord."

He stopped the Gemendi twenty paces from the tent with a tall central pole jutting twenty feet above the canvas. "Are the new long-talkers," he'd almost used the word *radio*, "an improvement over distance?"

"They are, my Lord."

"You will wait here." He removed his small leather-bound notepad. "I have my own codebook. Let no one approach. The Prelate needs to be assured of his privacy."

"As you command, my Lord."

The new Kaerin long-talkers operated in what Ocheltree had described to him as the short-wave, but its power was four-fold that of the older models and a tenth the size.

He didn't alter the channel—the operator had told him the airboats on the other end were no longer responding and assumed destroyed.

He took a deep breath, trying to formulate the words in a language he'd learned from a dead man.

"Edenites, this is Kaerin Lord Tima Bre'jana. I would speak to you."

*

Outside of Winchester, Chandra

"Kyle, you have been ordered back to the bird by Colonel Pretty. Immediately," Jiro's voice over his helmet's speakers surprised him. "I'm spinning up the engines."

They'd responded to reports of a Kaerin plane landing in the fields south of Winchester. The enemy plane hadn't so much as landed, as it had bounced to a stop. Its nose was buried in the soft ground of a wheat field. There'd only been four Kaerin warriors alive inside, and only one of them in any condition to put up a fight.

They'd had to deal with that. The other three were being given medical aid a few feet away from him, and he doubted if they'd make it. The entire squad had been mashed up into the front of the aircraft. Most had been impaled on broken and splintered pieces of the wooden fuselage.

All in all, it had been a false alarm, but he knew from listening to the radio reports—and even some distant gunfire—that some of the planes were managing to offload warriors.

"On my way," he called back.

Once in the air, he plugged his sat phone into his head set and dialed Hank.

"Lucky we weren't in a fight, sir. What gives?"

"The portal at Portsmouth is waiting for you and Audy. He's inbound as well. Get to Eden ASAP. I'll be sending you both back across the channel here via portal once I have the coordinates. Their Prelate-in-waiting just reached out via radio. Speaks rudimentary if basic English. I think we can assume he's been working with or on Ocheltree. He wants to talk."

"No shit?"

"No shit," Pretty answered. "He described a location—we think it's not far from where Ganz and his team have gone to ground. I've got them moving to the location. He'll provide the coordinates if it looks legit."

"Ganz understand the sensitivities involved?" Kyle asked.

"You mean does he know not to shoot on sight, or let the two Jema he's got with him do it for him? Yes, he does," Pretty replied. "I was very clear. I also told him that if it looked like a trap, avoid contact and report when safe. Kyle, if there's a chance he's legit—"

"I understand." Kyle's heart sped up a notch. Finally, something that might give them some understanding of their enemy beyond third-party assessments.

"Kyle—nothing but unconditional surrender. Invasion fleet turns around immediately. I've already spoken to Jomra and the Junata council. We are all in agreement. Nothing gets negotiated. Set up a commo plan with him if he's not looking to defect and intends to go back."

"You want to give him that option?" Kyle wasn't surprised at Pretty's order regarding a communications plan—they'd both attended the same tactical intelligence training classes. Rather, it was the idea that a Kaerin leader would take this step, with the intention or expectation of being allowed to return, that he had trouble getting his head around.

"The Kaerin leadership just opened up a channel of communication that would see him executed—so if it's not a trap—I think we let him go back."

Kyle could see the familiar landmarks passing by the small window. "Understood, Colonel, I agree. I'm ten minutes out from Portsmouth."

*

Normandy, Chandra

Tima's driver was a High Blood Dadu barely out of his regional training center. The young warrior seemed far more affected by the brooding presence of the large Kaerin Teark seated next to him in the front seat than by the Prelate-in-waiting in the backseat.

He found the dynamic illuminating. Power was recognized from the vector it was delivered. If the young Dadu offered offense to him, punishment would flow from Teark Wag'gast, and the young warrior knew it.

Tima was unable to see a path in which these two warriors survived the next few hours. Their deaths would hold no meaning weighed against the Kaerin who had been killed in the last two days, or against those who would die in the coming days. He kept that thought close to his heart—he had to. What he intended on doing might save countless Kaerin in the long run, but it would likely bring an end to their control of this world. How that occurred may very well be decided today. It all depended on the Edenites.

Given the disparity in numbers between Kaerin and subject clans, he had long believed his people's control over Chandra was untenable over the long-term, unless the subject clans could be culled. That had been his proffered solution to Lord S'kaeda. Tima had no doubt his logical solution in this regard—his will to do what was needed—was the primary reason the Prelate had elevated him.

The Edenites had upended everything, and he had come to doubt his people's ability to defeat an enemy that could appear anywhere on Chandra at will. He'd long wondered if Ocheltree's appearance had been engineered by the Edenites for the purpose of sowing doubt. If so, they were far more like the Kaerin than they imagined. In the end, it was his will to survive, not him personally, but for the Kaerin people that had brought him to this point.

"Take this next turn," he ordered from the back. "Towards the abandoned landing field."

"Yes, my Lord." The Dadu's voice sounded nervous, and Tima could see the hint of a smile on the Teark's face.

Teark Wag'gast turned to look over the back of his seat. "My Lord, are we expecting someone?"

"We are," he answered truthfully. "On your oaths, I trust that neither of you will share what you see here."

"Of course, my Lord." The Teark answered immediately and then faced the driver with what could only be a growl.

"Yes, my Lord. I understand," The Dadu answered quickly and looked to his Teark for some sign of approval. The veteran just let out a sigh and shook his head.

Tima felt the weight of his handgun at his waist. It was modeled after one of the Edenite weapons that had been returned by the Strema survivors two years ago. *Irony*, that was the English word that Ocheltree would have used to describe his planned actions—or perhaps *tragedy*. Then again, the prisoner Ocheltree had possessed a singular ability and naivete to believe that violence never solved anything. Tima knew better. Violence, and the will to enact it, was in the end the only thing that truly ever decided anything.

The abandoned airfield had been targeted for the last year by the Edenites. Its surface had been too recognizable for what it was, as were the scouting airboats that had launched from here. Even now, as their vehicle paralleled the landing strip, he could see the ridges of rain-filled bomb craters in the distance.

"Proceed up to the end of the landing field," he ordered.

"Yes, my Lord."

Soon after, the driver brought the car to a hard stop, out of either nervousness or a desire to do exactly as he'd been instructed.

"Dadus." The Teark was annoyed. "Do you think it's a good idea to park on the landing strip? Perhaps we could move off to the side, closer to where there is some cover."

"Yes, Teark. Apologies."

Tima remained silent until the car rolled to a gentle stop at the edge of the landing strip. "This will suffice. I'm going to stretch my legs. You should both do the same."

The area was entirely abandoned. A kamark or two from the channel, the steady breeze moved the almost-white grass growing up between the cracks in the landing surface strip.

Tima recognized the process underway. Within ten years, perhaps less, this place would be unrecognizable. Nature would reclaim its sovereignty. It wasn't too far removed from what would happen to the Kaerin if the Edenites succeeded in defeating them. His biggest fear was the subject clans. Armed with Edenite weapons, in their numbers, they would roll over the Kaerin in revenge born of centuries of repression. Tima had no choice but to trust the words of a dead traitor.

"My people wouldn't allow that to happen." Ocheltree had died believing that.

Tima walked to the front of the vehicle, wondering if the enemy was here already and watching. If he were in their place, he would need a sign. A gesture of trust. He pulled the weapon that Ocheltree had told him was referred to as a Glock, racked the slide, and shot the Teark in the back of the head. The Dadu stood there for a moment just staring at him.

"What is your name, Dadu?"

"Ket'tal, my… Lord."

"I will make certain your name will be entered next to Teark Wag'gast as serving with honor."

"My Lord?"

Another shot rang out and echoed across the expanse of the open area. Several birds were scared up from the tall grass growing beyond the edge of the landing strip. He hadn't even noticed the echo of the first shot.

"Forgive me," he whispered into the wind.

He held the handgun over his head and placed it on the hood of the vehicle. Turning back around, he took a seat on the front bumper and waited.

"Well, that's one way to deliver your bona fides," Sergeant Ganz whispered to himself.

The Jema probably wouldn't understand him, and the two Edenite soldiers were too green to know what he was talking about. They'd been watching the Kaerin since the car had driven past where they were hiding and disgorged its occupants less than a hundred yards away.

"Sergeant? What do we do now?" One of the Edenites—Cliff, or Charlie—spoke up. The two corporals were interchangeable to him at this point, though both had performed well enough over the last twenty-four hours that he'd mentally committed to learning which one was which.

He turned to look at all four of his charges. "Can I trust you guys to put your lasers on him, without shooting him?"

"No," The Jema Teark wearing the chevrons of an EDF Sergeant answered immediately.

Ganz felt himself smile as he nodded in appreciation at the remark. "Okay, points for honesty."

He wasn't entirely up on the whole of Jema history, but he'd seen enough during his short time on Eden and Chandra to realize that the Jema had been slave soldiers of some type to the Kaerin. He'd be pissed off as well.

Ganz pointed at the EDF Corporal he was almost certain was Cliff. The blonde, surfer-looking kid seemed to have the best language ability across Chandrian and English of any of the soldiers with him.

"Cliff, I want you with me to translate."

"I'm Charlie." The corporal grinned. "But can do."

"Whatever." They hadn't slept in nearly thirty hours, and, thanks to the Air Force, had been on the move almost the entire time. He could barely remember his own name at this point. "Okay, other Cliff, you stay back here with Jad—"

"Jad'osta," the stocky Kaerin who had admitted he couldn't be trusted not to shoot the Kaerin finished for him.

"Stay with Jad'osta—he's in charge." He faced both of them. "Do *not* shoot this guy. We've got officers, Kyle and Aud... Audy-something on their way to speak to him. If they say we can service the dude, we will. But until then, we just maintain security."

He pointed at the remaining Jema that reminded him of an oversized martial version of the dad character from American Pie—Damn, he was definitely getting squirrelly and just wanted this to be over so he could get some sleep.

"You are with me and... Charlie. Can I trust you not to put holes in this character?"

The Jema rubbed at his own eyes while nodding. Ganz was relieved to see the Jema soldiers could get worn down as well. "I am Bal'lorista. I am with you."

Ganz thumbed the magnification on his rifle scope to maximum and confirmed the handgun was still on the chitty-chitty-bang-bang-looking car's hood.

"Ok, Charlie and Ballerina—you are on me."

The Jema shook his head. "My Edenite friends call me Bal."

Ganz shouldered his rifle, half expecting to have to deliver a few warning shots if the Kaerin spooked and ran. "Why didn't you just say so?"

"It is amusing to watch you struggle with our names, and this place. You are newly arrived?"

"What gave it away?"

The Kaerin sitting against the bumper of his vehicle saw them as soon as they stood up in the brush. He didn't run, just stood up slowly and watched them expectantly.

Ganz lowered his rifle to a ready position and moved forward. "We walk down the runway, right? Leave our friends a clean line of sight to his forehead."

"Yes, Sergeant," Charlie answered. Bal gave a nod and walked up onto the cracked concrete surface on his other side.

"Bad guy is wearing one of those swords we were warned about," Ganz thought out loud.

"He will not lay his sword down." Bal made it sound like it was something he should already know, and Lord knew it probably was. Something else to add to the list.

"Charlie, when we get close enough to talk, first thing you tell the bastard is that I'm in charge, and if he so much as touches the hilt of that blade, he's dead."

The Kaerin watched them with open curiosity as they approached. Charlie spoke the words that Ganz had to assume were a fair representation of his request.

The Kaerin looked at him and nodded once slowly. "I will do as you ask." He spoke slowly but clearly in English. "I thought to be met with more… senior persons."

Eat a dick. "They are on their way." Ganz answered, still surprised the Kaerin knew any English at all. "Charlie, keep him covered. Bal, collect that sidearm."

Ganz pulled his sat phone from his waist bag and dialed the number he'd been given. He'd half expected Kyle to pick up. The voice on the other end identified herself as Portsmouth Portal Control."

"This is Sergeant Ganz. I was given this number to call. The HVT is here, location is secure. We are at the extreme north end, bay side of the old runway. Rest of the runway is clear and usable for insertion."

"Confirmed. I will portal coordinates to Eden." The voice responded coolly and hung up.

"Your airboat will land here?" The Kaerin sounded surprised. "It will be seen—our warriors will respond."

Ganz jerked a chin down the length of the runway. "Let us worry about that."

"What is H-V-T?" the Kaerin defector, or whatever the hell he was, asked. "One of your acronames?"

"Acronym." Bal spoke up for the first time. "They use them often. High Value Target."

The Kaerin regarded Bal closely. "You are of the Jema?"

"I am." Bal growled.

"And you are a Kaerin Lord," Ganz interrupted as he watched the Jema Sergeant tense. "Right now, that doesn't mean shit—do you understand me? As far as I know, we haven't killed any Kaerin Lords yet, but that's only because we haven't had the chance."

The Kaerin looked from Bal back to him and nodded. "I agree. At this moment, our ranks would not seem to—"

Crack! Boom! The echoing sound of the translation arrival of the *Phone Booth* caused them all to start. Ganz took his time enjoying the look of shock on their prisoner's face. Truth was, he'd been expecting the concussive noise, and he'd still nearly shit his own pants as the arrival had occurred directly behind him. He made sure Bal and Charlie had the guy covered before turning to look.

Kyle Lassiter and the Jema officer, Audrey... or something like that, who he hadn't met yet, stepped out onto the pavement from inside the same CONEX container-looking thing he'd first used to go to Eden. From a distance and dressed out in tactical gear, they looked like matching bookends. Things must have gotten interesting back in Portsmouth with all the planes they'd seen flying overhead to have involved the officers. Then again, he knew he was still thinking in Earth terms and drawing from his experience in the US Army. Things couldn't be more different here.

"And these are?" The Kaerin stood up a little straighter and pointed behind Ganz with his chin.

"How 'bout we let them introduce themselves," Ganz replied.

The prisoner made a shooing motion down the runway with both hands. "Should we not go to them?"

"Fuck that," Ganz replied. "We're tired. Your little stunt has had us running all morning. Besides, they're officers. They can probably use the exercise." The HVT seemed shocked by the fact that all three of the low-ranking soldiers guarding him shared a smile and a laugh.

"How about you lead the negotiations?" Kyle suggested when they were still forty yards out.

"You wish to shock him?"

"Yeah, he hears me—he'll have one more reason to think the Jema traded one overseer for another. I'll kick in enough to let him know he's dealing with a united front."

"This still makes no sense to us," Audy replied. "A Kaerin Lord would not defect... that is the word?"

"Yes."

"A Kaerin would sooner die than submit before losing everything in battle. I still believe that they can be made to surrender, as does Jomra—but as I said, they haven't lost yet. This is something else."

Kyle could hear the EDF planes overhead in the distance flying air cover and keeping their eyes open. The *Door Knocker* and a company of EDF soldiers were a phone call away. "I can't imagine what he thinks he's going to be able to say."

"Nor can I." Audy shrugged and then pointed forward as they drew closer. "You speak with the Sergeant. I will pretend to be Jake and have a dick-measuring contest with the Kaerin. I doubt he expects to talk to a Jema here."

Kyle controlled his laughter. "Channeling Jake? What could go wrong?"

"Sergeant Ganz!" Kyle called out. "Thank you. Pull your team back and maintain a perimeter. We've got friendly air cover on channel eleven and backup a phone call away, at the same number you just used to get us here."

"Yes, sir," Ganz replied before pointing at the two dead Kaerin in front of the vehicle. "The HVT took out his escorts himself."

"Their deaths are my responsibility." The Kaerin talked directly to Audy, who had taken a position directly in front of the man who their intel said would be the next Kaerin Prelate.

"I am Lord Tima Bre'jana, of Landing." The prisoner squared his shoulders as he spoke directly to Audy, in English. "I have been recognized as the official heir to Prelate Noka S'kaeda. You may be our enemy, but I am honored to be speaking to your leadership. Are you the Edenite known as Colonel Pretty? Or Perhaps Captain Lassiter?"

Kyle lifted his hand. "I'm Captain Lassiter."

The Kaerin gave him a nod and dismissed him just as quickly, turning back to Audy.

Kyle could see the grin playing on Audy's face. There was no doubting this scene of Audy confronting the Kaerin Prelate would be shared across the robust Jema RUMINT channel over the next few days. His friend was enjoying the moment.

"I am Audrin'ochal of the Jema. What is it you wish to say here?"

The Kaerin recovered quickly, but the look of annoyance that had run across his features would have been hard to miss.

"A Jema?" The Kaerin turned away from Audy and faced Kyle. "You would have me believe the Jema hold such a position of command in your alliance?"

"I don't care what you believe," Kyle answered. "But the Jema's role is a fact. We don't make a move on this world without their support or guidance. Audrin'ochal is who you should be taking to here and now."

"I see." The Kaerin nodded to himself after a long moment. "You don't know what to think after I make contact with you. You try to… what is the word? Confuse me?"

Kyle couldn't help but be impressed by the guy's reasoning. He still wanted Audy to bitch slap the Kaerin, but knew his friend wouldn't.

"Why did you initiate communications with us?" Audy asked.

"You know of our history?" The Kaerin switched to back to Chandrian, and Kyle was somewhat surprised he understood it. "That we are not from this world originally?"

"Speak English." Audy shook his head. "Ocheltree has clearly taught you well. My people have no desire to desire to speak a slave's language."

Frustration, maybe some anger, flashed across Lord Tima's face, but the Kaerin was savvy enough to stamp down on it in short order. Kyle hoped his helmet-mounted camera was picking it all up, because everyone was going to want to see this replay.

"He did," the Kaerin responded in English after a long moment of wrestling with his emotions. It was clear, this was a guy unused to having explain himself. The asshole had probably never heard the word no. "I'm sorry to say he was killed on the orders of the Prelate in response to your attack on our world gate."

Audy shrugged. "He was a traitor."

"Yes, he was. Yet it was the discussions I had with him that had led to me taking this step of communicating with you."

"I believe I asked *why* you have done so," Audy pushed.

A strange look passed over the Kaerin's face. "May I first ask you a question, Audrin'ochal? From another who calls this world home."

"You may ask a question."

Kyle had never seen this attitude of superiority from Audy—not from any high-ranking Jema. Audy was doing a great job of keeping the Kaerin pissed off.

"You have lived among the Edenites for several years—have you learned the game of chess?"

It was Audy's turn to be surprised. Kyle couldn't fault him—he couldn't imagine where the Kaerin was going with this.

"I know of the game," Audy answered. "I have not played it."

"Interesting…" The Kaerin responded, nodding to himself. Kyle remembered the briefing from Amona, who had worked closely with this guy: *Lord Tima served as a warrior, but he's a Gemendi at heart.*

"And the game puker? Have you played that?"

"If you are trying to say 'poker,' then yes," Audy answered, getting frustrated himself. "We play often."

The Kaerin smirked and looked back and forth at both of them. "Traitor or not, you can take comfort that Daryl Ocheltree did not forget where he was from. He kept what honor was left to him. It appears I've been playing the wrong game."

"His family will hear of this," Audy replied. "Now, answer my question. Why are you here?"

"You spoke of slaves a moment ago. That is why I am here. Our host at sea—one of our Lords, to be more accurate—possesses a beacon of ancient Kaerin design. It will… illuminate," Lord Tima paused, shaking his head, "no—that is not the right word—it will locate this world Chandra for the people who control our home world, Kaerus. If the beacon is activated, I fear, and you should fear, that they will be able to come here as we did."

"The old stories are true?" Audy asked.

"Stories and myths to the people of Chandra." Lord Tima gave a single nod. "For us, it is our history. Nearly a thousand years ago, when we first came here, our technology was more advanced than yours is now."

"Why would you fear that?" Audy asked. "This fantasy of a magic beacon would seem to be your only salvation."

"It is not a fantasy." The Kaerin shook his head. "And if it were truly a salvation for the Kaerin, I would have activated the beacon I possess, or my ancestors would have used it centuries ago. This was your fault." Lord Tima pointed at each of them in turn.

"When you destroyed our complex on the island of Landing, certain areas long-buried were rediscovered. A way to power the beacons was found, and among the Kaerin, only the Prelate, my father, and myself, know the truth of our history. The truth of why we fled our homeworld."

"Fled?" Audy asked, beating Kyle to the question. "What truth is that?" he continued.

"Our people fled that world during a horrific war that we were losing. Had, in fact, lost. We don't know why or how we traveled to this world—it was not the intended destination. We had no knowledge of this place. My ancestors were part of the Kaerin host marooned here. Now, a beacon capable of locating this world for our ancient enemy travels on the flagship of the fleet approaching Irinas. I came to alert you to the threat, and if needed—help you destroy it."

Audy smiled. "Our Edenite allies have a term called 'bullshit'. Did Ocheltree teach you that word?"

"He did." The Kaerin looked between them. "On my oath as a Kaerin Lord," he paused and shook his head. "On my honor as a man, what I say is true. Lord Oont'tal has a beacon. He has managed to power it, and if he should lose the coming battle, he will activate the beacon."

"You are asking us to let him win?" Audy scoffed.

"I'm more practical than that. I would ask you to destroy him before he can realize he has lost. I have the only other beacon, and I certainly have no intention of using it.

"I know what the arrival of our… people would mean. Though, in fact, they are not Kaerin. My ancestors of the Kaerin clan founded and ruled our world of Kaerus for generations—only to lose it to another clan, the Torpun. Whoever they are now, whatever they call themselves—they are not Kaerin."

"They sound as if they might be an improvement." Audy smiled.

The Kaerin swore in anger, using words Kyle couldn't follow, and then seemed to reset his emotions as he composed himself. "From your perspective, Edenite or Jema, it is true—they could be an improvement over a race you are at war with. It is a risk you are in a position to take."

"I am here in honor. I know the truth of our Kaerin history, what we have done on this world. What we became—it is not who we were. We believed in freedom and this *liberty*—Ocheltree told me about it. The survivors that arrived here were soldiers, all of them. They had just lost a war fighting for those ideals. Once here, marooned, and surrounded by enemies, decisions were made that we would never be weak again. Three hundred years of conquest on Chandra, followed by seven hundred years of rule." The Kaerin gave a shrug, as if in apology. "We became who we are—it does not change who we ran from, nor does it alter the technology of our homeworld that surpassed your own a thousand years ago."

"Who you are—who you became—is why we are at war," Audy fired back.

Kyle couldn't have said why, yet he believed the Kaerin, or at least felt the Kaerin believed it himself. All of it scared the shit out of him.

"So let us war, Jema. To the end." The presumptive Kaerin Prelate nodded in agreement. "We know little else—nor do your own people."

The Kaerin turned away from Audy and faced Kyle. "If there is any hope for my people in the future, it will need to be learned through war. I don't have the power to stop this fight, and I would not survive the attempt to end it in anything but victory. If you are victorious— which in my mind, I believe you will be—in the end, you will need someone who can speak for the Kaerin. Someone who knows the truth of what we once stood for, who we once were. Ocheltree believed that your people could be... merciful? In victory."

Kyle's head was spinning. The Kaerin was saying he knew his people would lose, would have to lose. As strange as it was, he could almost hear the old Jema Sri'tel's voice in the Kaerin's words. Jake had it right—Chandra was fucked up. Worse, in his mind—it was fucked. There was no short cut to end the war here.

"In victory," Kyle answered. "Yes, we can be merciful. How many of your people do we have to kill before your people will listen?"

"I don't know the answer to that." The Kaerin seemed to shrug. "We have known nothing but victory. I think the only honest answer I can give is… enough."

"What of the beacon?" Audy asked. "How could you possibly help us to destroy it?"

The Kaerin nodded quickly. "Our new ships have their primary cannon in revolving turrets—"

"We've seen them," Audy interrupted. "They sink just as fast as your older ships."

The Kaerin ignored the insult. "There is only one ship in our fleet that has two such large turrets. That is Lord Oont'tal's flagship. It is undoubtedly in the middle of his fleet and well-protected. I carry the opinion that Oont'tal expects to lose. In his heart, honor leaves him one choice. His pride is the only thing that has stopped him using the beacon before now. He will activate the beacon. He believes our home world would come to rescue us. If he were capable of thinking otherwise, I would have told him the truth of our history. If the Torpun come here, we would all—Kaerin, Jema, and Edenite—be killed or enslaved. I am here to seek a future that may yet be saved."

"Saved for who?" Audy asked.

"Perhaps all of us," Lord Tima Bre'jana answered. "We will try to win. There is no other way to earn the type of future I was told your people believe in." The Kaerin tuned to look at Kyle. "And your people, Edenite. Do you not tire of fighting a war that is not your own?"

"It's very much our war," Kyle answered. "It's our neighborhood, and we stand by our friends, to the end."

The Kaerin surprised them both by nodding in agreement. "I had hoped to speak to men who understood honor. In that, I believe I have succeeded."

*

Chapter 28

Portsmouth, Chandra

The conference room was quiet, considering the occupants. They'd all listened to Kyle and Audy's individual assessment of Tima Bre'jana. Hank clicked off the viewscreen, where they'd all just watched the video from Kyle's helmet cam for the second time. He turned in his chair to look down the table at where Amona sat between Doc Jensen and Elisabeth.

"Amona, you are the only person here who can claim to know Lord Tima. Do you believe what he says?"

"The story about the Kaerin's origins rings true, as far as it aligns with the stories that were told by my clan. Though the part about the Kaerin fleeing in defeat—I have no idea. It's not the sort of story the Kaerin would have allowed to survive."

"But the man himself," Hank pressed. "Could you make a judgement on whether he was being truthful?"

"I never knew Lord Bre'jana to lie." Amona held up both hands in supplication. "A Kaerin would have no need to lie to a subject. If they were displeased, you knew it. If it was worse, you were simply disposed of. I do know, among the Gemendi, he had a reputation of being a... I think you call it a 'troublemaker.' I once overheard the Prelate complain to Lord Bre'jana in person that 'he'd been warned not to ask him a question if he was not ready to hear the truth, no matter how uncomfortable the answer may be.'"

"This was when you hid behind the walls during their meeting on Landing?" Kyle asked. He remembered personally conducting Amona's intel debriefing.

"Yes, sir." Amona nodded, looking surprised that Kyle had remembered.

"Does it matter whether we believe him or not?" It was Elisabeth who spoke up. "There's a reason I'm headed back to Eden as soon as this meeting is over. The invasion fleet is bearing down on this place—wouldn't their flagship be our first target, at any rate?"

"Just the opposite." Hank shook his head. "I understand where you're coming from, Elisabeth, but everything we know of their command and control says the only people capable of turning the Kaerin armada around in retreat are the ones in command. Our plan has been to focus on the troop transports—with them destroyed, none of us can figure a reason of why the Kaerin warships would hang around in easy range of our planes and ships."

"Kill this Lord Oont'tal," Jomra spoke up "and his last command will hold. There may be others of high-enough rank in their fleet that could change the order, but that could also be wishful thinking. It is not something they have ever had to do."

"I wouldn't doubt if this Bre'jana character was playing several games with us," Kyle interjected. "He was smart, scary smart. That much was clear. I just can't get past the feeling that he believed what he was saying about the beacon."

"Dave?" Paul Stephens, at the head of the table, called on his chief scientist. "Is it even possible? Plausible? Could they have such a device, given that it comes from a time when the Kaerin were far more advanced?"

Jensen barked out a short laugh. "You mean do we have to worry about an alien invasion on top of a redo of the Spanish Armada, and oh, just for fun, a *Sink the Bismarck* scenario?" Jensen had been quiet, scribbling on his compad since the first mention of an interdimensional beacon.

"I don't know what a 'Bismarck' is," Jomra answered. "But yes, is an invasion from these Torpun of the Kaerin's homeworld something we need to prepare for?"

"Possibly?" Jensen shrugged. "And—I have to qualify that answer by saying that it's an entirely different thing than saying I have the least idea of how." He waved his compad at them as if there were another person in the room that would understand the scribblings. "We've looked at the problem set of trying to get a signal across the quantum intersection between worlds since we were back on Earth and had first discovered Eden. We can't do it, not yet, even though the models prove it is theoretically possible."

"There is no way, in my opinion—even theoretically—where I could explain a signal being sent between worlds that do not intersect. It's possible from Earth to Eden, or Eden to Chandra—but only because Eden's dimension somehow naturally intersects those two worlds. We know for certain that the world the Kaerin came from is not the world on the far side of Chandra in the chain. Frankly, how the Kaerin arrived here from their home world shouldn't have been possible either. We can't explain it."

"You finally said something that I agree with, Doctor Jensen." Jomra gave a solemn nod. "Yet, they are here. The came from elsewhere, somehow."

"I'm not arguing that, sir." They all thought it comical how Jomra was the sole individual in existence that Doc Jensen referred to as 'sir.' "They are here," Jensen continued. "My team has spent significant effort trying to determine how. The best theory we've come up with is some sort of high energy event in close proximity to the Kaerin's translation somehow created a quantum bridge between two disparate locations that couldn't possibly intersect. Best off-the-cuff theory we have—backed up by the fact that they were supposedly at war—is a fusion bomb cooking off at the point of origin, just as they translated."

"So not repeatable, or targetable?" Stephens asked for clarification.

"I still can't explain how it's possible." Jensen shook his head. "If

I'm right about how it happened the first time… no way they could repeat it with a specific destination in mind. But I could be dead wrong and these Torpun could have the ability to finger paint in the quantum foam."

"Quantum… foam?" Elisabeth looked down the table at Jensen. "That's a thing?"

"For lack of a better word." Jensen shrugged. "Yeah, it's real. Call it the potential energy that just appears in a given space devoid of all matter. It bubbles up out of nowhere, or from somewhere we can't explain yet—but it's there. We call it 'quantum foam.'"

Kyle was only half listening to Jensen's explanation about shit that may or may not even exist. However he looked at the problem, Chandra was fucked. Jake had told him that a year and a half ago. Tima Bre'jana, he was certain, had arrived at that same conclusion. The guy had risked everything in meeting with them, and had at least intimated about a potential path to an honorable defeat.

"Look," Kyle kicked in. "The relevant point is that the Kaerin leadership believes it's possible. We should act like we believe them and move accordingly—I think it is the only chance of dealing with the Kaerin that *are* here. We can win every fight in this war, but unless we have somebody who might, just might, be willing to push the Kaerin leadership towards peace—we are going to have to live with unleashing a war of extermination. These subject clans on Chandra get a taste for revenge—there will be no stopping them."

"I agree," Jomra noted. "I do not want to build a future on ash, even if it comes from Kaerin bones."

"Nor do I," Hank echoed.

"I believe we are all in agreement on that score." Paul sounded from the head of the table. "Alright, let's sink the Bismarck."

"An all-out strike," Jensen added. "Overwhelming, in as short a time as possible. I could be completely wrong about this beacon."

Everyone turned to look at Jensen's end of the table. Elisabeth threw her pen at him.

"For God's sake, Dave!" Stephens shouted. "You don't hedge like this."

"Hedge?" Jensen pulled on an ear. "We're talking about a type of quantum entanglement that we don't even have the math to explain. Guess is the best I can do."

"We still sink the Bismarck, yes?" Jomra asked.

*

Bay of Biscay, Chandra

"Lord Oont'tal, the *Alar'rimast* at our vanguard reports three enemy boats in sight. Small craft—descriptions match those we have of the boats that fire the guided rockets."

The enemy had waited longer than he thought they would to attack his fleet of warships. Perhaps their guess at the range of the enemy's airboats had been exaggerated. He had expected the first attacks to come from the air.

"It begins." He looked up from his map table and gazed out the heavy windows on a slate-gray sea and bright blue sky. "Maintain constant contact with the *Alar'rimast*—by relay if necessary. Get the names of the ships closest to her and make contact with them in advance. I want to know what form the attack takes."

The *Bel'lasstor* was the most powerful warship the Kaerin had ever built on this world. Many its innovations were the product of an Edenite traitor that had been hidden from him and who he wasn't supposed to know about. The stern-mounted propellors, the armor, the revolving turrets, they were all most useful, but at the moment it was his own addition that he relied upon.

The *Bel'lasstor* had been designed around a communications room stuffed with more than twenty long-talkers operating on different wavelengths. They'd asked him to command a fleet. Being able to communicate with multiple ships simultaneously was something he had long dreamed of.

Still, he worried the enemy may have waited so long to attack because they didn't view his fleet as a threat. He walked the short distance across his bridge and went down a single flight of stairs. A short walk brought him to Gemendi Yun'nay's quarters. The door was open, and Yun'nay sat with the beacon between his legs.

"It's time, Yun'nay. Bring the device to the bridge and stay with it. Our vanguard has sighted the enemy. We can be sure they know exactly where we are."

"I'm ready, Lord."

"Your standing orders?"

"If I feel the *Bel'lasstor* struck severely, I am to activate the beacon—even without your direct command."

"Just so, Yun'nay." He offered a rare smile. "There is none other I would trust with this."

"It is my honor. But Lord, how am I to distinguish a severe attack from one that merely strikes us? We are heavily armored."

"I don't think you will have any doubt, Yun'nay. If it happens, do not hesitate. If I am unable to give the order, you must act."

Yun'nay pulled the heavy leather bag up over the top of the beacon and picked it up. "I'm ready, Lord."

"Very well," he replied. "Follow me."

*

"EDF Navy, this Air Target Team- One. Passing coordinates to you. We have enemy ships below us, making due north." Jeremy, his squadron of eight planes strung out in a ten-mile-wide line to either side of him at an altitude of 9000 feet, turned on a wing so he could count the visible ship wakes the break in the sparse clouds afforded him. He got to twenty-two before the view was blocked by another cotton ball.

"Coordinates received, Air Target One, we are moving in but will wait to fire pending your strike."

"Copy all, Navy. Good hunting."

"You as well, Air Force. Captain Harper sends her regards."

He ignored the warships below him and stayed on course. Somewhere further south was the enemy flagship. He switched frequency to his squadron channel. "I know I'm always giving you shit, Arto—but we could really use those eyes to come through for us. We should be getting close any minute now."

Three minutes later, it was Milo'rana that spotted the large warship. He was two planes over, off Jeremy's starboard wing less than four miles away.

"I have it, the big one. Two large turrets, one forward, one aft of the superstructure."

"Okay, Target Team, track to Milo. We'll drop down to six thousand feet and confirm target once we're formed up." It wasn't fair, he was the squadron commander, and in every war movie he'd ever seen, the commander was supposed to spot the bad guys first.

"Strike Team, this is Target Team One. Potential target sighted—we are moving to confirm."

"Copy all, Target Team One. We are ready." Jeremy couldn't help but associate Adelmein's German accent with his recent ass chewing. He looked straight up out of his canopy and saw nothing but blue sky above. Adelmein and wingman were in their F-35s somewhere far above them at 35,000 feet, waiting.

Ten minutes later, they'd all confirmed Milo had spotted the right ship. Not only was it the only one they'd seen with two heavy gun turrets, there were another twelve smaller ships arranged in two rough concentric diamond patterns around it. He'd been told the enemy flagship would be well protected, and he had to assume that every one of those Kaerin escort vessels bristled with heavy machine guns. There would be a limit to how low they could go. The problem was, their targeting lasers had a range limit too.

"Target Team, lasers on. Light up the primary target and drop to eight thousand feet." They were flying in a loose circle above what looked like an ancient battleship—ancient as in pre-WWI. Jeremy focused on his own targeting system once he was sure he was level at eight thousand feet. The target was boxed, and the targeting laser in its rotating dome at the bottom of his fuselage was locked on.

"Strike Team, this is Target One—target is lit at eight thousand feet. Do you have a weapons lock?"

"Negative Target One, no light, I repeat—no light. Strike Team is holding at Angels 14."

Jeremy cursed to himself. During the pre-mission briefing, Adelmein had thought eight thousand feet might be low enough. "Target flight, this is Target One—hold altitude, I'm dropping to Angels 7." He nudged his stick forward, having no concept of how loud the wind, water and steam engines of a warship were. All he could think about was how much engine noise a flight of nine Wolverines put out. It was only going to take one asshole on that ship—or any of them, for that matter—to look up and spot them before every machine gun beneath them opened up.

"Target One—this is Strike One. We have a single strong signal."

Jeremy glanced at his altimeter. "Copy Strike One, I'm level at Angels seven point two. Target Team, circle down and join the band."

"Target One, this is Target Two—I've got flashes on the surface. They are firing."

Jeremy smiled to himself. Of course it was Arto who spotted that.

"Target Team, we knew they would—let's get this over with."

He was starting to wonder how much energy a large machine gun projectile would have after being fired almost a mile and a half straight up. He felt better with the answer that came to mind until he started realizing how little energy it would take to knock his thin-skinned carbon fiber airplane from the sky.

He listened to each of his team report in when they had dropped to his altitude, wondering what was taking the strike team so long.

"Weapons have lock, releasing in three, two, one, mark—weapons away." Adelmein sounded calm. Why wouldn't he? They weren't getting shot at. "Keep targeting lasers on target."

Adelmein couldn't help himself—the guy was a tool. Somewhere above Jeremy and his squadron, inside the circular track their planes were running, eight laser-guided missiles were on their way.

*

"They are too high, Lord," The warrior commanding the helm of the *Bel'lasstor* reported. "No signs they have fired any guided rockets, but we are beginning evasive turns."

"Very well," Oont'tal spoke from behind his field glasses.

He hadn't seen anything drop from the enemy's airboats either, but there were too many, too far apart to see all of them. They were, in fact, at a range that put them above his escort vessels and not the *Bel'lasstor*. What were they playing at? They were close enough he could see the tube-shaped objects slung under their wings with the field glasses. He lowered the glasses and glanced over at Yun'nay, sitting on the top step of the stairway leading below. His Gemendi was watching him closely.

He needn't have worried. Yun'nay could be trusted to act in the event he could not.

"Any report from the *Alar'rimash*?"

"Lord, they report the enemy vessels are maintaining their distance, they have—"

Oont'tal's world flashed white. There was no pain, no sound. He was dimly aware of his field glasses being driven back through his eyes, and his feet were no longer in contact with the deck. He felt his back slam against something hard with the detachment of a brain that hadn't figured out it was dead. His last thought was of Yun'nay.

Yun'nay regained consciousness and immediately became aware of his leg bone sticking out through his trousers six inches above where his knee used to be. He'd been thrown down the stairs and the narrow corridor's wall was nearly its floor—the *Bel'lasstor* was listing badly. Down the corridor, light from an opening in the hull that hadn't been there a moment ago showed him the device still in its leather shroud fifteen feet away. It might as well have been a kamark away. The corridor was filling with acrid smoke from the lower levels of the ship.

He tried to move and screamed. The ship itself seemed to have heard him. She was sinking bow first, and quickly. The device rolled a few spans closer. He reached out with the one arm that still worked and waited. The corridor behind him was filling with water, he could hear it surging upwards from behind. His mangled body caught in the twisted rungs of the ladder held him in place.

The ship groaned and vibrated beneath him. The scream of shearing steel was loud enough that it seemed to be a spike in his ears. Suddenly the open wound in the deck behind the device split further, and a bone-jarring pop tore the back half of the ship off, leaving him looking up at the open sky. His one working arm missed stopping the device as it hurtled towards him. It struck him in his gut, amidst already shattered ribs.

He was crying—screaming in pain—as he used his one hand and his teeth to pull the leather bag off the top of the device. He flipped off the cover—the button glowed red. Its charge from the ancient boat's hull had lasted. He pushed the button just as the sensation of ice cold water reached his back. He held the device as tight as he could, waiting for something to happen. It should do something, surely. The cold water shocked him into taking a deep breath, filling his pierced lungs with water as the light above him dimmed. I*t should have done something…*

"Holy Shit," Jeremy whispered behind his mask. The missiles had hit at nearly the same time. The stern of the ship was all that was left above water, and it had rolled upside down. Before it had gone under, parts of the forward half of the enemy's flagship looked to have melted. Jeremy had dipped down to five thousand feet for a closer look.

There was a solitary Kaerin warrior clinging to the exposed keel of the still floating stern. The warrior knelt, hanging on with one hand, waving his sword at him with the other. In all that destruction, all he could think about was how the warrior had managed to get up there.

"Okay, Target Team, we've got our pictures. We still have missiles of our own to unload. Don't waste them. Disable a target and move on. We need to get back for reloads. Hopefully the transports will be in range by the time we get back out here."

"Strike Team One to Target Team." Adelmein broke in on their squadron circuit. "This was a good mission. Strike Team is RTB for re-arming. Target Team One has tactical command."

This was a good mission? Jeremy shook his head in wonder. It was probably as close to praise as anything Adelmein had ever said.

"Copy, Strike Team," he replied. "Good shooting."

There was no response, and Jeremy began a casual climb back up to eight thousand feet. They had plenty of fuel left, but not so much as to be stupid about it. Besides, it wasn't like they had to go looking for targets.

"This is Target Team Two," Arto spoke up. "Taking target due north of primary."

Jeremy listened in on the calls, painting a picture in his head and making certain all his people would be firing at different azimuths. He was more squadron commander at the moment and figured his own missiles could be used as second-strike cleanups where needed. His turn brought the stern of the enemy flagship back into view, and he couldn't make out whether the warrior was still there or not. He found himself hoping the warrior would get picked up by one of the other ships in this wave, but then again, he doubted any Kaerin vessel would take the time to launch boats for survivors.

*

Chapter 29

Off the coast of Brest, Chandra

"Steve, do me a favor—run below and check the generator one more time." The EDF Navy officer he reported to tapped her earbud. "The crew boat says we are leaving in five—bad guys are getting close."

Steve stared back, wondering if Lieutenant Barton was pulling his leg. He liked her—she was easygoing and listened to her people—even people like him, a civilian contractor who had given up a great-paying job in California on Eden for double the salary working a one-year contract for the EDF on Chandra. He was pretty sure she liked him too, and he'd been trying to work up the courage to ask her out. So why would she ask him to go back down there, and not someone else? The answer was a given. Because he was a contractor… it went without saying.

"I know it's a little funky down there." She didn't look up from her own work where she was bent over an open laptop plugged into the firing control. "If the generators conk out, this is all for nothing."

A little funky? They had taken to calling the captured Kaerin paddle-wheeler the *SS Bucket*. The ship had been old when it had fallen into their hands after taking Portsmouth. The good parts of the ship, exposed to the disinfecting nature of regular sunshine, reeked of dead fish and rotting wood. Belowdecks was something else entirely. The leading theory held that the Kaerin had used the rotting hull to haul animal offal and fish guts for fertilizer. At any rate, the ship had been fixed up to look like a viable, ocean-going Kaerin transport from a distance, at least from the outside. It wasn't—not even close. They'd towed it out here during the night and were more than ready to abandon the wreck. Its deck had been reinforced to hold the missile launchers that needed the power from the generators below to operate.

"Right." He shook his head. "You won't leave without me?"

"Wouldn't think of it." She lifted her head and smiled at him. "When this is over, you are going to buy me the best steak in Portsmouth with all that money you make."

His impending terror at having to go below was momentarily forgotten. She liked him! "It's a date!"

He started down the wooden staircase headed below decks, stopping midway to turn his flashlight on. At the next step, he walked into an invisible, fetid wall of hate. The stench seemed alive. He shook his head and buried his face in the crook of his arm as his stomach revolted. The pathway back to the big diesel generator, running loudly, was clearly marked with new oak that had been installed to support its weight. He stayed on the new wood, noting hints of diesel exhaust amidst the unholy mixture he was breathing.

He checked the fuel level—all good. He checked the RPMs and output, all good. The fuse panel was all green. The generator pulled in fresh air from an intake vent they'd cut into the hull. It wouldn't run for more than a few minutes in this air and needed an outside source. Clearly, nobody thought a contractor deserved the same. He'd worked for a solid week, running the electrical lines between here and the deck, and he was fairly certain he'd scarred his lungs.

One of the lights on the fuse panel blinked, or maybe it had been his oxygen deprived brain. He stared at it, focused on the fact that he needed to take another breath. It blinked again. Fuck me! He was close enough to be able to read the numbered stickers on each fuse switch. Lucky number seven. He followed the heavy power cable with his flashlight out from the front of the junction box to where it coupled with the extension cable running up a support beam.

He diagnosed the issue immediately. One of the two torsion clasps had popped open. He took a breath, doing his best to ignore the taste, and ducked his head to run over and snap the clasp back down. He knelt there and turned back to the fusebox, praying that the circuit light stayed a solid green. It did. He waited long enough to require another breath. There should be a medal for this level of dedication.

"Generator is all good—circuits all green." It might have been his imagination, but he could have sworn that he could see his breath as he spoke into his radio, as if it were twenty below and not a very humid and sticky ninety degrees belowdecks.

"Okay, thanks Steve. Get a move on. Crew boat is loading."

He didn't have to be told twice. The stairway and the glow of sunlight above beckoned. He took a deep breath and ran. The wood beneath his feet was so rotten it gave way without a sound. For all the good it did him, he had time to realize that he should have backtracked to the fuse box to stay on the new wood. The lower hold was nearly pitch black and whatever he landed in was soft and had been there a very long time. He wanted to scream, but needed to needed to breathe. He puked instead.

It wasn't quite a panic to get down the rope net into the crew boat, but it was close. They were all in a hurry to get off the *Bucket* and its nightmare inducing stench. The small crew boat bobbed up and down, its rubber bumpers pounding against the worm-eaten hull of the paddle-wheeler. The Kaerin transport fleet had been spotted and was getting closer to the opposite, south facing side of the *Bucket* every second. Lieutenant Barton was fighting sea-sickness as she counted the bodies in the boat and the three still coming down the side of the ship. When her count hit twenty, she lurched forward. She made it to the side of the boat just in time before projectile vomiting into the Atlantic.

She'd hated this assignment since being posted here three months earlier. There wasn't a shower hot enough or long enough to get rid of the *SS Bucket's* stench. It usually took a day or two of fresh air before food started tasting right. She looked up at the sides of the hulk as they moved away, towards a friendly shore to the northeast and hoped she'd never have to see the thing ever again. She spit over the side and wiped her mouth on her sleeve before dialing Command in Portsmouth.

"*SS Bucket* is operational; crew boat is on our way home."

God, that felt good to say. She knew at least six missile-equipped patrol boats had made two or more naval strikes each against the invasion fleet. She knew because most of her peers served aboard those warships and they all stayed in touch as much as time allowed. They'd all been involved in attacking Kaerin harbors and shipbuilding centers for the last six months while she'd been assigned to the shore batteries and then, most recently, to the *SS Bucket*.

She didn't know how many Kaerin transports were left. The Air Force had been hammering at them as well, but she figured if the *Bucket* did her job, she'd have something to brag about. There were thirty-six missiles spread across her deck in nine four-pack launchers. She just hoped that the Navy ships providing the targeting waited until they had that many ships in range.

"Good Copy, *SS Bucket*. Targeting Team is in position and waiting for more of them to get in range. Safe travels."

*

"Kareel, lookouts have sighted another wreck ahead. It's close to our path. Two of the enemy boats have been spotted six kamarks to the east. They seem to holding position."

It wasn't the first wreck they had seen, and he doubted it would be the last. Kareel Jum'raga wasn't a sailor, and he was beginning to wonder if he'd survive to see the island of Irinas. Over the last day, transports making up their fleet had been destroyed or disabled all around him, and there was nothing he could do but watch and wonder how his own boat had continued on unscathed.

The attacks had come from the cursed airboats of the enemy, or worse, the small boats that danced in and out of cannon range on the water, seemingly toying with them as they launched their guided rockets. It rarely required more than one enemy rocket to disable a transport, and if the damnable weapons struck weapons stores or below the waterline, the boat was generally lost to fire or sunk outright.

Even now, the horizon behind them birthed columns of dark smoke visible from the last attack by two of the enemy's boats. One had flowed past them, bow to stern, so close his warriors on deck had tried to throw hand bombs at it. Their single cannon hadn't been able to depress its aim to even attempt a shot. Once again, he and his warriors had been spared, and the enemy had fired at other ships. His battle fortune had always been strong, but he was beginning to worry about what might await him on Irinas. Perhaps fortune would see them disabled, burning, or floating free only to starve to death, but he thought not. Not him—he would die in battle, on land with his sword in hand.

"I see it," he responded. He could just make out the wreck. No smoke came from its stacks. It was dead in the water. "Boat Master, we will not alter course. Send a message to the rest of the fleet that we are proceeding as ordered. All cannons should be ready to engage the enemy boats should they come within range."

He wasn't certain who was in command at this point, and it was becoming a problem. No other Lord or War Leader had issued any of their own commands via the long-talker or countered any of the commands he had issued. Jum'raga had to believe they would have, if they had been there. He knew there were several similarly ranked Kareel still afloat behind them, but none of them had challenged his command. He'd long served in Lord Oont'tal's own host, so among the other surviving Kareel ranked warriors – that fact probably explained why there hadn't yet been a dispute.

Lord Oont'tal had taken the battle fleet on ahead of the transports three days earlier, but there had been no word or response from any of those ships since yesterday morning. It was as if they'd steamed out of range, except that their intention had been to clear the seas of the enemy—something that clearly hadn't happened. If, as he feared, the Kaerin battle fleet sat on the dark bottom of this unforgiving sea, what hope did transport boats like his have?

"Require all boats to report in. I want a full count on what warriors we have."

"Yes, Kareel."

If this situation lasted much longer, he would have to officially claim the title War Leader. The warriors would need one. The scope of the fleet's writ demanded one. His ship was at the leading edge of the invasion fleet's formation, and if possible, he would be among the first to step ashore.

*

"The *Bunker Hill* and *Saratoga* report forty ships in range of the *Bucket*, sir."

Hank looked at the plot on the wall. The Kaerin transports were down to somewhere between 250 and 300 ships, and their best intelligence had each one carrying five hundred warriors. The invasion fleet was approaching Brest and the cape of Northwestern France with several hours of daylight left. If their speed held, the survivors of this attack would be positioned to land troops sometime late tomorrow.

"Ask the Navy how long before the *Bucket* falls within enemy cannon range."

He waited for the communications officer to get her response and looked over the faces of the darkened command center. Heads were bowed over their monitors, a couple of quiet conversations were taking place where folks had rolled their chairs together, and at least two people he could see were curled up on the floor, asleep under their desks. He couldn't have been prouder of the job they had all done. With the exception of the shore batteries, they were almost out of missiles to direct to the targets.

"*Bunker Hill* reports ten minutes, sir."

He nodded to himself. "We'll wait another five minutes. Start a clock. The more Kaerin ships see this attack—the better."

The enemy's morale was now his target every bit as much as their ships. Tima Bre'jana was presumably back in Kaerus by now. The Kaerin Prelate-to-be, if he was to be believed, was already having second thoughts. They needed that sentiment to spread.

*

"It looks abandoned," Barg'rasta opined.

The veteran Bastelta was Jum'raga's oldest friend. He would rely heavily on the man in the coming fight. Barg'rasta stood near the middle of the bridge, just behind the Gemendi shipmaster steering the paddle-wheeler.

"Has to have been one of the ships launched from a harbor nearby." Jum'raga lowered his own field glasses. He'd been trying to keep track of the two small enemy vessels that had been shadowing them. They seemed to have started moving south towards the main body of his force. So far, the enemy host hadn't come within cannon range, and he couldn't imagine any reason why they would. "Perhaps from one of the ports in Lord Atan'tal's holding?"

"Kareel," the ship master spoke up. "Atan'tal lands are only sixty kamarks to the east. There are a handful of ports it could have come from. From the looks of her, she's very old—they might have just floated her free to make room in the harbor."

Jum'raga grunted in response. The Gemendi could be right. Then again, he'd seen the writ firsthand. All the decoy launchings from the northern ports were to have been carrying local clan war hosts. Lord Oont'tal had referred to it by saying they were slaying two oxen with one blow—distract the Edenites, let them waste time and weapons while destroying worthless locals. He doubted if a Kaerin Lord would have deviated from that writ. Which begged the question, who would have stopped to rescue a bunch of Junata clan warriors? Or why?

"Gemendi, turn away. Approach no closer to the wreck." They'd been warned of fireships, and although the wreck was adrift, he saw no reason for a close inspection. "Barg'rasta, signal the other ships to stay at least two kamarks away from it."

He lifted his field glasses for another look at the hulk and saw a pillow of white gas suddenly bloom from its deck, near the stern. He'd seen a lot of those blooms from the smaller Edenite vessels. He recognized it immediately.

"Rocket attack!" he yelled. "Signal all ships! Alter course!"

Experience had taught them the small Edenite boats carried a maximum of eight rockets each, and sometimes only four. Indeed, with the two enemy vessels tracking his fleet, he'd already assumed he was going to lose another sixteen transports. How many of those damnable rockets could the enemy have put on that transport? He watched in silent fury as the rockets continued to launch, one after another. The entire vessel was almost obscured in white smoke, but with each launch, the billowing cloud grew and a dark object could be seen lancing upward until it was lost to speed.

"Gemendi! Get us in cannon range of that boat!"

"Yes, Kareel!"

He watched as the shipmaster spun his wheel half a turn and then pulled on a brake lever to slow one of their paddles. Slowly, ever so slowly, the horizon slid past the bridge's window until the wreck, still firing its deadly rockets, was aligned with their bow and cannon once again.

"Almost in range," Barg'rasta called out. "Cannon crew is ready."

They heard the rolling echoes of the first impacts behind them. Jum'raga forced himself to turn and look astern at the rest of "his" fleet. Two boats had been hit, and three more took rockets in the short span before he turned away. The last one's powder stores had been hit, and the boat had exploded into a spray of driftwood. He ground his teeth as seconds later the cacophonous boom of that explosion reached him across kamarks of open water.

"Fire when able!" He did his best to keep the emotion out of his voice. He'd long thought Lord Oont'tal was a model Kaerin Lord. No one doubted that man's will, and he'd rarely heard his Lord speak at above a whisper.

The single cannon on their forward deck fired. He watched as the projectile hit the water just short of the wreck, and then skipped into it. He couldn't be sure what had happened, as there was so much smoke obscuring their target. The light wind opened up a patch, and they all saw a dark, jagged hole in the enemy boat several spans above the waterline, just aft of its motionless paddles.

Forty seconds later, they fired again. In the interim, the rockets had continued to launch. Their second shot went through the wreck's pilothouse. Jum'raga counted six more rockets after that—their launches were almost synchronized with the echoing sounds of other rockets finding their targets behind him. The launches stopped as suddenly as they'd begun. The wind slowly cleared the smoke away just as they fired a third time. This shot hit near the bow, right at the waterline. Through his field glasses, he could see water pouring into the boat.

"Approach no closer!" he ordered. "Veer away."

"Kareel?" the ship master questioned. "Our cannon won't traverse more than ten points."

"Veer away," he repeated. "They are done."

"Yes, Kareel." The Gemendi ship master didn't sound happy. Jum'raga had been warned what a prickly bunch they were.

"That beast could take hours to sink, Kareel." The Gemendi added without being asked.

"We have our writ, Gemendi. You have your orders."

He turned to Barg'rasta. "If the Gemendi questions me again, take his hand."

His friend grinned back at him. "Yes, Kareel."

He paused before turning to look astern. He already knew what he was going to see. From the sounds, the rockets were still landing. Ships were burning across the southern horizon. He turned towards the setting sun. There had been no attacks during the previous night. If that practice held, and they could survive until nightfall, they might live to see the enemy's coastline.

"Shipmaster? Your best estimate at this speed to the primary target?"

"Late tomorrow afternoon, Kareel." the Gemendi answered quickly, frozen like a statue with both hands on the ship's wheel. "An hour or two before dusk."

Jum'raga walked over to the map on the wall. "And if we proceed directly to our secondary landing site?"

"Midday tomorrow, Kareel—at the latest. It is much closer."

That settled it. He was done being a target. He wanted off this cursed boat and didn't like the odds of attempting a landing in the dark. "Proceed to the secondary target. Barg'rasta, inform the fleet of our new destination. All warriors will be prepared to disembark by mid-morning. Also, until we make contact with the War Fleet, I am assuming the mantle of War Leader." With luck, there was another living Kareel out there who outranked him.

Barg'rasta nodded knowingly. They'd served together for almost a decade. "Yes, War Leader."

He signaled his Bastelta over to him as he watched the two enemy boats in the distance begin to launch their own rockets. Once again, it seemed his boat would be spared as they were focused on vessels to the south of him.

"War Leader?"

"Wait until this attack is over, then require all undamaged and underway boats to signal in. I'll still need that count of what's left to us."

"It will be done, War Leader." Barg'rasta lowered his voice further. "We'll need you with all your faculties tomorrow—you need sleep."

"I do," he admitted, shaking his head as two more distant rocket strikes echoed across the ocean lit by a sinking sun. Those would be the last salvo fired from the wreck. Those launching from the small ships had yet to strike. "Barg'rasta, don't harm the Gemendi. We'll need both his hands tomorrow."

His Bastelta smiled knowingly. "I won't be telling him that, of course."

He shared a smile with one of his oldest friends. "I would expect not. Leave orders that I am to be awakened if anything happens during the night, and be certain to get some sleep yourself."

Another powder magazine exploded in the distance as he turned to go below.

*

Chapter 30

Jeremy slid back his Wolverine's canopy as his engine sputtered to a stop. The ammo team was already moving. The fuel truck sat a hundred yards away, awaiting its turn.

"Any word from PJ?" he asked as soon as the ground crew rolled up the stepladder, Chief Bowman already riding on top.

"He's fine," Bowman answered, locking the canopy open and offering a hand to help him climb out. "He belly landed in a field not far from the farms at Exeter. There was an EDF company out there, and he got to their radio. I've got an aircar on the way to retrieve him—he says he's good to go."

Jeremy grinned to himself. What else would PJ say?

"We'll have a plane ready for him by the time we get him here."

"Missiles?" Jeremy asked, already knowing the answer.

Bowman spit a stream of whatever he was chewing on over the rail of the stepladder. "Nothing yet. You're getting rockets and bombs again."

Jeremy hid his frustration. "Can I trust you to make sure the doc checks PJ out before you let him get in another plane?"

"You can." Bowman pointed at the porta-potty at the edge of the apron. "Go—privilege of rank, beat the line."

He didn't have to be told twice. They'd taken off before sunrise and met the enemy fleet as it was coming around Pointe du Raz, the extreme northwest point of France. Intercepts of the Kaerin ship-to-ship communications during the night had let them know that the invasion fleet was no longer headed to Portsmouth, but would try to shorten their course on the water. They were now aiming for Plymouth, almost directly north of Brest.

The small Junata settlement there, and those all along the southern coast, had been evacuated days ago. The EDF had been portaling troops from Eden into the Plymouth area during the night, preparing a reception. The shore-based missile batteries strung out along the northern shores of the Channel weren't going to come into play, except for the few that could be moved in time, which left his and Callie's air squadrons the first and last line of defense.

Sure, the Navy was still out there, but he'd heard they were as short on missiles as his planes were. As the chief had said, they were down to rockets and bombs for the moment. This morning, the laser-guided rockets had worked well.

Three or four hits with the rockets and you had a decent shot of disabling one of the side-wheelers. Sometimes you missed, and sometimes you got a nice secondary that would turn the wood-hulled ships into kindling. It was a numbers game. The official count on the enemy ships had been just over two hundred when they'd arrived over the fleet. They'd destroyed or stopped another thirty ships in the morning's attack.

Their laser-guided rockets weren't fire-and-forget missiles. His pilots had to get a lot closer and stay in line with the target to use them. That was how PJ's plane had been shot up by machine guns operated by the Kaerin warriors on the deck of his target. Luckily, not at all the enemy ships had figured that trick out.

Once the rocket pods had been emptied, they'd been down to dive bombing—with 250-pound bombs. It was hard. His squadron's twelve planes had dropped a total of forty-eight bombs—only five had hit targets. As a group, they sucked at it. Callie's squadron hadn't fared any better, but at least they'd all gotten some practice in.

There'd been a rumor in the night that a shipment of more missiles from Eden was in route, but he wasn't counting on it to arrive in time. He knew 'in route' could mean from their nano-production facility to the closest portal on Eden, or from a portal on Caledonia to the airfield. He'd checked by radio on his way back in, and the answer had again been vague.

Lost in thought, he almost jumped out of his skin as somebody pounded on the porta-potty's door before jerking it open.

"Callie?"

"Relax! I've seen it," she teased. "Unless you want your girlfriend baring her ass to the whole squadron—take it outside!"

Jeremy was pretty much pulled through the open door and bounced outside as he was in the process of zipping up his flight suit. Carmen Amara, another pilot from Callie's squadron, almost ran him over. Other planes were still turning off the end of the runway and making their way to their respective service teams.

"Lieutenant Ocheltree! You're a guy!" Carmen yelled at him.

He held a hand up in apology and moved away quickly—lesson learned. Next time, he'd pee behind his plane. If they hurried, they had time for one more open ocean attack before they'd be helping defend the harbor at Plymouth.

*

Plymouth Harbor, Chandra

"How long before the missile battery is up?" Jeff Krouse shouted as he spotted Kyle and Audy approaching. The *whumpf-swoosh* sound of a Javelin missile firing from somewhere close by wasn't lost on Kyle. The enemy was close.

Jeff's group, the EDF's Black Division, was here to stop them. The Division had come by the name in several ways and had been waiting on Eden for the last week, ready to deploy wherever they were needed.

Two plus years earlier, they'd been the Jema Fist that had stood its ground against four Strema Fists along the shores of the Mississippi on Eden. They'd done it under a black flag that had signified to the Strema that they'd fight to the end. They had—the Strema's end.

The Jema Black Fist had been born that day. From that point forward, they'd bolstered their ranks with EDF personnel and been the first to fully integrate into the EDF. In the battle of Portsmouth a year earlier, they'd carried the heaviest load and performed to both Hank Pretty's and Jomra Sendai's satisfaction. There was no doubt they were the EDF's premier regular division. A lot of that had to do with its commanding officer.

Jeff had long been referred to as the Black Jema, not for the color of his skin but for the tenacity in which he prosecuted battles. Jeff's reputation of being a Jema at heart had been something he'd run with, and was in large part responsible for the evolution of Jema warriors into soldiers. Fighting under Jeff and his Jema named "Black Battle Heart," his soldiers knew they would get into the fight and make it count.

"Thirty minutes as of five minutes ago," Kyle answered as he came to a stop behind Jeff's command truck. "I was on the radio with them on our way in. We've got air support twenty minutes out, and they will do their best to maintain a presence for the duration."

Jeff was listening to him, nodding in acknowledgement, but he was staring at a Jema lieutenant next to him as he came to a decision.

"Do it," he spoke, leveling a finger at the lieutenant's face. "You've got Captain Majeski's brigade behind you. Your job is to pull your company back to his main defensive line—lead the dickheads right into our guns. Don't be a dead hero."

"Yes, sir!" The Jema didn't bother saluting before jogging off to a waiting aircar.

"Rope-a-Dope?" Kyle asked.

"Sort of." Jeff pointed down at the map. "They've already beached half a dozen ships along the sandy stretch on the far side of the peninsula."

He indicated across the bay at the distant swath of land that blocked most of the harbor's approach from the Channel. Kyle and Audy had seen the Kaerin ships headed directly at the broad strip of sand on their flight in from the air-car.

"More like a dozen by now," Kyle added.

"Good," Jeff spit. "I hope they're all headed that way. Dumb bastards are on a peninsula, and we've got our strongest lines set up on this neck of land, penning them in." Jeff slashed a hand north to south on the map over the neck of the peninsula. "We figured all those nice sandy beaches were going to be hard to ignore, given the pasting the Air Force and Navy gave them on the way in. I'd like to get a fight going there and hopefully pull more moths to the flame. God knows they run to the sound of a fight."

Audy grunted in appreciation. "Indeed."

"Glad you approve." Jeff pointed again at the bay. In between the mainland, the small Junata village, and the near coast of the peninsula were more than a dozen Kaerin vessels. Several were sinking or had run aground on sandbars where they were in the process of burning. But there were dozens more in sight behind them, rounding the headland and moving into the bay. "If we'd had that missile battery, we could have blocked a good part of that channel—made them bunch up even more."

"You did that with Javelins?" Kyle asked nodding out to the burning ships in the harbor.

"Yeah, but it took a lot of them." Jeff paused to take the time to tap his can of snuff against his leg. "First bunch we fired just took out the pilothouses. Fuckers kept coming. You know the javelin, it's hard to target a specific piece once it boxes the target. Having a hard time hitting the paddle wheels when they are head-on like this. At any rate, we're out of them for the moment. There's more coming in, but they are already late."

"You can still block the channel." Audy lifted his chin out towards the bay where the Kaerin vessels were creeping closer. "Most of their fleet is still well behind these that will have to be dealt with no matter what. Block the channel when the missile battery becomes available and force the ships behind this leading edge to land on the channel's side of the peninsula."

Jeff got his dip situated and gave his head a nod. "I thought that's what I just said. Don't you go and try taking credit for my plan."

It was a good plan, Kyle thought. Like any good tactical plan, it was defined by geography as much as anything.

"Alright." Kyle pointed out to the water. "We've got maybe ten minutes before these guys can land anywhere on the bay. Where do you want us?"

"I've tried to put two companies at every site that looks like you could drive one of those ships ashore inside the harbor. We've dug in as best we can. We rolled heavy with our gun trucks. With this mud, they are going to be better defending in place more than for any kind of maneuver. This shithole has one real road, and it's behind the village and heads back to Portsmouth. If we missed a landing location…" Jeff smiled and shook his head. "When they land at a place, we've missed. I have the two land yachts on speed dial."

Jeff looked directly at Kyle. "Speak to me. You've got more experience than me with this large force shit. What am I missing? I've got Jake's team as a local QRF in helos and Ospreys. Stant'ala and Hyrika have scout teams set up behind town in an arc about four miles inland. You know we'll have leakers."

Kyle nodded knowingly. If this went well, they'd probably be hunting small units of Kaerin a week from now. "What's left on Eden as a portal reserve?"

"Tom Souza and Hans have a brigade each right now. Most of Tom's Division had been waiting in Portsmouth—they are still portaling back to Eden with their gear. The colonel's go-to-hell plan is to drop that force in the path of the Nazis, should they break out of here."

"It's a good plan," Kyle acknowledged. "Especially given that they changed landing sites on us." He glanced over at Audy. "You see them doing what we think they will?"

Audy lifted an arm out towards the approaching ships. "They are already doing it. But I agree, we must make this harbor approach impossible for them and force their ships to land on the far beaches. We know their ships are communicating with each other. Hopefully, the message will spread that the harbor is not a viable alternative."

Jeff gave Audy a funny look, a grin slowly breaking out on his face. "Admiral Audy, I think I have a job for you."

Kyle started laughing. Audy looked back and forth at them. It took him a moment to figure out what was so funny. "You want me to speak as if I'm aboard one of those ships?"

"He's smarter than he looks." Jeff offered a grin.

Audy's eyebrow twitched. "It might work. I would be willing to try."

"That's the kind of enthusiasm I like." Jeff shook his head and laughed before looking at Kyle again. "I'm under direct orders to keep you both out of this fight. In Pretty's words, you're the only two people we have that could pick the next Kaerin Prelate out of a line-up." Jeff forestalled Audy's complaint with a raised hand. "Jomra was standing next to him when he said it. It was made very clear to me that it went for you too."

"That is not accurate," Audy took umbrage at the idea of being protected. Pretty had already threatened Kyle with weeks of paperwork within wi-fi range if he so much as picked up his weapon. "There were a number of soldiers there with us," Audy finished.

"Give it up, Audy." Kyle shook his head. "It's not a fight you are going to win."

"Just stay with me." Jeff nodded. "Feel free to scream when I fuck something up."

A truck convoy was coming through the village down the main road, its horn a constant bleating against the sound of heavy machine guns starting to open up on the approaching ships.

"That would be my Javelins." Jeff grinned and started off before pulling to a stop. He looked back at them. "Can you contact Portsmouth and ask the Navy to get into the harbor here to give us a hand? Say please if you think it will help."

Jeff paused and pointed at the approaching ships. "Missiles or not, they could at least drive around out there and get those bastards to turn sideways so we can get a decent shot at them."

"On it." Kyle reached for his phone. He knew the planes were in the process of re-arming, but there were ships that had left Portsmouth and should already be here. He paused in his dialing as an out-of-breath corporal ran up to Jeff.

"Sir! The missile batteries are having issues. Something about problems with their fire control and shitty roads—but they are working it."

"Wonderful…" Jeff spit.

Kyle overheard the message and tapped his head while looking at Jeff. He jerked a thumb at Audy. "We've got an idea."

Audy was shaking his head. "We do?"

Kyle pointed at the trucks behind Jeff. Troops were already pulling the hard-side carry cases off the back. "You got the Navy coming with dick-all for missiles, and you got missiles that don't do shit unless you can get a broadside."

It took Jeff half a second to reach the same conclusion he had. "I'm so not going to be the one to tell Pretty."

Kyle waved at the harbor behind him. "We have to stop these in the harbor if your plan is going to work."

"I know." Jeff nodded once and then grinned. "You know what they say—if it works, forgiveness is easier than permission."

"What are we talking about?" Audy almost yelled.

*

Dom Majeski had a full, heavy brigade holding a line two miles long, stretching across the peninsula from the shore of the inner harbor to the light surf of the Channel-side sandy beaches. They'd had four bulldozers running all night, creating a no-man's-land in front of his lines at the point where the peninsula narrowed. Most of his gun trucks were locked in place behind berms of mud and earth, and his 4500 men would be fighting from protected positions.

There'd been a screwup somewhere back on Eden. His brigade's artillery had been portaled somewhere behind the city of Plymouth. And yes, they were still in range of most of the peninsula, but he'd wanted them on the hills directly behind his position. In their place, he'd moved most of his heavy mortars, and they had a field of fire encompassing the whole approach to his line.

Friendly gunfire erupted to the east, beyond the cleared strip of land. Those were the 6.8 mm assault rifles of Lieutenant Kaj'jal's platoon, who were out there to lead the enemy on. There was an explosion of Kaerin fire in response. A good bit of that was automatic rifle fire as well, Dom noted. He doubted if the Kaerin's forward units were packing around one of the now infamous, and very large caliber, hummingbird guns. No, he listened more closely. Those would be the Kaerin's new assault rifles, patterned after captured M4s.

"Get the drone over that!" He yelled out.

"They're working on it," Brent Phillips answered next to him. "Tree cover is a bitch."

Dom doubted there'd be a tree left standing on the peninsula by the end of this fight. His job was to hold the this line while his mortars, artillery, and the EDF planes bombed the shit out of the enemy. But he hadn't seen or heard an airplane in nearly an hour.

"Mortar's ready to cover their exfil?"

"They're ready," Phillips answered. "They just need target coords."

He looked down at the monitor slaved to the drone flying over the Kaerin's beach landings. Twenty ships were beached, a handful were in the process of unloading, and a miles-long line of ships were offshore, steaming towards the beach.

"Where is the fucking Navy?"

Phillips pursed his lips and shrugged. "Where's the Air Force?"

*

Chapter 31

E.N. *Constitution*, **E.N** *Independence*

"Somebody needs to remind Portsmouth we can't portal from one base to another—we actually have to sail there."

Amelia Harper vented her frustrations at her husband Jack over the radio through her headset. Portsmouth had just asked for an update on their progress for the third time in the hour. Her E.N. *Constitution* was a quarter of a mile ahead of his E.N. *Independence* moving west at flank speed towards Plymouth. They were almost there.

They were carrying only two missiles each, but the extra empty launcher had been removed and replaced with the original 25mm auto cannon. The work to do it had taken an entire night, and the downtime on land had been more than welcome. They'd been running steady at thirty knots for the last eight hours. They were getting close, and this promised to be a knife fight in a phone booth compared to the long-range laser targeting and missile launches over the last week.

"They know it," Jack came back. "They're just trying to plan around our ETA. You're the belle of the ball."

"That'd be a first," she replied.

"Wait one," he came back. She rolled her eyes. If they were asking him for another update so soon, she was going to scream.

John was off the air for almost a minute before he came back on. "Change in plans, honey. Once our missile racks are dry, you are to proceed to the quay for a pickup. We'll go in behind you and keep the bad guys distracted."

"Are we Uber now?" She couldn't imagine what or who would be needing a ride.

"They got a plan, Amelia. You're not going to like it."

She listened to the "plan," thinking that somebody in charge had lost their mind.

*

"That's it! No more!" Amelia Harper squeezed past the Javelin carry cases that filled her bridge and managed to get her head out the small opening that had been the hatchway to her cramped forward deck. Every open space on her already small ship was taken up by the heavy plastic carry cases.

"Alright, we're good to go!" Kyle Lassiter shouted back to her from where he and the Jema Audrin'ochal were kneeling on the narrow foredeck directly in front of her sloped bridge windows.

They were surrounded by yet more missile cases that had been strapped down against the deck's outer railing, as if they were some sort of protection, not full of something that went boom by design.

"We aren't going anywhere until you two idiots snap into that safety line." She knew who they were, and she didn't care. She was beyond angry. This was a dumb idea, and she just knew that somehow, she was going to be held responsible for killing two of the EDF's leaders, not to mention the husband of one of her best friends on Chandra.

She turned to her one crewman who had volunteered to assist them on deck with the cases. "Seaman Mathers, radio me when they are snapped in—you as well. We won't be going anywhere until that happens."

"Yes, ma'am!" Mathers shouted back and started to add a salute before ducking instinctively as a Kaerin shell went overhead, exploding behind a line of Junata dwellings at the backside of the village.

Amelia pulled herself back inside the bridge and climbed over a stack of missile cases getting to her chair.

"Captain?!" Ensign Calderon, sitting at the helm, addressed her. "I think that was meant for us."

"Not yet!" she yelled back, craning her neck to try to get sight of the *Independence* as it surged past them, putting itself in between her ship and the line of Kaerin paddle-wheelers out in the bay. Most were making for different points of land, but at least half a dozen had decided to try to kill the foolish boat that had decided to dock in the middle of a fight.

"All tied in, Captain." Mathers' voice sounded excited in her ear. Stupid kid was probably going to enjoy this.

"Go, Andrew! Get us moving."

She watched her helm officer kill the station-keeping jets and push the throttle forward just as the wake from the *Independence* rocked them hard up against the stone quay. She ignored the sound of missile crates shifting behind her—she was far more worried about what would happen if one of those Kaerin shells hit one of the cases.

Andrew pulled them in a tight circle accelerating out from the dock that was probably covered in navy gray paint by now. Out her front window glacis, she took some satisfaction from the fact that both her idiot passengers had some trouble keeping their balance.

"Run us past that group shooting at us, no closer than a thousand yards."

"Aye, Captain."

"You are weapons-free, Monica. Give them what help you can."

"Aye, Captain."

On their way into the harbor, both the *Independence* and *Constitution* had scored hits with all four of their missiles. The rifle fire from the troops on the decks of the enemy ships had been heavy anytime they'd approached. Staying out of rifle range was going to be hard—the harbor was getting crowded.

She looked with longing at the relatively empty water beyond the flotilla of enemy ships. They had to work quickly—there were reports of a larger wave of ships coming in behind this one.

She watched as Audy and Kyle readied a missile. Mathers threw the empty case overboard and was already pulling another from the stack as a loose crate slid past him, almost taking him out below the knees. A spout of water from an exploding shell lanced upward a hundred yards off her port bow.

"Swing us further to port Andrew, our passengers can wait a bit longer."

The passengers weren't listening. Kyle fired his first missile—at what, she couldn't tell. She'd been expecting a roiling cloud of smoke from the launch, but there hadn't been anything beyond a loud pop that made its way through the thick ballistic glass.

They were already re-loading, and she watched in appreciation how fast they worked with Audy seating another missile and Harper getting the next crate open. The next fired about a minute after the first. Okay, maybe she'd been wrong. This could work. If they hit anything. If her passengers didn't catch a cannonball or a shot from a Kaerin long-gun. They'd just fired a third missile when Jack's voice broke in over the radio.

"Way to go, *Constitution*!"

"Oh yeah, that's a hit!" Monica added from her station.

Monica could see less out the windows than she could, but had the best view on the bridge at the moment from the camera on her stern-mounted remote cannon. "Those things have longer range than I would have guessed."

"Use the range, Andrew," Amelia ordered. "Keep us as far away from those things as you can. Remember, just because they may be burning, doesn't mean their troops won't be on deck firing."

"Yes, ma'am."

Kyle fired another missile, and then there was a delay as Mathers had to undo the straps on the next stack of crates. Audy glanced back through the window into the bridge. He was grinning like a kid on his first bicycle and holding out an upturned thumb.

Dumbass. She forced herself to smile and responded in kind, shaking her head. It would have been a great start to one of those old-world "hey, hold my beer videos" that her idiot brothers had liked so much.

*

"What the hell, Jeff!" Colonel Pretty wasn't happy. "I've got reports from pilots that they can see three assholes launching javelins from the deck of one of the patrol boats—tell me that isn't who I think it is."

Jeff was less concerned about Colonel Pretty's anger than he was glad to hear there were planes overhead. They'd taken their sweet time getting here.

"Colonel, order those planes to get over the peninsula. The Kaerin are attacking all across our defensive line. We almost have the missile battery up—the harbor is not the priority right now. Can you patch me in to them?"

"Ground Lead, this is Falcon One." The pilots broke in. "We are on this channel as well. We copy and are proceeding to the peninsula. We can see your lines."

"Glad to have you here, Falcon one." Jeff sent up a prayer of thanks. The Kaerin had massed for an attack against Dom's position a lot faster than any of them had thought they would. "Drop on any concentration of Kaerin east of our lines—ignore their ships for now. Let them beach, we're ready for them. Our troops will lay out red smoke on priority targets."

"Copy all, Falcon One—out."

"Jeff! Who's on the fucking boat?!" Yeah… the Colonel was pissed and forgotten why he'd called.

"Back to you in a moment, sir." Jeff clicked the microphone off and switched channels.

"Dom, you've got air support inbound—drop red, repeat—drop red smoke where you need them the most!"

"Is about time!" Dom came back after a pause that was becoming worrisome. Dom was nearly screaming over the sound of a nearby auto cannon and machine guns.

Further conversation wasn't possible, as one of the paddle-wheelers in the bay drove up onto the rocks a quarter mile east of his position. It announced its arrival with a shot from its main cannon pointed directly ahead. He couldn't see whether it hit anything or not, but the EDF dug in directly in front of it opened up with everything they had.

The 25 mm cannons from half a dozen JLTVs started chewing at the bow of the craft, working their way through the ship. The enemy vessel seemed to come apart as if it had run aground into the teeth of an invisible tree chipper, and the troops on deck didn't fare any better. Automatic grenade fire began lobbing shells onto the deck, even as every EDF trooper in range with a rifle opened up.

Jeff swallowed the bile rising in his gorge even as he hoped for another ship to run point-blank into one of their prepared positions. Right now, the Kaerin needed to be dissuaded from this avenue of attack.

"Sir, we've got two ships just starting a turn into the estuary."

One of the young Edenite runners was at his shoulder and pointing further east. It wasn't an area where there'd been anything to dig into. He'd been assured the *Door Knocker* and its sister ship the *Party Favor* could handle the water and mud.

"Alright, you got this." He calmed his voice and grabbed the trooper by the shoulder. "Send the coordinates to Portsmouth. Request one land yacht." He held up a single finger inches from the kid's nose. "Put it in the marsh right where we talked about. Let them know what they'll have coming at them, and remember the landing orientation—it's critical."

"Broadside towards the enemy. Yes, sir."

Jeff clapped the man's shoulder, repeating what he'd said to himself a minute ago. "Go, you got this."

He waited a few seconds, listening in on the soldier's conversation with the portal control in Portsmouth, before reaching for his own sat phone to call Hank back. He'd counted, and Kyle and Audy had hit seven ships before Colonel Pretty had called. More looked to be burning in the distance, and he could still see the two patrol boats motoring between and around the enemy ships. They were too far away for him to make out any figures on their decks.

"What the hell, Jeff? It's them, isn't it?"

Jeff pinched the bridge of his nose. "I was promised the missile battery will be up in twenty minutes, sir. That was an hour ago. We had to stop them here and force their main body to land on the channel-side beaches. The Javelins don't have enough punch unless they hit a broadside—we needed to get fire power out on the water... sir."

He was sure he could hear Pretty's jaw popping on the other end of the line. "I'm told five minutes on the missile battery."

"Your lips to God's ears, sir," Jeff replied.

Hank didn't say anything for a moment. Jeff wasn't too worried. If anybody understood what was needed, it was Hank Pretty. "Get them out of there the second you have the missiles up."

"Will do, sir."

*

Dom turned away and ducked as the oblong fuel-tank-looking bombs fell away off the wings of the three attack planes. They'd come in low from the harbor side. It looked to him like they were flying right down the treeless path of the cleared no-man's-land. Their defensive fire across the cleared strip into the tree line, swarming with Kaerin, dropped off in an instant as every soldier dropped to the bottom of their trenches. He couldn't help but think it wouldn't matter if the pilots missed.

The afternoon light suddenly got a lot brighter at the bottom of his trench, followed by the rolling explosions of the napalm bombs. He scrambled up the firing step inside the trench and looked over the edge of his mud-filled sandbags. Some of the bombs had dropped well to the east of where his people had marked with smoke. Several had found their mark and scorched a line north to south. He turned his head away as several Kaerin warriors ran from the conflagration out into the clearing aflame. Human torches moving out of instinct.

It was probably his imagination, but he thought he could hear screams over the rolling booms of the echoing explosions.

"Troops up!" he screamed. He wanted this over. They had to make them quit.

"Peninsula Control to Falcon Flight—you were on target. Next target is red smoke a quarter mile inland from the beach. Target that troop concentration!" He had to scream the last as his men up and down the line started firing again.

The pockets of Kaerin taken out by the bomb strikes were still burning, and the flames were spreading to the trees. The burning areas acted like traffic medians and the Kaerin tide just flowed around and between them, bunching up. His mortar fire began landing again just as the Kaerin mortars exploded in a line perpendicular to their trench a hundred yards north of his position. At least two of them landed directly on top of their lines.

Phillips saw it too and was already moving. "I got it."

The JLTVs behind where the enemy mortars had landed kept up their deadly fire even as the EDF troops in front of them died.

He grabbed up his radio. "Jeff—this is Dom. If you can spare them, I am going to need QRF support. Have them hold behind our guns. I'll be able to direct them on arrival."

"Have your lines been breached?"

"Negative, but they have mortars. A lot of them. We need additional reserves—my main reserve is near the beach where my people have less cover."

"Copy—QRF is on its way. Five minutes. More planes coming your way as well."

"Copy—thank you." It wasn't exactly military standard communication, but it was heartfelt.

*

In their haste to get the Javelins loaded on board and strapped down, Kyle had misplaced his ear protection and his ears were ringing painfully. They'd fired nearly twenty missiles and stopped at least fifteen ships. They had some breathing room in the harbor, which was good as they'd shot through what they had stored on deck and the process to transfer the cases from the bridge to where they needed them was taking longer.

There were three paddle-wheelers steaming around the headland of the peninsula, but the *Constitution* had to run past damaged and burning ships to get to them. The surviving Kaerin troops on board those vessels were stranded for the moment, but that meant they didn't have anything else to do besides take potshots at the two enemy ships in the harbor, especially the one with the morons standing out in the open on the forward deck. Mathers, the *Constitution's* crewman helping them, had already been grazed across his thigh, but the kid hadn't slowed down a bit.

Audy had gone down for a moment, taking a half spent round in the middle of his back. His backplate had caught the heavy slug after being slowed by the bulky safety water floats the ship's captain had insisted on, but Audy was hurt and definitely moving slower.

So far, Kyle had been lucky, it was probably better that he couldn't hear the potshot rounds zipping by. That said, there'd been one close enough to his head to feel. He didn't need his hearing to see the ships they were headed towards explode in quick succession. One, two, three—they went up in fireballs as shore-based missiles struck home. It was about time.

He grabbed Audy by the shoulder and pointed towards the bridge window. "Time to get you on the radio!"

Audy glanced ahead at the burning ships and nodded in agreement. They both stood to make their way slowly to the narrow walkway around the edge of the bow, when the *Constitution* began to turn away from its attack run. Kyle felt their safety wire get hit through his hand. The pencil-thick cable came alive for a moment like the worst foul-ball sting in history. It came apart between the two of them.

They were looking at each other in surprise as the ship's turn launched them over the railing. Between the instinctive thoughts of "oh shit," and "Pretty's going to be pissed," Kyle couldn't help but think Audy looked ridiculous.

*

"Say again?!"

Jeff wanted to scream, but there was a chance he'd misheard the captain of the *Constitution*. There was enough gunfire coming from half a dozen different points at the edge of the harbor—some less than two hundred yards away—that he couldn't be sure.

"They've both gone overboard!" The ship's captain was yelling *at him*. Why, he didn't know. "Their floaties are keeping them up—we have eyes on them."

Jeff lowered the radio to his waist and looked for something to hit. He took a deep breath. "Get them out of the water... please."

"Working on it. *Constitution* out."

He grabbed the first soldier he saw carrying a Jema blade. "You're coming with me, corporal!"

"Gat'taska, sir. I was ordered to report to the command tent."

"Why?"

"I'm to tell our commander," the corporal shook his head. "To tell *you,* sir, that the third scouts have spotted a platoon of Kaerin behind our lines. Landward of the estuary. They could not get confirmation of their sighting on the radio."

"Yeah, frequencies are getting walked on." Jeff nodded knowingly and turned the young man towards the radio truck. "We heard the report. Consider your writ fulfilled and come with me."

The *Door Knocker's* insertion into the battle had gone well enough, but a good number of Kaerin warriors had spilled off their ships and used their own sinking, bullet-riddled ships as shields as they waded to shore. They were probably still running.

"I need you to get on the radio and pretend you are a Kaerin captain on one of those ships burning out there." He pointed out into the bay.

"Me? Sir."

"I'd do it myself, but I'm told my accent is horrible," Jeff answered in Chandrian.

"Yes, sir."

"Yes, you can do it? Or yes, my Chandrian sucks?" He asked as pushed the man up the stepladder into the back of the commo truck.

The inside of the compartment smelled of sweaty stress and funky mud. Everything in this place smelled of mud.

"Which one of you is monitoring the Kaerin short wave?"

A short, chubby, bookish-looking kid with thick glasses raised his hand in the back.

"You stay!" Jeff pointed. "Everyone else out! Now!" he screamed. He grabbed Corporal Gat'taska's arm, who was just trying to follow orders and make a run for it. "Not you, Corporal, you're staying as well."

"Sir." Another radio operator raised a hand, an Edenite, from the look of him. They must have recruited a high school's AV club to run the radio truck. "I have Colonel Pretty on the line—he's demanding to talk to you, sir. 'Right the fuck now.' His words, sir."

The phone on Jeff's belt was vibrating as well. "Tell him you can't find me. Now you all get out—wait outside."

The operator with the headset and mic in his hand just stood there, looking back and forth from his mic to Jeff.

"He heard that, didn't he?"

"Yes! I fucking heard that!" Pretty's screaming was loud enough he could hear it through the radio operator's headset being held out to him.

"Two minutes, sir." Jeff bent over and yelled at the headset.

He turned on the remaining operator. "Corporal Gat'taska has a message to send the Kaerin fleet. Can you do that?"

"We have their channel—yes, sir."

"Do you know the name of any of the commanders or ships that were destroyed?"

"Yes, sir. It's a long list, but we were told to log all the names for the intel guys."

"Pick one!" he yelled. "Has to be one you know was in the bay."

He turned his gaze on the confused Jema and forced himself to relax. "You are going to say the harbor is impassable, the channel is blocked, and that the remaining ships can't close with the Shareki. No admission of being defeated—just short and sweet. 'You are unable to close with the enemy from the harbor—all ships to land on the channel-side beaches.' Say it back to me."

It took three tries. Corporal Gat'taska was not a natural actor.

"Bastelta Tak'delo," The kid with glasses held up his notes. "He was in command of one of the ships that turned into the estuary—he hasn't been heard from since."

"Perfect." Jeff nodded. "No way he made it through that."

He'd seen the pilothouses of those ships literally be taken apart board-by-board as the *Door Knocker's* mini-guns had gone to work.

"You are Bastelta Tak'del" he clapped a hand on the Jema's back and forced him down into the seat next to the Edenite kid.

"Tak'delo," the radio operator corrected him. "Bastelta Tak'delo. He spoke very slow, almost in a whisper when we heard him before. He was real calm, like some of them are." The Edenite radio operator explained that all to the Jema corporal in what to Jeff sounded like pitch-perfect Chandrian.

The Jema looked up at Jeff and pointed at the radio operator.

"Right!" He turned to the Edenite teenager. "You do it."

To his credit, the operator delayed only long enough to make an adjustment on his radio. "All boats, this is Bastelta Tak'delo. The harbor entrance is blocked. We cannot approach to kill the Shareki. Do not enter the harbor—it is a trap. All boats land on the channel beach and join the battle."

The kid switched something off before turning to look at Jeff, shrugging like he did this stuff all the time. "It'll probably take some time to confirm that the message is getting through—they do a lot of relaying between ships. We don't even think they all have radios."

"What's your name, kid?"

"Edwin, but everybody calls me Buddy. I mean, Private Moss, sir."

Jeff pointed a finger at back at him. "You're now Corporal Eddy Moss, kid. No more 'Buddy.' Well done!" Jeff flashed them both a thumbs up and reached for his sat phone.

"Thank you, sir."

Jeff had half a mind to ask the radio operator to call Hank for him. Corporal Gat'taska looked relieved he hadn't had to do the needful.

"They're fishing them out now," Hank said upon picking up.

"Thank God!" Jeff breathed a sigh of relief. If anything had happened to Kyle and Audy, he'd have been next in line to be the Colonel's sidekick, and that wasn't something he'd be any good at. As far as he was concerned, he was really good at only two things—and nobody needed a free safety these days.

"Sir, I'd like to portal in at least a brigade of Souza's division from Eden—now. Right behind our lines on the peninsula. Dom is going to need more help than our QRF can offer."

"They are still moving through the portal from Portsmouth to Eden." Hank answered. "He's only got four regiments prepped on Eden so far. And you are all a long way from any portal if we have to meet the Kaerin after they break out."

"With respect, sir—screw that. Give me the four regiments. They won't be going anywhere—I guarantee it. Dom has been stacking them up, but he could use the firepower, and ammo is going to be an issue soon. If they all land beachside, he's going to need help. We'll hold them there and kill them."

It was a good ten seconds before Hank came back. "I'm in agreement. Jomra heard you, and he's smiling. I'll get your reinforcements flowing. Meantime, you've got both land yachts at your call to start ferrying your bayside troops towards Majeski's line."

"The *Door Knocker* is disabled, sir. It's a landmark, half buried in mud. Its field generators are off line. But I copy, we've got the *Party Favor*."

"You've got the jets coming back as well. Dom's calling them in. I'm told you'll have another flight of planes in twenty minutes."

"Copy all, sir."

"Jeff?"

"Sir?"

"If you would, please have Audy and that idiot friend of his call me once they are standing back on land."

Jeff grinned. "Yes, sir. It will be my pleasure, sir."

*

Chapter 32

Kaerin War Leader Jum'raga was not smiling. His long-time brother-in-arms, Bastelta Barg'rasta, had led the first concentrated attack on the Shareki line that had them trapped on this dangerous spit of land. The attack had been savaged by the Shareki airboats before it had even begun in earnest. Even then, reports had come back that the attack had nearly succeeded, would have succeeded if the Shareki had not been able to reinforce the small breach in the line his warriors had forced. He should have waited until they'd had more troops gathered.

The failed effort had been costly—not just the numbers of warriors lost, or the fact Barg'rasta had been among the fallen. It was the time he needed to organize for another attack. The enemy was using the delay to reinforce their line. He could still hear the rolling echoes of gate arrivals behind the enemy line that heralded yet more Shareki warriors barring their path off this strip of land separating the bay from the channel. There was a booming echo every few minutes. He didn't know how many Shareki had been there to repulse the last attack, only that there would be far more to face during the next.

The enemy no longer had to split their defense between here and the multi-pronged bayside assault. One of the Bastelta assigned to attack the interior shores of the bay had messaged that it was a trap, and that the Shareki had blocked the channel. He didn't know how that was possible, but he had seen many things today that he could not have imagined. First among them, an attack by four Kaerin fists—twenty thousand High Blood warriors—had been stopped, turned back and chewed to pieces by the Shareki's firepower.

Much of his fleet was still in the process of beaching their boats and spilling their warriors onto sand mixed with blood and the contents of sea-sick stomachs. The enemy's airboats swooping down on the narrow beach, and the enemy's artillery chased his warriors into the trees where Tearks and Bastelta fought to restore battle order and move the men to points where they could ready themselves for the coming attack. Very soon, there would be no more space on the beach, and the portion of the fleet still holding offshore would be forced to offload warriors into the surf. It would only make the bloody gauntlet that much more difficult.

Hidden under the trees himself, half a kamark from the enemy's line, Jum'raga looked up, seeking the fast-moving airboats whose roar heralded their approach. Different from the other airboats that were present in much larger numbers, these sounded like the sky itself was being ripped apart. They had seen at least two of the terrible machines and they had carried bombs that were dropped during swooping attacks with an accuracy that seemed magical.

They were overmatched—there was no utility or honor to be found in denying it. Whoever had thought Kaerin warriors could overwhelm these Shareki was living in a world far from this place. A line of angry fireballs erupted a kamark away, and the crack of their explosions reached him seconds later. In the background was the thunderous roar of the enemy's airboat climbing away and preparing for another attack. How many warriors had he just lost? He did not know how, but somehow, the enemy had known they were coming here. They had been dug in and waiting for them. The Shareki wanted them here, trapped between water on three sides and certain death in the one direction they had left to them.

"Is the long-talker operational?"

He asked the trio standing behind him, a pair of Bastelta and a single Kareel. They were all from other boats—two were from other clans—

and he did not know them. They did not know him either, beyond the fact he had declared himself War Leader.

"It is, War Leader," the Kareel wearing the colors of the Prelate's S'kaeda Clan said. "Though there are only a handful of boats that have not yet landed that are so equipped."

He had no intention of communicating with those boats, at least not yet. "I am going to try to reach Lord Tima across the channel."

He watched the three warriors for any sign of dissent. If they as a group disagreed with his assessment, his life was forfeit. The thought of being killed by these three almost made him smile. His death was a foregone conclusion at this point—the only question was how.

It was time for honesty. "I can see no hope of penetrating their defensive line. If any of you disagree with that, please tell me what I am missing."

No one answered him, but the two Bastelta were looking to the other Kareel for some indication of how this discussion would proceed.

"I have no wish to summon the Prelate's host across the channel to face what we have in front of us," Jum'raga began again. "I'm told we cannot get our surviving boats off the beach until the next high tide. By then, there will be even fewer of them left to send back across."

"What are you suggesting?" The other Kareel, either out of habit or planning, moved his sword hand to his belt, a finger away from the hilt of his long knife.

Jum'raga glanced westward, where his warriors kept the enemy's lines under nearly constant fire. "We attack in the next few hours with everything we already have ashore. Let the outcome of that decide whether we land the rest of our boats and send for the Prelate's host to join us. If we can't break their line with the ten Fists we have now—how would the additional seven fists still afloat change that outcome?"

"We should wait until we have those extra fists," one of the Bastelta tried.

Jum'raga nodded in agreement. "I would like to…" He paused as one of the Shareki rocket-driven airboats screamed past less than a hundred feet above the neighboring line of hills. It released a single bomb before looping upward, its rocket engines screaming. They all felt the sharp crack of the bomb in their teeth, ears, and through the soles of their boots. Jum'raga waited for the rolling echo to fade as he looked at each of the warriors in turn.

He lifted an arm in the direction of the explosion. "Our warriors have yet to draw a blade. Most have died before they reach halfway across the killing field the Shareki have scratched across the land. Their airboats and cannons will not stop. They are killing us in numbers faster than we can land ships. We will never be as strong as we are now—and you have all heard the echoes of additional gate arrivals behind their lines. They are being reinforced." He paused again and met each of their gazes. "I ask you to tell me how I have misread the situation."

The Kareel he'd been worried about took half a step forward. "You are the War Leader. We will follow you. You see it true." Both Bastelta saluted smartly in unison.

He nodded in reply. "Prepare the warriors. We have ten Fists. We will launch a simultaneous attack—two Fists at their center, four at water's edge on both ends of their defensive line. I will confer with Lord Tima and return shortly to lead the attack on the beach-end of their lines."

*

"Go get Captain Krouse!" Newly promoted *Corporal* 'Eddy' Moss pulled off his earphones and swung them down to his desk. The rest of the radio operators in the back of the commo truck just looked at him. "Now! Their commander is talking to his boss across the channel."

Ten minutes later, Hank and Jomra were back on the phone with Jeff, Dom, Jake, and Tom.

"Our planes are reporting that the ships yet to land are turning south." Hank relayed the intercepted radio message. "They look to be headed back across the channel. Lord Tima just approved an all-out attack that they are going to kick off before dark. But that's it—the rest are returning to port."

"Sir," Dom started, "I know it's a long shot, but maybe we should get on the public announcement horns and let them know they can surrender. We'll let them leave."

"Screw that," Jomra spoke up. "Captain Krouse? Is that a correct usage of the phrase?"

"Yes, sir." Jeff chimed in. "I believe you've got the gist of it."

"Guys," Hank interjected. "Their leadership just blinked. It was Lord Tima again. We've got him thinking. We now have a chance to put a big hole in their warrior class' morale, and we are going to do it. There will be survivors, and we will treat them well—see them returned. This isn't a Strema host dying on another planet. They are not going to be able to hide the fact they got their asses kicked. Given their culture, it's an opportunity we are not going to throw away."

"Understood, sir," Dom answered. "Captain Souza's reinforcements are in place—we'll stop them."

"Hey not trying to bring up a sore subject or anything," Jake spoke up. "But where's Kyle and Audy? We heard they got fished out of the bay."

"They are on their way back to Portsmouth," Jomra answered, sounding like he was trying not to laugh. "By truck."

*

The sound of the mini-gun going silent, its electrically driven barrel assembly winding down to a full stop, was punctuated by a handful of mortar shells exploding in the distance. The shells had been fired before Jake's order to cease fire had fully propagated up and down the length of the EDF line.

The impossible had just happened. The tail end of the Kaerin attack had broken and ran. By then many, if not most, of the EDF soldiers

419

who had just stopped the attack were weeping behind their guns. The reality of the slaughter couldn't be denied. Jema soldiers had been among the first to stop firing and start shouting across the killing strip, imploring the Kaerin to retreat. There was no celebration, just a quiet relief and a blanket of moral terror that they might have to do it again.

Along the rocky shore of the inner bay, the Kaerin high-water mark had come within twenty yards of the first trench line. Close enough to throw grenades and kill ten soldiers as they'd advanced with their swords drawn. The machine guns and .25 mm auto cannons behind the line made certain the advance went no further. At the opposite end of the line, on the channel-side beaches, there had been no cover for the Kaerin advance. There, the High Blood human wave had gone down like rows of wheat in a field—most before firing a shot. War Leader Jum'raga had led the attack from the front and been killed after stepping out from behind one of their beached ships, waving his long sword.

Near the center of their defensive line, Tom Souza put a hand on Dom Majeski's shoulder, overlooking the death and destruction in front of them. The younger man had just emptied his stomach into the bottom of their trench.

"Have to think long run, Dom. We have to believe this just saved a lot of lives. Kaerin lives."

Jake was standing nearby, looking down the shallow slope at the piled Kaerin dead. He'd overheard Tom and shared the same hope, but doubted if the poor dead bastards piled waist-high in places had figured that out or would have cared.

*

Normandy, Chandra

Lord Tima Bre'jana stood looking out the windows of the harbor control office. Camped in the town behind him, and at harbors to his east and west, were nearly 400,000 warriors that were waiting for word that a landing site had been secured and that they would board the expected ships returning from victory on Irinas.

He had yet to share his decision that the invasion had been called off. He was still coming to terms that it *had* been his decision. Prelate Noka S'kaeda was dead. He had collapsed with the news of the missing, and presumed destroyed, battle fleet three days earlier and had not recovered.

An hour before War Leader Jum'raga had messaged him from Irinas with news that the attack had failed utterly, news had arrived that Lord Noka had died. That news had spread like wildfire. Now, his first pronouncement as Prelate was not going to be one of victory or promised retribution. It would be one of retreat, of caution, and it would in all likelihood create a series of rivals that he would have to deal with.

That prospect worried him far less than the Edenite's next move. They would no doubt do exactly what his ancestors had done—take apart this world one region at a time, co-opting local clans as they went. There was nothing his people could do to stop them. All that was left to Tima was the forlorn hope he could convince enough Kaerin that there was perhaps some honor to be found in fighting the Edenites for some sort of peace.

He pulled the single chess piece from his pocket. He'd taken it from Ocheltree's rooms for reasons he didn't want to think about. It was the white king. All this time, they'd been convinced the Edenite's strategy was dictated by the weakness of their numbers and avoiding a battle they couldn't win. The enemy had been playing a different game from the very beginning—luring him and the Kaerin into a battle *they* couldn't win. Now, the Kaerin were left with the threat of subjugated peoples that would soon be holding knives to their throats. It had long been his greatest fear.

He dropped the game piece to the floor and snapped it in-two under the heel of his boot. A small part of him hoped Lord Oont'tal had managed to get the beacon's signal to the Kaerin home world. The ancient enemy that had driven the Kaerin to this place wouldn't care what games the Edenites played—perhaps some vindication could be found in that outcome. There would be no honor. It wouldn't be his fight. Fighting the ancient enemy that had driven them here or the Edenites—it would not matter. His people's days were numbered.

*

Chapter 33

Somewhere off the coast of Northwest France, Chandra

Steve had been clinging to the slimy, fetid beam for nearly two days, and his strength was fading. The last time he'd slid off the rough squared beam, it had taken everything he had to get back on it. If it had happened at night, he'd have drowned. The *Bucket* hadn't broken up as it slowly sank as much as it had seemed to dissolve. The water in the hold had risen slowly enough that he'd managed to float back up to the rotten hole he'd fallen through. He'd made it onto the deck and awaited the inevitable. He'd had time to rope a few old timbers stacked on deck together. His knot tying skills hadn't been up to the task, and an hour after he'd floated free, he was down to a single piece of rotten timber that had been part of the original ship.

After two days in the water, the timber was so slick it seemed to exude slime. It took strength he no longer had to hang on. He should have stayed in New San Diego. The job wiring up a tidal generator system had been boring, but at least the air had been breathable. Like an idiot, he'd jumped at the chance to work as an electrician on Chandra. After his first day on board the *Bucket*, he'd been ready to break his contract. Lieutenant Annie Barton had been the only reason he'd stayed.

Images of her inviting herself to a date with him had been playing through his head a lot lately. Damn if that steak didn't sound good about now, but only after a few gallons of water to drink. Sometimes, like right now, it seemed like he could hear her talking to him.

Something heavy and soft hit him in the head. He managed to break the vacuum seal the side of his face had with the slimy log and turn his head. An image of Annie hovered above him. There seemed to be other people behind her.

"Steve!" she yelled. "Can you hear me? Grab the floaty! You owe me a steak!"

*

Kaerus—Kaerin Home World, Capital City of Ro'delus

The morning sun broke over the hills to the east, lighting the sky in a fiery orange. The sunrise promised a beautiful day. A perfect day, thought Mur'ell Otak'rino, the 31st Director of the Great War Museum. Perfect, except for the fact that she had to personally direct a tour this morning for the first-year students of the Academy's school. The children of the Kaerin Academy were often as gifted as their parents, and she was not about to assign their tour to one of her deputies.

As always with young children, there'd be several parents present acting as chaperones, and it never hurt to make a good impression on the people that ultimately funded her life's work. The museum sat at the edge of the Academy's sprawling campus. Open to officials and citizens on an equal footing, this morning it was reserved for the nearly two hundred six-year-old children who would get their first official taste of their rich history.

"One of the children has a parent that's a guardian."

She hadn't even heard her Prime Deputy walk up behind her. She was glad to see Dur'mak was wearing his suit, the same one she'd made him buy for last year's New Year celebration. The academic usually showed up to work looking like one of the custodial staff.

She smiled in greeting. "I'm sure there will be several children of guardians in the group."

"No, I mean, yes." Dur'mak gave his head a shake. "I was just informed by the security people that they'd been contacted by Academy security. A guardian is going to be part of the group as one of the chaperones. They didn't want his security detail to alarm us."

"Oh." She nodded. "That's a first."

"If you'd like—" Dur'mak started, but she raised a hand, stopping him.

"I'll take whatever group he is in," she countered. "Unless you are volunteering to be the one that has to defend our budget request this year."

"Thank you, no."

The children, offspring of the Kaerin elite, came through the lobby doors like a flock of wingless birds—all noise and pandemonium—herded by instructors that already looked exhausted at mid-morning.

Mur'ell's particular group started in the grand gallery. She'd give the history lesson first, and then lead them around the rest of the museum. She'd done this before—but never with an actual guardian standing in the audience.

The high-ranking elite would no doubt be able to give her talk as easily as she could, with more detail and context as well—but the silver-haired, late middle-aged man seemed entirely focused on his daughter. *I suppose guardians are people too,* she thought. *He's probably looking forward to a day off spent with his child.* She waited a moment for the instructors to bring the group to some level of focus before starting.

"Welcome to the Museum of the Great Civil War. I'm the Director here, and you can address me as Director Otak'rino. Who can tell me why we have this museum?"

She called on a young girl raising her arm in the front row. "To make us remember."

"Yes, I suppose that's part of what a museum does. But why is this museum so important?"

"So we can have a field trip!" A young boy shouted out from the back.

"Another good reason." She kept her smile and exchanged a friendly look with the Guardian, who seemed to appreciate the young boy's honesty.

"We are the Kaerin," she began. "All of us, across this world and on Kaerus Minor as well. We are one people, forged from many, who have lived in peace for centuries. But that peace came at great cost in a struggle we almost lost—in fact, a struggle we did lose. Who remembers who the Torpun were?"

"Children? We've studied this…" One of the instructors, no doubt looking to score points with the Guardian as well, spoke up, sounding almost nervous.

"They were the bad people who fought us."

Mur'ell nodded her thanks. "Yes, that right. Did you know that they won? For almost two centuries, the Torpun ruled Kaerus. They took away many of the freedoms we all enjoy now, but theirs was a system based solely on power and control, and without an external enemy to fight, they began to fight each other for control of our world.

"But the Kaerin," she added a smile, "we remembered why we had fought them in the first place—and nearly five centuries ago, we started to fight back. Can anyone tell me what the rallying cry was of those Kaerin who fought back and defeated the Torpun?"

"You have to find what you lose," A young boy in the front row shouted loudly.

"That is close," she responded once the laughter settled down. "It was, '*What was lost, will be found.*'"

She lifted a hand, indicating the panoply of military equipment in the displays behind her. Some of it was melted to slag, and even after all these centuries, much of it stood behind four inches of specially designed transparent metal due to its radioactivity.

"All this you can see behind me belonged to those brave Kaerin who made a last stand on the island of Grata during the Torpun's war of conquest—the war we lost. Those Kaerin were trying to transport to Kaerus Minor from where they planned to continue the fight. They all died in an atomic attack launched by the Torpun.

"From that day forward, our creed, 'What was lost,' did not only signify the freedoms the Torpun took from us, but the people we lost—our ancestors who died fighting for the ideals we hold to this day. It took centuries before we retook our world and regained our sacred rights granted to us by our creator—but it all started with a war we lost."

"The tour you are going to go on today," she continued after a moment of taking in the wide-eyed faces, "is focused on the later struggle—the war we won, and the Torpun defeat. But I think it is important to start the story here at the war we lost, at this monument to the people we lost. The seeds of our world were planted then."

She glanced across the crowd, careful to be circumspect as she tried to gauge the reaction of the Guardian, who, dressed in civilian clothes, could have been anyone, if not for the two uniformed security guards standing at rest a few feet behind him. He smiled back at her and gave her a nod that seemed to say he appreciated the lesson.

"Now, if you're all quiet and well-behaved for your instructors, you can follow me into the next room where you'll get to take turns climbing into a real mech suit."

Her crowd exploded in excitement, and she moved to the side to let them file past. A young boy grabbed the hem of her jacket and gave it a tug just as the Guardian and his charge were coming down the steps.

"Miss Director, why is that thingy there blinking?" The young boy's arm was outstretched towards the display behind her.

She flashed a look of apology at the Guardian—she'd really wanted to thank him for coming—as she turned to look.

Many of the ancient devices were kept powered. It made for a better display. But she was as confused as the young boy at the large blinking light on a piece of communication gear—she wasn't certain what its function was, but knew it had never blinked like that.

"Well… I'm not entirely certain. I believe it was a communications relay of some sort." She smiled down at the child and glanced up at the

Guardian, who was suddenly standing very still, staring at the object. "It must be picking up a signal from the outside."

"No," the Guardian spoke up absently as he stepped past her, closer to the display. "It's a quantum-paired beacon." She watched as he tilted his head in confusion.

"Paired with?" she asked.

The Guardian's face seemed to harden before her. His eyes lost the warmth his earlier smile had carried. "Director Otak'rino, I think we'll need to exclude this gallery from the tour for the other groups. I'll have some people here shortly who are going to want access to the," he paused, adding a smile that didn't reach his eyes, "this display."

"Of course, Guardian." He knew what it was—that much was clear to her. "We serve."

***

A note

I want to thank everyone for their patience with regards to this book. The last year has been crazy and more than a little challenging. I could detail the reasons, but I think at the end of the day all that matters is that the loved ones whose health scares took priority for a while are all doing well.

Mostly, I just wanted to take a moment to thank you, the reader. Gone are the days, when I had to pimp out my children with a promise to wash your car in exchange for a review. That said, if you feel you are on the fence about writing a positive review – I'm certain we could work something out. Those reviews on Amazon, but also on Goodreads are important to keeping a series alive - but so is word of mouth.

I'm anxious to finish this series and start several others that have been cooking – but rest assured, it's all Eden Chronicles until it's complete.

Best regards, S.M. "Scott" Anderson

Made in United States
Troutdale, OR
10/08/2023

13485160R00268